Praise for Katie MacAlister's
Matchmaker in Wonderland Romances

A Midsummer Night's Romp

"Gut-wrenchingly funny! . . . If you want romance, some hilarious sex scenes, a bit of a mystery, and to have a goofy grin . . . then by all means read this book!"
—Open Book Society

"Charming, sexy, and laugh-out-loud funny."
—Fresh Fiction

"As entertaining as the romance, comedy of dialogue and action, and amusing cast of characters prove to be . . . the intriguing underlying setting and mystery provide something extra for the reader to enjoy."
—Heroes and Heartbreakers

The Importance of Being Alice

"Witty, charming, and erotically tender . . . [a] sparkling romance." —*Publishers Weekly*

"Hilarious and seductive in all the right places . . . a funny, adventurous, sensuous romance with something for everyone." —Fresh Fiction

continued . . .

"Mutual attraction, madcap adventures, and sexy fun ensue. This delightfully fluffy romance . . . is the perfect antidote to the blues." —*Booklist*

THE PERILS OF PAULIE

Katie MacAlister

JOVE
New York

A JOVE BOOK
Published by Berkley
An imprint of Penguin Random House LLC
375 Hudson Street, New York, New York 10014

Copyright © 2017 by Katie MacAlister
Excerpt from *The Importance of Being Alice* copyright © 2015 by Katie MacAlister
Penguin Random House supports copyright. Copyright fuels creativity, encourages
diverse voices, promotes free speech, and creates a vibrant culture. Thank you for buying
an authorized edition of this book and for complying with copyright laws by not
reproducing, scanning, or distributing any part of it in any form without permission.
You are supporting writers and allowing Penguin Random House to continue to
publish books for every reader.

A JOVE BOOK and BERKLEY are registered trademarks and the B colophon
is a trademark of Penguin Random House LLC.

ISBN 9781101990681

First Printing: January 2017

Printed in the United States of America
1   3   5   7   9   10   8   6   4   2

Cover art by: woman in a red dress © wacpan/Shutterstock Images;
green meadow, blue sky with asphalt © Sergeyit/Shutterstock Images;
1909 Thomas Flyer Flyabout © Car Culture/Getty Images
Cover design by Adam Auerbach

This and so many of my other books would never have been possible without the love and support of my darling agent, Michelle Grajkowski. She is not only the best agent in the world—she's also the nicest woman I know. I want to be her when I grow up.

Acknowledgments

No man is an island, and no author is . . . well, I guess an island . . . without her street team to help spread the word. Mine is particularly fabulous, and so it's with much gratitude that I thank the following ladies for all their help: Mary S. McCormick, Amy Lochmann, Patricica Doose, Barbara Bass, Amanda Whitbeck, Cathy Brown, Dawn Oliver, Gabrielle Lee, Katie Chasteen, Susanna Jolicoeur, Veronica Godinez-Woltman, Erin Havey, Rebecca Taylor, Leona Merrow, Sabrina Ford, Tracy Goll, Cadra Hebert, Andrea Denmon, Monett Wray, Tori Lhota, Tammy Gahagan, Peg E. Olkonen, Julie Atagi, Lisa Partridge, Candice Allen, Dawn Henry, Amy Hallmark, Andrea Long, Misty Snell, Jennifer Quirke Clavell, Susan Baez Randleman, Shiloh Gibson, Nikki Lhota, Nikki Harris, Teri Robinson, Laura Hondl, Cely Havens, Teresita Reynolds, Mandy Johnson, Sarah Cromley, and Sandy Musil.

Paulina Rostakova's Adventures

"This," I announced to Angela at breakfast, "is definitely the worst day of my life. No, worse than worst . . . it's the pinnacle of horribleness. It's hell and a nightmare combined. It's serial-killer awful."

That's how it all started two days ago, with me complaining about my life. I have to say, it feels a bit weird writing everything that happened down in a journal, but hey, if it was good enough for a certain intrepid lady reporter, it's good enough for me.

"Serial-killer awful?" Angela is the best stepmother a girl could have, if only for the fact that she is used to dealing with the drama queen that is Dad. So rather than calling me on my dramatic statements—which I admit were a bit over-the-top—she simply looked up from her laptop and gave me a sympathetic look. "I'm sorry, dear. You don't have to help your father, you know. He simply said if you needed an occupation, you could help with the inventory. I will admit that there are few things I'd rather do less than spend the next four days inventorying flooring materials stacked in five warehouses, but if you are as bored as you say you are—"

"Of course I'm bored. I have nothing to do!" I said, slapping my hands down on the marble counter.

She pursed her lips, making me feel like a spoiled brat. "I'm sure if you needed something to fill your time, I could find a charity—"

"I volunteer everywhere," I said, despair making me feel like I was floating in a sea of molasses. "I read to the old folks at the assisted-living place, I was a Big Sister until my kid moved to the other side of the country, I walk dogs at the old-dog sanctuary, and I bundle stuff at the women's shelter. I help at the library with the special-needs kids' hour, and once a week I get a cardio workout by mucking out stables at the horse rescue. I hate to seem ungrateful, but . . . but . . ."

"But you want something to do other than volunteer at charities," Angela finished for me, nodding. "I wish I could help you, dear, but charities are all I have experience with, especially now that we've founded the group to oversee all of the local area charitable organizations."

I sighed and slumped down on a barstool that sat at the counter. The remains of my meager breakfast lay before me. "And now I sound petulant and spoiled."

"Not spoiled—not in the sense that you grew up with affluence around you," Angela said kindly. "You can't help it if your father is the flooring king of Northern California. And I do understand your ennui. Your father is a bit . . ."

"Overprotective? Maniacally intent on ruining my life by not letting me have any freedom? Borderline obsessive about keeping me away from anything even remotely interesting?"

"He is afraid for you," she said, giving me a gently chiding glance. "He fears you will be kidnapped again."

"He's just using that as an excuse," I said, rolling my eyes. "I was six when that happened, and it was my mother's parents who took me. They weren't trying to extort any of his millions. They just wanted to see me since Mom had died and Dad was being his usual paranoid self."

"If he is a bit overprotective—and I will grant you that not allowing you to choose a career that will take you away from us is not healthy for either you or him—it comes from a good place. He loves you, Paulie. He fears for your well-being."

"He worries I'll hook up with some man who wants me for his money, you mean," I said sourly. "He's beyond unrealistic if he thinks he can keep me stuck at home until I'm an old lady. I'm going to be thirty in a year! Thirty! Who else do you know who lives at home until she's thirty?"

Angela had gone back to reading her e-mails, but she did pause long enough to cock an eyebrow at me.

"OK," I admitted, not bothering to look around a kitchen that was bigger than most of the apartments in San Francisco. "I will give you that living in a house that is borderline mansion and having my own suite of rooms makes it ludicrous to complain, but the point remains that he's got a stranglehold on me, and I want out. I want to be free. I want to go places, and meet people, and . . . and have adventures!"

"Like that Nancy Bly," Angela said, nodding as she continued to peruse her in-box.

"Nellie Bly," I corrected, sighing. "*She* didn't let anyone tell her she couldn't do anything. She wanted to be an investigative journalist, so she just marched into a newspaper and demanded the editor give her a job. And he did, despite the fact that in the late 1800s there were no women reporters."

"It's not that your father doesn't want you to be happy," Angela said absently. "He loves you very much. He just wants to make sure you're protected against those who might wish to do ill to you."

"He wouldn't be so paranoid if he hadn't been part of the Russian Mafia," I muttered under my breath.

"What's that, dear?"

"Nothing. I swear, Angela, if it didn't sound too ridiculous for words to say this, one of these days I'd tell Daddy that I'm going to run away from home."

"Oh, I wouldn't do that," she said, tapping on the laptop's keyboard, her mind obviously on her work. "Your father would insist you take a bodyguard with you."

"Bodyguard," I said, snorting derisively. Daddy had threatened me with that particular atrocity every single time I told him I wanted to move out on my own. As it was, every time I left the house I ended up having one of my father's goons (as I thought of them) trailing me everywhere, every day, "just in the case," as Daddy said. Only recently had Angela and I managed to convince him that I could do my volunteer duties without a steroid-swilling ex-military Russian muscleman accompanying me. "I just want to have a life. Is that so much to ask?"

Angela didn't answer, being thoroughly engrossed in her correspondence. So, feeling like an overgrown child, I glumly made my way back to the three-room suite where I spent my time at home and pulled out a well-worn copy of one of Nellie Bly's books. "I bet *she* would have made Dad listen to her if she was in my shoes," I grumbled to the book, then felt a thousand times worse because what did it say about me that I couldn't get out from under his thumb?

"I'm doomed," I said morosely two hours later, lying on the floor with my cell phone held to my ear.

"What, again?" asked Julia, my closest friend, who

ran the women's shelter where I volunteered twice a week.

"I'm never going to get out of this house. Fifty years from now, I'll be rattling around the big old empty place, just me and about four dozen cats."

Julia laughed, but sobered up quickly enough. "I've told you that you're welcome to seek shelter here, Pauls. You don't have to have been in an abusive relationship with a romantic partner to qualify for our program—"

"I know, but my father isn't abusive. He's just super overprotective because he used to be in with a bunch of bad people before he left Russia and he thinks everyone in the world is just lurking outside the house, waiting to nab me and hold me for ransom."

"Maybe they are," she answered lightly, then spoke rapidly to someone who had evidently come into her office before returning to me. "He is the flooring king of Sacramento, after all."

"And environs," I said glumly. "He's very big about making sure people know how far-reaching his flooring empire is."

"That doesn't mean you have to remain a captive in your own home."

"I'm not a captive," I pointed out.

"You might as well be one. Paulie, you can leave! I keep telling you that. I'll help you break free."

"It's not quite that simple," I said with a sigh. Sometimes it was difficult making people understand my father. "Dad is very old-school. Daughters, to him, stay at home until they get married."

Julia snorted. "This is not Soviet-era Russia. You don't have to give in to outdated and misguided thinking. You are a modern woman."

"I know, I know. It's just that the couple of times I started to move out, Dad made himself sick with worry.

I mean physically ill. Cardiac-unit kind of ill. I just couldn't put him through that again."

"That's emotional blackmail, and you know it," she argued.

"Yes, but it's easier to deal by staying here than to risk killing my dad with worry."

"Pfft," she scoffed. "He'd survive. You're just too devoted to family—that's what it is."

"Mmm-hmm," I said, not wanting to continue the argument. We'd had it before, and nothing would change until Dad finally saw reason. "Change of subject time— oh hell."

"Your life again?"

"No, Angela just texted me. She said she wants to talk to me at dinner about a new opportunity that just came to her attention. Probably she has another charity for me to spend time with. Ugh. Speaking of that, I have to get to the farm and help out with the horses. Today is the farrier's day."

"I'll talk to you later. Maybe we could go see a movie."

"Ha! Without escort?" I mimicked my father's heavy accent. "Is not reasonable. Pipples want to take what is not theirs. Pipples want to break Rostakov, to make him much pain. Is not good to go out without protection."

She giggled. "Well, then we can just get a pizza and binge-watch something on Netflix."

"We'll see. Maybe some handsome stranger will be at the stables and want to sweep me off my feet in a nonkid-napping sort of way, and then I can escape the Rostakova Dictatorship."

"Laters," Julia said, and hung up.

I spent the day at the rescue stable, enjoyed my time among the horses, donkeys, and other four-legged beasts, chatted with the other volunteers, and returned home in time to find a raging argument going on in what my father called his study (but was really just a large panic room that he'd outfitted as if he was a nineteenth-century British lord).

"—is not safe!" my father was saying in his loud, gruff voice. "You want her dead? Or worse? You work with my enemies? You want her fingers cut off slowly and sent to me, one by one?"

"No, of course not," Angela said, her voice as calm as my father's was emotional. Two large men with no necks and distressingly gruesome tattoos on their arms and hands stood flanking the door to the study. "But this opportunity seems heaven-sent, and I would hate to see her miss out on it. You remember me speaking of my niece Mercedes, don't you?"

"Boys," I said, deliberately being obnoxious. Boris—the no-neck on the right—had frequently been assigned to follow after me when I threw caution to the wind and went out on my own. He had no sense of humor and delighted in tattling on me to my father. Igor, his buddy, was almost as bad, although he was less bright, and sometimes I could bribe him into leaving me alone in a store for an hour.

"Paulina Petrovna," Boris acknowledged in return, using both my first and patronymic names in the manner that he knew I disliked.

"I bet there's a wall outside you guys could find to hold up," I said, sailing through the doorway. "Preferably the one where the revolutionaries are taken to be shot."

Igor cast a worried look to his comrade. "How does she know about the wall?"

I spun around to look at them in horror. Boris just smirked at me and closed the door in my face, leaving me trapped in an L-shaped room that was partially lined with floor-to-ceiling bookcases filled with books that had never felt the touch of human hands. I stalked forward, making a mental note to ask my father if the boys had been joking, but the argument soon drove that thought away.

"Is not your niece I worry for," Daddy was saying when I rounded the bend of the room and found them both standing at a massive oak desk. "Is others. You want her to go to Belarus? To Russia? She would be taken from me instantly."

"Not if people didn't know who she was, and there's no reason to tell anyone her surname. She can use her mother's name, after all."

"Who can? Are you guys talking about me? Dad, you're going to have a stroke if you don't stop huffing and puffing like that. Your face is bright red." I stopped at the desk, my interest piqued at the word "Russia."

"You do not your mind about my face," he snapped, but sat down with a grunt. "Your stepmama is crazy. Without brains at all. Is crazy idea."

"It is not crazy. It is perfect. Paulie, dear, do you remember me telling you how my niece Mercy married an Englishman and went to live in England?"

"She wants me to visit her? I'll do it!" I said, not caring about pesky things like details.

"No, it's not that." Angela smiled, and I was distracted enough by the genuine affection in her eyes to slip my arm through hers.

"Sorry I interrupted you, darling. You go ahead and tell me what it is you want me to do that Dad thinks is so crazy."

"Is crazy." Daddy waved his big hands around in the air, his eyes narrowing until he was squinting at us. "Will not happen. Too dangerous. Rostakov has too many enemies."

She patted my arm. "It really is ideal, because you'd have people around you, you see, so your father couldn't say you weren't protected. And Mercy's brothers-in-law—two or three of them, I don't remember exactly—would be there, too, and I just know they'd watch after you."

"I don't need watching after—" I started to object, but bit it off so she'd continue.

"And then of course there is the film crew. They'd be with you every step of the way, too."

"You want me to be in a movie?" I asked, confused. "With your niece and her English family?"

"No, no, I'm not explaining myself well at all," she said, a bit flustered now. "Let me tell it from the beginning."

"Is no matter. Paulina is not go to Russia," Daddy said darkly, slamming his fist down on the desk. "I am spoken."

"Have spoken, dear," Angela corrected automatically, then led me over to a red-and-yellow-striped love seat and sat down with me. "Mercy's husband's family is some sort of minor nobility. They had a television crew filming them at an archaeological dig two years ago, and now that same film crew wants to make a reality show about a race."

"Like *The Amazing Race* TV show, where people go all over the world and do weird things?" I frowned. "I really don't want to eat bugs or repulsive parts of animals."

"Not that sort of a reality show. Oh, let me show you Mercy's e-mail." Angela pulled out a piece of paper from her pocket and gave it to me.

I smoothed it out over my knee while my father rumbled objections and threats, both of which Angela and I ignored.

Relive one of the greatest races of all time! [the promotional copy read] *From the studio that brought you* A Month in the Life of a Victorian Duke *and the*

wildly popular Ainslie Castle Dig *comes the re-cre-
ation to end all re-creations! Relive the thrilling 1908
New York City to Paris race that spawned legends!*

"Wait a minute," I said, pausing to look up at Angela.
"Is this about that movie with Jack Lemmon and Tony
Curtis? The one where they race all over the place?"

"It's all there," Angela said, smiling and nodding at
the paper.

*Watch as participants don the clothing of a century
ago and race across continents in authentic period
cars! Thrill as they fight for superiority across dangerous lands! This one-month race will take its participants from the flat Midwest plains of the United States
to the exotic locations of China, Russia, and Europe.*

"Oooh," I said, my blood seeming to come alight with
the sense of adventure that fairly oozed off the paper. "It
is like that movie!"

"Is dangerous!" Daddy growled. "Too dangerous. Better you stay home with Papa and Mama."

"I'll do it," I told Angela, not even bothering to read
the rest of the information.

"But, dear, you don't know what it will entail—"

"It doesn't matter," I said, standing up, my heart beating so fast I wanted to dance and sing and crow to the
world that, at last, adventure was going to be mine! "I'll
do whatever job this production company wants. I'll be
a gofer. I'll be a script girl. I'll be a personal assistant. I
don't care—I just want to be a part of it."

"They will want you to be in one of the cars," Angela said
in her placid voice. "I'm afraid you will need to dress up."

"Like Nellie Bly?" I asked, my spirits soaring. "Oh
my god, could this *be* any more perfect?"

"Read Mercy's information," she said, nudging my hand.

"No. Is no good to read. She stays here, where she is safe," Daddy said, getting to his feet again.

"I'm twenty-nine years old, Dad," I said, snapping at him. "I'm an adult, and you do *not* have a say in this."

"I have say," he said, reeling back in a dramatic manner. He's such a drama queen. "I am Papa!"

"You are a domineering man who thinks he gets his own way on everything, but I'm not a little girl anymore. I'm going."

"You are not!" he bellowed, loud enough that the door opened and Boris stuck his head into the room.

"Go upstairs and take her message so you can read the information," Angela said, urging me toward the door.

I obediently went toward the hall but cast a worried glance back at my father, who was now shouting to Boris and Igor that he would not allow Angela to throw his only child into the hands of his enemies. "Are you going to be OK with him in that mood?"

"Oh, heavens yes," she said with a chuckle. "He just wants a little soothing. Once you've read the information, if you still want to do it, let me know and I'll have Mercy connect you with the production company."

"Tell her to connect away, because I'm doing it no matter what it takes!" I announced, then turned on my heels and ran up the stairs, my imagination already flying.

Paulina Rostakova's Adventures

JULY 16
1:45 p.m.
My bedroom

So much to do! So many things to get ready! I'm all aflutter, and probably would be running around like a chicken without its head if not for Julia and her magical planner o' organization. At least, that was the idea.

"So," Julia said after I demanded she come to my house two days after the Great Emancipation, as I shall henceforth think of it. "I get the part about the global race, which is really a cool idea so long as you don't have to eat any bugs or camels' scrotums."

"I know, right?" I made a face and pulled up the Web site that Mercy had sent me to for more information. "But this show doesn't sound like that sort of thing at all. Here, see? They are going to duplicate the route of the original 1908 race, and use cars of the same time period, although Mercy says the producers are going to put modern engines in the cars so that it doesn't take months to finish the race."

"That doesn't sound bad," Julia said, looking at the Web site. "You get to go through a lot of countries."

"Thank god I managed to get a passport a couple of years ago without Dad knowing."

"All right, so you're following the same race path, but why don't you need to take a lot of clothes with you? You're going to be gone for over a month."

"That's the best part. The production company wants to make this like that *Great Race* movie that had themed cars. Because this is reality TV, the producers are creating teams of people so they have lots of interaction to film, like people fighting and storming off, and making googly eyes at each other, and having jealous scenes, and all that sort of thing."

"Typical reality TV fodder," Julia said, nodding. "I still don't understand about the clothing."

"Well, Mercy has arranged for me to be in a car with two other women. We're supposed to be suffragettes, you see, so we get to wear 1908 suffragette clothing."

"Oooh," she said, her eyes alighting with costuming fervor. "Big hats."

"Feather boas," I said, nodding.

"Long skirts, though," she warned.

"Flattering to the figure," I pointed out, looking down at where my abundant curves were lolling about.

"There is that."

"According to the e-mail I got from the producer, I can wear my own clothes in off periods, but during the race hours I have to be in costume."

"That doesn't sound too bad." She squinted at the screen and read aloud, "'There will be checkpoints where teams must rendezvous for interaction with the camera crew. Avoidance of these points will earn the team negative points.' What's all that about?"

"The teams get points for going through various cities, and if you don't stop and let them film you, you get demerits or something." I waved away that concern and piled a bunch of underwear into a large duffel bag. "I don't really care about the race per se, although the winners do get twenty grand each, but it's the experience I'm excited about. I'll be out there doing the same thing that Nellie Bly did. She made an around-the-world journey, too, and wrote a book about it. I'll be able to take notes, and interview my fellow racers, and post things to a blog that I'll later turn into a book. It'll be just like I'm a modern-day Nellie."

"Mmm-hmm." Julia scrolled down the page. "Holy moly, will you look at that!"

"What?" I asked, setting down a handful of bras to look at where she was pointing.

"There's a list of teams with pictures of the racers. Well, a couple of pictures—the rest are blank."

"That's because they're filling in people who dropped out or who they haven't booked yet, or so Mercy told me," I said, going into my bathroom to sweep up a collection of body washes, shampoo, conditioner, and various other sundries. Those I dumped in a cosmetics bag, and tossed that into the duffel as well.

"Yeah, but these two are booked already. And aren't they yummy?"

I looked, blinked a couple of times, and agreed. "Wow. Dibs on the one on the right."

"Silly, you can dibs them both, since I won't be in the race and you will. I wonder if they're single. Oh, wait—you can click on their names. Let's see . . . Mr. Right—ha!—is Dixon Ainslie, thirty-two, estate agent at Ainslie Castle in England."

"That must be one of Mercy's brothers-in-law. I think Angela said the family name was Ainslie."

"It doesn't say anything about a wife . . ."

I returned to the bed, where I'd dumped the entire contents of my closet and dressers. "Put your list-making skills to work and help me decide what to take and what I don't need."

"Hmm . . . I don't see anything bad in his bio. You have my blessing to pounce on him." Julia's eyes glittered with mirth. "If you hooked up with him, you could live at a castle!"

"Meh," I said, shrugging, feeling a bit overwhelmed trying to decide what to take with me. "I live in a huge house. I'd much rather have a small little cottage with an adorable garden filled with rabbits and hedgehogs and friendly deer."

"If you had all that, you wouldn't have much of a garden left," Julia said, clicking on the other man. "Looks like Mr. Left is Dixon's brother. He's two years younger and is a commercial artist."

"Bully for him. Come on, you organizing fiend, let's get the to-do and to-take lists going. I was thinking a couple of pairs of jeans, one nice dress for any dinners out, and a couple of skirts that won't wrinkle. Two blouses, two sweaters in case it's chilly at night, a couple of tees, and my flats and tennis shoes." I started sorting clothes into stacks.

"How can you be worried about mundane things like clothing when there are handsome Englishmen to ogle?" she asked, clicking on other people shown on the race site. "Nope. Those two are definitely the cream of the crop."

"I'm not interested because I'm looking for adventure, not a man," I said, holding up a gauzy broomstick skirt. "Is this too casual to wear in Europe? You know how stylish everyone there is. I don't want to look like a back-water boob."

"You're not married, not dating anyone, and not gay. *Of course* you're looking for a man."

"Not me. Do you know the sort of background check my crazy father would demand for anyone I was inter-ested in?" I gave a little shudder and tossed the skirt into the no-go stack, picking up instead a maxi skirt made of a pretty blue-and-purple-paisley cotton. "It's just not worth it."

"You can't tell me you don't get lonely, because I've seen you go googly-eyed at those superhero movies where the yummy actors wear skintight suits," Julia persisted, looking at me over the top of the glasses she wore to read things on the computer.

"Pfft," I said, trying to dismiss the subject. The last thing I wanted to do was focus on my lack of a love life.

"You haven't dated anyone in almost four years."

"Blame my father for that," I said, picking out the best of my jeans.

"I won't, because you've had boyfriends. It can be done. You just won't put yourself to the trouble of finding a man." I was about to protest when she continued, stabbing a finger toward the screen. "Here's the answer. You'll be thrown together with a bunch of men without your father being able to have a say in who or what you do."

"Boy, you really want me to get laid, don't you?" I asked, laughing.

"Are you saying you don't?"

"No, of course not. I enjoy sex as much as anyone. It's just that . . . men are so much work. You have to be on your best behavior for the first few months, lest you scare them off. You have to consider their needs before yours because that's how men are. And you have to let them think they're smarter than you, which is almost always not the case. I just don't have time for that."

"That's because you're meeting the wrong type of man. I don't have to do any of that with Sanjay."

"That's because your Sanjay is a saint, and a very smart man."

She smiled smugly. "He is that. But this is about you, not me. Don't be so stubborn about hooking up with someone who turns your starter crank."

"Ha! Starter crank. I see what you did," I said, stuffing the reject clothing back into the dresser.

"After all, you must get . . . *needy*."

"That, my dear, is what battery-operated devices are for." I shook out a forest green floor-length dress and posed with it. "What do you think? It looks pretty nice on me, and it's made of material that doesn't hold its wrinkles."

"Fine, fine," Julia said, giving it a swift glance before returning to the screen. "Oooh, there's some guy from a TV show going to be racing, too."

"You're a poop," I told her, laying the dress next to the duffel bag. "You're the one with all the planning expertise, and here you are spending all your time drooling over a bunch of men you've never met."

"I'm just trying to help you become as deliriously happy as I am with Sanjay," she said, and laughed when I threw a button-down oxford shirt at her head. "All right, all right, I'll leave your potential husbands alone and start the list making. Where's the paper? Thanks. OK, let's start with the necessities. Toothpaste and toothbrush."

"Check."

"Tampons and ibuprofen."

"Check."

"Cleansing products: facial, body, and hoohaw."

I paused in the act of stuffing pairs of socks into a side pocket. "Why do I need vaginal cleanser?"

She tipped her head toward the laptop. "You'll want to feel springtime fresh if you're going to snag yourself a hunky Englishman."

"For the love of Pete, Julia!"

She giggled. "Now, about your underwear. I've seen it, and I think you should dump it and go with thongs. Men like thongs."

"That's it," I said, taking the tablet of paper away from

her. "I'll go unorganized. You're clearly too overcome with smutty thoughts to be of any practical use."

"Fine, but don't blame me if your granny pants scare off any potential suitor!"

"I'll take that risk," I told her, and spent the rest of the afternoon happily arguing with her over every garment.

Life was looking good, and nothing could dim my happiness.

Paulina Rostakova's Adventures

JULY 18
11:18 a.m.
Row 7, Seat B on the plane to New York City

Crap! Crap, crap, crappity crap! Big fat hairy balls of crap! Boris is on the plane with me! He's hiding behind a magazine, but I just know it's him.

> July 18
> To: Daddy
> *Why is Boris on the plane? Dad! I am almost 30! I don't need a bodyguard!!!*

> July 18
> To: Angela
> *Is Boris there?*

> July 18
> From: Angela
> *I don't know. Let me ask your father.*

July 18
From: Angela
Peter says Boris has taken a vacation for a few weeks. Why? Did you change your mind about a bodyguard?

July 18
To: Angela
I knew it! Dad sent Boris here! He's on the plane! Globules!

July 18
From: Angela
Globules? Boris has globules?

July 18
To: Angela
Autocorrect, sorry. That was supposed to be goddammit.

July 18
From: Angela
Ah. I will speak to Peter about Boris.

July 18
From: Daddy
You are Rostakov woman. You are valuable. Mens from film company are not protection. Ignore Boris. Pretend he is not there. Do not talk to anyone. Use Mama's name. You have Taser?

July 18
To: Daddy
No, I did not bring the tater!

July 18
To: Daddy
*Damn you, autocorrect! TASTER! I did not bring the
TASTER.*

July 18
From: Daddy
*What are you tasting? Let Boris eat first in case of
drugs.*

July 18
To: Daddy
Gah!

Paulina Rostakova's Adventures

"Would you like to switch seats with me?" The woman in the seat next to me must have heard me swearing under my breath, not to mention periodically rising up to twist around and glare at the seats toward the back of the plane.

"Hmm?" I stopped shaking my phone in an attempt to get my idiotic father to understand that I was an adult and capable of taking care of myself, and looked at the woman. "Oh, sorry. Have I been bothering you? No, this seat is fine. It's just that I want to throttle my father and can't because he's back in California."

"Ah." She smiled. "I understand how family can drive you nuts. I was just in Seattle visiting family who I haven't seen in a long time, and now I know why I moved to the other side of the world. I'm Tessa, by the way."

"Paulie," I said, smiling in return. "I so wish I could move away from my family, but my father has issues."

"Oh, don't I know it? My stepdaughter is nineteen, but her father still treats her like she's a child. We have to remind him now and again that she's an adult."

"It's like she's living my life," I said with a sigh. "Although I'm a lot older than nineteen. Would you excuse me? I have to go yell at a man."

She obligingly swung her legs to the side and allowed me to crawl out from my middle seat. Although I could have charged a first-class ticket to New York City, I was trying to make a point by not relying on my father's money to undertake this adventure. Instead, I accepted the production company's economy-class ticket, enjoying my father's sputtered comments about the dangers of mingling with people. I fixed my eyes on a large shape in the very last row and marched down the narrow aisle, dodging and sidestepping people's arms and legs and two flight attendants before finally stopping next to Boris.

"It's no good hiding behind a magazine," I told him, plucking the flight magazine from his fingers. Boris, wearing a pair of sunglasses and a hoodie, glared back at me. "I know that you're here, and I know what you and Dad are planning. It's not going to work. You can't come along with me on the race. I will tell the production people as soon as I get to New York that you are a stalker and need to be kept away at all costs."

His jaw tightened. "You wouldn't."

"Try me!" I shoved the magazine back at him. "If I so much as glimpse you hanging around the fringes, I will report you as a dangerous stalker. I'd advise you to take the vacation you're supposed to be on, and forget about my father's paranoia." I smiled tightly. "Have a nice time in New York!"

He swore under his breath when I turned and made my way back to my seat, but we both knew that he was fighting a lost cause.

"Problem?" Tessa asked when I climbed over her legs. "I shouldn't be so nosy, but if there's something I can do to help you—"

"It's just my father's idea of protection," I said, waving away the subject. "He doesn't like me traveling on my own. I, on the other hand, am very excited to be going to New York. I've only ever been there with family."

"It's not my favorite city, but it does have a lot to do and see. Unfortunately, we won't have much time to do any sightseeing."

"We?" I asked, settling in for a pleasant chat. I hadn't flown much—and never on my own—but I didn't at all find Tessa the stereotypical unpleasant seatmate. The man sitting on my other side had fallen asleep as soon as the plane took off and showed no signs of waking anytime soon.

"My husband and stepdaughter are meeting me there. We're going to be part of a special event—a road rally that's being filmed."

I gawked at her, an unpleasant look to be sure, but I couldn't help myself. "You're . . . you're in the race, too?"

"Too?" Surprise lit her eyes. "You're in it?"

"I'm one of the suffragettes," I said, delighted.

"So is my stepdaughter!" she answered, laughing. "What a small world!"

We compared our stories. "And your stepdaughter's name is . . . ?"

"Melody. You'll like her—she's very smart, and very knowledgeable about the suffragette movement. She's studying history at college."

"I'm surprised she's not part of your team."

"Oh, Max—my husband—would have loved for her to be on our team, but she wanted desperately to be in the suffragette car. Instead we have a delightful woman who used to be our maid. Well, on the show she was our maid."

"Show?"

"Max and I met on a reality show filmed by the same production company."

"Very cool. I think I remember reading something about that."

Tessa smiled again, and I warmed even more to her. Like me, she had an abundance of curves, but unlike my black-haired bob, she possessed long brown hair, which she wore in an intricate braid. I was envious of that hair. We chatted for the duration of the flight, with her telling me what it was like to be filmed for a month.

"They won't watch you during intimate times, like bathroom and bedroom events, but everything else is fair game."

I shook my head. "I don't think I'm going to be able to act natural knowing people are filming me."

"Oh, you forget about it fast enough. Tabby and Sam— the sound-and-camera team—are awesome that way. And they're really nice. If there's something super embarrassing, they will conveniently erase that part."

"I don't know what could be that embarrassing, so long as they don't film me in the shower."

"You have no idea," she said with a rueful laugh, shaking her head. "With us, it was catching Max and me in compromising positions. It seemed like any time we went in for a lip-lock, or something more physical, the cameras were there. Sam was most obliging, though, and didn't pass on that footage to Roger, the producer."

"That won't be a problem with me," I reassured her. "I don't have a romantic partner."

"But you never know who you might fancy in the race," she said with a little waggle of her eyebrows. "Have you seen the Italian team? Holy moly, they are straight from the cover of *GQ*. And there are a couple of gorgeous Brits, and the French team looks pretty nice if you like 'em Gallic."

I made no comment, instead exclaiming when she pulled a black journal out of her bag to show me a picture of her husband. "Oh, do you write in a journal, too? I just started one."

"Yup. I've done so ever since I was a girl. Max keeps telling me I should publish them, but there's a lot of intimate stuff in there."

I raised my eyebrows. "You write about your . . . uh . . ."

"Sure, why not?" She gave a little half shrug. "Sex is just as much a part of life as everything else. Besides, Max likes to reread those sections."

I was quiet for a bit while she told me about her life in England, the house, her husband, and how she hated wearing a corset even though it did wonders for her figure. I decided that if—and that was a very big if—I had any moments of romance during the next month, I'd document them. I was fairly sure that Nellie Bly would have, although, naturally, she'd have kept that out of any book she published.

"Still," I said to myself when Tessa was off using the bathroom, "I bet she wrote that stuff down, too. Oh well. It's not like I'll have anything to document, sultry Italians and handsome Frenchmen aside."

From: AliceWonderland@ainsliecastle.com
Subject: FWD: So?
To: Dixon
CC: Rupert

Dixon, would you show this e-mail to your obstinate brother? He refuses to respond, and we're dying back here to know what's going on.
　　ORIGINAL MESSAGE
　　Rupert! You were supposed to e-mail us as soon as you got to New York City and met the other racers, and it's been almost four hours. Have you met Mercy's

stepcousin-in-law or whatever relation Paulie is to her? What did you think? Are you not e-mailing because you're disappointed? Everything that Mercy said her aunt told her about Paulie sounded like she's wonderful, and you guys share all sorts of interests. You like horses— she works with horses! You like art—Mercy's aunt says Paulie used to draw. You're almost the same age, so stop being silent and tell me what you think. You know my matchmaking mojo is on the line here.

Elliott says to tell Dixon that the order for fertilizer came in, but they dumped it on the south lawn, so we've closed that off from the tourists, so he said not to worry if there's a dip in revenues for the month.

E-mail me as soon as you get this. I'm dying to know what your first impression of Paulie is. I think she's just perfect for you!

Paulina Rostakova's Adventures

JULY 18
6:14 p.m.
Dorcet Hotel, New York City, Room 1107

Tessa told me that the dinner tonight with the production company would allow all the participants to meet one another, and then we'd go off to be measured for costumes. I was going to wear my maxi skirt, but decided I'd better trot out the fancy green dress instead.

"Good idea," Julia approved, her voice tinny and distant since I had her on speakerphone while I hurriedly got dressed. "Not that the skirt isn't cute, but you might as well have your first impression be one of elegance and charm."

"I am anything but either of those two, but thank you for the vote of confidence."

"You're welcome. Now go forth and conquer Mr. Right."

I rolled my eyes. "Tessa said there were some handsome Italians, too."

"Oooh. I'll look at the Web site and see if they have their pictures. Just don't drop a wall down, OK, lovey?"

"A wall?"

"The kind you erect to keep men out of your life."

"I don't do any such thing," I protested.

"You may not know it, but you do. I understand—I really do—but now that you've finally made your break from your father, don't slip into old defense mechanisms. You're free—let down your hair and enjoy yourself."

"I'm not as free as you think," I muttered, and told her about Boris.

"I'd like to say I'm surprised, but honestly, given your father's behavior, I'm not. Are you sure you ditched him?"

"I hope so. I made it pretty clear I'd have him removed from the area if he tried to follow me."

"Good for you. Whoops—Sanjay just got here. Have a great time, and text me later, OK?"

"Will do. Laters!"

I'm not a shy person, but I was a bit hesitant about entering the hotel ballroom that had been reserved for the production company. A dozen or so round tables were set up, as were a big whiteboard and a screen for a laptop projector. People bustled about, laughing, chatting, and generally making the sort of happy sounds that indicated a successful party.

"Name?"

I jumped a little when I entered the room and a young man with a clipboard popped up.

"Oh. Hi. Um, Paulina Rosta—uh—" I stopped and remembered that, except with immigration officials, I was supposed to use my mother's maiden name.

"Paulina Rosta?" The man frowned at his paper and flipped through a couple of sheets.

"No, it's Paulina Lewes. Sorry."

"Ah. Yes, you're here. You're at table six." He nodded into the room. "The meet and greet will go on for another twenty minutes; then Roger will welcome you."

"Gotcha." I entered the room, my head up, my stomach knotted with nerves, and my palms sweaty. "Steady,"

I told myself. "Nellie wouldn't have blanched at the idea of a bunch of strangers in a room."

"I totally agree," a voice said behind me. "Although I don't know this Nellie person. Is she famous?"

I spun around to see a blond woman in her mid-twenties pouting at her phone, clearly taking pictures of herself. "Hi. Um. Nellie is Nellie Bly. She was an intrepid woman reporter in the 1880s."

"Oh." The girl rolled her eyes and took another selfie. "Why do you care what she thinks? She's got to be, like, almost dead now."

"She is dead. She died in 1922."

"So thrilling." The girl stopped admiring herself in her phone's camera and looked around the room. "Oh god, they're here. They're sure to want to drool all over my tits."

I blinked at both her comment and the way she hoisted up her substantial bosomage, generously displayed in a skintight spandex dress. "Uh . . ."

"The Italians. They're animals, all of them," she said, striking a pose when one of them lifted his hand to wave at her. "All they want to do is get in my pants. As if. I'm holding out for the lord's brother."

"The who now?"

"One of the English teams has two brothers of a real English lord on it. Can you imagine being a lady with a real castle? You could totally have a show about that."

"A show," I repeated, feeling particularly stupid. "A TV show?"

"Yeah. My dad's the producer," she said, suddenly raking me over with a scathing glance. "You one of the crew?"

"I guess so. I'm going to be in the suffragette car."

She stared at me for a minute, then made a disgusted noise in the back of her throat. "No offense, but you aren't at all the sort of person who should be in my car."

"*Your* car?"

"I'm the lead suffragette." She tapped at her phone, sliding through a number of texts. "Dad was going to make me be in the U.S. car, but Mom put a stop to that. As if I was going to ride around in a car where you can't even see me?"

"I don't think I know what you're talking about," I said, confused. "You mean the car had a top? I thought they were all convertibles back then?"

She flipped through more text messages. "The U.S. car—you know, the modern one?" I must have looked as puzzled as I felt, because she continued, with another irritated noise. "There are two races. One for the old cars, and one two months later for the new ones. Mom says the cameras are going to be on the old cars more because we'll be wearing costumes, and it's all very *Downton Abbey*, and people like that sort of thing. The new-car race is just a race, you know."

"Huh. I had no idea there were two separate races, but I guess it makes sense."

"So." She tucked away her phone and gave me a pointed look. "You'll be on my team, then. Naturally, I'll be the driver and the spokeswoman for the group, and the English girl said she can do the navigation stuff, which means you get to be the mechanic. I hope you're handy with tools."

"Uh . . ." She sashayed off before I could answer, making for a cluster of men in identical shiny midnight blue suits. I gathered by the way they greeted her that they were the Italian team, and had to admit that Tessa was right—they were easy on the eyes.

Just as I was thinking of joining the group in order to meet my fellow race contestants, a small gaggle of women and a man entered the ballroom. The man stopped to talk to the guy at the door, but the three women made a beeline for the Italians, who greeted them with cries of joy.

"Well, hell," I said aloud to myself, my spirits dropping at the sight of the women clinging to the men. "There goes my shot at sexual gratification with a handsome foreigner."

I felt a movement at my side and turned to see the man who had entered with the women was now next to me, giving me a quizzical look that included a raised eyebrow.

"Tell me you didn't just hear me say that," I said, blushing like crazy.

"I'm afraid I did."

"Oh god. And you're . . . British?"

"I am," he said, inclining his head in agreement. One side of his mouth twitched. "I believe that, technically, that makes me a foreigner."

"Oh god," I repeated, and covered my face.

He gave a hoarse little chuckle, a sound that was oddly pleasing despite the fact that I wished the ground would open up before me so I could fling myself in. "I'm sorry—that was unfair of me."

"Unfair?" I opened my fingers so I could look at him through them. "How so?"

"'Unkind,' perhaps, is a better word," he said after a moment's thought. "I've embarrassed you either way, and for that I apologize."

I dropped my hands and considered him. He was a little taller than me and had short auburn hair, hazel eyes that were mostly grayish blue, and a strong jaw that made my stomach quiver a little. "I'm the one who says something inappropriate, and you apologize? You definitely are British." I smiled to make sure he understood I was gently teasing him, and added, "I'm Paulina Rostakova, by the way, but I go by Paulie. Oh crap. I meant Paulie Lewes."

"Indeed?" He looked somewhat surprised by my correction.

"Yeah, it's a bit complicated. My dad won't let me use my name because . . . well, because reasons."

He offered his hand, which I shook while he said, "I'm Dixon Ainslie. It's a pleasure to meet you, Paulie Lewes."

"Oh, you're one of Mercy's brothers-in-law."

He froze for a couple of seconds. "You know Mercy? Do you also know Alice?"

"I can't say that I do. Know anyone named Alice, that is."

"Good," he said, relaxing. "I thought she might have decided that since Rupert wasn't answering . . . I thought you might be . . ."

I waited for him to finish. "What?" I asked when he didn't continue.

He made a face. "My sister-in-law has a habit of trying to pair off all of us. My brothers and me. She's been riding on a high ever since she sent Mercy down to help Alden, and lately she's turned her attention to my brother Rupert and me."

"A matchmaker, huh? I have a friend like that, only she just wants me to hook up with people. Hence the comment about getting it on with a handsome foreigner." It struck me at that moment that he was the man who I had dibsed on the race Web site, which of course made my blush go even hotter. "Well, this is definitely going to be one for the journal."

"Pardon?"

I shook my head and made a vague waving gesture. "Just ignore me. The jet lag has clearly turned off the filter between my brain and mouth."

"I understand that." He glanced at his watch. "It's the middle of the night for me."

"Ugh."

"Are you a writer, then?"

"Me? No."

"You mentioned a journal, so I thought perhaps you were a writer, too. My brother writes thrillers."

"Very cool. I'm a cozy mystery lover myself, but every now and again I dip my toes into thrillers. What's his name?"

"Elliott. Are you one of those . . . what do they call them . . . scrapbookers?"

"I wish I was—some of those people go crazy wild with decorations and things. My journal is new—I'm recording everything that happens during the race. All the conversations, all the stuff I do and see, all the exciting adventures we have. And then, when it's over, I hope to publish it. I'm a big fan of Nellie Bly—have you heard of her?"

He shook his head, so I spent a few minutes telling him about her and her exploits.

"She sounds quite intrepid. The journal idea is . . . interesting."

"You should do one as well," I told him, smiling. "You could do the man's perspective and publish it, too!"

He looked thoughtful. "It's something to consider. I've always liked record keeping, and in fact one of the few perks of my job is annotating Elliott's estate books with notes about the tenants, crops, and so on."

"You work on an estate? Oh, that's right—your brother is a lord."

"Just a baron, actually, and yes, I'm the estate manager." His expression warned it wasn't something he enjoyed.

"You don't look like you're super happy about that fact," I said.

"It's a job. We all have them," he pointed out.

"Not me." I made a little grimace. "Unless you call being a serial volunteer a job, which I guess in a way it is. So you like journaling—have you done much of it?"

"None. You?"

"I'm a journaling virgin, too," I said, excited to have a journal buddy. "You can always give it a try, and if you don't like it, let it go."

"I'll give it a thought," he said. "So you don't know Alice, but you are a friend of Mercy? I've only met her once, but she makes my brother very happy and is quite charming."

"I don't know her, as a matter of fact." Together, we strolled toward one of the tables set up with a variety of beverages. "She's the niece of my stepmom. I chatted with her via e-mail, but that's about it. Why, is she a matchmaker, too?"

He gave a faux shudder. "Not that I know of. I take it if you've been in contact with Mercy that you're the American she mentioned who is joining the women's team?"

"Suffragettes, that's right. I just met the leader of the team." I dropped the volume of my voice, glancing around to make sure no one could hear me, and leaned in to him to whisper, "She's a bit of a diva, I think."

Dixon, to my horror, stepped back just as if I had been covered in cooties. I blushed again and busied myself with examining the bottles and glasses on the table, telling myself that I was a fool, a big, awkward, idiotic fool who spoke without thinking and leaned close to men who didn't like that sort of thing.

"Sorry," Dixon murmured, looking extremely uncomfortable.

"No, it's my fault," I said, taking the high ground and apologizing. "I shouldn't have leaned into you that way. Not everyone likes it. Just so you know, I have a couple of gay friends."

His eyes widened. "I'm not gay."

"No? Well, then I guess it's just me." I swallowed down the hurt sting of that knowledge and turned away to grab an open bottle. I had no idea what was in it, but at that moment I didn't care so long as it was alcoholic.

"This is horribly awkward. I suppose I should—"

I didn't find out what he should do because at that moment a man with a fringe of red hair around a mostly bald head tapped on a microphone set up in the middle of the ballroom and said, "Hello? Is this on? Ah, it is. Hello, old friends, members of the crew, and new recruits. Welcome to what is going to be the greatest show on earth! If I could get everyone to grab a seat, we can get on with the orientation."

A quick glance at Dixon showed me he was avoiding looking at me, which stung even more. I headed off to the nearest table, still yelling at myself mentally, although, to be honest, I couldn't figure out what I'd done that had so offended him. Maybe I smelled of body odor?

I took my seat and used the opportunity of setting my purse on the ground to take a covert sniff of my armpits. Nothing was amiss there, so I pulled out a small pocket mirror and made sure I didn't have anything unsavory poking out from my nose, or obnoxious eye grit, or potatoes growing out of my ears.

Dixon took another seat at my table. Not next to me, but one away, and just as I was thinking of how to say something to him, Tessa bustled up with a tall dark-haired man in tow. "There you are! We were looking for you. Paulie, this is my husband, Max."

"Pleasure," Max said, giving me a little head nod before holding out a chair for Tessa. She sat directly next to me, chatting happily as her husband took the chair on the other side of her. I looked at Tessa and, suddenly feeling annoyed, looked at Dixon and cocked an eyebrow at him.

His jaw tightened, but he couldn't do more because at that moment Tessa asked his name and he had to respond.

"You must be the third English team! Max and I and

a friend are in the duke's car. Awesome. Jeez, Roger, keep your knickers on! We were just meeting and greeting!"

The last was in response to the bald man saying pointedly into the microphone that they would get started just as soon as the noise died down.

The man—who must have been Roger d'Espry, the producer—made a face at Tessa. She blew him a kiss.

"Welcome, again, everyone. I'm so glad to say that, as of four o'clock this afternoon, we've filled the last position of team members. The modern race teams are still being pulled together, but as they are being filmed by a different production company, we will have little to do with them." He gave us a warm smile. "I think we all know which race the public will prefer! Now, I thought we'd have some brief introductions first, just so everyone knows who everyone else is. I am Roger d'Espry, producer with Vision! Studios, and this is Graham Strey, our resident mechanical genius responsible for our fine mostly vintage automobiles. Graham, stand up."

A harassed man of about fifty or so stood, a pair of glasses pushed to the top of his head. He waved wanly.

"Next is our beloved crew. Tabby, Sam, Dermott, and Clarissa are our film-and-sound teams, and they are the people who'll be capturing your every word, so make sure they're good ones." Roger laughed heartily. There were a few polite titters, but most of us just looked uncomfortable.

Four people who were at the far table stood up and waved. One of the women pointed at Tessa, who gave her a thumbs-up.

"There are seven production members connected with the studios. Stand up, gang."

I kind of zoned out at the introduction of a bunch of people who were evidently responsible for all the work to keep the production going, as well as a handful of race officials who would be keeping tabs on the racers.

"More about that later at the race meeting," Roger said when the five men and women who were the officials retook their seats. "And now, the talent! I see that you're somewhat mixed up at various tables, so if you'll just stand when I call out your team names, we can zip through the intros. First we have the Essex Esses: Samuel, Stephen, and Sanders. Gentlemen, if you would stand . . ."

Three men in their mid-thirties stood, their hands held up in triumph.

"Next we have the Ravishing Romeos, our friends from Italy in the form of Carlo, Luca, and Francesco." The three dark-haired men rose and bowed. Several women cheered loudly, which made them preen.

"The fine country of Germany has given us the Hessen Hausfraus: Anna, Martina, and Claudia. Ladies?"

Three women rose, all of them in their forties or later, and each wearing an identical purple tracksuit. They looked like comfortable moms, and I wondered what on earth they were doing on an around-the-world race. "Empty nesters, do you think?" I murmured to Tessa.

"Probably. I bet they're going to be hellish competition, though," she whispered back. "They look sweet, but that probably means they're ruthless and will beat us all."

"Representing Britain we have three teams. First up is the Engaging Englishmen in the form of brothers Dixon and Rupert, and a man who is no doubt familiar to anyone who watches reality TV, star of both *Strictly Come Dancing* and the hit reality show *Three Men in a Flat*: Kell! Gentlemen?" With a little sigh, Dixon got to his feet. Across the room, a man I assumed was his brother bobbed up, while seated centrally to Roger was a third, a goateed man with long blond hair pulled back in a man-bun. He rose, waved, blew some kisses, bowed, and made the Namaste gesture before bowing a few more times.

"The ham element of the show," Tessa said in an undertone.

"You think?" I asked, not at all impressed by Kell.

"Oh, definitely. Roger told us he made all sorts of demands about guaranteed amount of time on camera, saying he was bringing his sizable audience to the show."

"So he's a real celebrity, not just one of those reality people who like to post pictures of their asses on social media and believe their every move is of vital interest to the world?"

"On the contrary, he's exactly like that. He was thrown off of the *Three Men* show after the fourth week, and likewise only lasted a few weeks on the dance show. Roger said it was because he kept having meltdowns over the costumes."

"Ugh."

"Exactly. I feel for Dixon and his brother having to ride with him."

We both turned to look at Dixon, who did a double take at the sudden attention, and in response looked moderately startled.

"Now we have a couple that I'm sure I need not introduce to anyone—Team Ducal Daimler with our former duke Max Edgerton, his lovely wife, Tessa, and Abbie Teller, who played Alice the maid on the award-winning *A Month in the Life of a Victorian Duke*."

Tessa and Max stood to genuinely enthusiastic applause. Across the room, another woman rose and waved before sitting down.

"How do you feel being back on camera again?" I asked Tessa quietly.

"So long as I don't have to wear the Victorian corsets,

I'm fine with it. The wardrobe group did an astonishing job the last time, and I'm sure the Edwardian clothes will be just as gorgeous but a lot comfier to wear."

"Our French cousins are amply represented by the Gallivanting Gourmets, who are Armand, Etienne, and Yves." Three men who were at one of the beverage tables clearly flirting with the women waitstaff turned and waved, then resumed their previous activities.

"And last but certainly not least, we have Team Sufferin' Suffragettes, with Melody Edgerton—whom I'm sure you all remember from *Life of a Victorian Duke*—Paulina Lewes, and my own daughter, Louise d'Espry."

Louise shot up from her seat at the table and smirked, waving and doing a 360-degree survey of the room, blowing kisses to all and sundry, and generally eating up all the attention. Across the room next to the woman named Abbie, a dark-haired girl rose and gave a cursory wave. I could see she had a port-wine stain on one side of her face and a serious mien that warned she was not at all in the same attention-seeking class as Louise.

"Well, that, at least, is reassuring," I said under my breath.

Dixon must have had very quick ears, because he glanced at me, but the second our gazes met, his dropped, leaving me feeling like I'd been punched in the gut.

And how ridiculous is that? I thought to myself an hour later when I stood in nothing but my underwear and bra in a room filled with racks of partially finished clothes, stacks of shoes and boots, and boxes and boxes filled with large-brimmed hats. I held my arms out obediently while two different women took my measurements. I felt more than a little self-conscious, but mostly distracted by how upset I was over Dixon's reaction to me.

"It's not like I really do have cooties," I said to myself.

"No, of course you don't," one of the wardrobe ladies said absently, jotting down a note about the length of my upper arm. "Right. Let's have you without your bra. We'll need to make sure the corset fits right."

"Ugh. The corset. Tessa warned me about it."

"I don't doubt it. She really hated wearing it during the *Victorian Duke* show." The woman handed me a kind of linen undershirt, which I slipped on after peeling off my sports bra. She then held up a corset that wasn't yet finished and consulted with another woman while they held it on my torso. One of them said, "Well, let's see if Tessa's old corset will fit."

"It's the wrong shape, though," the second woman objected.

"I know, but at this point a corset is a corset is a corset."

"Huh?" I asked as they fished a pretty pink brocade corset out of a wicker basket and deftly wrapped it around my torso. It wasn't bad until they started tightening the laces at the back, and then all of a sudden I felt as if a piece of steel had me in its grip, crushing my ribs, squeezing my guts together, and pushing my boobs higher than they'd ever been. "Dear god. Are those my boobs?"

"A good corset does wonders for the girls," the main wardrobe lady (who I later found out was named Joan) said, grunting a little when she hauled on the corset laces. "Right. I think that's as good as we're going to get. What do you think, Maeve?"

Maeve, a young woman with red hair and a plethora of freckles, tipped her head to the side and considered me. "I think we should be able to get her into the premades without too much trouble."

"Premades?" I asked, wanting desperately to take a

breath but knowing without a doubt that I'd never get actual air into my lungs while wearing the corset.

"The frocks," Joan said, waving toward the racks of clothing. "We make them roughly to your size and finish them up once we have you try them on. Right. Let's start with the main driving dress."

Maeve went to fetch a dress. I stood in my underwear and corset and eyed myself in the full-length mirror that was propped up against a wall. Behind me, the door opened and a man walked into the room, a piece of paper in his hand.

"I believe I'm supposed to be—" He stopped when he saw me, his eyes widening.

It was Dixon. And facing him, with appalling naked-ness, was my butt. I met his gaze in the mirror, then whirled around so he couldn't see how big my ass was, which of course meant it was reflected back to him.

"Eek!" I said, unable to think of any actual words. My hands went first to cover my boobs, then my crotch, and then finally behind me to my butt. I couldn't decide what I wanted to cover more, so my hands fluttered back and forth for a few seconds.

"Sorry. I thought . . . I was supposed to get fitted . . . Sorry," he stammered, and spun around to march out of the room.

"And there goes Mr. Right," I said with a sigh, know-ing that I'd just lost any chance I ever had with him. Not that I really had a chance—or for that matter wanted one—but still, it dinged my pride to know that he found me so repugnant he couldn't even be bothered to ogle my boobs.

I looked down at the girls and sighed again. I had a feeling the monthlong race was going to end up feeling more like half a year.

JOURNAL OF DIXON AINSLEY
20 July
9:44 a.m.
New York City

I'm not quite sure how to start this. Or why I'm doing it, other than that it will be a good way to track expenses. And I suppose experiences.

JOURNAL OF DIXON AINSLEY
20 July
9:46 a.m.
New York City

I suppose I could write down my expenses. That would be a reasonable thing to track.
    Expenses to date:
    One journal, bought in hotel gift shop, $15
    Three-pack of pens (black), same, $7
    I guess that's really the sum total of my expenses, since the production company is paying for lodging and food. I don't know what else to write.

JOURNAL OF DIXON AINSLEY
20 July
10:13 a.m.
New York City

The weather is nice. Very sunny. Heard it's raining back home.

JOURNAL OF DIXON AINSLEY
20 July
10:14 a.m.
New York City

Maybe this journal thing isn't for me. I can't think of anything more to talk about.

What I just wrote looks so lame. I wish I knew how people did this.

Those last two sentences also look lame.

JOURNAL OF DIXON AINSLEY
20 July
12:55 p.m.
New York City

Google has a lot of examples of people's journals. Most of them are too . . . personal. But there was a nice example of a travel journal that a man did about his family's journey across the States, so I will try to emulate him. He had conversations, and maps, and drawings, and lots of observations. I can't draw, but I can find maps, and I have a good memory, so I should be able to write down conversations. Plus, I'm used to observing people.

OK. Decision made. I will make a travel journal.

I have to go back a little bit, though. Damn. I could have postdated this if I'd thought about it.

JOURNAL OF DIXON AINSLEY
20 July
1:01 p.m.
New York City, day one

"You need a vacation, Dix," Elliott said in April. I was working on the projections for the upcoming wedding season, and although I'd already printed out the summary of our reservations for the Dower House bookings for the next six months, as well as the crop forecasts, livestock assessment, and income due in from tenants, I felt I was missing something.

"I had a vacation," I said, hitting the print button on a pie chart illustration of the various sources of estate income. I hated pie charts. I also hated crop forecasts, livestock assessments, and tenant income schedules.

"Two years ago. It's time for another."

"I'm busy," I said, waving my hand at the printer. "We're coming up to summer, and you know how popular the Dower House is for weddings."

"You have everything planned to an inch. Besides, Alice is itching for something to do."

"Surely Jenna is keeping her busy?"

"Yes, but as Alice is the first to say, there's more to life than chasing after our daughter." Elliott gave me a look that was part pity and part warning. "I'm obligated by brotherly love to warn you that if Rupert continues to resist her attempts to make him settle down to just one woman, she's planning on turning her sights on you."

I dropped the printout I'd just plucked from the printer and spun around to face him fully. "What? Why? She knows about Rose, doesn't she?"

"Yes, but she considers nine years long enough to move past your grief at losing a fiancée to cancer and opening yourself up to love again. Those are her words, not mine, by the way."

"She has nothing to do with the matter," I said firmly. "My romantic life is none of her business."

"Not strictly so, I agree, but you know Alice—she wants *all* my brothers happily paired up with the woman or man of their choice."

"*Choice* being the key word of that statement," I said with surly distaste, and typed furiously at a report on the status of the fields currently lying fallow.

"Which is why I suggest you take a vacation. For about six weeks."

"What? I couldn't possibly be away that long," I said, waving my hand at the computer.

"Why?"

"I'm the estate manager," I said, glaring a little at him. Elliott might have been my elder brother, but he was also woefully ignorant as to what it took to run an estate this size, especially since now we were focused on tourists. "I have things to manage."

"Fine, but I warn you—Alice is already reaching out to friends to find someone for Rupert. She's even drawn Mercy into the scheme, and you're next."

A sort of dread-riddled panic filled me at the thought of the two women joining forces to match me up. "But I don't want to find a woman! I'm happy on my own. And I had a woman I wanted. She died. End of story."

"Not so far as Alice is concerned," Elliott said, perusing some of the charts I'd printed out. "Looks to me like things are in pretty good shape and that you could easily take six weeks off for the race."

"Race?" I snatched the papers from his fingers and put them into a file folder. "What race?"

"Some around-the-world thing that Roger d'Espry is doing. You remember him?"

"No."

"That's right—you were gone when the film crew was here watching Gunner and Lorina dig up Roman remains. Well, it's the man who has a production company that specializes in reality TV reenactments of a sort. They did one with a Victorian setting, and now they want to do a New York to Paris race that follows the route of a 1908 race."

"Hrmph," I said. "Not interested."

"You would get to race in an authentic period car," Elliott said in a persuasive tone.

That made me sit up. There's nothing I love so much as antique cars. "What kind of authentic period car?"

"Er . . ." Elliott pulled a folded scrap of paper from his pocket. "Nineteen twelve De Dion-Bouton."

"What?" I took the paper from him and whistled. "It has an Antoinette aircraft engine. This is amazing. The car should be in a museum."

"I gather that d'Espry made arrangements to have cars restored that were in bad shape, so it's not in original form."

"Still, parts of it are real." I pursed my lips and thought. "What's this race entail?"

He told me. In fact, he dragged me back to his office, where, after working our way through the obstacle course of baby toys, he pulled up an e-mail and let me read all about it.

I decided that it might be fun and, after making sure that Alice (who volunteered as my replacement while I

was gone) was up to speed on monitoring the tourist
activities and bookings, found myself packing for a
monthlong race.

Rupert had also been roped into joining the team, although his reasons for doing so were less than sterling.

"Birds will dig it," he said, shoving my elbow off the
shared armrest between our seats on the plane flying us
to New York City. "Plus it gets me away from Alice. She
keeps throwing women at me."

"I wasn't aware you had any problem finding women,"
I said, giving him a brotherly once-over. He had combed
the wild mop of hair that usually stuck out at all angles
and put on something other than the knee-length shorts
and T-shirt that were his habitual costume.

"I don't, but this is a free trip around the world. I'll
be able to take tons of pictures, and I've got my tablet
with me, so I can draw as I go."

"I'm surprised you got the time away from your job."

He shrugged and pushed his seat back, much to the
annoyance of the person behind him. "I left it. They
wanted me to design the most obnoxious dreck you've
ever seen. It's time I go out on my own anyway. Freelance
design is where it's at."

I spent a good hour trying to make him see that dumping his job to gallivant around on a reality show for a
month wasn't, perhaps, the best career choice, but Rupert
had always been one to go his own way.

He said as much when we arrived at our hotel, dumping
his bag in the room next to mine and not even bothering
to unpack before he appeared in my doorway. "Right.
That's me sorted. I'm off to see the ladies of New York."

"I thought perhaps we could see some of the sights—"

He grinned. "Oh, I'm going to. But the last thing I
need is a misery guts hanging around my neck like an
albatross."

"I am not a misery guts," I said, annoyed.

"You are when it comes to meeting women. Hell, you don't even like them touching you."

"I don't like *anyone* touching me," I pointed out. "I don't understand why people do not respect one's personal space."

"And that is exactly why you are the worst wingman in the world," Rupert said, dashing in to ruffle my hair and give me a huge bear hug. "Have fun, brother."

"Dammit, Ru!" I yelled after his fleeing figure, trying to restore order to my hair and my shirt, which he'd deliberately rumpled.

"I can't help it if I don't like to be touched," I told my reflection. "People touch too much anyway. They're always patting an arm or hugging or touching a shoulder—there's no reason to be so exuberant. Moderacy, that's what's needed in this world—moderacy in shows of affection, and in the invasion of another person's space."

After putting my things away in the closet and dresser, I had a quick shower, shaved, and went down to the ballroom for the welcome party.

A gaggle of women was at the doorway, and I made sure to let them go first. By the time I was checked in by an assistant at the door, I could see the party was already going. I wondered if Rupert had remembered about it and was going to look for him when I heard a woman say in what I believe is called a smoky voice, "There goes my shot at sexual gratification with a handsome foreigner."

She saw me as soon as she spoke, and was visibly embarrassed. I did my best to put her at ease, even going so far as apologizing for making the matter worse by chatting with her, and fortunately her blush faded quickly.

Unlike some women, she blushed prettily. In fact, she was very pretty, with high Slavic cheekbones, a pointed little chin, and a smattering of freckles across the bridge of her nose and upper cheeks. Her hair was shoulder length and straight, a glossy black that looked as if it felt like silk. But it was her eyes that gave me pause. They were brown, but a beautiful brown with all sorts of different colors mixed into it . . . reds, golds, even a little black flecked her irises. I quite enjoyed looking into her eyes, as ridiculous as that sounds.

"I'm Paulie," she said, and we shook hands. She had a surprisingly strong grip for a woman, which was a nice change. Since there was no sign of Rupert, I spent a few minutes talking with Paulie. She told me about her plan to keep a journal on the race, an idea that appealed almost immediately to me.

Just as I was enjoying myself with her, we wandered over to the drinks table, and she suddenly leaned in to me, her straight black hair brushing against my cheek. It was as if she had been made of fire—a bolt of heat shot down my neck and settled in my belly. I took a step backward, startled by both the touch and my reaction to it.

I mumbled an apology, the hurt in her eyes making me feel like I was the biggest heel in the world.

That look haunted me, and I tried to explain that I was just startled and didn't dislike her, as she seemed to think, but by that time Roger d'Espry had started talking and introducing the teams.

I was pleased to see, when it was time for my team to stand, that Rupert had made it to the party in time, although judging by the women at his table, he'd had no problem making new friends.

"Look, I want to explain about earlier," I said to Paulie when it was all over, but she didn't seem to hear me . . . or she chose not to. Either way, she hurried off with Tessa.

"Well? What do you think? Looks like it's going to be

fun, eh?" Rupert stopped next to me as people received their costuming appointments.

"That has yet to be determined," I answered, glancing at my watch. "I have to be fitted for my costume in twenty minutes."

"Mine is in an hour. Good. Gives me time to work on my new friends." He grinned and waved across the room, where a clutch of people stood around the doors chatting.

"Yes, I noticed you didn't have any trouble finding a couple of women to coo over you," I said dryly.

"Finding them? No, but I did have a bit of a fight to get them past the bloke at the door since they weren't on the list. Looked like you aren't doing too bad yourself. That bird you were with is a looker. Where'd you find her?"

"Paulie? She's one of the racers."

"*Really,*" Rupert drawled, looking thoughtful. "Maybe Alice is right."

For some reason that I refused to examine any further, I wanted to punch him in the shoulder. *Hard.*

"She's out of your league," I told him instead, and quickly changed the subject. "What did you think of Roger d'Espry?"

Rupert shrugged. "Seemed just like Elliott and Gunner described him—scattered, but competent enough. You going to the bar after your fitting?"

"I hadn't planned on it."

"Your loss if you don't. I'll be there with the twins, and from the sounds of it, the Italians are planning on hosting a party there. You could do a lot worse than to show up and meet a few bits of delectable flesh."

I gave him a look of jaded exasperation and started toward the door. "You may get by thinking of nothing but sex, but some of us have other things on our minds."

"Like I said, your loss." Rupert punched me on the

arm, then went to the corner to collect his twins and join the group surrounding the Italian team. I wondered idly where the third member of our team was, then went out to find the conference rooms that were currently housing the wardrobe department.

I consulted my assignment sheet and opened the door listed. "I believe I'm supposed to be—"

The words died on my tongue. Standing in the center of the room, facing a tall mirror, and clad only in a pair of skimpy lace underwear and a corset, stood Paulie.

Note to self: Expunge the following paragraph so as to avoid lawsuits regarding inappropriate thoughts.

I've seen naked women in my time, but never have I seen a woman who looked like a Greek statue brought to life. No, not Greek—that was too antiseptic and cold. Paulie was anything but that—she was warm, with curves everywhere, rounded breasts rising high above the corset, beautiful arms that she used in an attempt to hide first her bits, then her breasts, then finally her ass. And what an ass it was—gloriously round and smooth and . . . I had the worst urge to take it into my hands and just squeeze. She whipped around, a blush sweeping upward from her chest. I realized I was staring at her breasts and dropped my gaze, but that just led me to admire the sweep of her hips (good birthing hips, my mother would call them) and then down to two delicious thighs, round and silky looking, and for a moment I had an insane vision of me kissing my way up those thighs.

The look of horror on her face stopped those thoughts dead.

"Sorry. I thought . . . I was supposed to get fitted . . . Sorry." I ran out of the room before I could embarrass Paulie any further, and ran into Roger d'Espry a few doors down the hall. He was chatting with the couple who had been at my table, and turned to wave me over.

"Have you met Dixon? He's the earl's brother."

"Elliott is a baron, actually," I murmured.

"We have met," Tessa said, smiling at him. "He was at our table with Paulie. Where is she?"

"Being fitted," I answered, making a face. "I'm afraid I inadvertently walked in on her while she was . . . er . . ." I waved a hand at my torso. "Being corseted."

"Oh lord." Tessa gave a little laugh. "Don't worry. I'm sure she'll survive. If the corset was anything like what I wore, it covered up a lot."

"I owe her an apology, but I doubt if she wants to hear that now."

"Let's see . . ." While we had been speaking, Roger had consulted a tablet computer. "You are scheduled to be in the Rosewood room five minutes ago. That's around the corner and on the right."

"My instructions are incorrect, then," I told him, and shoved at him the piece of paper that had directed me to Paulie's room.

"Ah. Yes, I believe that the rooms were switched around at the last minute due to storage constraints. Now, Max, let me talk to you about what I want you and Tessa to do to officially start the race . . ."

Dismissed, I left them discussing the festivities and went into the correct room.

An hour later I emerged, having been measured literally up one side and down the other and having tried on several pairs of trousers, waistcoats, and jackets, as well as Edwardian driver's togs. I objected to the giant hat that puffed up on my head like a bloated mushroom, but felt somewhat dashing in the duster and goggles.

"This is rather nice," I told the two wardrobe women, who slipped the dark chocolate brown duster over a matching suit. The suit was a bit short on me, and they hastily made notes and muttered things about ripping out the temporary stitching. "Arms are too long, Lydia. Half inch."

"I see that. Legs are too short. Another inch and a half, I think. What about the waist?"

"Looks good," the unnamed wardrobe woman said. She was probably in her mid-fifties and had the reassuringly impersonal demeanor of a nurse, or someone else used to nudity.

The other woman, however, began fluttering her eyelashes at me the second I disrobed. I don't have any pretentions to being an Adonis, but work on the estate does keep me relatively fit, and I've never had a woman vomit upon beholding sight of me. Still, there was nothing in my appearance to merit such blatant flirting.

I coughed gently and tried to avoid Lydia's attempts to catch my eye. "Goggles, too? Very steampunk."

"So trendy!" Lydia said, and batted her eyes. "They look good on you."

"The camera will like you—that's for sure," the other woman said, standing back and looking me over critically. "You're tall without being too tall. Shoulders are good—we won't need to add any padding there. Your torso is a little short, but that just means you have longer legs."

"Long inseam," Lydia said, nodding and fluttering her eyelashes. I gritted my teeth and avoided glancing at her, instead donning the goggles and eyeing my reflection.

"Selfie!" Lydia said, and put an arm around me, leaning against me to take her picture. I held on to a smile while she took a couple of pictures, then tried to ease away from her without it being too obvious.

"Well, that's you done," Lydia said at last, her eyelashes going a mile a minute.

"Thank you," I said politely, and began to take off the brown worsted suit. "I'm sure the wardrobe will be, if not exciting, at least accurate and stylish."

"Very stylish," Lydia said.

I handed her the suit and began to pull on my own clothing, but when the older woman said something about fetching the last basket of shoes, I waited until she left the room before saying with as much gentleness as I could, "I much appreciate the offer, but I'm afraid I'm not what you want."

"What I want?" Lydia paused in the act of hanging the suit, giving me a come-hither look. "What do you mean?"

I shook my head, keeping my expression kind. "I'm aware that many women find an English accent irresistible—my brother Rupert is a perfect example of that—and while I appreciate the interest, I just want to warn you that I'm not available. Well, I am, but I had a fiancée, and she died. So I'm not really on the market."

Lydia stared at me a minute, then fluttered her lashes. "What are you talking about?"

"Your . . . for lack of a better word . . . flirtation."

"I'm not flirting with you," she said, and held up her hand. "I'm married. See?"

It was at that moment that I realized the excruciating truth—the woman had some sort of physical tic that made her appear to be batting her eyelashes like a coquette straight out of *Gone With the Wind*. I stared in horror at her for a second, then smiled weakly and said, "Silly me. And here I thought my charms were irresistible."

She watched with (madly blinking) wariness while I finished dressing and exited the room. As I was leaving, the other woman came in, and I heard Lydia saying, "It's amazing a hat will fit on that guy's fat head. You wouldn't believe what he said . . ."

I hurried down the hall, not wanting to hear any more. "I just wish this hellish day would come to an end," I growled to myself as I approached the elevators.

Naturally, the door opened while I was speaking, and Paulie emerged, carrying a pair of shoes.

"You having that sort of a day, too?" she asked, strolling past me. "Look at it this way: at least you didn't have someone find you physically repellent."

She turned the corner and was gone before I could apologize.

There's going to be a lot of this journal that I can't publish.

Maybe I made a mistake. Maybe I should have stayed home, where it was safe.

Dammit, I don't find her physically repellent! Far from it.

Right. That's enough of that sort of talk. Time for a cold shower, then bed. Things will be better in the morning.

God, I hope they're better in the morning.

Paulina Rostakova's Adventures

JULY 20
1:44 p.m.
Dorcet Hotel, New York City, parking garage

"I think we all agree that I'm the head suffragette." Louise tossed her head and gave Melody and me a look that dared us to dispute that statement. "And Melody is the studious one who knows all the stuff, like navigation and all that."

"I'm so delighted being the stuff-knowing one," Melody said dryly, her face deadpan.

I bit back a giggle, knowing from my time with her that anything remotely humorous completely missed Louise. She had to be the single most self-centered person I'd ever met, and I grew up in California!

"Which makes me the rogue suffragette," I said, trying to spin a wrench around my fingers, but ending up flinging it at Louise's foot. She shrieked and leaped back, giving me a mean look in return. "Sorry."

"I should hope so!"

I fetched the wrench back and held tight to it while Louise made a note on her phone. "You're the handy one," she finally told me, giving me a less-than-happy face. "I hope you pay attention at the mechanic class."

"From what I understand, Graham the mechanic will be traveling with Roger's entourage. I only have to know how to do a couple of things, like tighten lug nuts or those pointy things in the engine."

"Spark plugs," Melody said, sighing under her breath.

"Right, those. Don't worry—I'll be the queen of suffragette mechanics."

"If you could do it without damaging my Jimmy Choos, that would be awesome," Louise said in a sickly-sweet voice, then did another hair flip and plastered a smile on her face when she saw the camera crew heading our way.

Two other teams were in the garage, each going through the rule book and getting acquainted with the cars. I was a bit surprised to see the film crews following Roger around. "Why are they filming this? We're not in costume, and we are just learning about the cars," I said.

"It's all prep work," Melody explained with a nod toward Roger, who was at the car next to ours. "Behind-the-scenes stuff to be used on the director's commentary version of the DVD."

"We're going to be on a DVD?" I asked, surprised. I thought it was just a British reality show, although Louise had said earlier that she'd heard there was a chance a U.S. network was going to pick up the show.

"Most likely." Melody consulted the printed handbook that we'd all been given. "I'm looking forward to crossing the country. I've never been here, but Tessa talks a lot about it. Is this I-80 road that we spend some time on interesting?"

"I don't know. I've never been on it, but from the map I looked at this morning, it seems to go relatively straight across the country, so I imagine there will be some pretty scenes." I looked askance at the car next to us. "I just don't know how they expect us to get across the country in two weeks in this giant white behemoth. I know it's not a complete antique, but its body parts are. Can a car that old make the trip?"

Melody patted the car's long hood. "I think it has character."

I gave the car a thorough examination. It looked a lot like the car from the famous movie: gleaming cream-colored metal with leather straps holding the hood down, great sweeping sideboards that you could stand on if you wanted, two rows of red leather seats, with one of the narrow old-timey tires strapped to the back. On the front hood, a sign painter was carefully writing THOMAS FLYER in fancy black script, outlined in gold. "At least the seats look comfy."

Melody didn't answer because at that moment Roger d'Espry approached with Sam and Tabby, one of the two camera-and-sound teams.

"Well, ladies, what do you think of our Thomas Flyer? Isn't she a beauty? The shell of the car is all original, although we had to have part of the frame and most of the engine work redone."

"I'm glad to hear I won't have to be a real mechanic," I said, feeling awkward when Sam swung the camera around to me. I tried hard not to look directly at it, per instruction.

"Oh, but you will be called on to do simple maintenance. And that's why Graham is here—Graham?" The mechanic hurried forward. "Graham will show you how to fill the oil, check the water, change a tire, and so on."

"Oh. Gotcha. Hi," I said, still feeling awkward . . . At least I did until I caught sight of a couple of men who emerged from the elevator halfway down the garage. Dixon Ainslie was dressed in a pair of black pants and a plaid cotton shirt, looking as coolly confident as ever, and twice as annoying. Another man was with him, one with wild brown hair that seemed to stick out in all directions and a short goatee—his brother no doubt. Both men approached while Roger was telling Melody how they had merged together the old and new to make the cars, and what elements were true to form (steering, tires, and some basic mechanicals) and what was more current (engine, so we could go faster than forty miles an hour, seat belts, and transmission).

"Shall we get started?" Graham asked, handing me a small can of oil. "I'll show you how to check the oil first. We'll top her up before you leave, but it's good for you to know how to do this in case you're out in the wilds of Russia and need it."

My attention was divided between the lesson and Dixon, who strolled over to watch behind the camera. His brother had stopped to chat with two pretty production assistants, giving me the impression he was a lady's man.

"The hood straps connect here. See that?"

"That buckle, yes?"

"Right. Take that off; then you can push the hood back onto itself. And there you see a very modern engine."

"Hopefully, you'll keep that off camera," Roger interrupted himself to say. "Viewers like to believe what they're seeing, so it's vitally important that you maintain the image of an actual antique car."

"All righty." I moved so my body was between the camera and the open hood. "Like this?"

"Perfect." Roger turned his attention to his daughter, who had finished a phone conversation and come over to preen before the camera. "Louise, dear, perhaps you'd like to take the wheel and familiarize yourself with the method of driving. You other ladies will learn as well, but since Louise will be the pilot, we'll get a few shots of her learning her stuff."

Louise was more than happy to oblige, and climbed into the car, pausing to say, "The steering wheel is on the wrong side!"

"That's how they were made then, love," Roger said soothingly, and hurried over to her side to point out various elements of the steering and acceleration.

"Would you mind if I peered over your shoulder?" Dixon asked when Graham showed me where the oil cap was. "Evidently I'm to be the mechanic on my team as well, and I assume the engines are the same even if the outer car is not."

"Good idea," Graham said. "Will save me time. Now, do you see that gauge there? Just draw a line straight to the left and you'll find the oil cap."

I was very aware of Dixon leaning next to me as we peered into the engine and had to keep my attention firmly focused lest it wander to thinking of snarky things to say to him . . . and wanting to casually brush my arm against his. By the time we had a lesson on how to add water, where the car horn could be unplugged, and how the big brass-contained headlights were replaced, I stopped wanting to be rude to Dixon and instead admired his fascination with the car. He asked several questions about the rebuild, how the cars would operate in inclement conditions, and what sort of facilities were being arranged for repairs.

"I'll be riding with the film crew," Graham told him. "Ideally, any repairs we have to make we can do at night, off camera."

"I understood that the real racers had endless trouble with their cars," I said, recalling the Web site I'd read the night before. "Breakdowns constantly, getting stuck in snow and mud and so on."

"So I understand, although we're not concerned with

duplicating that for the television audience," Graham said, moving around to the rear of the car to show me how to attach and remove a spare tire from the block that would be affixed to the back of the car. "Viewers want action and drama, not sitting around in the mud waiting for a tow."

"I'm glad to hear that, because the original race sounds like it was a hellish nightmare."

Dixon gave me a look that seemed oddly approving, then bent to see the connectors that would hold a stack of tires onto the back of the car. After another half hour of instruction, Graham went off to see the car that Dixon and his team would use, promising to show him some of the differences between the vehicles.

Before he left, Dixon said softly, "Do you have a moment?"

"Sure." I put a smile on my face, well aware that the camera was nearby, now filming Roger in front of a large map of the U.S., ostensibly showing Louise the route across the country.

He nodded at a spot about ten yards away, and I followed after him, curious now if he was going to say something that would annoy me after we'd spent a nice half hour learning basic car stuff. "What is it? Not something bad, I hope."

"I hope not as well. I wanted to apologize about last night. For the . . . erm . . . reaction I had when you leaned in to speak quietly. I wanted to reassure you that it was nothing about you personally. It's just that I have . . . I don't like . . . Boundaries are important to me."

"Boundaries?" I asked, confused.

"Personal space." He waved a hand around the front of him. "I am uncomfortable when people I don't know well breach that."

"Are you saying you don't like to be touched?"

"Yes, but I generally try not to say it like that. It sounds so misanthropic."

I relaxed. "Is that all it is? One of the directors for a charity I work for is like that. She's super antitouchy, but she's also a germophobe, so I've learned to not touch anything in her office."

"I'm not that bad," he said, grimacing. "I don't back away if people touch me—at least not normally. It's just when I'm taken by surprise that I react without thinking."

"So . . . if I was to put my hand on you now, you wouldn't react?" I asked, eyeing his chest. For some reason, it seemed to hold an unholy fascination for me. I couldn't help but imagine it naked. The hint of reddish brown hair peeping from the top of his shirt told me he wasn't a hairless wonder, but also wasn't the Amazing Monkey Man.

His lips twisted into a half smile. "I can't promise that, but I wouldn't flinch."

I stared at him in surprise for a moment. "Did you just flirt with me?"

"What?" He looked startled. "No. Did I? I'm not sure now."

"You said you couldn't promise you wouldn't react if I touched you. I just want to know if you meant that like you might have a nice reaction." I glanced over at the others, but no one was even looking in our direction. "Like a turn-you-on sort of touch."

He cleared his throat. "As to that, I suspect it would depend on how you were touching me."

"OK." I pursed my lips a little, not to entice him, but because that's what I did when I thought hard. "I'm going to touch you now."

"Very well." He straightened up.

"Well, that's not going to help," I told him.

"What isn't?"

"Standing there all stiff like you're facing the firing squad." I put my hand on his biceps. "Relax. Breathe. Nothing bad is going to happen."

He visibly relaxed, and even gave me a little smile. "You're making too much of what is really just an annoying personality quirk."

"I'm not the one who flinched when I leaned in to you." I smiled reassuringly at him. "Second hand coming in for a landing."

"I shall endeavor to survive the experience," he said in that plummy English accent that made me feel all warm and fuzzy. I put my other hand on his chest.

"Well? What are you feeling?" I asked.

He looked thoughtful for a moment. "Hungry. I missed breakfast."

"Nothing . . . erotic?"

"No. I'm sorry."

"I'm not." I took my hands off him, giving him a friendly smile. "It wasn't meant to be erotic, so I think you're fine, mentally speaking, except for the personal-space issue, which a lot of people have, to be honest."

"Thank you for that diagnosis. Are you . . . erm . . . doing anything for dinner?"

"Good lord, Dixon," I said, feigning amazement. "First you flirt with me, and now you're asking me out to dinner? Whatever will be next? Holding hands in Times Square? Necking in the back of the Thomas Flyer? Rubbing your naked chest against mine while stroking your hand up my leg, your mouth nibbling on that sweet spot behind my left ear, and your other hand gently, oh so gently toying with my nipple?"

The silence that followed that was really loud.

"That was strangely specific," he said at last.

"Sorry," I said, fanning myself. "I have a very active imagination."

"I see." To my utter delight, he waggled his eyebrows for a few seconds. "You never know what might happen, although I suspect Roger will not approve of racers engaging in those sorts of activities."

"Are you kidding? Have you never seen reality TV?"

"No, I don't watch much TV at all."

"Then you wouldn't know that people eat that stuff up with a spoon and beg for more. The bigger the drama, the higher the conflict, and the more naughty the high jinks, the better the viewing."

"I draw the line at having sex in the cars just to improve ratings," Dixon said with a serious face that I thought indicated he was annoyed until I saw the glint of humor in his eyes.

"Fine, but don't complain later that I turned you down. I'd say yes to dinner, but my dad and stepmom are flying out to see the start of the race tomorrow. We're doing dinner together."

"Ah," he said, his expression smooth and unreadable. "Another time, perhaps."

I threw caution to the wind. I mean, I grabbed it with both hands, dug my fingers into it to get it to pay attention, and flung it away from me as hard as I could. "Why don't you join us?"

"You want me to meet your parents?" Something flashed through his eyes. It might have been surprise, or it might have been fear.

"Not like that. I just thought if you don't have anyone to eat dinner with, you're welcome to come along with us. But perhaps you'd like to stay with your brother?"

"I doubt Rupert would welcome me," he said with a wry twist of his lips and a glance at where his brother was now very clearly flirting with Louise.

"Then it's settled. Dad said he'd meet me in the lobby of the hotel at seven. Is that OK with you?"

"Yes, although it means missing the embarkation party with the other teams."

"That starts at eight, and we should be done with dinner by nine. We can go after that, if you like."

"That sounds agreeable," he said politely, and I was suddenly possessed with the urge to grab him by his prim and proper head and kiss the daylights out of him. But instead of doing that, I simply gave him an innocent smile and returned to the Thomas Flyer to watch while Melody got a brief lowdown on how to drive the car.

The rest of the morning was spent in final fittings for the costumes and a lunch where the official race rules were discussed.

Unfortunately, I didn't see Dixon at the lunch until it was over, so I sat with Tessa and Max and their friend.

"Now, I know you're all aware this is a race," Roger told us as we finished off some excellent salmon en croute. "But we don't want anyone risking his or her life just to garner the prize. Therefore, the official race committee has declared that the U.S. segment will consist of points which you obtain by hitting checkpoints in the allotted time. So there's no sense in racing flat out to get to San Francisco as fast as you can—each night we'll have a designated stop, and your time getting to that stop will be recorded. If you get to it too quickly, it means you have been speeding, and you will be penalized. Likewise, if you get there past the allowed time, you will also receive a penalty."

"That sounds smart," Tessa told Max, who nodded.

"We'll see if it works. I suspect that most people will be champing at the bit to be the first one to each day's destination."

"You can say that again," I said. "Louise told Melody and me that if we make her lose any camera time, she'll gut us with her nail scissors."

Max looked startled, but Tessa laughed. "I suspect your car is going to have the most fun."

"As you know," Roger continued, "we will drive across the country on a variety of interstate highways. Although the original racers varied slightly from our route, for the most part our journey will mimic the path they took across the country. The route isn't as direct as modern roads provide, so be sure to follow the instructions we give you and not a GPS unit's directions. Once all active racers are in San Francisco, cars and drivers—as well as the film crew—will be loaded onto the two transport planes generously provided by our sponsor." He named a company that I later found out provided petroleum to the Western world. "The flight to Beijing should take about sixteen hours. Following that, both you and the cars will be cleared through customs and the race will pick up anew. This time, however, it will be a race in the truest sense of the word, although, of course, we expect you to adhere to all local traffic laws and speed limits. The first person to follow the course route and reach Paris will win not only the race, but the twenty-thousand-dollar prize award for each member of the team."

"We could get the roof redone," Tessa told Max. "Or maybe throw it toward that cottage in Scotland you've been eyeing."

"New car, and a trip to the Azores," Max replied.

"I could put a down payment on a flat," Melody mused. "And go to Australia."

"What would you do with your money, Paulie?" Tessa asked.

I thought. It wasn't enough for me to get my own house,

and I had a car. "I think I'd use it to send my dad and stepmom on an around-the-world cruise. Or at least as long of a cruise as the money would buy."

"How altruistic of you," Tessa cried.

I didn't correct her by telling her my motive would be to get Daddy out of my hair for a few months. Instead I smiled and turned my attention back to Roger.

"This afternoon we'll allow you all to actually drive your cars at a location free from public traffic. Graham will be on hand in case there are any questions. This evening is the embarkation party, where we will film each of you on the eve of the great undertaking. You will not be in costume, but any thoughts you have about setting off on such a momentous journey should be saved for your individual filmed session."

I thought about what I'd say for that, but couldn't think of much that would interest anyone.

Paulina Rostakova's Adventures

Just a quickie update before I get ready for my date . . .
er . . . dinner with Dixon. And Daddy and Angela, of
course.

We drove around an abandoned strip mall on Long
Island and practiced parking, turning, backing up, and
accelerating and stopping. Driving in the Thomas Flyer
is an absolute hoot. Hard, but a hoot.

"The first thing you're going to notice are the three
pedals on the floor," Graham said when it was my turn
to learn how to drive.

"Yup," I said. "Gas, brake, and—what, a clutch?"

"No. Right is your brake, middle is your reverse, and
left is the clutch."

"Um . . ." I looked down at my feet. "Where's the gas,
then?"

"That lever on the right side of the steering wheel.
What you do is push the clutch all the way to the floor,
give it some gas, then let up on the gas and lift up your
clutch foot."

I stalled it the first couple of times I tried to get

moving, but at last I got the dance down and was soon zipping across the parking lot at a heady twenty miles an hour.

"Louise worries me," I told Melody later, once we were out of the subject's hearing.

Melody cast her a thoughtful look. "She doesn't seem to be very good at telling the clutch from the brake, does she?"

"That, and she's so busy smiling at the car with the camera, she's not paying attention to where she's driving."

"Perhaps we can suggest she let us do the bulk of the driving," Melody suggested.

"She's not going to want to do that if the cameras are on."

"No, but they won't be filming us all of the time. If we can limit her driving to just film times, then we should have a greater chance at completing the race without . . . problems."

"Like crashing into something," I added grimly.

Crap. Must go fling myself in the shower and put my hair up. I wonder if it's too late to add some color to it.

Paulina Rostakova's Adventures

JULY 20
7:31 p.m.
Dandie's Lion Restaurant, Manhattan, ladies' room

My father is an idiot.

Paulina Rostakova's Adventures

JULY 20
7:44 p.m.
Dandie's Lion Restaurant, Manhattan, ladies' room

Dixon is an idiot, too.

Paulina Rostakova's Adventures

JULY 20
8:02 p.m.
Dandie's Lion Restaurant, Manhattan, ladies' room (the attendant just asked if I have a UTI)

Although he does know his cars. Dixon, that is, not Daddy. Hell. There's Angela. More later.

JOURNAL OF DIXON AINSLEY
21 July
12:55 a.m.
New York City

I'm at a loss as to where to start about the evening's events. I'd prefer never to remember some of them, but that's cowardice speaking, so I will ignore my desire to heavily edit the happenings. I can do that when I publish the diary, after all.

Let us begin with a full retelling of the evening.

Paulie invited me to dinner with her after I explained about how I dislike people invading my personal space. At first, I was taken aback—how could she interpret a simple apology as an expressed desire to date her? I like her, despite the fact that she herself stated that she wants to get laid by one of the non-U.S. racers, but I'm determined not to let that color my opinion of her. After all, Rupert is already working his way through any and all American women who are willing, so why shouldn't Paulie do the same? Perhaps Alice has more matchmaking skills than I previously thought.

I'm going to have to delete the above paragraph from a finished book. Not only do I sound self-righteously priggish, but it makes Paulie sound like a trollop of the worst color, and she's anything but. I speak, of course, with the hindsight of the dinner behind me, which I understand isn't at all allowable in narrative retelling.

Right. I shall have to delete *that* paragraph as well. Where was I?

I met Paulie in the lobby of the hotel. She looked quite nice in a red dress that was, perhaps, a shade too short, considering it showed off a lot of those long, long legs of hers, but I suppose she is free to wear what she likes. Come to think of it, it had a low neckline that more or less demanded that everyone admire her breasts. Surely she had to be aware of just how much breast she was exposing? Is that the way they dress in the States? I admit I didn't have the opportunity to look at how other women were dressed, what with Paulie's breasts sitting right there, gleaming at me in the subdued lighting of the restaurant, not to mention the occasional flashes of leg that were quite distracting.

But I'm jumping ahead of myself.

"Hi," Paulie said by way of greeting in the lobby of the hotel. "You look nice."

"Thank you. I wasn't prepared for a black-tie event, so I hope a simple suit would suffice."

"More than suffice," she said, smiling broadly. The admiration in her eyes was more than a little warming. "You look like James Bond."

"I assure you that I have no skills that would qualify me for that persona. I'm a simple estate manager. That dress is quite . . ."

"Fun? It is, isn't it?" She did a little twirl that showed off even more leg. Heat pooled in my groin, an effect that I ignored. The last thing I needed was an untoward erection.

"You have the funniest look on your face," she said, frowning a little. "Are you in pain?"

"Not yet, but I will be if you keep spinning around," I muttered.

She stared at me in surprise a second, looked down at her dress, then back up to me with a slightly opened mouth. It took her a second before she reached out and whapped me on the arm. "You're flirting with me again! Golly, Dixon! Is this a record for you?"

"I don't know why you interpret having definite personal boundaries with disliking women or, rather, not being interested in women, but I can assure you that the truth is far from that. I like women just fine. I met and proposed to a woman twelve years ago. She died of brain cancer four months before our wedding."

I hadn't meant to blurt all of that out, especially not standing in the middle of a busy hotel lobby, but out it came, and I had the dissatisfaction of seeing her playful expression turn to one of embarrassment.

Dammit, I'd done it again. I was the world's biggest ass.

"I'm sorry," I said with a sigh at my inability to speak without making a fool of myself. "I didn't mean to snap at you like that when you were simply teasing me."

"You didn't really snap so much as put me in my place," she said after a moment's thought. "Can I put my hand on your arm?"

"What? Yes."

"Good." She put her hand on my lower arm, giving it a gentle squeeze. "I'm sorry about your fiancée, Dixon. I didn't know that you were grieving, or I wouldn't have poked fun about you flirting. Wait. Was it a flirt? Oh god, it wasn't, was it? I totally misinterpreted it? Argh! I could just die of embarrassment!"

"We seem to be quite adept at making each other feel uncomfortable," I said, putting my hand over her fingers where they still sat on my arm. It was a pleasant sensation, and I wondered how long it had been since I had touched someone's hand. "Let me at least relieve you of any guilt you might be feeling. My fiancée died a little more than nine years ago, so yes, perhaps that was a little flirting on my part. I will admit that I don't have the easy manner that Rupert has with women, so I find things a bit difficult, socially speaking. Do you . . . er . . . want to be flirted with? By me, that is, since I know your goal is to have sex with one of the foreign contestants."

She stared at me in growing disbelief, her fingers digging painfully into my arm before she released it. "I beg your pardon?"

"What have I said now?" I asked, feeling even more like a clod even though I'd just asked a simple question.

She hit me on the arm again. "You basically said I'm in the race just so I can hook up with one of you guys with plummy accents, and chests that could drive a virgin to drink, and butts that you just want to bounce quarters off of."

"You yourself said—"

"I know what I said!" she snarled and, grabbing my wrist, hauled me through the doors to the sidewalk, where she must have noticed a limousine that had pulled up. "That was an aberration, and I'd appreciate it if you'd forget it. Dad, this is Dixon. He's not my date, so stop puffing yourself up. He's just one of the fellow racers who thinks women are trying like mad to get into his pants even when they aren't. Dixon, this is Angela, my stepmom."

She released my wrist and climbed into the back of the limo (exposing a lot of thigh in the process), leaving me on the sidewalk with a man slightly shorter than me but almost twice as broad. He wore a scowl that could probably darken the brightest summer day, and I was aware that another man emerged from the front of the car.

"Hello, Mr.—" I started to say, but at that moment the man behind me began frisking me, grabbing me under the arms, and roughly patting his way down to my legs, whereupon he proceeded to check out each leg before moving around to the front of me to pull open my suit jacket, pulling out first my wallet, then the small notebook in which I'm making these notes. He flipped open the wallet and studied it for a moment.

"Dixon Ainslie," he said, and handed me back my things.

"What is country of birth?" Paulie's father asked me.

"Might I inquire what—"

"COUNTRY OF BIRTH?" he repeated at a much louder volume.

"England, but I don't see what that— Are you Googling me?" Outrage was, I'm sure, quite evident in my voice when I saw the henchman tapping away on his phone.

"Sure," Paulie's father said, eyeing me with profound suspicion. "You maybe don't want to be Googled? You have something to hide?"

"I have nothing to hide—"

"Dad, come on! I'm starving, and I told you that Dixon wasn't a boyfriend, so you don't need to do a background check on him. He's just one of the racers."

"Is good to be careful. I have enemies," he said darkly, his eyes narrowing on me. "You know what I do to enemies?"

"No, but I assume it's something extremely violent and quite possibly illegal."

"Right," he said, giving me a push to the car. I thought about turning around and making my excuses, but the sight of Paulie's legs had me climbing in. I was going to sit next to her, but her father gave me another shove, and he and I ended up on the seat facing the two women.

"It's a pleasure to meet you, Dixon," the woman next to Paulie said. "I'm so glad Paulie's made a friend already, and you're more than welcome to join us for dinner despite what Peter may imply. You're English? It's been a long time since we visited that country, but I have fond memories of the Lake District. Do you live near there?"

"No, but I've been there, and agree it's quite nice."

Conversation to the restaurant consisted of Paulie's stepmother chatting about her trip to England, and which BBC America shows she enjoys. Paulie was content to sit there and frown at her father, who spent his time grunting single-syllable replies to his wife, all the while watching me with so much suspicion, I wouldn't have been surprised if he had asked to see my passport and a copy of my fingerprints.

The restaurant was evidently a trendy place, filled with what Elliott would call the Beautiful People, most of them prancing about as if the paparazzi were watching their every move. Who knows? Perhaps they were, although I didn't see anyone with a camera. We were escorted into an alcove set off the main dining area, providing privacy and yet still open to the rest of the restaurant, a fact I found comforting, given the reaction of Mr. Rostakova toward me.

"Well, isn't this nice?" Angela said once we were seated.

"What are they doing here?" Paulie asked, staring pointedly at the two men who accompanied us. One was the driver, while the other was the man who'd patted me down. Neither was introduced.

Mr. Rostakova ignored her question. "Sit," he told me, and pointed to a chair as far from Paulie as possible. I had a feeling he would have placed me in a nearby alcove, had he been given the chance.

"Oh, for god's sake, Dad! I told you twice already: he's not a boyfriend! Dixon, ignore my father, please. He's deranged."

"Am not deranged," Mr. Rostakova said, clearly outraged. "Am protective. Is good thing to be protective."

I sat next to Paulie, not wishing to give in to the sort of behavior performed by a man who has another man frisked. "I'm looking forward to dinner. My internal clock is still a bit confused, and somehow I seem to have missed lunch," I said conversationally.

"Yeah, I'm super hungry, too," Paulie said, looking over the menu. I had a bit of a moment when I saw the prices, but decided that my savings account would withstand the hit it would take when I insisted on paying for dinner.

"You want water? Here, you have water."

"He has his own water glass, Dad," Paulie said without looking away from the menu. Her father pursed his lips and reclaimed the glass he was trying to press on me. Behind him, his two men stood, hands crossed, their eyes on me. It reminded me of a scene out of *The Godfather*.

There was a discussion of what meals appealed to everyone, and both Angela and I settled on steaks while Paulie opted for a seafood pasta dish, and her father had tripe.

Yes, tripe. Actual tripe.

"So, you driver in race. You have job in real life, yes?" Peter Rostakova asked once our orders were given and a wine had been settled on.

"Yes, I do. I manage my brother's estate. He's a baron," I said as casually as I could. Normally I dislike mentioning Elliott's title in that manner, but Rostakova had irritated me to the point where I threw manners out the window.

"Oooh, a real baron? Did you hear that, Paulie?"

"No, of course I didn't. I'm only sitting a foot away from him with perfectly normal hearing."

"You like fine things in life?" Rostakova asked, pulling out a silver card case. "You like this, yes? Is pretty?"

He offered me the case, but before I could take it, Paulie snatched it out of his hand and rubbed her hands all over it.

"You ought to be ashamed of yourself! No fingerprints!

Not this time! I refuse to let you drive away another man with your paranoid imaginings. Not, as I have said about a hundred times now, that we are dating. Dixon is here because his brother is a horn dawg and he's by himself. Got that?"

"Is my job to see you are protected," her father said with a hurt look at her. "You are only daughter. You are heiress!"

"Oh, for the love of god! *Dad!*"

"I have to powder my nose, dear. Why don't you come with me," Angela said, getting to her feet.

Paulie looked like she wanted to continue ranting at her father, but she followed her stepmother readily enough. The second they were gone, Rostakova moved over to Paulie's seat, his goons sliding in on the other side.

"You like my daughter, eh? Paulie is pretty girl, yes? You want to get close to her, to do things to her that a husband does?"

"Do you know, I don't believe that's any of your business?" I said calmly, which was a miracle, considering I was seething inside. How dared this man confront me as if I was the worst sort of pervert? Especially after Paulie had told him multiple times that we weren't dating.

"I see you look at her breasts. I see you look at her legs. I know that look." Rostakova leaned in close. "Is look that says man wants to take her to bed. She is good girl. She will not go to bed with you."

"I'm sure she is old enough to make up her own mind who she desires to pursue an intimate relationship with," I agreed, hanging on to the cool demeanor I'd seen Elliott use.

"She is young mentally," he replied, tapping his head. "She is innocent, pure of knowledge of bad things."

I had a feeling that Paulie wasn't quite as innocent as her father thought, but kept that to myself.

"Dad," Paulie said, reappearing with her stepmother. Her tone was sharp. "You're in my chair."

"Is good. English and me, we have talk. We understand." Rostakova gave me a look that warned I'd better agree.

And it was that look that did it. I'm not proud of it, but at that moment I decided that, as long as Rostakova lit a fire under me, I might as well throw on a bit more fuel.

"Oh? About what?" Paulie asked. I had stood when the ladies returned to the table and pushed Paulie's chair in after she reclaimed it.

The view of her cleavage from above was memorable, but it was for Rostakova's benefit that I bent over her and kissed her on the cheek very near her ear, with my other hand on her almost bare shoulder. "Why, you, of course," I said, enjoying both her quick intake of breath and her father's red face and sputtered protestations. Luckily, they were in Russian, but the fury in his eyes gave me a great deal of satisfaction nonetheless.

"What the hell?" Paulie asked when I took my seat.

I was taken aback by the anger in her voice and eyes— so taken aback that I didn't answer immediately.

"Do you think I talk just to hear myself?" she asked, and snapped her napkin open with violence. "I told my father we aren't dating, and then you go and peer down my dress and kiss me? Is that the sort of shit you pull in England? Because if it is, I'm here to tell you that it's not going to be tolerated here."

"I'm—I'm sorry," I stammered, ashamed of my behavior. "I hadn't thought—"

"No, that's very clear that you haven't!" She threw down her napkin and shoved back her chair, quickly getting to her feet. "I have to use the restroom."

"But, dear—" Angela got only those two words out before Paulie stormed off.

I thought of going after her to apologize, but realized I couldn't stand outside the ladies' room and beg for her forgiveness.

"Igor," Rostakova said, his gaze never wavering from my face, "you have the knife I wanted? The one to make stallions not stallions?"

Igor smirked.

"Dear," Angela said, putting her hand on her husband's, her voice filled with amused exasperation. "It's not polite to threaten people with a gelding knife over dinner."

"Gelding knife," Rostakova said, rolling the words lovingly over his tongue. "Very much gelding knife. Yes."

"Are you looking forward to driving the antique car?" Angela asked me, clearly feeling a change of subject was due.

I greeted it with much pleasure, for many reasons. "Very much so, yes. The De Dion is a lovely car. It ran in both the 1907 and 1908 races, you know, although it didn't finish well."

"I didn't realize there was another race," Angela said, smiling up at Paulie when she returned.

I half rose, but Paulie was seated before I could do more than cast an anxious glance her way.

"It ran from Peking to Paris and was the inspiration for the race we are duplicating. The De Dion company was one of the largest car manufacturers of the time, although primarily European in make. They were the first to have a V-8 engine."

"I assume that's good?" Angela asked.

"It was at the time, yes. Made for a very powerful car."

"Not as powerful as the Thomas Flyer," Paulie said quickly. "The car that actually won the New York to Paris race."

"Very true," I said, and when Angela turned her attention to her husband, I leaned closer to Paulie and said,

"I'm truly sorry for my little show. I'm afraid it was in reaction to your father's less-than-subtle threats."

She turned her eyes, a beautiful rich brown, to me. "Oh! So you weren't overcome by my charms into expressing your admiration."

There was a twinkle in her eyes that caused me to smile in response. "No, although I will say your charms are very . . . erm . . . charming."

She laughed aloud, garnering a huge scowl from her father, and relaxed back into her chair. We spent an enjoyable half hour talking about the original race and how much Paulie was looking forward to traveling across the country.

"You've never done so?" I asked quietly when Rosta-kova was on the phone with someone and Angela was at another table talking to an acquaintance. "Without sounding crass, it would appear you come from a family that has the means to travel when you desire."

"Oh, Dad's a bajillionaire—floors in California can be very lucrative, especially when you use your illicit background to get expensive hardwoods at a very cheap price—but he's also the king of paranoia. He's convinced that if I were to do anything on my own, I would imme-diately be kidnapped and held for ransom."

"Good lord. That seems a rather insular view."

"Oh, it's beyond insular and smack-dab in the land of batshit crazy, but there's not a lot I can do about it. I don't have any money of my own, and due to a lack of oomph, my college degree—history—has just sat around doing squat. I volunteer a lot at Angela's charities, but this race is really the first time I'll be able to do what I want to do."

"And that is?"

"I want to be an adventuring journalist. I plan on emu-lating Nellie Bly, who was a Victorian reporter."

"That's right. You mentioned her earlier. I have a vague memory of her exploits. Didn't she attempt to duplicate Jules Verne's fictional around-the-world journey?"

"She didn't just attempt it. She beat Phileas Fogg by more than a week. And a gold star to you for knowing about Nellie. Not a lot of folks do." Her smile was warm, and it touched me.

Our food came at that moment, halting conversation until everyone had their meals before them and the servers had left.

"But surely . . ." I hesitated, trying to find words that wouldn't offend. "You'll pardon me if this sounds like an insult, because it isn't intended as one, but you don't look like you're straight out of college."

She bristled up for a moment, then gave a short laugh—at herself, I suspected. "I'm not, much though I wish I looked like a dewy twenty-two. I'm twenty-nine, which, yes, means I've been living as an adult for a long time. I know what you're going to say—why didn't I just walk out and get a job and support myself like everyone else? The answer is the price I'd have to pay."

"I've heard it was expensive to live here—"

"No, not that. Can I lean close?"

"Absolutely," I answered, charmed that she acknowledged my oddities by asking permission. She leaned in, and I caught a brief whiff of a light perfume that seemed to coil around me. "I was kidnapped once, you see. By my maternal grandparents. They just wanted to see me, but Dad is convinced that his nefarious past in Russia means everyone is gunning for him and his family. And to be honest, I'm not absolutely sure he's not right. Regardless, if I moved out, he would insist I had round-the-clock bodyguards, and I don't know about you, but that's not a living arrangement I could stomach for long. The pretense of freedom but reality of imprisonment . . ." She gave a little shudder. "It's better to just stay at home and slip out when I can. Plus, Dad would worry himself to death if I left. He ended up in the hospital once when I tried, so I stay home rather than fight it."

"I'm surprised if that's your father's attitude that you are doing this race around the world, especially when so much of it will be through Russia."

Rostakova finished his conversation before I had ended the sentence, and roared an oath in response. "You see? Even English knows the danger of you going to Russia. You go home with us. Will be safe then."

"Ignore him," Paulie said, flashing an annoyed look at her father. "He's on my list anyway."

"List?" Rostakova's expression changed quickly from antagonism to pure innocence, his lips pursed and his eyebrows raised. "What list is this?"

"My shit list for you sending Boris after me. Don't even bother, Dad—I saw him on the plane. Although I will say that, thankfully, he took my threat seriously and hasn't been pestering me here."

Rostakova pursed his lips even harder.

Paulie must have noticed it because she set down her fork to slap the table. "Dammit, Dad! If you've hired someone else to tail me—someone I don't know—I swear to heaven I won't go back home. I'll just wander the world indefinitely!"

"Is my job to protect—"

"Oh, for god's sake!"

The rest of dinner was mostly a continued argument between Paulie and her father, although after a few minutes Paulie decided to ignore her father and spoke only to Angela or me. It was exhausting and uncomfortable, and I was relieved when the meal was over and we could leave.

"You and Dixon go back to the hotel," Angela said after Rostakova had wrestled the check away from me. I made a legitimate attempt to get it back, but one of his bodyguards moved between us, effectively blocking me off. "I want to take a drive through the park before we turn in. Peter, dear, modulate your voice! The other diners are being disturbed."

"Come on," Paulie said, nodding to me, and I hurried after her when she bolted to the exit. She didn't wait around to find a cab, simply glanced up and down the street and took off at a fast walk in the direction that I believed headed for Times Square, where we'd be starting our race in the morning. "Do you mind walking?"

"Not at all. Would you mind if I took your arm?"

"No, but you don't have to ask," she said with a smile. "I don't have any personal space issues."

I took her hand in mine, not quite sure why I felt it necessary to do so, but pleased that I had. Chivalry, I told myself as we turned the corner and Paulie slowed down to a reasonable walk. I was being chivalrous, nothing more.

"I felt it was only polite, since you ask before touching me. Although I should say that you really needn't feel like you must do that. I'm only skittish around strangers, and I feel that, after going through the baptism of fire that was dinner with your father, I know you."

She laughed and we spent an enjoyable hour seeing New York City at night, avoiding the street people, sidewalk touts, and inebriated partygoers, as we enjoyed the amazing mix of cultures that was Manhattan. By the time we returned to the hotel, I was definitely looking forward to the coming month. It wasn't being unfaithful to Rose by simply enjoying a woman's company, I told myself. I was, after all, a human being and, as such, needed the pleasure that another person's company brought. I'd limited myself the last nine years to just the company of a few close male friends and family, but I felt that taking pleasure in sightseeing with Paulie wasn't tantamount to a declaration of undying affection.

That could never happen. My heart had shriveled up long ago or, at least, the romantic part had.

I glanced at Paulie, noting the excitement in her face and voice as we entered the hotel lobby.

"—going to be so much fun, although I have to admit I'm a bit worried about the cameras filming us. I have a horrible feeling I'm going to pick my nose or scratch my crotch or something, and everyone in England will know that Americans are just as uncouth as they'd thought."

"I don't think you're uncouth," I said. "I think you're rather splendid."

She stopped and turned to me, surprise and delight giving her additional color, making her cheeks a lovely pale pink. "Why, Dixon Ainslie, you devil. First flirting, then a kiss on the cheek, and now an all-out compliment? If you keep on this way, you're going to turn my head."

"It was a heartfelt compliment, so I'm not going to apologize for it."

She glanced around. The lobby was mostly empty. "You have only yourself to blame for this."

Before I could react, she stepped forward and kissed me, very gently and quickly. The pressure of her lips on mine, fleeting as it was, seemed to release something deep in my belly. It was a yearning, a want that I hadn't felt in a very long time.

She was gone almost immediately after that, running up the stairs to her room two floors above. I walked slowly to the elevator, absently pushing the button for the eleventh floor while I considered the kiss.

Frankly, it scared me, because it meant my heart wasn't quite as dead as I'd thought it was.

And I didn't know what to do about that. I didn't want to relive the memory of the time Rose and I had had together, and yet . . .

I don't know how to finish that sentence. I can't think anymore. I just want to go to sleep and forget everything.

Paulina Rostakova's Adventures

JULY 21
10:11 p.m.
Room 438 of local motel

Well, I'm freakin' exhausted. Who knew that driving from New York City to Buffalo would be so tiring, but holy hellballs was it!

Getting ahead of myself. Let me do this in proper order.

"Don't you look sharp!" Angela said at six forty-five a.m., when we were gathering in Times Square to set off on our great adventure. There were a few local news crews in attendance, most of whom were talking to Roger. Kell, in his attempt to increase his importance, stood next to Roger and could be seen posturing and mouthing inanities. I wished I'd remembered to ask Dixon what he'd thought of his carmate and made a note to do so at a later time.

"How pretty those dresses are," Angela added.

"Do you like it?" I did a twirl. "I have to admit the lace top is pretty, although I'm not sure how much I'm going to like being in an ankle-length skirt all day. Did you see my cool boots? They're very steampunk." I lifted the navy blue twill skirt, which bore twin lines of brass buttons down the front, and showed Angela my lace-up boots.

"Very nice, dear. You look so elegant. Doesn't she, Peter?"

Daddy growled something. "You take this. You stay safe."

"If that's a gun," I said, pointing at the small leather pouch he tried to press into my hands, "then I absolutely will not take it. Dad, I am not in any danger. The film crew will be with us, and I'll have Melody and Louise with me all day long, and Melody says she has a black belt."

"What about night?" he asked, his scowl black with suspicion. "English stays with you?"

"I'm sure he'll be at the same hotel, but if you are asking if we'll be spending the night together, then you can just stop being so worried. I have no intention of hooking up with him. He's just a nice man."

"Hooking up? What is?"

"Sex! As in, having sex with Dixon! Which I won't be doing!" I said loudly, slapping my hands on my skirt-covered thighs. Lucky me, right at that moment not only did Sam and Tabby come over to film us getting into the suffragette car, but so did the local news station.

Everyone stared at me for the count of four.

Tabby raised her eyebrows and looked at Sam, who had lowered the camera. "Five bucks says they're shacked up before we get to the other coast."

"Ten says they won't even make it that far," Sam answered.

I pointed a finger at them, saying, "Don't you start with me! I'm in a corset with my internal organs smooshed together and have a deranged father to deal with."

Tabby laughed.

"You take," Dad said, and shoved the leather pouch at me.

"No!" I kissed Angela on the cheek, then turned to repeat the gesture with my father. "Go home. I'll e-mail and text you periodically and let you know I'm alive, have all my fingers, and haven't been kidnapped. I love you both. Good-bye."

Dad started making a fuss, but Angela pulled him back. Sam resumed filming and caught about a minute of Melody and me posing next to our gleaming white car, which now had a huge decal on the hood announcing we were part of the New York to Paris race. The car itself was heavily laden with various boxes strapped to the running boards containing things like tools, spare water and oil, a tiny bit of gas in case we ran out in an inhospitable place, a first aid kit, some emergency food and drinking water, and a waterproof map. Onto the back were strapped six spare tires and a small American flag.

Louise, who had been posing with her father while the news crew interviewed him, hurried over when she saw Sam and Tabby and immediately began telling them what an honor it was for her, the leader of this team, to be the person to start the race.

"Think she'll lighten up any during the trip?" I asked Melody in an undertone. She was wearing a cute black-and-white shirt and skirt, with a straw boater hat bearing the purple and green colors of the suffragettes. My hat was a big cream affair with lashings of white net veil and a pair of goggles in cream and brass.

Melody wrapped her own modest bit of net around her hat, anchoring it to her head with a long hat pin. "We can hope, but I rather doubt she's going to let any chance in front of the camera escape her. Does it bother you much?"

"Not really. I don't mind being in the background. It gives me a chance to watch everyone and take notes."

"Goggles on, ladies!" Roger announced, marching over

to us. "It's almost seven, and we need to get you all on your way by eight when the street is reopened."

Our goggles had buckles at the back, so I slipped mine on and got them buckled up underneath the veil. Then, with a wave at my parents, I climbed into the backseat with my notebook in hand. Melody took the navigator's seat while Louise made a great show of getting behind the wheel, her enormous pink-and-cream hat with flowers, feathers, and a couple of fake birds now swathed in veil.

I waved to the crowd and crew members and caught a glimpse of Dixon when he emerged from behind a group of tourists. He was dressed in a dark brown suit with vest and coat and had a derby hat on his head. He looked absolutely at ease in his Edwardian clothes, and I had the worst urge to ask him if they made him wear period underwear, too.

OK. I admit that ever since that kiss last night, visions of him parading around without clothes, Edwardian or otherwise, occupied my mind. I banished those thoughts, knowing full well that although Dixon might be a little flirty, it didn't mean anything. He'd made it quite clear that he was still mourning his lost love.

"Such a shame, too," I said to myself as I strapped on very nonperiod seat belts that the insurance people had insisted be installed in all the cars.

"What's that?" Melody turned around, yelling over the sound of the engine. Although the people who made the cars had used more modern engines so that it wouldn't take us six months to make the journey, there was no room for things like mufflers (or, as I found out a few hours later, shocks), so the motor was quite loud.

"Go!" Roger said, consulting his watch.

With a cheer from the crowd and a grinding from the gearbox as Louise did the clutch/acceleration dance, we set off, Tabby and Sam right behind us in an open convertible.

Clipped to the front of the flat windscreen was a black video camera that caught our conversation and actions in the car. Louise started a stream-of-consciousness talk to the camera, telling it all about herself and how she loved driving, simply loved driving, and was very competitive, and just hoped that the rest of her team would be up for the long hours she planned to spend driving so that we would win the race and all the glory.

Cars honked as we proceeded out of the city. Almost immediately, we were sucked up in New York City traffic and came to a standstill, hemmed in on all sides by taxis, cars, delivery trucks, and lots and lots of people.

"Well, this is disappointing," Louise complained as we crawled our way toward one of the tunnels out of the city. "You'd think they would have cleared a path for us since we're filming a show."

"Reality TV at its best," I yelled from the backseat, and made a few notes on just what my thoughts were at this exciting moment. Somehow, they ended up being mostly focused on Dixon's clothes, what he looked like without them, and a speculation of just how long it took a person to stop grieving over a dead fiancée.

The openness of our Thomas Flyer made it a bit difficult to write when we were actually moving, so once we had cleared the city I tucked away my journal, only to find the leather pouch that my father had evidently slipped down beside the seat without me seeing.

"Dammit, Daddy . . ." I opened up the pouch and saw, as I had expected, a small gun. My father had made sure I knew how to shoot most firearms early on in my life, so I just rolled my eyes at this one, made sure to remove the clip from it, and stuffed it down between the two red leather seats at the same time I made a mental note to hand it over to Roger later.

We had made it out of the city (just) when all hell

broke loose. We'd been driving along at the speed limit, waving when passing cars honked at us and making sure to make some comments to the in-car camera (when Louise wasn't soliloquizing), but all of a sudden there was an ugly metal sound and the car swerved violently to the right, almost sending us through a guardrail. Louise screamed and started pumping what she thought was the brake but later determined was the clutch. Melody, with presence of mind, grabbed the wheel when Louise covered her face, screaming, "We're going to crash! We're going to crash!"

She must have hit the brake in her frenzy of pedal-pushing, because we slowed down almost instantly and Melody got us pulled over onto the shoulder.

"What the hell happened?" I asked, unbuckling my seat belt. Behind us, the convertible with Tabby and Sam pulled up.

"I don't know, but I suspect it was something to do with the tires or suspension," Melody said, and looked meaningfully at me.

"Oh. Mechanical stuff. That's me, huh?" I got to my feet, grabbed the small notebook I'd used to take notes on how to do things on the car, and hopped over the side to the ground. Sure enough, the right back tire looked like an alien had exploded from it.

"We blew a tire!" I yelled over the sound of traffic as it raced past us.

"Well, get busy with the repair," Louise demanded in a bossy sort of tone that I could tell was going to jangle my nerves.

"Do you need help?" Melody asked, crawling over the front seat to the back.

"No, no, I have this under control," I said, propping open my notebook and reading the tire changing instructions. "Let's see, wrench, jack, grease pot . . . got it." I opened up one of the boxes strapped to the running board and dug around until I found the wrench and grease pot. The next box gave up the jack and a long light olive green apron that I was told to put on so as not to get my costumes dirty. I set my hat, veil, and goggles on the seat, smiled at Sam and the camera, donned the apron, and tried out another wrench twirl. "Right! Suffragette power time, ladies and gentlemen."

"Oh, get on with it!" Louise snapped.

"Sheesh," I said, kneeling painfully on the gravel. "Hold your girdle on, lady. Er . . . corset." I grinned for the camera and, using the hand pump, got the jack under the side of the car nearest the tire. Another car pulled up behind us while I was wrestling with the bolts in the center of the tire.

"Need a hand?"

I glanced up to see Dixon. "Oh, hi."

"Hello." He glanced at Sam and Tabby. "That looks like difficult work. Might I lend some assistance?"

I couldn't hold back a little giggle, saying softly, "That sounded very Edwardian."

"Thank you. I tried." He cleared his throat and said louder, "Would you like me to try my hand on those bolts?"

"Sure thing," I said, handing him the wrench. "These clincher tires are a pain in the butt, if you want to know the truth."

"I'm sure they are."

"What the hell is going on?" Kell stormed over, saw the cameras, and immediately ratcheted up his anger a few notches. "Do you have any idea of how much time we are losing, Ainslie? Not to mention the fact that you are helping the competition." He turned to face the camera dead-on. "I'd like to formally complain that my teammate is trying to sabotage our team!"

"Oh, for god's sake," Dixon said, grunting when he put his weight on the wrench. One of the bolts was being obstinate, but he got it loosened just as Kell was demanding to see Roger to have Dixon thrown out of the race.

"Look, buster," I said, getting to my feet. Louise, who realized that a scene was being enacted and wanted to be a part of it, had climbed out of the car and was twirling her veil while standing next to Kell. "I realize this is a race, but it doesn't mean that people have to act like asshats."

Tabby snickered. Sam raised an eyebrow.

"Can I say asshat on TV?" I asked them.

Sam shrugged.

"You stay out of this, you . . . suffragette," Kell said, hissing the word.

I straightened up. "Dude. This is my tire that Dixon kindly—because he's a gentleman, not a poseur—is helping me with. So take your drama elsewhere, preferably out of hearing because I have things to do."

Kell sputtered a few choice phrases. Louise nodded and preened for the camera. Melody, looking over the edge of the car, smothered a laugh.

"Where's the spare?" Dixon asked, having successfully removed the offending bolt. He pulled the tire off and looked up expectantly.

"Right here, but I can put it on. You guys had better get on your way, so Mr. Antsy-Pants there doesn't have a stroke because you were being thoughtful and nice."

"Are you sure? I can—"

"We are leaving," Kell announced, and stalked back to the car. "With or without you!"

"Go," I said, shooing him after Kell. "It's way too early to encounter this sort of trouble."

He smiled and took himself off.

I picked up one of the spares I'd removed from the

rear of the car and called after him, "Thanks for your help, Mr. Ainslie. Good manners and sportsmanship are always pleasing to witness!"

"Nice touch," Melody pronounced, nodding her approval.

"Is this going to take much longer?" Louise asked, frowning when Dixon's car rolled past us. "I don't want us to get behind. We have something to prove, after all."

"Not long," I said, forcing the wheel onto the plate. "Just have to tighten the bolts a few times . . ."

The "few times" took five minutes before I was convinced the wheel wouldn't fall off while we drove at high speeds, but at last we were on our way, Tabby and Sam in their convertible zooming on ahead to catch up with some of the other racers.

"That was just annoying as hell," Louise said, gritting her teeth as she ground the gears together trying to shift up. "Just my luck, I get saddled with the lame car."

"It's not lame," I said loudly, winding my veil around my head a few times before tucking it into itself. "It's a gorgeous car, and incidentally it's the same kind that won the original race."

"Hrmph," she said, and spent the remainder of the day telling the windscreen camera her every little thought, from what it was like to have all the responsibility of success on her shoulders to how stupid Thomas Flyers drove and how she wanted to race in a sixties sports car and call her team Vlad the Impala.

With a brief stop at a Starbucks for some much-needed caffeine (and a potty break), Melody took over driving a few hours later, and I took my turn late in the afternoon.

"Hey," I said about an hour into my stint at being the driver. "That looks like one of us ahead."

"Where?" Louise, who had been reclining on the backseat with her phone, sat up straight.

I pointed to the side of the road about an eighth of a mile ahead and began to slow down.

"What are you doing? You can't stop!" Louise shrieked, pounding me on the shoulder.

"Are you kidding? Did you forget that Dixon stopped to help us just a few hours ago?" I pulled up behind them, putting on the massive hand brake. "I'm not going to just blaze past them."

"That was the English team's choice. Our team is going for the win. Don't you dare leave this car! Paulie! Dammit! Melody, stop her!"

"Sorry. I'm with Paulie on this," Melody said, following me. She had the presence of mind to snag the big flat metal key that was used to trigger the ignition mechanism.

"You guys need some help?" I asked, approaching the car ahead of us. The three Italians, dressed in sporty white Edwardian motoring suits, each embroidered with their names, turned, their goggles glinting in the afternoon sun.

"The radiator, she is not happy," the one named Luca said, flashing me a brief smile.

"It's not the radiator—it's the gas. We are out," said Carlo.

"We have some extra gas—" I started to say.

"No! We do not!" Louise stomped over to us. She punched me painfully on the arm. "You are not giving away our gas. What if we need it? Then we'd be stuck and would lose the race, and all because you want to play hide the Italian salami with Rico here."

"The name is Carlo—" he started to protest.

"You are seriously offensive—do you know that?" I told Louise. "I just hope the cameras didn't get any of that, because you'll be hearing from the Italian-American community if it did."

"It is not petrol," the third member, Francesco, said. They all spoke English very well, but had thick Italian accents that, had I not preferred a nice crisp English accent, might have melted my knees. "We have petrol."

"I thought we all had extra emergency petrol?" Melody asked, glancing at their car.

"We have, yes," Francesco said. "It is something with the engine."

"Oh. Well, I'm not going to be much help with that," I said.

"It's all right," he said, giving his car a rueful look.

"I wish there was something we could do to help you. I have a cell phone if you need to call Roger—"

"Speak of the devil," Melody said, looking behind us. "There're the Germans, and Roger is right behind them."

Indeed, at that moment the German ladies drove by with a blast of their horn and friendly waves. Behind them drove the sedan bearing Roger and an assistant. Their car pulled up in front of the Italians, and Roger emerged with Graham the mechanic.

"Oh, good. The cavalry has arrived, gentlemen."

Immediately they went to consult with Roger and Graham, and with nothing more to do, we returned to our car. Louise said nothing more about the incident, but I felt her glaring daggers into the back of my head as we drove along.

Driving the Thomas Flyer was kind of a mixed bag: it was a fun old car, and people honked and waved and gave us thumbs-up signs, but the actual act of steering, not to mention shifting into other gears, was a huge strain on the shoulders and arms. We agreed to limit our driving time to just two hours before switching to eliminate fatigue.

"All right, but if the cameraman is with us, then I drive," Louise said, punching viciously at her phone. "After all, I am supposed to be the driver."

"I'll be happy to let you have my shift if you're so anxious to be seen driving," I said sweetly, pulling into the parking lot of the hotel we were to stay at that night. At the far end of the lot, a station had been set up for the racers to check in. I glanced at Melody as we rolled over to the waiting crew. "How bad is it?"

She consulted her watch and a clipboard holding the race information. "Well, we're twenty minutes late. That's two infractions. But given that we had a blowout, I don't think that's too bad."

"Two infractions?" Louise's voice went up a whole octave as I pulled up. "Two effing infractions? This is bullshit! Where's my dad? I am not going to stay with a team that can't be bothered to try to adhere to the rules. Two infractions on the first effing day!"

"Team Sufferin' Suffragettes," the crew member said, checking us in. "I'm afraid that you are twenty minutes past your allotted time."

"I know. We had a tire issue."

"And then she—" Louise scrambled out of the car and pointed dramatically at me. "She made us lose time by stopping to help another team. I shouldn't be punished for that! I wanted to keep going, but she made us stop. I want those infractions taken off of my name. I refuse to be a victim!"

Melody rolled her eyes and made a note of our score on the car's logbook.

"I'm afraid the scoring is based on teams, not individuals," the poor crew person tried to explain, but Louise was in full drama mode and stormed around insisting that someone get ahold of her father, who would straighten everything out.

"If you would pull over to the section of the parking lot that is secured," another crew person told me, pointing to the far end where a couple of RVs had been set up.

I remembered vaguely hearing that the crew people would be watching the cars for us while we were in the U.S., but it would be up to us to keep the cars safe when we were abroad.

"Looks like we're the last people," I said, noting the cars already parked.

"Second to last. I think the Italian team is still behind us. At least, I haven't seen them pass us." Melody collected her things and left the car.

I stretched, greeted the woman who came over to take the car's flat key, and asked if we were second to last.

"I'm afraid so," the crew member said, giving me a cheerful smile. "But don't worry—it's only the first day, and you have a long way to go. You can make it up."

"True that." I chatted for a few minutes more, then went to find my hotel room. On my way there, a white car pulled into a parking spot ahead of me. I wouldn't have noticed it except for the fact that, as I approached, the person inside the car ducked down. I caught the movement out of the corner of my eye as I was about to round the corner to the hotel's lobby and paused to glance back.

A bald head bobbed up, saw me standing still, and disappeared again.

"He didn't! Dad, this time you have gone too far!" Anger fired inside me at the sight of that bald head. Quickly, I walked to the car and wrenched the door open, saying as I did, "Boris, so help me god, if you think I was kidding when I said I'd tell the producers you were stalking—oh. Uh . . ."

A man sat up, a bald man to be true, but this one was most definitely not my father's henchman.

One of his black eyebrows rose in question.

"Oh my god, I'm so sorry," I said, stammering a little when my words tumbled over one another in their haste to apologize. "I thought you were someone else. I'm so, so sorry. I'll just shut your door now, all right? You can go back to . . . er . . . whatever it is you were doing bent over like that."

I closed the car door and, with flaming cheeks, marched into the lobby, cursing myself under my breath, which continued mentally while I collected my room key, was informed that there would be a meeting the following morning at seven a.m. before the day's racing started, and took the elevator to the fourth floor, where the production company had reserved the entire floor for racers and crew.

"What room are you in?" Melody asked, an empty ice bucket in her hand as she came toward me, clearly on her way to the ice machine.

I looked at the plastic key card in my hand. "Four thirty-eight."

"Oh, good. I'm across the hall from you. Take a left at the end of this hallway. I'm just getting some ice for some cold drinks with the French team. You're welcome to join us."

"Sounds awesome, but first I'm going to get out of this corset and then take a long, cool shower. I may join you later, if that's OK."

"Absolutely. I'm going to hop in the shower as well. I feel all gritty from the open car." She gave me a smile and tapped her chest. "There's one benefit to being the bluestocking character, and that's the fact that my corset is the Rational style, and not at all bad to wear."

I wiggled my shoulders uncomfortably and continued my way down the corridor, saying as I left, "I sure wish I'd had the presence of mind to claim that character. This thing is ghastly."

"I'll lace you up tomorrow if you like," she called after me. "And I'll do it looser than wardrobe did for you this morning."

"Just so I fit into the pretty clothes." I toddled on to my room, immediately switching on the air-conditioning, pleased to see that my suitcase had been delivered by the production company. In addition, a wicker basket sat on the bed, as well as a large round hatbox. One of the production assistants handled mending and spot cleaning as needed, but for the most part we were expected to take care of our outfits ourselves. With the exception of our underclothes, which were collected every three days and returned to us laundered.

I removed the lace shirt and tried desperately to reach the cords of my corset, tied in such a way that I was supposed to be able to undo it myself (Melody and I had already agreed to be corset buddies and lace each other up in the morning), but I couldn't get my arms twisted around to untie the laces.

"Dammit," I muttered, spinning around to try to get at them. After five frustrating minutes, I gave up and peeked out into the hallway. It was empty, but there were two doors across from me, neither of which was directly opposite me. I frowned at them, hesitated, then figured that, even if I got the room that wasn't inhabited by Melody, whoever was there would be able to help me.

I tapped at the door just as a man came around the corner. It was the bald man from the car. He stopped, gave me a hard stare, then did an about-face and returned the way he came.

"Well, that's odd," I said aloud.

"What is? It couldn't be the fact that you're all but baring your breasts to me, could it?"

The door had opened while I was staring after the odd man, revealing Dixon in a pair of jeans and an open shirt. I stared at his naked chest for a moment, all thoughts fleeing my brain except for the wonder and awe at how gorgeous his chest was.

"Paulie?" he asked.

"Hmm?" Really, he had the nicest chest I'd ever seen on a man. He wasn't smooth shaved, but wasn't hugely hairy, either. He had a nice light dusting of reddish brown hair across his pectorals, sweeping down in a line to his belly button. He had the faintest hint of a six-pack, not ripped like someone who spent hours at a gym but enough definition that my fingers itched to stroke down the silky line of hair. I took a deep breath, curling my fingers into fists in order to keep from reaching out and touching his chest.

"Don't do that," he said, his voice kind of rough.

"Do what?" I asked, wrenching my gaze from his chest to his face.

"Take deep breaths." He closed his eyes for a second. "It . . . does things."

"It does?" I wondered if he'd gotten too much sun while driving.

"Yes. To your . . ." He waved a hand toward my chest and opened his eyes. "Did you want something in particular, or did you just drop by to flaunt your breasts at me?"

I looked down. I'd forgotten what the corset did to them, presenting them front and center. "No, actually. I was hoping you were Melody so I could get help taking off the corset."

His eyes seemed to glaze over for a few seconds. He opened his mouth to speak, closed it again, gave a little cough, then said, "Can I be of assistance?"

I was in his room before my brain could even alert my mouth that there were words coming. "Sure! That would be awesome. I'd appreciate it a lot. You have no idea how rib-crushing these things are."

His eyebrows rose a little, but after hesitating a second he closed the door and followed me into the room. "Not that I'm not happy to help you, but aren't there hooks on the front you can undo? My sister used to be part of a reenactors group, and her corset had hooks she used to get in and out of it."

"This isn't one of those kinds of corsets, unfortunately." I spun around so that he could have access to my back. "The laces seem to be knotted. I can't get them undone. If you can take care of the knot, I can probably do the rest."

"No need," he said in a rather breathless voice as he started to work on the knot. "I'm happy to help."

All sorts of smutty thoughts passed through my head while he tugged on the laces, everything from licking that wonderful chest to flinging him onto the bed and rubbing myself all over him. I was a little shocked at such thoughts, because I hadn't at all intended on pursuing a romance with anyone, let alone the men in the race, but there was something about Dixon that caused my brain to override my common sense.

"I think—yes, I think this will do it."

"Ahhh," I said, sighing in relief as he got the laces undone and pulled the corset open wide. It sagged down in the front, revealing the skimpy fine-lawn camisole I wore underneath it. I scratched at my front beneath my boobs and took a couple of experimental deep breaths. "You have no idea how good this feels."

"You have . . . erm . . . some red marks on your back."

"Red marks?" I tried to see over my shoulder. "What sort of red marks? Oh god, they aren't pimples, are they?"

"No, marks made by the corset, I believe. They're above the line of your vest."

"My vest . . . oh, undershirt. It's a camisole, actually. Where are the marks? I can't see them. Can you put a finger next to them so I can tell Roger where the corset is rubbing?"

"Just here." His fingers swept along a spot on my left shoulder blade. I shivered. "And here."

It was as if his fingers were made of molten gold, making my skin tingle where he touched.

"And . . . here." His hand brushed a line down my spine, inside the camisole. I shivered again.

"Really? My whole back?" My breath seemed to be somewhat sparse, not enough of it filling my lungs.

"No. I just wanted to touch you."

I turned around at that, pulling the loosened corset off over my head. We stared at each other for the count of seven, he with his bare chest and I almost bare with what was tantamount to a see-through camisole.

His eyes dilated. My breath caught even more, and suddenly I reached out with both hands and slid them up his chest to his shoulders.

He made an inarticulate noise, and that's all it took. I knew I shouldn't give in to the sudden rush of desire that seemed to grip me with burning fingers, but sanity—or even forethought—didn't matter at that moment. What *did* matter was Dixon, specifically the ways and means his body was applied to mine. Without warning, I was against him, the camisole doing nothing to keep the heat of his chest from soaking into my breasts. His hands slid underneath my camisole to stroke my back while his mouth—oh lordy, his mouth! He tasted hot and spicy and slightly sweet, and did I mention hot? Hoo! We're talking steaming-the-drapes sort of hot, and when his tongue got into the action, it went from steam to an inferno in a flash.

I pushed off his shirt, trying to touch all of him that I could reach, even while he kissed the very thoughts out of my head.

A noise in the hallway had us parting, but thankfully only briefly. I stared at him, one hand on my lips. "Wow," I finally managed to say. My brain was too befuddled to come up with any other words.

"Indeed," he said, and then we were smooshed together

again and he was kissing me the way I'd secretly been wanting to be kissed ever since I'd set eyes on him.

"This is wrong," he murmured at one point. I had
paused stroking his chest and arms long enough for him
to pull my camisole off, his hands instantly taking pos-
session of my breasts.

"On the contrary," I said with a little moan of happiness when his head dipped down so he could swirl his
tongue over nipples that suddenly demanded that very
act. "It's so, so right. And left. Do the left."

He did the left nipple, warm waves of pleasure rippling
out from my breasts to pool deep in my stomach. My girl
parts were tingling for all they were worth, demanding
equal time with Dixon's mouth and complaining that the
breasts got all the fun.

"You're right. I'm wrong. This is good. Very good," he
said, his breath hot when he kissed a path back up to my
neck. He hit the spot behind my ear and I swear my legs
turned to pudding. His hands left my breasts and went
around to the back of me, fumbling with the skirt hooks.

"I'm so glad you agree. Shoes?" I had managed to get
his fly unzipped and was sliding his jeans down, hooking
my fingers into his underwear at the same time, but
paused when I realized he was still wearing a pair of
brogues.

"Yes, shoes," he said, gently biting on my earlobe.

"Shoes are so good," I said, squirming when my skirt
sagged and slithered down to the floor with a rustle.
Beneath it were a petticoat and bloomers, both of which
Dixon handily dealt with.

I shoved his pants down over his hips, too caught up
with the overwhelming surge of need topped with a huge
dollop of lust to even think about the words that my
mouth was babbling. All I knew was that I wanted him,
and wanted him right then. Not a second later.

We stumbled our way over to the bed, half tripping over clothing, until I tumbled onto the bed, Dixon pausing only to shuck his shoes, pants, and underwear before joining me. I used the time to hastily fight at the laces of one of my boots. He obliged with the other one, and then we were both naked on the bed together, his body half covering mine as his mouth returned to pepper me with kisses of fire.

"This . . . To the left a little, please. Yes, right there . . . This escalated quickly," I said in between pants.

Dixon lifted his head from where he was once again tormenting my breasts. He froze, confusion and some other emotion filling his face. "It did, didn't it? Does that make you uncomfortable?"

"I was going to ask you the same thing." A wee bit of common sense returned to me, or at least if not common sense, then thoughts of what Dixon might be feeling.

He stared at me for a moment. "You mean because of Rose?"

I nodded, feeling more naked than I ever had in my life, the sort of naked that went beyond a mere removal of clothing.

His expression was shuttered.

I didn't want to press him if he truly wasn't ready for a physical relationship, but I also didn't want him thinking that a little sheet tangoing meant we'd be spending the rest of our lives together. "The way I see it is that we're both adults, neither one of us is in a relationship, and we're doing, for lack of a better term, a little mutual itch-scratching. That's all. There's no commitment on either side."

"That sounds . . . reasonable." His face cleared.

"That's how I see it, at least." I slid my hand up his arm. "Not that I intended on doing this at all, because despite what you overheard me saying at the welcome meeting, I really wasn't planning on getting involved with anyone. But I like you. I like the way you talk, and you look really good in Edwardian clothing."

He smiled, and I felt as if my body was bathed in sunshine. "I like you as well. I never know what you're going to say."

"I get that from my dad, unfortunately." I made a little face. "I'm never going to hear the end of it if he hears that after all my protesting we ended up in bed together. If you don't mind, I'd like to keep it quiet."

"I have no objection," he said, dipping his head now to gently nibble on my neck. "I'm not keen on everyone knowing my private business."

I giggled and slid my hands down his chest to his belly. "I notice you seem to have dropped your personal boundary limit."

"I do that sometimes." He waggled his eyebrows, then kissed me again, setting my tingly parts alive with desire. My breasts felt heavy and needy, and I wiggled against him in silent protest.

"What?" he asked after a minute of me tugging at his arms and back.

"What *what*?" I asked, my brain wholly focused on the sensations he was stirring within me.

"You're squirming around like you are uncomfortable. Am I too heavy? Should I move off you?"

I blinked at him a couple of times, trying to process his words. Was he saying he wanted to stop? "Don't stop. Oh hell, that sounds like I'm begging. Dammit, I don't care—I'll beg. Don't stop. Do more. Much, much more."

"You are the oddest woman . . ." The rest of his words were lost when he moved down my body, kissing a path.

My inner bits sent up a cheer when they realized where he was headed, and although I'd never been entirely comfortable with oral sex—while knowing it was foolish to worry whether someone else thought the view was scenic or not—none of those thoughts even broached my mind. Instead I stopped him because I didn't want to lie around being passive—I had a burning need to touch and taste him.

"My turn!" I said loudly, and pushed him over onto his back. "Dear god, you're gorgeous. Just look at you! Your chest is awesome, and you have muscles, but not *muscles,* and you're not so hairy that I want to break out a razor, and your legs are really nice, too."

"Not as nice as yours," he said, doing some sort of wrestling move that ended up with me on my back and him over me again. "Your legs, that is. You don't have any hair that I see, other than your . . . er . . ."

"Tingle-bits is what I'm calling them now," I said, breathless, and bit his shoulder before shoving him again and following him so that I straddled his hips. "Stay put, will you?"

"But I want to give you pleasure," he said, his hands instantly taking hold of my breasts.

"Oh, you're already doing that. You're not giving me time to do the same."

"On the contrary, I'm enjoying myself immensely."

"Good." I smiled. "Then you're going to love this."

"You're not doing this right," he complained. "You should let me have my turn first; then I will allow you to molest me, and after that we will work together and—"

I slid backward and grasped his penis with a firm but gentle grip and licked the underside.

He sucked in a huge quantity of air and with both hands gripped the sheets beneath him.

"What was that about not doing it right?" I asked.

"I was wrong. So wrong. Very wrong. I've never been this wrong in my life," he babbled, his eyes full of hope.

I smiled again, a very womanly smile, one chock-full of the power that women held over men, and then applied myself to make him babble even more. By the time I was done fully investigating his genitals, he was almost incoherent.

"I like how you thrash around when I do this," I commented at one point, and gently squeezed his testicles while running my tongue the length of his penis.

He groaned and his hips bucked.

"Now, how about I do this—" Before I could finish my sentence and put action to (unspoken) word, he sat up and said loudly, "No! It's my turn now."

"But—"

I was on my back before I realized what was happening. He spread my legs and swung them over his shoulder, grinning wickedly at me over my pubic mound. "No buts, my fair little temptress. Now it's your turn to thrash around and moan and groan and not be able to think straight. We shall commence thusly."

"I love how you talk," I said, my eyes rolling back in my head when he stuck a finger into my depths at the same time his tongue started investigated the outer tingly bits. And that pretty much was the last thing I said that made any sense. Dixon curled another finger into me, which sent me lurching upward. I grabbed his arm and said, the words tumbling over one another, "Oh my god, that's good! That's really good! Stop doing that right now because if you don't—"

"Stay there," he said and, to my intense sadness, rolled off and disappeared into the bathroom. He returned almost instantly with a strip of condoms, one of which he was trying to roll onto himself as he ran back to the bed.

"Hurry!" I said, my body rife with demands for his body to return to its right and proper place.

"I'm trying. I'm trying, but the blasted thing . . . Got it."

"Thank god." I almost sobbed, and welcomed him back onto me with little cries of happiness. He sank into me with a move that seemed so right, and yet not nearly enough. I moved with him as he let his hips go wild, my mouth busy with nibbling along his collarbone, the feel and scent and taste of him wrapping me up in a haze of purest pleasure. I bit his ear when he made a little swiveling move and dug my fingers into his shoulders, wanting to yell and sing and dance and never move from the spot all at the same time.

"I hope," he said, panting into my ear, "I hope you're . . . I hope . . ."

"Oh yes," I said, wrapping my legs around his and thrusting upward, my back arching as my orgasm spiraled out in ripples of sensation. My muscles tightened and spasmed around him, forcing him to thrust hard a couple of times, murmuring something into my neck as he shuddered his own pleasure.

"Well, that," I said a few minutes later, when Dixon rolled off me, "was seriously awesome."

He lifted his head and squinted at me. "How is it you can talk when I can barely catch my breath?"

"I'm a woman," I said, turning to my side so I could trace a finger down his lovely chest. "We are superior that way."

"I think you're cheating somehow," he said, closing his eyes again.

"That's because your poor man's brain can't cope with a life-changing orgasm and still be able to indulge in pillow talk."

"Life-changing, eh?" he asked.

"That's right." I poked him in the side until he opened his eyes. "Can I say again that this was totally unexpected? I don't want you thinking I've been laying a trap for you just because you're a handsome Englishman."

He stared at me for a minute. "You think I'm handsome?"

"Of course I do. You're all yummy and you have pretty gray-blue eyes with black lashes that I can tell you make me intensely jealous."

"My eyes are plain hazel, not pretty gray and blue."

I pinched his arm. "You are supposed to accept compliments nicely, not argue."

"Ah. I apologize, then. Thank you for thinking that I'm handsome when everyone else tells me I'm barely passable."

"Now you're going to make me think you're fishing for compliments." I bit his shoulder gently.

"On the contrary, I'm trying to be honest." A little smile quirked up one side of his mouth. "I do think that, of the two of us, you are the more attractive. You have lovely brown eyes with perfectly suited eyelashes, so you have no need to be jealous of mine. And your hair is like liquid silk. I won't go into how your legs leave me weak with desire, or what the sight of your breasts does to me, because I wouldn't want you getting a fat head."

I laughed, and pinched him again. "Thank you for that, and thank you for also not mentioning the fact that there is an overabundance of me. Not that I think you would do any body shaming, but I appreciate that you didn't feel the need to swing to the opposite and tell me how much you like chunky women."

"You're not chunky in the least, and I do happen to like the fact that you aren't one of those rail-thin women who are obsessed with their appearances."

"And that gets you a gold star for the day," I said, glancing at the clock radio next to the bed. "Crap. The dinner is supposed to start in half an hour. I suppose I should go get my shower at last."

"We could stay here instead," he offered, and for a moment I was tempted.

"Sounds lovely, but I think it would be pretty obvious

if we were both missing. I'm not a super-private person, but I really don't like the idea of the cameras catching us together, and they'd be bound to if they noticed we were off on our own. I know how these reality shows work, you know. They love to film any fights, general drama, or couples who try to sneak off together."

I got up while I was speaking and slipped the petticoat over my head, followed by the camisole, collecting the other garments and my boots.

"I understand," Dixon said, watching me with avid eyes. "I am not looking for any attention, either. Kell is welcome to it."

"And I thought Louise was bad—you definitely got the worst carmate of the two." I opened the door and peered out into the hallway. With my card key in hand for a speedy entrance, I blew Dixon a kiss and hurried across to my room.

JOURNAL OF DIXON AINSLEY
23 July
5:30 a.m.
Buffalo, New York

The drive to Buffalo yesterday was interesting. Scenery was fairly rural. We stopped to help Paulie and her team. Kell screamed about that for an hour afterward. No time infractions. Car ran fine.

I'm not sure I'm cut out for travel journaling. I can't think of anything more to say about the trip out.

JOURNAL OF DIXON AINSLEY
23 July
5:36 a.m.
Buffalo, New York

I can think of a lot of things to say about Paulie, though.

JOURNAL OF DIXON AINSLEY
23 July
11:18 p.m.
Sandusky, Ohio

Privacy warning notice. The next couple of paragraphs are not to be included in travel journal and are just for my own reference. And insight—not that it's done anything but make me feel horrible.

How can I let Paulie go on believing what she believes? That's the big question that was giving me hell after Paulie knocked on my door last night and we ended up in a lovemaking session. Except there I was, feeling horrible afterward once Paulie had left to return to her own room.

"You ass," I told myself as I got dressed. "She thinks you're mourning the loss of your dead fiancée. She doesn't know the truth. Tell her. Tell her the truth."

A little voice in me disputed that suggestion, saying that things were going so nicely, it would be a shame to screw them up so soon in the relationship.

"Not that there is a relationship," I said to my reflection, getting out a razor and shaving cream. "It's just physical pleasure. Nothing more. No emotional entanglements."

My reflection looked skeptical at that.

"I'll tell her," I said later, when I was pulling on my shoes and checking to make sure I had my wallet and passport. "I'll her the truth. Then she won't have to feel guilty about me feeling guilty, and she can wrap those gorgeous legs around me with abandon."

The production company had chosen a hotel that had a banquet room, which was where our first night's dinner was held. I scanned the room for Paulie, but didn't see her. I intended on waiting around the door so that I could be there when she arrived, but Rupert beckoned me over. Reluctantly, and with an eye on the door, I wound my way around the tables to where he sat with the other English team.

"This is Dixon," he said, introducing me. "Dix, I told Stephen here that you'd be able to help him with a spreadsheet."

The man in question smirked. "Would you mind terribly? The hub here insists that we keep our plans ordered, so that we can check them off as we get to them, and I can't get the damned thing to do anything but clump the text up as a wad."

I gave Rupert a telling look, which he ignored. He mumbled something about saying hello to one of the personal assistants and headed off while I took the seat next to balding Stephen. I glanced at the other two men, unsure of which was the husband. "Er . . . hello. Nice to see some fellow countrymen. I don't think we met earlier?"

"No, we were present for the first night's dinner only," one of the other two men said, "and fittings of course." He was dark haired, with a beard and thick black glasses, looking like a stereotypical geek.

"We had plans, you see," said the third, a man whose origins were probably somewhere in the Caribbean, if the slight accent was anything to go by. "Hub three wanted to go to Atlantic City quite badly."

"Hub three?" I asked, confused as hell.

"We're polyamorous," Stephen said with a bright smile. "We're all married to each other. I'm hub three, Sanders is hub one, and Sammy is hub two."

"I see." I looked at the tablet, squinting at the tiny window of spreadsheet. I made it bigger and tried to decipher the jumbled text.

"We shock ever so many people back home when we tell them," Sanders (dark hair and glasses) said with obvious complacency. "But here no one will turn a hair to us."

"Except for the fact that we're the villains," the last one said. By process of elimination, I figured he must have been Sammy. "People'll have a thing or two to say about us because of that—don't you know?"

I managed to get the text spread out so that it was readable. The words I saw there and the ones spoken had me looking up in surprise. "You're the villains?"

"Yes, isn't it exciting?" Stephen beamed at me and ruffled his fringe of light brown hair until it stood on end.

"We're ever so thrilled to have the part, and as I said, the hub—hub two—wants to keep our list straight so we don't repeat ourselves."

"I think," I said, setting the tablet down, "I'm going to need this explained to me. I wasn't aware we were assigned specific roles. I thought we were just racing."

"Oh, we are," said Stephen. "Didn't you see that movie *The Great Race*? We're the villains just like Jack Lemmon and Peter Falk were the villains. We're here to win the race at all cost, and we will do whatever it takes to do so."

"But that was a movie," I protested.

"Yes, but this is TV," Sammy pointed out. "It's almost the same thing."

"Even if we ignore that, we're still left with the fact that this race is based on a real one, one in which there were a handful of people traveling around the world, and I don't recall hearing anything about any of them being self-declared villains." I looked from one to another of them. They all stared back at me with blithe indifference.

"It'll make for good TV," Sammy insisted. "Roger thinks it's an excellent idea."

"Then he's insane if he thinks I'm going to aid and abet you attempting to sabotage my team or any other team." I held up the tablet. "These plans are downright actionable."

"Oh, they're not that bad," Stephen said, waving away my concern. "It's not like we're going to hurt anyone, after all. We're not psychopaths! We just want to throw a few spanners in the works."

"Nice ones," Sammy agreed, nodding. "Ones that slow people down."

"That's cheating," I said, my voice rife with disbelief and outrage.

Sanders shrugged. "There's nothing to stop any of you from throwing spanners in our works, you know."

"Only the fact that we value good sportsmanship and common decency," I snapped, and thought seriously of handing the tablet back when a thought occurred to me.

"Now, don't take that attitude," Stephen said in a voice that I assumed was meant to be soothing. "It's all part of the reality TV game, Dixon. You need to open yourself up to the sorts of shenanigans that go on in front of the camera. You'll see—our plans will spice things up just enough to keep you all on your toes and to provide for some truly epic footage."

I glanced down at the spreadsheet, automatically formatting it so the text was arranged properly. *Banana in tailpipe*, read the first item, followed by: *loosen bolts on steering wheel, slip laxative to team, lock team into room on third floor or higher, dispose of spare tires, replace radiator water with vodka, get team members fighting amongst selves, accuse a team of theft (NB: must plant something on them first), encourage members of rival teams to sleep together in order to foster jealousy and ill feelings, tell press members are felons, write slurs on cars when teams aren't looking.* "This is a hell of a list," I said slowly. I looked up to see three pairs of eyes on me, speculation in all of them.

"No," I said quickly.

"No what?" Stephen asked.

"No to whatever it was you were going to say. I don't want to have any part of this. I don't hold with cheating of any sort, and no matter what you say, that's what this is."

"Oh well," Sammy said, and held out his hand for the tablet. Reluctantly, I handed it over. "We had to try, you know."

"I'm going to have to report this," I said with a nod at the tablet. I don't know what I expected them to do at that statement, but it certainly wasn't smile at me.

"You go right ahead and tell Roger about it all," Stephen said, the others nodding with him.

I rose and was about to leave when something occurred to me. "What's to stop me from warning the other teams what you have in mind? You just let me see your plans, after all, and if I tell them that you intend on attempting to eliminate their chances at winning, they will simply watch out for you."

"That's what makes it all so delicious, don't you think?" Sanders asked, his eyes holding a look that I remembered well in a bully from my school years. "You'll all be on guard, but you won't have an idea when or where or how we'll strike."

"Thanks for the help with the spreadsheet," Sammy added, tapping on the tablet. "It's much more readable this way. I wonder if we should get a printout?"

I shook my head and left them, going straight to Roger, who was busily talking to two other members of the production company.

"A word in your ear if I might," I told him, and gave him no option to refuse. Quickly, I explained what had happened with the Essex Esses team. "I don't like to be the one to tell tales about another team, but the blatant statement of intent to cheat surely excuses it."

"It would—it would indeed, if that's what will really happen," Roger said calmly, giving me a patient smile. "The boys came to me with their idea, naturally, and I couldn't help but give it the green light. Oh, not any actual sabotages—that would be quite against the rules of the race—but their intent to play the villains before the cameras will be pure gold. Everyone loves to hate the villain of a piece, and here we have three!"

"But their plans," I protested. "Their list of what they plan on doing—have you seen it?"

"All just part of their personas, I assure you. Why else would they show it to you?" He shook his head. "Think, man—if they truly wished to damage anyone's chances, they'd hardly tell you, then express no concern when you said you'd tell the rest of the racers."

"I didn't say I would tell everyone; I just asked them what was to stop me from doing so." I had to admit, he had a point. If I was planning some sabotage, the last thing I'd do was tell people about it. "If they weren't serious about it, why go to all the trouble of creating a spreadsheet?"

Roger shrugged, and pulled out his phone when it burbled. "Padding their parts so they will get more camera time? Which they will, of course, because, as I said, everyone loves to hate the villain. Ah, Barry. Yes, I'm here. Buffalo, actually. First day of shooting was a bit rocky, but overall good . . ."

He moved away to take his call, leaving me to stand with a vaguely dissatisfied emotion. I glanced around the room and saw Paulie, but her table was full. Disappointed, I lifted my hand in a wave, but she was laughing at something her tablemates—two of the Italians and her teammates—had said.

I felt alone and somewhat peevish, and sat with the Ducal team for dinner. Roger recapped the events of the day for everyone, made a few announcements about what was coming up for the following few days, and talked a bit about the local news stations that would be catching us up. I didn't pay much attention; I was too busy wondering why Paulie didn't even look over at me.

Kell stopped by my table as the meal was coming to an end and said acidly, "I hope you will have more team spirit tomorrow and not attempt to make us lose again. I didn't come all this way just to sit around in a car and see a country full of idiots."

"That's rather rough, don't you think?" I asked calmly, instinctively knowing that the best way to deal with his temper was to keep a firm grip on mine. "I've enjoyed the people I've met here thus far, and the scenery will get quite spectacular when we approach mountains, or so my brother told me."

Kell's lips were thin when he snapped out, "Shows what you know. Just do your job and don't get in my way."

I thought about suggesting to Paulie that we spend the night together, but since she had already left, I figured she had other things to do.

Better things. More interesting things.

"God, I hate it when I get maudlin," I said aloud on the way back to my room, and shook the glum mood off.

By the next morning, I'd given myself several lectures reminding myself that I had no intention to get involved with anyone and that, although a little mutually satisfying sex wasn't wrong, it was better if I had no intentions beyond that.

"The race is only for a month," I told myself when I loaded my things into the car for the early-morning start. "After that, you return home and she goes back to California. There's no future there."

"Talking to yourself again, old man?" Rupert asked, taking his place in the backseat of the car.

"Shut it," I told him amiably, ignoring the glare that Kell gave me as he climbed in behind the steering wheel.

"Right," Kell said, glancing at his phone before tucking it away inside his motoring jacket. "Let's try something a little different today. The cameras like action, so we're going to give them some."

"What the hell are you talking about?" Rupert asked, leaning forward to hear the answer over the sound of the engine roaring to life.

"We're not getting nearly enough camera time. That daughter of d'Espry is hogging all the attention, and if she thinks I'm going to put up with the antics of an amateur, she can think again. Either we get the bulk of the filming, or I'll leave. My agent has leads on a couple of new reality shows starting up, so I don't need a show where I'm hardly seen."

The car lurched forward to the waiting crew, who were sending racers off in five-minute intervals. We took our place in line, Rupert and I exchanging glances while Kell outlined a plan that was frankly fantastic. "There's a town named Rudsville that we'll pass in the afternoon. While we're there, two men are going to pretend to rob a petrol station and will speed away. We'll hop into action and chase them down. After calling d'Espry to let him know what's going on, of course, so he can be sure to film us in pursuit."

"Are you out of your mind?" I asked him. "That's the most ridiculous setup I've ever heard. Who did you find to agree to that?"

"Two mates of a friend of mine. They won't really rob the station," Kell snapped. "You don't have to get all holy on me. God! If I'd known I was going to be forced to be part of a team that had no idea what it's like to be on a reality show, I'd never have agreed to this."

"I don't think Dixon is out of line questioning this plan," Rupert yelled as we hit the motorway and Kell shifted into a higher gear. "What do you expect to get out of that plan?"

"Camera time. I thought I made that clear!" Kell bellowed.

"But what's it going to look like?" I asked, also yelling. "We chase down a car, and then what? We can't arrest the people, and I doubt if these men are going to agree to being arrested just to make you look heroic."

"They'll get away. We'll express our regret that we couldn't do more and then will continue on our way—an example of British justice at its best."

"*What* justice?" Rupert asked, but Kell didn't answer.

We drove on. I tried to make notes on the scenery, but there wasn't much that elicited interest. By the time we hit Ohio, I was contemplating throwing Kell out of the car.

"Maybe that would give him the camera time he wants," I complained to Rupert while we were stopped for Kell to have a toilet break behind some blackberry bushes alongside the road.

"I hear you, Dix. Maybe if we talk to d'Espry—"

"It won't do any good," I said wearily, looking up when the white Thomas Flyer sailed past us. From the back of the car, an arm shot up and waved. I smiled and lifted a hand in return, even though I knew that Paulie wouldn't see it.

"What's this?" Rupert asked, cocking an eyebrow at me before looking after the car. "If I didn't know better, I'd say that was a smile of a man who was interested in a woman. That was the suffragette car, wasn't it?"

"What are we going to do about this mad plan of Kell's?" I asked, blatantly changing the subject.

Rupert shrugged. "Nothing we can do to stop him if he insists on doing it. Best I can say is that we stay out of it if he does bring the cameras in to watch us. That way, we won't look like the fool he will most certainly appear."

"I don't know why he can't be content with focusing on the race. There's enough here to keep us interested, especially once we get done with this timed business and can truly race."

"I heard a rumor that we won't be doing the part through China," Rupert said, taking his place behind the wheel when Kell emerged from behind the bushes.

"Why? I was looking forward to seeing China, even if we were only going to be there for a few days."

"Word is that the visas that Roger had applied for are not coming in. Something about the government not wanting to give permission for the film crew to be there."

"What's this about the film crew?" Kell plopped himself down in the backseat and took up his phone, glancing up and swearing under his breath when the Italian car passed us, the camera car right behind them. "Dammit, get going! Let's not waste any more time."

"You're the one with the weak bladder," Rupert said, but obediently started the car and pulled out into the traffic. "Kim said we might be skipping China."

"Who's Kim?" Kell yelled.

"Production assistant. Blond. Big tits. Visa trouble with China," Rupert recapped at the top of his lungs.

"Oh. Good. Never wanted to go there in the first place."

An hour later, Kell insisted we pull over to the shoulder. We'd just passed the Thomas Flyer at a roadside stand (I assumed it was stopped for a restroom break), and all was well until Kell became agitated. Reluctantly, I pulled over, surprised when he shoved me out of the seat. "Just going to call d'Espry and tell him we witnessed a station robbery and are in pursuit."

"Kell, don't do this—" I started to say, but Kell held up an imperious hand and proceeded to tell Roger a tissue of lies. "Roger! It's Kell! Where are you? Good, you're ahead of us. You're not going to believe this, but we're at a petrol station just outside of Rudsville, and two men ran out of the station with guns waving and hopped in a car to race off. Clearly they just robbed the place, and we're chasing them now. If you get a camera crew up here, you should be able to get some exciting footage!"

"For the love of god," I murmured, and moved to let him take the driver's seat. I looked straight at the camera on the windscreen and said loudly, "I want a record that I'm dead against this deception."

"Me too," Rupert said, leaning over the backseat. "It's a mad plan."

"The robbers are in a small white sedan. There are two of them. The car has a bunch of bumper stickers on the back," Kell told the phone, and yanked hard on the acceleration lever, sending us jerking forward. "Look, lads—there they are! Let's get 'em!"

To the right of us, a small white car sat waiting at a petrol station. It was exactly as Kell described, and as we passed it Kell waved his arm wildly. The driver of the white car responded with a similar signal. It pulled out and quickly overtook us.

"Hanging up now, Roger," Kell yelled. "It's too dangerous to talk and drive. We could be killed if I don't give this wild chase all of my attention."

I couldn't help it—I rolled my eyes . . . at least I did until we passed another petrol station. This one had a familiar long white car sitting at a pump. Coming around the side of the building, Paulie emerged at a run. Standing in their car, d'Espry's daughter waved her hand, clearly calling to Paulie. At the wheel was the woman named Melody, hurriedly wrapping a big white veil of netting around her head.

"There's the suffragette car," I called as we sped past.

"Good! They were ahead of us. It means we'll make up some time," Kell bellowed in reply.

The wind ripped away the rest of his words. I glanced worriedly at the dials set behind the steering wheel, noting that we were now speeding along at a rate of fifty miles per hour. Although the cars more or less were equipped with modern engines that didn't require hand cranking and were infinitely more powerful and reliable, the frames of the cars were original and not built for high speeds. We'd all been warned about pushing the cars over the limit of fifty-five, a speed that we found made the De Dion shake horribly.

"Slow down!" I yelled, pointing at the gauge when Kell applied more pressure to the accelerator lever. The car began to make a horrible rattling noise.

"We have to make a show of it," Kell answered.

"He's going to shake the tires off," Rupert shouted, leaning over the back of my seat. "What the hell is he thinking?"

"He's not. That's the whole prob—"

The word stopped in my mouth as a white bonnet appeared to my left and a raucous horn sounded.

Rupert and I both turned to watch, astonished, as the Thomas Flyer pulled past us. In the backseat, swathed in white veil, Paulie waved and mouthed something, giving us a thumbs-up as their car pulled past.

Kell snarled something anatomically impossible and wrenched on the lever to give the car more speed. Snatches of words could be heard over the sound of the rattling and wind: ". . . they think they are doing . . . Roger told them. I will have my agent . . . stupid bitches getting in the . . ."

"Slow down!" I screamed, clutching the windscreen when it began to vibrate furiously. I was afraid the damned thing would come out of its frame and smash over us. "Kell, you're going to tear the car apart!"

"We're fine! It's just noise! I'm not going to let those bitches beat me to the camera!"

I turned my head. Next to my shoulder, Rupert was gripping the back of my seat, his knuckles white. "Call d'Espry," I yelled. "Tell him Kell is trying to kill us."

"You do, and I really will!" Kell screamed over the noise of the engine, car, and wind.

Rupert ignored him and pulled out his mobile phone and dialed.

A high-pitched scream of anguish emerged from Kell's open mouth. At the same time, I saw ahead of us the Thomas Flyer on the side of the road along with a small white sedan and a third car belonging to the camera crew. The cameraman stood on the hood of their car, filming as the ladies bounded over tall grass edging the road. Beyond them, two dark shapes bolted into a dense growth of trees.

A car approaching from the opposite direction screeched to a halt on the shoulder, and Roger emerged.

Kell began pounding on the steering wheel, obscenities polluting the air around him. I relaxed my hold on the windscreen as we started to slow, then suddenly was thrown forward, my head hitting the wooden dash of the car. Kell slammed on the brakes, still swearing profanely. The car fishtailed and skidded, one of the tires exploding loudly while we continued to skid to an eventual stop halfway off the shoulder into a shallow ditch.

"Christ!" Rupert yelled, fighting with his seat belt. "What the hell do you think you are doing? You could have killed us! Dixon, are you all right? There's blood all over your face."

The car shuddered slightly when a large lorry passed us. I sat up and felt my forehead, my fingers coming away red. "I'm all right despite Kell's attempt to send me through the windscreen."

Kell didn't wait to hear more from us. He ripped his seat belt off and leaped out of the car, running to where Roger was standing with the film crew. Across the field of tall grass, the three ladies were slowly returning.

"That's it," Rupert said, his face grim. "I'm done with this race. I hate to be a quitter, but life is too valuable to be riding around with that madman."

"I agree, but I'm not going to quit." With shaking hands, I got my seat belt undone and crawled out the side of the car away from passing traffic. "I am, however, going to demand that Roger replace Kell. He's a downright menace."

The cameras had turned from the women, now almost back to their car, to where Kell was storming up and down in front of Roger, his hands waving wildly, his face contorted with anger.

One of the women veered away and trotted over to where I stood clutching the side of our car.

"Dixon, the most exciting thing happened! Roger called us to say that someone had just robbed a gas station just down the road from us—holy shitake! You're bleeding!"

My head throbbed now, causing me to flinch back when she ran up and reached for my head. "Don't," I said, more roughly than I'd intended, especially when I saw the hurt in her face. I grabbed her wrist and continued. "Not because I don't want you invading my space. My head hurts. I don't want it touched."

"Oh," she said, relaxing, and pulled a couple of tissues from between her breasts. "How about if I dab up the blood running down your cheek? I won't come near the cut. What happened to you?"

I let her dab at my face, flinching when she got close to the wound. "My head hit the dash. I'm sure it looks worse than it is."

"You'd better see a doctor anyway."

"Perhaps."

5:43 a.m.

Fell asleep last night writing up the day's adventures. No time to add to it now. Must remember to pick up the story later.

Paulina Rostakova's Adventures

JULY 24
6:22 p.m.
Room 28 of local motel somewhere in Wyoming

Well! So much has happened in the last couple of days. I haven't had time to write it all down, but I'm going to catch up now while I'm waiting for Dixon.

The most interesting was the day that Dixon and I got together in his hotel room (the second day of the race) when I was all sorts of conflicted. Not for myself, but for him. He said it wasn't a problem, us being all itch-scratchy with each other, but I can't help but wonder if he's one of those men who holds on to grieving to protect themselves from ever being hurt again.

I wanted to talk to him about that, but we had to get down to the dinner that night, so instead I dashed across the hall into my room and took a shower. I was late to the dinner and could see that Dixon was busy with other people, so I sat with Melody. Louise and two of the Italian team joined us almost immediately.

"How did your first day go?" Luca asked when Louise stopped hogging all the conversation. "You had the flat tire, yes?"

"It was a bit hairy because I was worried the bolts would come off, but fine otherwise."

"Hairy?" he asked, his face screwing up.

"Sorry. In that circumstance it means difficult. How did your day go before your engine crisis?"

He shrugged. "Carlo, he wants to drive all the time, but he is bad at it. Francesco misses his wife, and talks to her on the phone the whole day. Me, I don't like driving the old car, but it is part of the day, so I do it."

"Sounds like there are personality clashes in more than just our car," I said, my eyes on Louise where she was leaning over while talking to Carlo, giving him the opportunity to see down her sleeveless shirt. "We did have some excitement when Roger told us about a gas station holdup. We lit out after the robbers and caught up with them, but they ditched their car and bolted before we could get to them. It was all very thrilling, if slightly anticlimactic at the end."

"Ah, yes, I heard about that. Carlo, he says that the TV star will leave the show because it wasn't him that ran the robbers off the road, but Fra and I don't think he will leave. He likes that camera much, that one."

"Fra?" I asked; then it clicked. "Oh, Francesco. I'm kind of in your camp on that—he's like someone else I could mention, and very caught up with who has the maximum exposure on camera."

I refrained from looking at Louise, who was, at this moment, scanning the room to see if anyone had a live camera (they didn't).

"It is so. You have a husband?"

I was a bit startled by the change of subject. "No, I don't."

"Boyfriend? Girlfriend?"

I hesitated for a couple of seconds. "No boyfriend or girlfriend."

"Good." He flashed extremely white teeth at me in a

broad smile. "We go to bed, then? I like the ladies with plumpness."

I sat up straight, sucking in my gut as I did so, then immediately released it, because I'd be damned if I let some man's idea of what women should look like matter to me. "I beg your pardon?" I said stiffly.

He made a gesture in the breast region. "Plumpness. Is not the word? I like women with bodies like in the paintings of Raphael, yes?"

"Bully for you," I said, then amended it by adding, "Look, I appreciate that you like women of size, but I'm not interested."

He frowned. "You said you do not have boyfriend?"

"That doesn't mean I'm going to hop into bed with you." I glanced toward where Dixon was sitting, wondering if there was room at his table for one more, and if there was, if it would appear clingy on my part to go sit with him.

"You don't like me?" He looked offended now. "There is something else you like? Ladyboys?"

"No! Look, I'm just not interested. OK? It's nothing personal—I'm sure you're a charming lover, but I'm just not looking for a man." Not while Dixon was around, anyway.

"I am a charming lover," he said complacently. "Very good. I give womens much pleasure, you know? With my mouth and hands. The womens, they like that very much. My jaw is quite strong."

"OK, one, ew. And two, I have no doubt you're the king of oral sex, but that doesn't change anything."

Movement at the corner of my eye had me turning to glance at the doorway. A man stood there, holding a sheaf of papers.

It was the man from the hallway.

"Right. Twice is odd; three times says my father hasn't

learned that he can't run my life," I said, ignoring Luca's questions when I jumped to my feet and began to wend my way through the packed room to the door. The man stared at me for the count of four, then turned on his heel and left. "That's right—you'd better run," I growled to myself, and gave chase.

"Stop!" I yelled when I whipped around a corner and saw the man standing at an elevator. He gave me an odd look as I puffed my way over to him. (Note to self: Really have to get back to Pilates class.) "OK, that was extraneous since you were stopped when I yelled that, but still, stop! As in, stop running from me!"

"Madam," he said in a deep voice with an edge to it that I recognized instantly. "I do not know you."

"Aha!" I pointed a finger and shook it at him. A woman with a housekeeping cart wheeled past us, giving us both a suspicious look. "I knew it! You're Russian!"

"I do not know you," he repeated.

"No? I bet you know my father, and you can just tell him for me that this is not going to work. I'm onto you, buckaroo, and I have no qualms in telling the production people you're following me any more than I'd have qualms about doing the same to Boris. So just put that in your samovar and smoke it!"

"A samovar is not a pipe," he said with maddening calm.

"And you can just stop that, too," I said, shaking a finger again.

"Stop what?"

"Acting like I'm the deranged one here, when it's you who is trailing me at my father's behest." I straightened up my shoulders and tipped my head back so I could look down my nose at him. "If I so much as see you again, I'll report you."

"You will be doing quite a bit of reporting, then, since

I have been recruited to join one of the racing teams," he said mildly.

"You have not," I said on a horrified gasp. How the hell had Dad managed that?

He indicated his paperwork. "I have my contract here, as a matter of fact. Now, if you don't mind, I have left my phone in my room and want to get it before I attend the evening's events."

The elevator opened. He entered and turned around to face me.

I glared at him. He let one eyebrow rise slightly before the doors closed.

"Bastard," I growled, and immediately sent a text to my father.

July 24
To: Daddy
You think you're so smart, don't you? Well, I'm onto you. I don't know who you had to pay off, but it won't work.

July 24
From: Daddy
What is wrong? You are OK? You have fingers?

July 24
To: Daddy
Yes, I have all my fingers. Dammit, don't pretend you don't know what I'm talking about! I know you sent the mysterious bald man!

July 24
From: Daddy
What bald man? Who is bald man? You are sleeping with bald man?

July 24
To: Daddy
Nice attempt to Disraeli me.

July 24
From: Daddy
Is Disraeli bald boyfriend? What happened to English? Take picture of driver license. Text to me. I take care of bald Disraeli.

July 24
To: Daddy
Autocorrect, dammit. Why does it always autocorrect me? There is no Disraeli. Well, there was, but he's dead.

July 24
From: Daddy
You kill Disraeli? Is fine. I call peoples. They make body disappear. You wait twenty, maybe thirty minutes, then go to lobby and stay there for half hour. When you go back to room, Disraeli will be no more.

July 24
To: Angela
Please tell Dad that I did not just kill a bald man named Disraeli, and stop him from sending whatever sort of illegal cleanup crew he's about to fire into action.

July 24
From: Angela
Very well. Did you kill someone not named Disraeli?

July 24
To: Angela
*No! There is no Disraeli! It was an autocorrect, and
you know Dad, he instantly saw a man spear.*

July 24
To: Angela
Dammit! Cold spire not man spear!

July 24
From: Angela
What?

July 24
To: Angela
CONS piracy. That's what I was trying to say.

July 24
To: Angela
I give up. I'm throwing away my phone.

After my experience with the man who I just knew my
father had sent to watch me, I tried to find Roger to
complain about letting the man in the race, but couldn't
find him. Then I texted Dixon to see what he was up to
(and hope he'd invite me to his room), but he didn't
answer.

In the end, I went to bed. Alone. My formerly tingly
parts were glum and cheerless, and threatened to start
writing emo poetry if I didn't bring Dixon around to visit
them again. It was very sad.

Today I was up early because we had the first takeoff
time. I wandered into the hotel's tiny dining area, where
they had laid out a breakfast spread. Melody was already

at a small round table, but I knew from the previous morning's experience not to try to talk to her until she'd had at least two cups of coffee, so I grabbed a bowl of granola and a cup of yogurt and was about to sit down at an empty table when I saw Dixon.

"Hello, stranger," I said, setting down my food.

"I'm sorry," he said, glancing around to make sure we weren't overheard. Fortunately, Sam and Tabby were chowing down and both busy with their tablets, no doubt catching up on the latest news and such.

"For what?"

"Missing your text last night. I fell asleep writing in my journal. I must have been more tired than I thought."

I glanced at the mark on his head. "You don't still have a headache, do you?"

"No, my head is fine." He grimaced. "Well, as fine as it ever is. But I do regret not being awake to . . . er . . . talk to you."

"I had a lot more than talking in mind," I said, giving him a flirtatious look that should have steamed his shorts. "I suppose, given your experience in the car, it was better that you get the rest. But tonight . . ."

"Tonight I definitely will not fall asleep early," he said, his voice rumbling in a way that made me feel very warm.

"I'm delighted to hear it." I sat down and, with an eye on the clock, hurriedly ate my breakfast. Dixon returned from the buffet with a plate of eggs and toast and a small bowl of fruit. "We're going first today, so I can't stay to chat long. Looks like we have a nice straight run today."

"Hopefully without encountering any bandits," Dixon said, touching his forehead gingerly.

"Sometimes I feel like we're in a movie rather than filming a reality show," I said, dabbing my lips and removing the four napkins I'd used to cover as much of my dress as was likely to get food on it. "Robbers, in-car dramas, dashing men and women in stylish costumes—I like yours today, by the way."

Dixon looked down at his gold vest and forest green suit. "Thank you. I'm told this is what was called a one-button suit, and all the stylish gents wore it in 1907. You look nice as well. The plaid suits you."

"It does, doesn't it? Let me see if I can remember what the wardrobe ladies said about my outfit." I got up and did a little twirl for him. "The skirt has six groups of four pleats each, and a bolero jacket. There is a blue silk belt, and my hat for today is a straw boater decorated with heather and yards and yards of this white net stuff that—let me tell you—sucks in all the bugs within a five-mile radius. The last part wasn't the official description, by the way."

"It's very charming," he said gravely, although I noticed a certain amount of approving heat in his eyes.

"I like it, but not as much as your pretty vest."

"Waistcoat," he corrected gently.

"You're in America now. Here it's a vest. And a dapper one, too. All you need is one of those wax-tipped mustaches, and you'd be at home in any Edwardian drama."

"We have enough drama already, thank you." He looked mildly unhappy. "I heard that Kell did not go easily."

"Go?" I swallowed the last of my granola, glancing again at the clock. I had ten minutes before we were due at the start. "Go where?"

"You didn't hear? Roger mentioned it at the dinner last night."

"I had to . . . er . . . duck out for a bit. It was over by the time I was done. What did I miss?"

"Kell being formally removed from competition. He claimed he had done nothing wrong and wasn't in the least to blame for yesterday's incident, but luckily the dash cam evidence was enough to prove he violated the terms of participating by putting Rupert, me, and the car in danger."

"Wow. So it's just you and your brother now?" I had a horrible suspicion what he was going to say next.

"And a new man, Anton Serik. I haven't met him, but Roger said he had been originally on the list to race but had been bumped in favor of Kell."

"Is he about five foot eight and bald, and has suspicious little eyes?" I asked, nodding when Melody tapped her watch at me and left the room.

"I don't know. Why?" He gave me an odd look.

"I think my dad sent him. Although he wouldn't have been on the original list if that was the case. Damn. Maybe I was wrong about him, in which case he probably thinks I'm certifiable. Crapstones! I have to go. Good luck today!"

"And to you," he said, half rising when I leaped up to dash away. I wondered for a minute if he had been about to kiss me, and turned back to him. He had sat down, but noticed me clearly standing there, waiting for a good-bye smooch. He rose just as I figured he wasn't going to kiss me and turned to go to the door. I caught the movement from the corner of my eye and, having taken three steps, stopped to look back at him. He was sitting again, but at my look back to him, he started to rise, freezing halfway as if he was not sure what I was going to do.

"Oh, for heaven's sake, this is worse than a slapstick movie!" I said loudly, and ran back to him where he was lowering himself back into the chair, grabbed his ears, and laid my lips on his in a fast-and-furious kiss.

I was out the door before I remembered that we weren't going to give anyone an idea of what we were doing in private, cursing to myself all the way to the car.

I'm happy to report the day's drive passed without any untoward events, although Louise was increasingly unhappy.

"I don't know why the film crew is spending all its time on other people when we are the ones who are interesting."

"Wow. Self-centered much?" I murmured in the backseat.

She slapped her hands on the wheel, causing the car to jerk dangerously to the side. "It's just not like what Mom said it would be. Look at me, sitting here doing nothing but driving all day long. How am I ever going to get the Instagram followers I need by doing nothing but driving a moldy old car?"

Melody cast a glance over her shoulder to me. I shrugged.

"Mom said it was going to be like *The Amazing Race*, only with costumes. This is nothing like it, nothing at all. There are no challenges, no excitement, and not nearly enough cameras. I'm the producer's daughter, for god's sake! I should have a dedicated camera of my own. I was almost on *Housewives of Catalina*, except I'm not married." She slapped her hands again.

"I don't quite know—" Melody started to say, but it would take a stronger woman than she to stop Louise once she was in one of her soliloquys.

"I'm going to tell Dad that things have to change, or else. I'm not going to waste a whole four weeks just *driving*."

I wanted to ask her what she thought a round-the-world car race would entail, but decided I really didn't want the answer. Instead, I tuned out her continued complaints and spent my time making character sketches of everyone I'd met, talking to Melody, and taking copious amounts of photos.

Since we'd made good time—too good, as a matter of fact, which would have left us arriving before the allowed time (and thus earned another infraction)—we stopped at a coffee shop outside the city and enjoyed an hour of

Wi-Fi, lattes, and the attention of everyone present. Louise posed for pictures with patrons, while Melody and I showed off the Thomas Flyer. Louise was miffed that the camera crews were not there to catch her doing her thing, and drove the rest of the way ranting about it being a conspiracy to keep her off the screen.

We rolled into our hotel checkpoint during the time allowed, and after a bit of mechanical talk from Graham (who wanted me to check oil, water, and gas levels, since there were no modern-day gauges), I toddled off to remove the corset and pretty outfit.

I stopped by the minuscule desk and picked up a key. Evidently this hotel—more of a motel than anything else—was built around the turn of the twentieth century and hadn't upgraded its doors to modern standards. I climbed the stairs to the first floor, turned down a long hallway, and toward the middle of it saw Dixon talking to his brother at the door of a room. Judging by the numbers on the doors, my own room was a few beyond the two men.

"Hello," I said politely as I scooted past them.

"Hullo," Rupert said. He'd already peeled off his high collar and necktie and opened his vest and shirt. He didn't look anything like his brother, and although he was handsome enough, he couldn't hold a candle to Dixon. "How was your drive?"

"Fine. I think the probability is quite high that Melody might murder Louise if she continues to narrate her every thought all day long into the dash cam, but I'm OK with that. How was your guys' trip? No problems with the new guy? Speaking of him, where is he?" I looked around, but it was only the two brothers and at the other end of the hall the German ladies all going into their rooms.

"Anton? He's around somewhere." Rupert gave Dixon

an odd look. "I'm off to take a shower and then commiserate with the French team before they fly home."

"What? They're leaving?"

"Didn't you hear? Their car was flattened by a lorry."

"A what now?"

"'Semitruck' is, I believe, the term used here," Dixon added.

"Oh my god. Are they all right?" I was shocked to my core. For some reason, I didn't think anything serious would happen to the racers. Flat tires, yes. Chases through fields, sure. But not cars smashed to bits by huge behemoths of the road.

"They're fine. They were out of the car. They were off taking what Roger calls a nature break and a lorry passing too close smashed the car into the guardrail."

"Holy crap. What a lucky escape."

"Yes," he said, his eyes dipping to where my breasts were mounded high inside my tight-fitting white lace blouse.

Casually, I peeled off the bolero jacket.

Dixon sucked in his breath. Rupert headed to his room, leaving Dixon and me standing in the hallway.

"Erm." He cleared his throat. "Which room is yours?"

"That way," I said, pointing past him with my key. "You're here?"

"Yes." An awkward, sexually charged silence fell. My whole body seemed to hold its breath.

"Perhaps you would like to come by my room later," Dixon said at the same time I asked, "Wanna do a sheet tango?"

We stared at each other; then I burst into laughter.

"Your way sounds so much more sophisticated," I said, twirling the bolero and moving off toward my room. "Think I'll see if my corset buddy is around. I'm so anxious to get out of it . . ."

Dixon was in front of me before I even realized he'd moved, snatching the key from my hand and jamming it into the lock on the door. "Allow me," he said, his eyes a stormy bluish green.

"Don't tell me—you're a corset devotee and you can't wait to see which one I have on today?" I asked, entering my room. My suitcase was sitting on the rack where the crew had placed it, but I didn't get to it before Dixon was at my back unhooking the blouse.

"I'm more a devotee of what's inside the corset. Arms up."

I lifted my arms and allowed him to whip the blouse off over my head. While he was laying it neatly on the dresser, I undid the silk belt and started on the skirt buttons. In no time I was scratching my ribs through my camisole, heaving big sighs of relief as I did so.

"You have no idea how good it is to take that beastly thing off," I said after I'd had a good scratch. I turned to face Dixon. "What on earth is wrong?"

"Nothing," he said, squinting at my lower half.

I glanced down, suddenly worried that something was amiss. I was still in my knee-length bloomers, but since they had a couple of rows of lace ruffles and were tied with pretty blue ribbons, I didn't see what there was to frown at. "Then why are you looking at me like you're suddenly horrified at my pubic zone? Surely you must have seen it the other night. I don't wax, but I do trim it so that I don't have a bird's nest down there."

"No, it's not that at all. I highly approve of your ... er ... pubic zone. It's that garment. I'm trying to decide if it's alluring or amusing."

I struck a pose, wiggling my derriere, which sounded a lot more risqué than it looked, since the bloomers were gathered at the waist and poufed out in the back. "The answer is that my allure is not such that mere mortal man can resist it. Why don't you take off some of your clothes? You have too many on."

"If you wish," he said in that proper English accent that made me giggle. "It is a warm day, after all, and I wish to be comfortable while I ogle your womanly curves, noncurves, and general allure."

"And my curves and noncurves want you to be comfortable," I agreed, and helped him out of his suit jacket, collar, tie, vest, and shirt. I abandoned him to remove my boots, wiggling my toes happily while sitting on the edge of my bed, watching him hop one-footed while he tried to pull off the other shoe. The underwear they'd given the men was evidently an extended version of boxer shorts, these ending just above his knee. The front had buttons on it, while, to my surprise, there was an escape hatch on the rear side. "I am having no judgment qualms on your undies, by the way. You look incredibly sexy in yours."

"But you like me better out of them?" he asked.

"Oh, hell yes." I stared with wide eyes when he shucked his underwear. "So very much better this way."

"It does have its advantages."

I cleared my throat and tried to look like I didn't want him just for his really fabulous body. "I missed you last night, by the way."

"As did I. I had hoped we could get together, but evidently it was not to be—"

He paused when a knock sounded on my door.

"It's probably Melody," I told him, getting to my feet.

Dixon glanced around and moved into the bathroom. "Oh?"

"Yeah. She has no problem getting out of her corset but knows I have a hard time with mine."

The last words were spoken as I opened the door.

Unfortunately, it was not Melody at the door. Standing with his back to me was Roger.

"—it saddens us all, but I am sure the other members of Team Sufferin' Suffragettes will continue on gamely. And here is the team mechanic, Paulie, to give us her reaction to this news. Paulie—"

Roger had turned around at that point, revealing not only Tabby and Sam filming him (and now me, in my underwear), but also his expression, which went from slightly worried to flat-out dumbfounded when Dixon emerged from the bathroom, a white towel around his waist.

"Uh . . ." I said, my eyes huge and my brain going utterly blank. "Um . . . hi."

"Hello," Roger said absently, looking quickly from Dixon to me and back again. "What . . . er . . . apparently you're . . ."

"Busy," Dixon said, and calmly came to stand behind me. "Was there something in particular you wanted?"

Roger managed to collect himself. Behind him, Sam rustled in a pocket and withdrew some money, which he handed to Tabby. The latter gave me a thumbs-up.

"Yes, actually, I wanted to get Paulie's reaction to the news that team leader Louise has decided to step down and return to California, where she will pursue an acting career." Roger's eyes had an oddly speculative look.

"Louise left? I can't say I'm surprised, since she was so clearly unhappy." I remembered that I was speaking to her father and that a little kindness would not hurt. "Naturally, she will be missed. She was . . . uh . . ." I couldn't bring myself to outright lie and say that she was a good driver, or even good company, and finally decided on, "She was a natural in front of the camera, and very comfortable at being the center of attention. I'm sure she'll be an outstanding actress."

"Normally, the production would bring in the backup female driver to replace Louise, but unfortunately our backup has decided she is unable to participate and thus we're going to have to leave the suffragette team with just two members." He put his arm around me and swung around so we were both facing the camera. "It will mean longer hours driving for both you and Melody. How do you feel about that?"

"Just fine," I said, wondering if he thought I was going to protest the loss of Louise. I'd gladly pick up more time driving just to be rid of her, and had a feeling Melody would be of the same mind.

"Excellent, excellent," he said, glancing at Sam and the camera. "As our viewers know, in addition to the entire French team, we've lost another racer today in the form of Abbie, who had to return home to attend to her ailing mother. It's been a hard day for the teams who've lost a member, but I'm sure everyone will rise to the challenge. And now I'll let you return to . . . er . . ."

"Dixon," I said, and, disentangling myself from him, smiled broadly at the camera while backing up into my room. "He was helping me with my corset. It's impossible to take off on my own, you see, and normally I have Melody do it, but she doesn't have any problem with hers, and sometimes she gets busy and doesn't have time to help me get rid of the corset, and Dixon was in the hall when I came in, so it seemed only natural to have him help me get it off."

Behind me, Dixon made a noise that was part laughter and part sigh.

"Er . . . just so," Roger said, the speculation still rife in his eyes. Tabby doubled over in silent laughter.

"These corsets are a real pain to wear," I started to say, but Dixon ended the conversation by reaching around me and closing the door. I turned on him. "Dixon! I was trying to explain why you're here in my room."

"Which would make sense if I wasn't standing here in a towel and nothing else," he said, his eyes filled with amusement.

"I was coming to that," I said in a grandiose manner. "I had a whole story lined up about how I spilled coffee on your clothes and you had to take them off because you didn't want the coffee to stain, and that it looked like we were in a compromising position, but, really, it was all innocent."

"But it isn't innocent," he said, sliding the strap of my camisole down. "It's not innocent in the least."

"Dear god, I hope not." I tugged on his towel, wrapping my arms around his waist and tipping my head back to kiss him.

Another knock sounded at the door.

Dixon swore and grabbed the towel from the floor.

I stalked to the door, annoyed.

"Did you hear the— Oh!" Melody stood at the door in street clothes, her eyes widening when she saw Dixon. "Sorry. I didn't know you were occupied."

I sighed. "It's OK. We just entertained Roger and the camera crew. I assume you're going to ask me if I heard about Louise? The answer is yes, I have. Roger filmed me getting the news."

"I see." Her gaze flickered to Dixon for a moment before she said apologetically, "We can talk about it later. Sorry to disturb you."

She pulled the door closed. I eyed it for a moment. "Who else is left to disturb us? Your brother?"

"No, he was with us in the hallway."

"Right." I turned around and leaned against the door in as seductive a pose as possible. "Then I think we're safe."

"We may be alone," he said with a suggestive waggle of his eyebrows, "but I don't know how safe you are. At least, not where it concerns my desires."

"Oooh," I said, shimmying forward until I was once again pressed up against him. The thin lawn of the camisole did nothing to diminish the sensation of his chest rubbing against my breasts. "Are we going to role-play? I've never done it, but always wanted to."

"We can if—" He stopped and we both stared at the door.

"Really, this is getting too much," I complained, and handed Dixon his towel before going to the door. I opened it just enough to glare through it and said tersely, "What the hell do you want?"

The bald-headed man named Anton stood there, a mildly pleasant smile on his face. "It occurred to me that we got off to a bad start, and since we are likely to see each other daily, it would be best for me to introduce myself and correct any misimpression you have."

"Busy now," I said, and slammed the door. My conscience pricked enough to make me open it up and add, "Sorry. It's a bad time. Later I'm going to want to have a long talk with you, especially about any contacts you have in Russia."

He blinked at me.

I gave him a pointed look, then closed the door again.

Dixon's lips were thinned, his expression annoyed in a way that made me want to giggle. He strode to the door, took up the DO NOT DISTURB sign, and opened the door to hang it on the handle. Standing in the middle of the hallway, looking in the other direction, was Anton. His eyebrows rose at the sight of Dixon.

"Ainslie," he said with a little nod of acknowledgment.

"Serik," Dixon answered, and, without saying anything more, closed the door, locking it, and putting the chain on for good measure. "Do you ever have the feeling the fates are against you?"

"I hadn't before this, but I'm now mentally running down a list of everyone in the cast and crew and figuring out who's likely to come knocking at my door next. Maybe we should hurry."

He sighed and, to my intense sadness, pulled on his pants. "I don't want to hurry. I want to take my time exploring every delicious inch of you."

"Then why are you leaving?" I asked, watching unhappily as he put on his shoes and slipped into the shirt, leaving it unbuttoned while he gathered the rest of his things. "You can't explore if I'm not in the same room, and I wanted to do a little wandering around your landscape, too."

"Someone, somehow, will interrupt us again, and as I said, I don't want to be rushed." He opened the door and looked back at me. "Two hours. My room. Don't tell anyone where you're going. Bring ice."

"Ice? Why?"

He was gone, the door closing quietly behind him, leaving me to tell my lady parts to cool their jets for a couple of hours, and to ponder just exactly how he intended on using the ice.

I've been neglectful in recording the events of the journey. To be honest, I considered giving up the whole journaling project, but Paulie urged me to continue, saying she was having fun with her own journal and that it gets easier with practice.

I asked her if she was recording conversations. "It seems I have a knack for remembering them, and it makes for more interesting reading than 'I asked this and so-and-so answered that,' so I make sure to include as much dialogue as I can recall."

"I do that, too, although sometimes I have to sit and think about what people said. And of course, I write about us."

"Us? How so?"

"You know." She waved a hand around and tickled my ribs. "Us. This. What we do together. The way you used the ice on me, for example. I'll be sure to include that, although I'm not sure if I'll ever recover from you popping that ice cube up the ol' hoohaw."

"You record our intimate details? Is that wise?" I asked, looking down at the top of her head. We were in my bed, having gone to my room after repeated interruptions in our attempt to engage in lovemaking, and, having completed said lovemaking (complete with a couple of very enlightening ice cubes), were now lying together, our bodies tangled in that way that lovers have, and a towel underneath us to soak up the results of melted ice.

"Wise how? Or rather, how would it *not* be wise?"

"You said you intended on publishing your diary of the trip. I was considering doing the same, but I would not wish to expose you to improper attention via it."

She rolled over to lie on top of me, her delicious breasts pressing into my chest in a way that instantly had me thinking about whether or not I could manage a second go-round. "Improper attention. Hee hee hee."

I swatted her ass. "You know what I mean."

"I do, and I appreciate your concern. As for my journal, I'm going to edit out all the naughty bits. That'll be just for me . . . and you, if you'd like a copy."

"Of course." I slid my hands down her back to her plump ass. I loved that ass with all its curves and enticing softness. "Would you like me to do the same?"

"Let me read your journal, or write up our smutty bits? Because the answer to both is yes, please."

"You are an odd woman," I commented, smiling a little to let her know I meant it in a positive way.

"And you're just noticing this?" She smiled and drew a pattern on my chest. My penis stirred, leaving me to think thoughts that a second round wasn't as far-fetched as I might have considered. "I didn't think I'd like erotic literature, as I prefer to think of our writings, but I have to admit that reading back to that lovely night, it really got my motor running."

She wiggled against me in a way that definitely made me think I could perform miracles.

"If you keep moving like that, you'll do more than get my motor running," I said with a bit of masculine pride.

"Really?" She rolled off me and inspected my penis. "Holy cow, you're right. I didn't think men could do that more than once in an hour."

"Most men can't, I'm sure," I said in an insufferably smug voice, but one I felt was fully allowable given the circumstances. "I, however, am a superior sort of man, one who is aroused only by a superior type of woman, and you are most definitely that woman."

"Goodness," she said, all admiration. She looked down to my penis, up to my face, and back down to it. "Do you need some help? I should help, shouldn't I? This isn't all your responsibility."

"Your assistance is always welcome," I said graciously.

"Right." She got to her knees and seemed to have some trouble deciding what to do. "Should we do some role-playing? That would be exciting and different, wouldn't it?"

"It would, but I'm not sure we need that—"

"Good! I've always wanted to try, and never had a boyfriend who was into it. Let's see . . . what should we role-play?"

"How about you be a sexy American woman with the loveliest legs in the country, and I will be a visiting Englishman who loves the way your legs wrap around my hips?"

She batted away that suggestion. "Naw, that's too realistic. What's exotic and out of the ordinary? Pirates! You can be a pirate captain and I'll be your buxom first mate."

"No pirates," I said quickly, shaking my head at her to emphasize the point. "My brother had a bad experience role-playing pirates."

"Pooh. Well . . . King Henry VIII?"

"The one who ordered the deaths of many of his wives?"

She made a face. "Yeah, as soon as I said it I knew it was bad. *Downton Abbey*?"

"Never watched it."

"Crap. I would suggest milkmaid and shepherd boy, but I have no idea what either does."

"How about," I said, rolling her over until my mouth was hovering over one of her round breasts, "we leave the role-playing for another time, and instead I kiss every inch of you?"

"That sounds jim-dandy fine with me," she agreed quickly, and dug her fingers into my shoulders when I took a nipple gently between my teeth. "Oh lord, yes! To hell with role play! Kiss my inches! Kiss my inches!"

I did so. It was glorious. She tasted of salt and woman and something that I couldn't define, a slightly sweet scent that seemed to wind itself around me and hold me in bonds. Silken bonds. Silken bonds of desire . . . No, that sounds too trite and purple.

But it was true. I felt bound to her in some way that went beyond just the physical pleasure I found in kissing and tasting and in some cases nibbling on her. It was as if she satisfied me at a level that I couldn't explain. I still can't. It doesn't make sense, because I know she isn't interested in a long-term relationship. She's made it perfectly clear that she enjoys our time together, but that she's a free spirit.

That's fine. I'm a free spirit, too. I am not looking for a girlfriend or, god help me, a wife.

One thing did bother me while I was doing all the nibbling and kissing and touching and rubbing her silken legs alongside my aching flesh, and that was the need to tell her the truth about Rose.

"You are so beautiful," I murmured against her thigh, feeling like I was going to burst soon if I didn't plant myself inside her. "I love the way you taste and feel."

She pulled me upward, her hands caressing my back, and then lower to my ass. "That is very sweet of you, especially since I'm not beyond mildly pretty, but I appreciate it nonetheless. And I love how you taste, too. I've never thought much about it before, but you are all hot and spicy and salty at the same time, and it kind of drives me crazy. It has to be some primitive thing, and if you don't put that condom on right now, I'm likely to die right here of unrequited lust."

I smiled and got the condom on without incident, the feeling of her heat when I sank into her sending little streaks of fire up my groin and straight to my spine. It was a glorious feeling, and when I lifted her hips to better position myself, she went wild underneath me, her legs tightening around me until I found myself on my back with her riding me.

"Do you mind?" she said in little panting breaths. Hell, she even panted in a sexy manner.

What was going on that I found panting arousing?

"Not at all, just so long as you don't stop that little twirl you do," I managed to answer. It wasn't easy, because at that point my brain felt like it was full of treacle and operating at one-eighth the normal speed and, frankly, I was a bit surprised I could even get coherent words out.

"I like the twirl, too. What about this?" She shifted forward a little when she sank down on me.

My eyes rolled back in my head, and despite my attempts to put them back where they belonged, they stayed there happily, as I enjoyed the sensations she was sending firing out to all points on my body.

"I'll take it that the groan is a good sign. Wait. There's something else I want to try . . ." She leaned to the back and with one hand took my balls and gave them a gentle squeeze.

I damn near came off the bed at that.

I sat bolt upright, my hands on her luscious thighs, and demanded, "Don't ever stop doing that!"

She laughed—she actually laughed. "I'm glad you like it."

"Now I know that women are truly the superior sex, because it's all I can do to keep my autonomous functions like breathing and my heartbeat going, and here you are not only laughing and coming up with inventive and incredibly arousing things to do to my poor man's body, but you can also talk in actual sentences and not just grunt noises of rapturous pleasure like I am doing."

"You're actually talking now, you know," she said, her breath hitching when I took her breasts in my hand and lay down again, bringing her with me. "Oh man, that's really good at this angle. Dixon, I hope you're not going to be long, because I'm about ready to blow up into a thousand orgasm pieces."

"Now," I said, reverting to what I thought of as single-syllable caveman words. I thrust upward into her, my hips working overtime. "Do it now."

"If you insist . . ." She did another twist and arched her back over me, her inner muscles trembling and tightening around me in waves that pushed me into my own orgasm.

One of the things I like best about Paulie is how she smiles after we've had sex. It's not a grin, or even a happy-go-lucky greeting . . . It's the lazy, exhausted smile of a woman who has been pleasured from the tips of her adorable toes to the top of her head. She smiled now, her body draped across mine as if she was a toga, one that was custom-made for me.

I stroked her back, my own body feeling like it was made of lead. The thought flitted through my head that now would be the perfect moment to come clean about Rose.

"Erm," I said after a couple of minutes to catch my breath and let my heart stop racing.

"I know," she said, stretching languidly and sliding off me to curl up at my side, one of her legs still across mine.

"It was very *erm*, wasn't it? Although I swear I'm going to walk funny tomorrow after two times in one night." She yawned and snuggled tighter against me.

"I might do so as well," I said, shifting my arm so it wouldn't go to sleep under her. Sleep pulled at me with tiny but persistent fingers, urging me to fall fully into its grasp, but I felt the need to be honest with Paulie. "Not to take anything away from what we just did, there's something I wanted to tell you."

"OK. Tell away."

I looked up at the ceiling, trying to decide how best to put it. "You know, of course, that I was engaged to be married when I was in my early twenties."

"Yup."

"Rose was a few years older than me, divorced, and ready to settle down. I assumed I was as well, because I fell in love with her while I was in university. She was the daughter of one of my professors, and I thought she was the most glamorous woman I'd ever met."

"Mmm." Paulie shifted slightly, her breath warm on my shoulder.

"She suggested we get married, and I reckoned that was a good idea. I've never been like Rupert—interested in a number of women—and Rose was, after all, more worldly than me. So we announced our engagement and set a date for the following year. Almost immediately after that, I realized I'd made a mistake. What I'd thought was a worldly woman was one who wanted absolute control over me, what I did, what I wore, who I saw. When I thought she was settled and centered, I didn't realize she was simply set in her ways and unwilling to compromise. We started fighting, at first over silly things, but she would never let anything go. The arguments increased and became more serious. I actually suggested that we put off the wedding while we sought couple's counseling to work out our issues—she refused, saying that we were two intelligent people, and if we couldn't work things out by ourselves, then no one could help us. This went on for months. I was miserable. I think now she was just as unhappy as I was, but for some reason she clung tight to the wedding as a point of salvation."

Paulie murmured something unintelligible.

I stroked her arm, feeling a sense of comfort from her nearness despite the bad memories. "Four months before the wedding, I decided to break things off. I knew it would be the best thing for both of us, but before I could do so, Rose was diagnosed with ovarian cancer. Quite an aggressive cancer. Naturally, I couldn't leave her then. She became a different woman—distant and cold and bitter. I could understand it; after all, she'd just been given a death sentence. I stayed with her to the end, but by that time she was telling me daily how much she hated me."

The room fell silent. My heart ached at the memory of that dark time. "I know it was the cancer and harsh drugs talking, but it still hurt. Around others, she was fine—calm and collected, and saying she was ready to face her end. But when we were alone, she was simply . . . cruel."

My throat closed up a little. I gave a cough to loosen it up.

"I didn't tell anyone how she had changed. I didn't want them thinking of her being so hateful. I didn't want to remember her that way. We did have some good times, after all. And of course, all of this meant that everyone—my family, her family, my friends—all believed I was deeply grieving her loss. I couldn't tell them the truth. But I can tell you, because I know that you will understand."

I waited for her to say that she wholly and completely understood why I did what I did, and that she thought it was damned nice of me to keep Rose's memory positive despite what I'd gone through, and many other suitably nice things, but Paulie was silent.

Horribly, wrenchingly silent.

"You don't . . . understand?" I asked at last, rising slightly on one elbow to peer into her face.

She was sound asleep, her mouth open slightly, a tiny little puddle of drool forming on my arm.

I'd sexed her into sleep. There was something satisfying about that, even if my soul baring had been so uncaptivating that it had put her to sleep. I closed her mouth, wiped up the drool with the pillowcase, and rolled her over onto her side, spooning behind her. She murmured something and wiggled backward into me.

"I'll tell you tomorrow," I said, allowing myself to sink downward into sleep. "I'll explain it all then, and you will stop worrying that I'm pining for a woman I haven't loved for a very long time."

The following day (today), was hectic, to be sure . . . Ah. There is Paulie, at last. I will resume this at a later time.

Paulina Rostakova's Adventures

JULY 27
4:42 a.m.
San Francisco, California, hotel room

I can't sleep. Stupid body not being able to get rest when it needs it. Yesterday was . . . hoo, baby. I can't remember a worse day in a long time. But I'm foreshadowing again. Let's go back to the beginning of the "hoo, baby" bit, which was yesterday morning.

"Did you hear?" Melody asked when I rolled out of my room in Salt Lake City (which didn't get used, thanks to Dixon being the Irresistible Mr. Sexy Pants), deposited my luggage with the crew, and with the great big wads of veil in hand toddled out to the Thomas Flyer. Melody paused and added, "That's a very pretty dress."

"Thank you." I did a pirouette to make the sky blue skirt, which was heavily pleated, swirl out. A coat cut in what the wardrobe ladies described as military style hit me at midhip, while the blouse underneath was a pretty pale cream embroidered with matching blue flowers. They had tried to convince me to wear the stiff collar similar to the sort that the men wore, but I felt like I was being strangled in it, so I had been given a wide lace choker to wear instead. I plunked the hat on my head and began to wind the veil around it. "Did I hear what?"

"Hmm?" Melody looked down at her plain navy blue walking skirt, white shirt with stiff collar and tie, and knee-length coat with black piping. "I don't know why the wardrobe people thought I needed to dress in such a utilitarian style. I understand I'm supposed to be the bluestocking, but really, would it hurt my image to have a pretty embroidered blouse like you have?"

"You're smaller than me, but if you like, I can lend it to you to wear another day. Maybe under a jacket it wouldn't look too big on you," I offered generously, feeling quite the stylish Edwardian lady as I climbed into the passenger seat.

"No, that's all right." She got behind the steering wheel and started up the car, nodding when a frazzled-looking crew member came over to tell her we were going third today. "I'll stick with what they made up for me. After all, I don't mind being the studious and serious member of the team . . . which is odd, considering that now it's just you and me."

"Yeah. It's so quiet here." I glanced at the dash cam and gave it a toothy grin. "What were you asking me about?"

"Oh!" She turned to face me, clearly excited. "We've lost more people!"

"Lost *more*? You mean people left the show?"

"Yes! The Ravishing Romeos' car wouldn't start this morning, and when Graham went to look at it, he said the whole engine had been corroded by some sort of acid. There's no way to repair it, and they can't replace it easily since the engines were custom-made to fit in the old cars."

"Holy crapballs! Someone sabotaged them? Is Graham sure it was sabotage and not just . . . I don't know . . . some sort of engine meltdown?"

"It was sabotage." Melody shifted us into gear when someone waved us forward. Ahead, just taking off, was the car with Dixon and the possibly nefarious Anton (I really needed to have a talk with him to find out once and for all if he was in my father's employment). Following them were the German ladies, and behind us, just getting into their Daimler, were Melody's parents. Bringing up the rear was the other English team.

"Who would do that?"

"I don't know, but Dad told me that Roger is in a state of panic because we are going to be responsible for guarding the cars once we leave the U.S." She gave me a significant look.

"We'll take turns doing four-hour watches," I said immediately.

"That's what I was thinking. It'll mean for broken sleep, but that's better than losing the race because someone decided to take out our Flyer." She patted the dashboard, looking somewhat embarrassed at the gesture, but it was one I wholeheartedly understood. I was becoming very fond of our car. Other than a few minor troubles—and a tendency to blow out tires with a frequency that meant I was getting very proficient at changing them—the Flyer was a pleasure to ride around in. Driving was still a bit of a struggle, but even that was becoming easier now that we knew the car's ways.

"You do have to wonder what we will be able to do that the crew watching the cars couldn't do," I said as we moved up a spot. The German ladies were waiting for their cue to start. "If someone managed to destroy a whole engine while the cars were under the production team's eyes, how are we supposed to keep our Flyer safe?"

"I don't know, but we can't be any worse than the guy who was supposed to watch the cars overnight. Oh, there's Roger."

Roger burst out of the motel and dashed over to consult with the starter before having a brief word with the German ladies. He stepped back as they rolled off, then gestured for us to pull up.

"You heard, I expect?" he asked us when Melody came to a stop. The starter made a note on our timesheet and handed it back to Melody. "It's terrible—terrible. I can't imagine who has it in for me now. It's always something! Every production, there's always *someone* who wants me to fail."

Melody and I murmured platitudes.

"Not that it'll stop, but I wanted to warn you ladies to be extra-special careful about the car. Don't leave it alone for a moment unless a member of the production team is around to watch it." He clutched the car door with fervor. "We spent too much money on these cars to have them destroyed willy-nilly."

"It sounds like it was a targeted attack," Melody said gently. "Corrosive materials don't just happen to find themselves on engines."

"Have you checked into the background of everyone here?" I asked, and immediately realized how awful that sounded. "That is, the new people. Like Anton what's-his-name?"

"Anton?" Roger's face went blank for a couple of seconds. "Why do you mention him?"

"Well, he is the newest member of the group. I believe someone said that he was supposed to be in the race to begin with but couldn't do it?"

"Eh? Oh, yes." Roger pulled out his phone, sighed heavily, and put it up to his ear. "I have to take this. Yes, Sheriff? Did you find out anything?"

"Why did you mention Anton?" Melody asked when Roger walked off quickly. "Do you know something about him?"

"No, that's just it." I hesitated for a moment, then gave her a brief rundown on my father's habit of insisting I have a bodyguard with me. "And I think that since I outed Boris, my father's normal flunky, he found someone else, and that someone is Anton."

"But he couldn't be, not if he was originally lined up to race," Melody said.

I was silent for a few minutes while she got the car going, and we pulled out of the parking lot to the street leading to the interstate highway. "That's why I was trying to pump Roger for information," I said loudly over the sound of the wind and engine.

"Sounds fairly implausible to me," she yelled back. "I can't believe anyone in the race would do something so heinous. It has to be a madman who heard about us and wanted to do something to give us grief."

"It could be. This country certainly has its crackpots."

I mulled over the issue for the next few hours, wanting to talk about it to Dixon but hesitant to spend what little time we had together talking about something so frustrating. Plus, I had a sneaking suspicion that it made me sound overly paranoid. What if Anton wasn't working with Dad? Then *I* would be the crackpot.

The hours passed swiftly as we drove the last U.S. stretch. We chatted periodically, much more relaxed than we had been with Louise, and although we both had to drive more each day, it was worth the tired shoulders and arms to have her negative personality elsewhere.

At one point we stopped for a quick lunch, only to see the German ladies outside a restaurant with the camera crew and Roger. A few people had gathered around them, so, hesitating to intrude on what was obviously their time to be filmed attracting attention from the locals, we drove on a block to find another place to stop and get a sandwich.

"Gives us time to get ahead of them," Melody said as

we bolted our lunch and hit the road again. "Not that it matters at this stage, but once we hit Kazakhstan, all bets are off."

"What's all this about Kazakhstan? Are we definitely not going to China, then?" I asked, tying my veil in a jaunty bow under my chin. Today's hat was a smaller-brimmed straw boater, but it had enough lift in the wind to keep trying to escape from my head.

"No, didn't you hear last night at the meeting?"

I thought of the night before. Dixon and I hadn't made it to the daily meeting, instead having a wonderful time in his room. "Um . . . no, we . . . I . . . missed it."

She grinned. "I'd make a comment, but I think I know from experience just how well a reality show romance can turn out."

"Well, it's not like Dixon and I are going to get married like your dad and Tessa did," I said, waving away that idea. "We're just . . . enjoying ourselves."

"That's the goal of life, isn't it?" she said simply. "Roger said that he simply couldn't get all the visas he needed, and permission for part of the trip through China was still under negotiation, so he decided to scrap that whole bit of the race and start us off in Almaty instead."

"That's the big town in Kazakhstan?"

"One of the two. Astana is the capital, but we'll fly with the cars to Almaty and then head off on our own." She grinned at me. "It's going to be quite the adventure."

"I can't wait!" I said, doing a little fist pump. "Adventure is my middle name! Well, not really, but it should have been."

It was approaching eight p.m. by the time we made it into San Francisco, to a hotel on the outskirts by the airport. Given the late hour, we were pleased to see that we were the first ones in, even though at that point it didn't matter.

"Let's keep this up, though," Melody said as we got out of the car. I noticed there were only two members of the crew about, and no cameras. Usually one of the camera teams was on hand to record everyone coming in, frequently catching us peeling off our goggles to expose two clean patches in faces made dirty by road dust.

"Where is everyone?" Melody asked the person checking us in.

"Accident," he said tersely, and waved us forward to the parking area where the cars would be kept until they were put on the chartered cargo plane.

"Oh no! Not another accident like the French team, I hope?"

"Is it serious?" Melody asked at the same time.

"Don't know." He shrugged. "Roger is at the hospital now with one of the brothers."

"Brothers?" My blood ran cold as I dug through my bag for my cell phone. "Not Dixon and Rupert?"

"That's it." He waved us on again. "Get parked. We have to clean up the cars, have Graham go over them for any problems, and get them to the airport so they can be loaded into the containers."

I hopped out of the car, dialing Dixon's number as Melody, with a worried expression, drove over to the section of the parking lot reserved for us. The second team member immediately began unstrapping the tires and boxes and placing them in a pile.

"Paulie?"

"Oh, thank god," I said, relief swamping me at the sound of Dixon's voice. "You're OK. Wait. Are you OK?"

"Yes." His voice was clipped, a sure sign he was either angry or upset. "Rupert has a broken leg. Samuel has two broken ribs and a suspected collarbone fracture. Anton is being looked at now, but he might have a broken wrist."

"Holy shit! What happened to you all?"

"Who's hurt?" Melody asked, running up to me as best she could in the corset and long skirt. "It's not my dad and Tessa?"

I covered the mouthpiece. "No, it's Rupert, Samuel, and Anton. They're all at the hospital. Dixon, what happened? Are you hurt?"

"I'm fine. I was out of the way getting a tire ready to change when the damned Essex car started rolling forward and plowed over Rupert and Anton."

"The Essex guys drove over you?"

"No, they weren't in the car at the time."

"Then what—never mind. What hospital are you at?" I asked, and made a mental note when he told me. I glanced around frantically, needing to be with Dixon, but knowing I couldn't take the Flyer out. I covered the phone again and yelled at the crew member to call me a cab before continuing with Dixon. "OK. I'm going to get a taxi and get out to you."

"I'll come with you," Melody said, pulling out her phone to text her parents.

"Melody is coming, too."

"There's no reason for either of you to go to that trouble," he said, exhaustion and despair rich in his voice.

"Of course we'll come. I want to be there to help you with Rupert. I assume that he'll have to go home, which is such a shame. Is it a bad break?"

"No, just a hairline fracture, but he can't drive. Paulie . . ." His voice broke, and for a moment I thought he might be crying. "Paulie, if Anton is hurt and can't drive, either, that leaves only me to drive our car. Roger won't allow me to drive the whole way by myself, and there's no one else to fill in. We'll be out of the race."

"No!" I shouted, then apologized. "Sorry. Didn't

mean to blast your earballs that way. Hold tight, Dixon. Don't worry about what might happen until we know the worst about Anton. We'll be there as soon as we can."

I won't go into the hellish nightmare of the next hour trying to get a taxi at a busy time of night and finally getting to the hospital a good forty miles away. By the time we found Dixon, I had worked myself up into a righteous swivet. I would not let Roger send Dixon home!

"Oh! Your pretty face!" I exclaimed when I rounded the emergency room curtain to find Dixon sitting on a chair next to an empty bed. "I thought you said you weren't hurt? Where's Rupert?"

"Off having a walking boot put on." Dixon grimaced, a cut above his eye already having been cleaned up and taped closed. He had what looked like a bruise forming on his cheekbone, and the faintest hint of a black eye. "I hit my head on the car when it was jammed forward, that's all. It's nothing like what the others have experienced."

"Good news!" Roger stuck his head into Rupert's cubicle. "Anton just has a mildly sprained wrist. Should be OK in a few days with icing treatment."

"Thank god," Dixon said, starting to rub his face wearily, but flinching when he hit a bruised spot.

"That's great," I said, relieved that Dixon's team wouldn't be out of the race. "How's Samuel?"

Roger's expression turned serious. "Broken ribs and collarbone. He's going to spend the night in the hospital, but he'll definitely not be in any shape to continue on. The other two Esses are spending the night with him, I understand. Must get one of the PAs to take their car to the hotel . . . Now what?" He had been looking at a text message while he was talking and quickly punched in a number to call someone. "What's going on? Where are the Hausfraus? What? That's impossible! How did that— Well, *were* they drinking?"

Dixon, Melody, and I all looked at one another.

"Drinking?" Melody asked softly. "The German ladies?"

"For Christ's sake . . . no, it is a direct violation—we'll have to enforce it, but this is just the last straw. If we lose any more teams there won't be a race left."

We waited in anticipatory silence for him to hang up, which he did, and turned to face us. "The Germans are out. They were tagged by some off-duty cop and the driver failed a Breathalyzer test."

"Man," I said, not knowing what to say. "That's awful."

Roger ran a hand over his bald head, riffling the fringe. "I made it quite clear to everyone what the rules were. I didn't just have you lot sign a statement saying you knew the rules. We had two meetings going over them—two meetings." He turned to us. "You knew, didn't you? You knew if you were caught drinking and driving that the whole team would be disqualified?"

"Yes, absolutely," I answered at the same time that Dixon and Melody added their affirmations. "That's why we wouldn't let Louise have wine with lunches. I feel awful for the Fraus, though."

"Then you can feel bloody terrible for me, since the whole race is falling apart around me!" Roger said before stalking away, the phone to his ear again.

Rupert was wheeled in just as Roger left.

"How do you feel?" I asked. "Stupid question, I know, but it's all I have right now."

"I've been better, although the pain meds are working now," he answered, getting to his feet. He looked tired, with lines of pain around his mouth as he stood and made some tentative steps under the auspices of a nurse. I waited until she gave him the final instructions and went to get him his paperwork before saying, "I'm so sorry about this, Rupert. The race won't be nearly as entertaining without you."

"Can't be helped," he said with a sigh, then gave me half a smile. "To be honest, there weren't as many women as I thought there would be. This—" He lifted his foot a little, then made a face. "This should be worth some serious sympathy points at home, however."

"You'll go to Elliott and Alice?" Dixon asked, gathering up Rupert's coat along with his.

"Probably. Alice and Mum will fuss over me to no end, whereas there's no one in my flat but two blokes who'd tell me to get off my arse if I asked them for anything." He gave Dixon a long look. "I expect you to win this blasted race in my honor—you know that, don't you?"

Dixon looked tired. "I'll try, but no promises. Come on. Let's get you back to the hotel."

"Where's the De Dion?" I asked when we slowly worked our way out of the emergency room, meeting up with Roger, Tabby and Sam, and Anton at the entrance. All four looked grim. One of the production assistants had gone to get Roger's car.

"It's here. There's a PA guarding it and the other car."

"I think our wounded heroes should travel in comfort back to the hotel," Roger decided when his car arrived. "Dixon, can you take the ladies with you in the De Dion?"

"We'll drive," I said, glancing quickly at Dixon's battered face and general demeanor of exhaustion.

Roger got Anton and Rupert installed in the back of his comfortable car and headed off with them, while the production assistant who had been left with the car faced the Esses' Zust car with disfavor. "I've never driven it before," she said, looking hesitant.

Melody patted her on the arm. "I'll drive it. You can ride with me, all right?"

"That would be lovely. Thank you," the PA said, and they went off.

I was a bit nervous about driving a car I wasn't used

to, especially given the nature of the last few hours, but the De Dion was a smaller car than the Thomas Flyer and it was a dream to drive in comparison with our big white beast. "Now you can tell me exactly what happened," I yelled over the engine as my phone's GPS found a route that avoided the freeway back to the hotel (I knew the De Dion wouldn't be able to cope with freeway speeds). "What happened to the Zust that it ran into you if no one was in it? And what were they doing with you?"

"We'd stopped to fix a tire. Turned out it was two tires. The Esses stopped behind us to see if we were all right, and when they found out it was just a blowout, they started getting back into the car. Something happened, though, and the brakes slipped, causing it to roll forward." He ran a hand over his face again. I badly wanted to tuck him into bed and kiss his owies. "Samuel was between the cars and threw himself down, but the front grille of the Zust caught him and pushed him against the De Dion, which in turned rolled forward, knocking Rupert down and going over his leg. Anton was standing a bit off to the side, and he lunged toward Rupe to pull him out of the way but hurt his wrist in the process."

I digested this picture of disaster, frowning with both the concentration and the thought needed to drive a strange car. "The Essex car slipped its brakes? How is that possible?"

"I don't know." Dixon looked bleakly out at the night, making my soul hurt with the need to comfort him. "Sanders was just climbing in behind the steering wheel when it started to roll forward. He said that perhaps the brakes hadn't set right and the movement of him getting in might have bumped something."

"But . . ." I made an inarticulate gesture. "How can brakes come undone like that?"

"Evidently they didn't do much to modernize the

brakes." Dixon sounded so tired, I hated to make him talk, but I didn't quite understand what had happened. "They were refreshed, as Roger calls it, to make sure they worked, but they weren't wholly modernized. From what I understand, it's entirely possible that the brakes can give way in certain circumstances. That's why we were told to always put large stones in front of or behind the wheels when they were parked."

"I thought that was just because it looked period for the cameras," I said, horrified at the thought that the Flyer could suddenly take off on its own, and made a mental note to never park it on even the slightest incline without several rocks to hold its tires in place.

"It isn't just for show, although . . ." He stopped, looking thoughtful.

"Although what?"

It took him a good two minutes before he answered. "I can't help but wonder if the Esses intended something to happen, and Samuel just got unlucky."

I flashed him a horrified glance. "You think they deliberately ran into you?"

"No," he said, shaking his head, then immediately added, "It's just that I had an odd conversation with them at the beginning of the race, and it keeps coming back to me."

"What on earth did they say?"

He took a deep breath. "They said they were the villains of the race, that they intended on acting in such a manner, noting that it had Roger's approval because it would make for interesting film, and they proceeded to pick my brain as to ways they could sabotage other racers."

"They didn't! Holy crapballs. Did you tell Roger?"

"Almost immediately, and the fact that he wasn't in the least bit concerned gave truth to Sanders's claim that they were doing so with Roger's blessing."

"Yeah, but that's playacting villainy, surely," I said,

negotiating a roundabout carefully before striking out on a highway that would lead us to our hotel. "Just for the cameras, not real actions intended to hurt people."

"I came to that conclusion after speaking to Roger, but now I'm not so sure. You have to admit, the race has been hit with a number of disasters."

"Yes, but I think that's par for the course. Did you read up on the original race? They lost all but two cars in the trip across the U.S. We still have three left, and we started out with less cars than in 1908. Plus, there's the issue of Samuel. Would they be willing to risk him just to take out Rupert?"

"I don't think the plan was to harm any of us, per se. Rather, I think that if the attack was deliberate—and we can't know that it was—then it was focused on the De Dion and not its human occupants. None of us were in the car at the time, after all."

"Which means you would be vulnerable if it moved," I pointed out, but had to agree with him. "I just can't believe any of the Esses would do that. They seem like such nice guys."

Dixon was silent, but I could see he was thinking deep thoughts. I left him to it while I focused on getting us back to the hotel in one piece, an hour later handing over the car to the waiting crew member with much relief.

"My room or yours?" Dixon asked once we had picked up our room key cards, and followed me to the elevator.

"Yours, I think, but I'll go to mine to change once I get the corset off," I said, eyeing him. He looked at the end of his strength. I made a resolve to not tire him out, knowing he needed rest more than he needed mind-blowingly fabulous sex.

I followed him to his room, asked him to unlace me, and then told him to take a shower and relax. "I'll bring us some dinner, and we can eat here, OK?"

"That would be wonderful," he said, smothering a yawn.

By the time I took a shower, got into comfy jeans and a sweatshirt, and had room service deliver a couple of burgers to my room, an hour had passed. I carried the food to Dixon, who was still awake, but barely.

"I think you need sleep," I said after we had eaten, collecting the trays and depositing them outside the room. "I'm going to my own bed, if you don't mind."

"Why don't you sleep here?" he asked, not making any protest about the lack of sexy-times.

"You'll sleep better without me bumping into you and waking you up," I told him, and blew him a kiss from the door. "Get lots of sleep, Dixon. Because tomorrow I might not be so considerate of your tender sensibilities."

He chuckled tiredly. "I'm counting on that. I'll just check on Rupert to make sure he's all right, then turn in for the night."

"Sleep well." I closed the door softly and made a beeline to the front desk, where I forced a clerk to tell me which room Roger was in.

"I have a few things to say," I told him when he answered the door, pushing past him uninvited. Inside were two of the production assistants, both film teams, Graham, and one of the wardrobe ladies who I knew had flown out to check our garments before we left the U.S. "Sorry if I'm interrupting a meeting, but I want to know what's going on with the Esses trying to kill Dixon's team. Did you look at their car?"

"Yes, of course," he answered, surprising me. He waved toward Graham, who was sitting on the bed with a laptop perched on his knees. "We went over it, as well as the Engaging Englishmen's car, to make sure it didn't suffer any damage."

"There's nothing wrong with the Essex car's brakes that was at all evident," Graham said in agreement.

"Which means it was done deliberately? Dammit, Roger, those men could have been killed or permanently injured! You can't let the Essex team go on being villains, not if they are taking very real actions to eliminate the competition."

"Pish," Roger said, startling me a little. I hadn't pegged him for the sort of man who said words like "pish" in serious conversation. "It was an accident, nothing more. The Essex Esses simply neglected to put the stones in front of the wheels, and since there was evidently a slight incline, the car simply slipped its brakes with the result that, sadly, two more racers are going home."

For the first time, I noticed a frazzled component to Roger's expression. No doubt he was feeling the stresses and strains of all the accidents. "How do you know it wasn't a deliberate accident? I know Dixon told you what the Esses said about being villains and working up plans for eliminating people—"

"They were rehearsing bits for the camera, nothing more," Roger said, waving my concern away. "Now, Paulie, dear, as much as I'd love to stand here and chat with you, we really must proceed with our production meeting. We have the cars to get loaded on the plane tonight, and we're waiting for a fax from the Kazakhstan embassy, and of course there is everything to get packed and loaded onto the charter plane by morning." While he spoke, he shooed me to the door, giving me a gentle push through it before adding, "It's all very tragic, I agree, but I assure you that with the exception of the engine corrosion, none of the accidents were intentional. The police are very confident they will track down the source of the acid used on the engine, so you can sleep tonight secure in the knowledge that there is no nefarious plan afoot."

"But—"

He closed the door in my face. I considered knocking until he opened up so I could continue my argument, but the realization that I had no more proof that the Esses were behind the accident any more than I had proof that Anton was working for my father had me turning and walking quickly to my room.

July 26
From: Julia
Hey, babe! Angela says you're in SF tomorrow? I can pop into town and meet you for lunch. Am dying to see you in your suffragette threads.

July 26
To: Julia
We get on plane at 8 a.m., so no time for lunch. I sent you selfies!

July 26
From: Julia
Yeah, but it's not the same as seeing you in person. How was cross-country drive?

July 26
To: Julia
It would take hours to tell you. This evening one car ran into boyfriend's and took out his brother and other car's member. Germans got snockered and were given boob.

July 26
To: Julia
Boot! They were given the boot!

July 26
From: Julia
Who cares about boobs! You have boyfriend? Who is boyfriend? When did this happen? Wait. Calling you.

July 26
To: Julia
No, don't. I'm wiped out and in bed and ready to crash. Will call you from airport in morning.

July 26
From: Julia
TELL ME ABOUT BOYFRIEND!

July 26
To: Julia
You are so demanding.

July 26
To: Julia
No other friend would be so mean when I was tired and just want to sleep and scratch the spot where one of the iron girders holding in corset poked into side.

July 26
From: Julia
I will get into my car and drive to your hotel if you do not tell me about boyfriend. RIGHT. NOW.
Sorry. Caps.

July 26
To: Julia
Fine. Quickly, though. Didn't get much sleep and was a long day.

July 26
To: Julia
Boyfriend is loose term. Don't like to call him just lover. It's Dixon. Englishman. From England.

July 26
From: Julia
That's where Englishmen are from, you didio.

July 26
To: Julia
Didio?

July 26
From: Julia
Idiot not didio. Couldn't type, was looking at race Web site. Oh! He's the one you liked! Oooh. Link to video interview with him.

July 27
From: Julia
Holy shmoly, he's hot! You scored, girlfriend.

July 27
To: Julia
Yes, he is hot. He's also banged up from accident. After midnight now, Jules. Gotta be up at 5 to get to airport early. Call you in morning. Smooches.

July 27
From: Julia
Smooches backatcha, babe. Kiss the BF for me. Lots and lots of times. Will want pics of him, too. Happy flight!

Paulina Rostakova's Adventures

JULY 30
7:11 p.m.
Astana, Kazakhstan, hotel room

Taking the opportunity to write this while Dixon snoozes.
Poor guy, he was up all night guarding the car, not letting
me take a turn like we'd agreed to do.

Crap. I shouldn't have written that there. Now it's out
of order. OK. Starting over.

We arrived in Kazakhstan with what I'm coming to
think of as the standard amount of issues, or as Roger
calls it, "The damned curse that someone has placed on
me, and if I find out who has done it, I'll string him or
her up by his respective balls!"

I would have giggled at the "his or her" part of his
conversation, but at the time I was too worried about
Dixon being kicked out of the race . . . dammit! I did it
again. Gah! Starting over again again.

The flight from San Francisco to Kazakhstan took
almost a day to complete, even with a charter flight carrying just the remaining racers and crew, our luggage,
and the cars in the hold. The problem was that once we
got to Almaty, bleary-eyed and groggy from being on a

plane for so long, the containers holding the cars in the cargo section were minus one.

"So this is Eurasia," I said to Dixon, huddled into my jacket and shivering. It was about five a.m. when we arrived, and thankfully Roger didn't make us get into period clothing for the arrival.

"It's not very Asian looking, is it?" Dixon asked with a yawn. "I wonder if there's any tea to be had."

"Ha." I nudged him with my elbow. He gave me a curious glance. "Tea? Asia? We're in Asia, the biggest tea consumers in the world. I think. Maybe. If not, they have to be close to it."

"Ah." He gave me a pitying look and went off to a table set up with a coffeepot to see if he could scrounge a cup of tea.

We were all gathered in a small glass-walled room evidently set aside for folks arriving on international charter flights, having just handed over our passports and visas, Roger speaking with the interpreter who had met our flight. Through the glass, we could see the plane on the tarmac, the handlers busy moving the containers off the plane. I watched them idly, trying to sort through my impressions of my arrival on not just a continent new to me, but one halfway around the world from my father.

I frowned when the baggage handlers pulled the last of our bags from the cargo hold and drove it off to what I assumed were customs. I looked back at the large cargo containers, counting them, then turned to face the room behind me.

"Um," I said to no one in particular.

Sitting on a row of molded plastic seats, Melody and her parents hunkered together, talking softly to one another. Beyond them the two remaining Esses chatted with Anton, who wore a sheepskin hat that looked like some architect's idea of a modern take on an opera house. Roger, two of the production assistants, and Graham were talking to the interpreter and a couple of officials who were idly flipping through our passports.

"Uh . . ." I cleared my throat loudly. "Hello? People? Where's the fourth car?"

It took a minute for my words to filter through to everyone's consciousness. Dixon was the first to glance over at me, then out the window, a Styrofoam cup of tea in his hand.

I waved a hand at the window. "Three containers. There are four teams, right? Suffragettes, Esses, Englishmen, and the Duke . . . did someone drop out and I didn't hear about it?"

There was a moment of complete silence; then all hell broke loose as everyone leaped up and ran to the window, all talking at once. Roger swore loudly and profanely, then, with the interpreter in his grasp, bolted for the tarmac. The two airport officials called after him and took off on his heels. The rest of us clustered at the windows, watching while Roger danced around the cargo containers, his hands gesturing wildly until one of the airline people hurried out and began unlocking the containers.

"What do you think happened?" I asked Dixon.

"I don't know. Perhaps they haven't unloaded the fourth car yet."

"Maybe." I frowned, leaning into him to say softly, "I have a bad feeling about this, though."

"Bad how?"

"Bad as in I think Roger may be partially right. I think someone has cursed the race. Oh, don't look at me like I'm a talking potato—I meant cursed in the sense that someone is deliberately causing problems to the race and racers." I couldn't help but slide a look down the windows to where the two Esses were talking with Anton and Max.

"Hmm." Dixon looked thoughtful. "Perhaps I should speak to Roger—"

"About the Esses? Yeah . . . uh . . . I might have done that last night after you went to bed."

He turned to give me a look filled with disbelief. "You did? Why?"

"Because you were almost killed! Or you could have been killed, and I wanted Roger to stop the Esses before they struck again."

He was silent for a moment. "I can't believe I'm going to say this in light of the fact that right now my brother is flying home to England with his leg in a cast, but I don't think the accident yesterday was intentional. You didn't see Sanders's face when he climbed into the car and it started rolling forward. Not to mention the fact that I doubt if he'd put his own partner—one of them—in such danger. Even if we do credit the Essex team with the most nefarious of motives, it seems counterproductive to take out one of their own."

"Yeah, that bothers me about the whole thing, too, but maybe that part was the accident, and they really intended on slamming into your car to disable you guys or it, or both."

He didn't have a chance to respond before Roger turned on the tarmac and bolted for the building, the airport people once again trailing after him.

"Oh dear," Tessa said, moving toward us. "This doesn't look good, does it?"

"It doesn't appear the fourth car is in the plane, no," Dixon answered. I had the worst urge to snuggle into him for comfort and warmth, or even just to hold his hand, but there were too many people around us.

Not, I mused to myself, that there were many people left who hadn't seen Dixon naked in my hotel room, but

I was determined to try to maintain some form of decorum.

"What's going to happen?" Melody asked, coming over with her dad. "There are only three cars? What does that mean for the race?"

"Unfortunately," Max said, rubbing his jaw, "I believe it means that someone won't be continuing."

We all looked at one another, then as a group turned to look at where the Esses were still talking with Anton.

"I know who I'd like to see get voted off the island," I said darkly, glancing quickly at the slight bruising still visible on Dixon's face.

"You heard the rumors, too, then?" Tessa asked, her voice dropping to an intimate level. "Tabby said that there are rumors they deliberately sabotaged the French team's car with acid and ran over Rupert in an attempt to break the team up."

"Tessa," Max said in a stern tone that was belied by the look of adoration he cast her way. She flashed him an equally adoring look. "That's just a rumor, and an unfounded one at that."

"Not so unfounded," Dixon said, and quickly explained his experience with the Esses in New York City.

"Holy moly," Tessa said, her eyes on the other British team. "Do you think they're picking off the teams one by one? What are they going to do to us? Max, we have to talk to Roger. This has to end!"

"I highly doubt the Essex team is sabotaging everyone else," Max said in what I thought of as an annoyingly calm tone. "You have to keep in mind how excitable Roger is and take everything he says with a grain of salt."

"It was Dixon who told us what the Esses team said, not Roger," Melody pointed out.

"Regardless, Roger is prone to making drama out of

every little thing. I agree the race has been fraught with unfortunate accidents, but much of that is perfectly normal, given the state of the cars we're using."

"Roger was right the last time he said the production was being sabotaged," Tessa said firmly, glaring at the Esses. "I see no reason to discount him now."

I slid a glance toward Dixon. He was frowning in thought. "Do you think that—" I started to say, but stopped when Roger and some airport officials burst into the room. Roger's fringe stood on end as if he'd stuck his finger into a light socket.

"My friends," he said, looking horribly frazzled. "Terrible news. As best we can figure it out, it appears that one of the containers bearing the Engaging Englishmen's car has been loaded onto a cargo plane that was sent to China."

"What?" I exclaimed at the same time the others started hurtling questions and comments at Roger.

Dixon looked stunned.

"I know, you have a hundred questions as to how this could have happened, and unfortunately I have no answers. Somehow, the original manifest—the one to China—was placed on the car instead of the correct one to Kazakhstan." Roger held up his hands until everyone shut up. "The car was put into a container but it didn't make it onto the plane. Regrettably, this means that although Anton and Dixon are perfectly capable of carrying on the race, they have no vehicle."

A stunned silence fell on us all. I scooted closer to Dixon and, damning circumspection, took his hand, giving his fingers a supportive squeeze.

"I'm sorry, Dixon. I'm sorry, Anton. I'm afraid this means that you are both out of the race."

"No!" a voice shrieked out, and I was startled to find it belonged to me. I'd also marched forward to stand in front of Roger, my hand still in Dixon's, which meant he was hauled along with me. "You can't do that! It's not fair! Get them another car."

The look Roger settled on me was filled with pity and exasperation. "I would if I could, darling, but unfortunately running antique cars capable of traveling from here to Paris are nonexistent."

"You don't know!" I argued.

"It's all right, Paulie," Dixon said quietly, tugging me back to his side. "It's an unfortunate circumstance, nothing more."

"Like hell it's an unfortunate circumstance!" I turned to face him to make my case, but beyond his shoulder I saw the two Esses watching, their faces identical masks of concern. I pointed and demanded, "It's their fault! They did this! They should be the ones to pay by giving up their car to Dixon and Anton."

"Us?" Stephen looked shocked, his hand touching his chest as if he couldn't believe my accusation. "My dear, I assure you that we had nothing to do with the loss of the Engaging team car."

"Bullshit," I snapped.

"There's nothing I can do," Roger said, spreading his hands wide. "I'm truly sorry, but they must have an appropriate car, and there is none to be had."

"How long would it take to get the car flown in from China?" Melody asked, earning from me a look of approval.

"You see?" I said in an undertone, for Dixon's ears only. "She's not giving up on you any more than I am."

"It's not a matter of giving up," he answered softly. "I'm only being realistic, Paulie. If I have no car, I can't race."

"That means you'd go home, and we . . ." I searched his eyes, hoping to see the same warm emotion that was growing in me every day we were together.

"Yes, I know." His expression was as bleak as his eyes.

Roger replied to Melody's question, "Too long, given how long their government stalled on giving us information about sending the cars to Beijing."

"Dixon can ride with us," I said, pointing at Melody. "You don't mind, do you, Melody? Excellent. It's all settled. Dixon can join our team, and Anton . . . Anton can go with the Esses." I would have been perfectly happy to leave Anton behind, but I had grudgingly decided that, until I had proof he was working for my father, I'd give him the benefit of the doubt.

Although I still kept my eye on him. Right now he looked placidly undisturbed, as if this had nothing to do with him.

"He can't do that," Roger said, shaking his head at Dixon. "Your car is a suffragettes' car. He is not a suffragette."

"No, but there *were* men supporters," Melody said quickly.

"That's right—I read about them just before I flew to New York." I nodded my continued approval of Melody's thought processes. "The husbands of a lot of the suffragettes also supported the cause."

"He is not a husband of a suffragette—" Roger stopped dead in the middle of his sentence, his eyes widening and his mouth forming a little O.

"Oooh," Tessa said on a long breath, and looked at Max. He looked confused. She elbowed him. "Your Grace."

"What? Oh." Max's eyebrows rose. "That might do it."

"What? What would do what?" I asked.

"Excellent idea," Melody said, smiling at Roger.

"What is?" Dixon asked, his brow furrowed.

"You know we did a reality show for Roger, right?" Tessa asked, tapping Max on the chest. "Max and I? He played a Victorian duke—who really was one of Max's ancestors—and I was his American wife. The show was a huge hit, and viewers ate us up with a spoon and asked for seconds. So if Dixon . . ."

She let the sentence trail off, looking expectantly at both Melody and me.

"If Dixon what?" I asked. Then it struck me, with an almost physical blow. I turned my gaze onto Dixon, who had evidently arrived at the thought well before me. He looked wary, and hesitant, and aroused, all at the same time.

"Not many men could pull off that expression," I told him quietly while Melody announced what a good idea it was. "But you do it in spades."

"I feel like I was hit upside the head with the De Dion," he admitted.

"The question is," Roger said excitedly, "which lady will Dixon marry?"

I stood up straight and glared at Roger. "Excuse me?"

"Well," he said with a wave of his hand, "I thought he might like to have a choice."

"Of course he has a choice. He has all the choices in the world," I said airily. "There is no pressure, none whatsoever."

To my intense discomfort, Dixon was silent for at least a minute. "You are talking about a pretend marriage, are you not?" he finally asked, gesturing toward Tessa and Max. "The same they had on their show?"

"Yeees," Roger said slowly, an odd light in his eyes. He pulled at an earlobe while he clearly thought the idea over. "Although the viewers would go crazy for . . . Kim!"

One of the production assistants who had traveled with us snapped to attention and bustled over with her clipboard. "Yes, sir?"

"Find me someone to officiate a wedding. Not a real officiant, one of those crackpot people who belong to weird religions. Dixon's brother is one of them, but we couldn't get him here fast enough."

She grabbed the interpreter and began grilling him.

"Wait. What? You want us to have a wedding? A real wedding?" I blinked fast, my insides squirreling around. "I'm not sure . . . I don't think . . . I mean, I like Dixon a lot—"

"We do not want a real wedding," Dixon said smoothly, cutting across my incoherent babble. "Not even for your show, Roger."

A little spike of pain bit deep inside me. I looked at Dixon from under my eyelashes, knowing full well how he felt on the subject of weddings. He'd never had the one he had wanted, and now here he was going to have to pretend to be married to me. Did I really want to put him through that? Did I want to risk whatever our ten-uous relationship was just for the sake of the show?

I would leave it up to Dixon, I decided, and accordingly took him by the arm, pulling him to a corner of the room while telling Roger, "Give us a couple of minutes."

"I know what you're going to say," Dixon announced when we were cloistered from the rest of the group. "You don't want to get married, least of all to me, and I want to reassure you that I'm of the same mind."

Now that hurt. I had to swallow back the pain, remembering that he was grieving a lost love. "I can honestly say that marriage isn't uppermost in my mind," I said after a moment's thought. "But a pretend one—one that is just for the show—is something different, don't you think? I mean, it's not at all the same thing as what you and your late fiancée planned, so it's not like you're betraying her memory."

He looked like he wanted to be sick. "No, of course not. You are completely different from Rose. And as for the wedding we didn't have . . . I tried to tell you the other night about that . . ."

"It's decided, then," Roger announced, clapping his hands and calling us back. "Dixon, Paulie, we'll film an impromptu wedding just as soon as the officiant arrives, no later than noon. That will put us three hours behind schedule, but it can't be helped, and the resulting excitement around the show should do wonders for ratings. I'll do a brief on-camera piece explaining that you and Dixon fell in love during the race across the States and that you decided to marry before another day passed."

"That seems rather deceptive," I commented, returning to the group with Dixon. "I don't like lying, and saying flat out that we're madly in love is doing just that."

"You *are* spending your nights together," Roger said dryly. "I assume there is some form of affection between you."

I blushed like mad, while Dixon looked mildly furious.

"Our relationship is no one's business, certainly not yours," he said stiffly.

"On the contrary, it's very much my business when it affects the show, as you will have noticed in article fifteen of the contract you signed," Roger said tersely, then lightened up to add, "It's all a moot point, isn't it? Whether or not you two are in love, you are fond of each other, and that's all we need for the cameras. Kim! Are you done finding the officiant? We must consult with the hotel venue to see if we can conscript one of their ballrooms for the wedding. Let's look lively, people! We have less than four hours to plan and film this wedding . . ."

Dixon and I stared at each other as Roger swept the production team, interpreter, and airport officials before him, casting orders hither and thither.

"Congratulations, I think," Melody said with a wry smile, and stuck out her hand for Dixon to shake. "Welcome to Team Suffragette."

"Thank you," he said, clearly a bit overwhelmed. I stopped him when he was about to follow the others out to claim the cars and drive to the hotel, where we would have a few hours to get into costume before the next stage of the race began.

"Dixon, if this makes you uncomfortable, we can simply tell Roger no. There must be some other way we can keep you in the race. Maybe you and Anton can both ride with the Esses . . ."

"Do you not want to do it?" he asked, hesitation in his eyes when he put his hand over mine. "It's playacting, true, but if it seems a bit too real to you—"

"No, I don't mind it at all. Are you kidding? It means we don't have to keep sneaking into each other's rooms at night and worrying that people will notice us. I am concerned about you."

"Don't be—I'm fine," he reassured me, and, heeding a call from Graham, hurried out to get a fast lesson in driving the Thomas Flyer.

"Did you ever think you'd be dressing for your Edwardian wedding in Kazakhstan?" Melody asked almost an hour later when she helped me into what I thought of as the hardcore corset, the one that lifted my boobs almost up to my chin and that was needed to wear my best gown, one that was a lovely silver gauze and lace over a periwinkle velvet undergown. The skirt part of the dress fell away in gentle ripples and a two-foot train bedecked with tiny little silver embroidered knots. The bodice was ruched, presenting the girls in a way that was extremely flattering. My shoulders were bare, but there was a pair of long white gloves that went to my biceps, with about a million buttons each.

"No," I answered, working on the buttons on one of the gloves. "But then, I never thought I'd be in Kazakhstan in the first place. Did you get the top hooked up?"

"Yes." Melody patted my back and stood with her head tipped to consider my reflection in the hotel mirror. "I swear the wardrobe people love you. That dress is gorgeous. You look every inch the bride of 1908."

"Whereas I feel like an aggravated woman of the twenty-first century. I just know the Esses had something to do with the loss of Dixon's car."

She adjusted the pleated collar that prettily framed her head and brushed a hand down her best dress, which was a dark navy with faint green stripes, decorated with a beaded black braid. "I don't see how they could do that, to be honest."

"Me either, but that doesn't mean they didn't do it." I glanced at the clock. "I guess we'd better get going. No, leave the plaid dress out. I'll want that to drive in, since this corset will kill me if I have to wear it for more than an hour or two."

She smirked. "I'm telling you—you should have been the bluestocking. This rational corset has improved my posture to no end."

"No one likes a smug suffragette," I told her, pointing a gloved finger at her. "Let's go, maid of honor, and get this wedding over so we can be on our way and leave the others in our dust."

She laughed, and we walked arm in arm to the small conference room that Roger was able to convince the hotel to let us use for filming.

I was feeling strangely elated even though the wedding was wholly pretend. There's just something about being dressed to the nines and going to meet a handsome, sexy man to make a girl feel pretty damned special.

Writing this quickly while Paulie is having a bath. Today was one of the longest days of my life, even though the hours conform to normality. It started on the plane, where we flew over the polar cap and down over Eurasia to Almaty, Kazakhstan.

"I'm looking forward to the real racing starting," I told Paulie when we were about to land in Kazakhstan. "Although I do regret the loss of Rupert."

"Of course you do, and I totally agree." Paulie made a face, then gave me a considering look. "You do know, of course, that we won't be able to continue our previous nights' activities?"

I was surprised by that statement for a moment until I understood what it was she was saying, and felt a little teasing was in order. "We will if you and Melody are able to keep up with the De Dion."

"Ha ha—oh, how I laugh at your misguided notion," she said with a snort, and pinched my hand. "The Thomas Flyer is, after all, the car that won the original race. There's no way your little French car can keep up with us once we let the Flyer have his head."

"His? Most cars are traditionally thought of as being female," I pointed out.

"Ours is male. He's a pain in the ass to drive and is constantly needing attention in the form of replaced tires," she answered, giving me a roguish smile. "And he's fast. Very fast. And speaking of fast males, I suppose we could try for a quickie before we start the race, because that's likely to be the last bit of action we get until you catch up with us in Paris."

"Bold words, but not at all realistic," I said with a complacence that I knew she would find objectionable. "Time will show which team is full of bravado, and which has the power to back up its claims."

She spoke a rude word then, and for the first time in a very long time, I felt a deep well of emotion blossom in what I thought of as the cold remains of my heart. Paulie seemed to light up all the dark corners of my life with a gentle glow of wit, intelligence, and long, long legs.

In short, she was just about the most perfect woman I'd ever met.

That's one reason why I didn't kick up a fuss when, after Roger discovered that our car was mysteriously missing, he suggested I join the suffragette team by the act of a pretend marriage to Paulie.

"You understand that I'm doing this only because I'm already pretending to be something I'm not, and adding a fake marriage is nothing more than an extension of the Edwardian gentleman persona you have created for me," I told Roger later, when he supervised my dressing in what he called my formal wear.

"That's the spirit," he said cheerfully, although I couldn't help but notice lines of strain radiating out from his eyes. "It's better than having to send your team back home, isn't it?"

"Yes, although I'm not sure how happy Anton is about going to the Essex team." I pulled on the pearl gray Edwardian version of a morning coat and spurned the matching gloves that Roger held out. "You are, I sincerely hope, talking to them about the accidents?"

He sighed dramatically. "I've told you. I've told Paulie. Hell, I've told everyone that the Essex Esses are not
to blame for all our bad luck. Yes, it was their car that
ran into your brother, but I'm convinced that was a simple accident brought on by a bit of unintentional negli-
gence. This idea that you have of putting the Essex team
squarely behind every problem that has blighted us is
simply unrealistic, and, trust me, if it was possible to pin
this curse on any one person or team, I'd gladly do so."
He ran a hand through what was left of his hair. "I don't
know why I can't conduct a simple television shoot without bringing out all the crackpots intent on destroying
my career."

"If it's not the Essex team behind it, then who is?" I
asked, accepting a top hat that was so glossy, I could see
a distorted version of my face in its gleaming curves.

"I wish I knew, Dixon. I really wish I knew. No doubt
it was an ill-wisher who followed us across country, but
now that we're in Kazakhstan, we should be rid of that
evil influence. I'm not saying everything will go smoothly
from here on out, because that's just tempting the fates,
but at least we should be rid of our saboteur, whoever
that is."

I wasn't at all the least bit convinced of that, but said
nothing more on the subject. After all, neither Paulie nor
I had any proof other than circumstantial evidence that
the Essex team was working through their list to eliminate the cast members.

The so-called wedding was short, mostly because neither Paulie nor I understood the Russian spoken by the
person Roger had found to pretend to officiate, but I had
to admit that it was an oddly touching ceremony nonetheless. Paulie looked more beautiful than I thought
possible in a dress of purple with a fussy bit over the top,
her eyes almost luminous when she stood next to me at

the great arched windows that overlooked the hotel's garden.

"Your responses to all the questions are '*da*,' which is basically you saying yes," Roger had told us before the cameras started filming. "I'm told it's not strictly the proper response, but since this wedding isn't real, it doesn't matter, does it?"

"Not in the least," I told him. A thought occurred to me, and I asked Paulie, "Do you speak Russian?"

"Only a few swearwords. Dad said I was American, so I needed to learn English, not Russian." She shrugged. "I only speak a little French and German."

"I have to say I wish you had a little Russian under your belt, because I'm afraid the only words I know are the ones I read in the phrase book flying to New York."

"Eh. We'll be OK. I have an electronic translator thingie on my phone, and part of the fun of an adventure is to overcome obstacles, right?"

"Right," I agreed, and took her hand. Tucked away in my pocket was a ring Paulie had worn, since there was no time to go shopping for one. She held a small bouquet of white and blue flowers and smiled at me throughout the ceremony.

Oddly reflective, I took stock of my life at that moment. There I was, a glorified accountant for my brother's estate, standing in the middle of a country far removed from my roots, holding the hand of a woman whose shining spirit filled me not just with happiness, but with a sense of rightness that I'd never experienced.

I decided I was getting sentimental over a faux wedding, and took my emotions in a firm hand.

"Right," Roger said, consulting his watch once the filming had stopped and Paulie and I had been pronounced reality TV husband and wife. "We have just enough time for a wedding breakfast, and then we'll have the official setoff at noon. I believe the hotel has managed to pull together a meal for us . . ."

We followed him into another room where a group of round tables had been set up. The Esses were already there, perusing the dishes that servers were setting up. Other servers were quickly putting down place settings and arranging wineglasses.

"No wine!" Roger said sternly, and, with the interpreter in tow, herded the server who was wheeling out a cart filled with bottles back toward the kitchen.

"I feel like I should be toasting you, or at least giving a speech, since I was the best man," Max said, lifting his water glass at Paulie and me. "But since the cameras are off, and time is at a premium, I'll just say good racing."

"Good racing," everyone murmured.

There wasn't a lot of conversation after that—I suspect people were tired from the long flight, but also nervous.

I glanced at Paulie, next to me. She was pushing her food around, not eating any of it, but moving it around on the plate in artistic mounds.

"Not hungry?" I asked her.

"No." She bit her lower lip, making me instantly want to kiss her. Dammit, since when had I allowed my self-control to slip in that way? "To be honest, I'm a bit jumpy."

"Frightened?"

"No, more . . . I don't know. Nervy, I guess. I feel like my skin is about to twitch with irritation."

"I'm a bit on edge myself." I pushed back my plate. There was some sort of seafood stew, which I hadn't partaken of due to a shellfish allergy, as well as a quiche and a beet dish that was tasty despite its appearance. "I think it's the combination of our first day of out-and-out racing and the disasters of the last couple of days."

Her glance slid over to where the Essex team sat, but

she said nothing, just nodded and pushed her food around into a different arrangement.

An hour later, we were assembled in the parking lot, listening while Roger went over the course of the race from this point out.

"Naturally, we can't cover three cars with two camera crews, although I will say that it is quite a bit easier filming the three of you than the original seven."

Sam was filming Roger while he spoke, but spun around to catch Paulie and me. Behind Sam, Tabby, holding the big boom microphone, gestured toward her face while she smiled widely. Obediently, I put a smile on my face and my arm around Paulie. She shot me a startled look.

"As you all know, this is where the race truly becomes a race," Roger continued. "Henceforth, there are no time checks, no speed limits that you must adhere to—other than those of the countries you'll pass through—and most importantly there is no starting and stopping time. That said, I will remind you that you all signed a statement guaranteeing that you will not drive more than eighteen hours in a single day. While I know you all want to win, we don't want anyone else being injured."

"Urgh."

Beyond Paulie, Melody stood with Max and Tessa. There was a distinctively unpleasant cast to Melody's face, an expression that just got worse when she wrapped her arms around herself.

"You are also bound to follow the route set down by the race officials. You should reach the northern oblast city of Petropavlovsk this afternoon. If you wish to push on to Kurgan, you will be well inside the borders of Siberia. Following that, you will proceed through Yekaterinburg, Izhevsk, Novgorod, and Moscow. After that, you

leave Russia behind and travel through Latvia, Lithuania, Poland, Germany, the Czech Republic, Switzerland,
and of course France. This follows much of the route of
the 1908 race, which of course will thrill our viewers."

Paulie's fingers bit into my arm. I raised my eyebrows
at her, mouthing, "Scared?" at her.

"Are you kidding?" she whispered. "I'm so excited, I
could scream. I feel just like Nellie Bly!"

"Erp."

We both turned to look at Melody.

"You OK?" Paulie asked her.

"I think something I ate didn't agree with me," Melody answered back.

"You can sleep in the backseat while Dixon and I
drive," Paulie told her. She nodded, but didn't look in
the least bit enthusiastic.

I cast a worried eye over Melody. She was looking
worse, if that was possible, a light sheen of perspiration
now glistening on her upper lip.

"Naturally, we expect good sportsmanship to be the
credo that you live by, at least during the race." Roger
chuckled at his own joke. No one else so much as smiled.
"It's up to you whether or not you wish to take pity on a
fellow racer on the side of the road with a blowout, but
keep in mind that the cameras will be filming those adver-
sities over other, more mundane possibilities."

"What's the matter?" Max leaned to the side and
looked worriedly at his daughter. "You look as green as
a frog."

"I feel green." Melody moaned, clutching herself
tighter.

"As mentioned in the itinerary, the support vehicles—
that is, my car and the two cars with the camera crews—
will be changed at each border. But fear not—the GPS

trackers on your cars will allow us to quickly locate you and catch up for filming purposes."

Melody swayed and put her hand over her mouth. She was sweating profusely now, and both Tess and Max had moved next to her, murmuring questions and suggestions of treatment.

Roger consulted a clipboard. "I believe that's it. You all know the rules, and I know you will adhere faithfully to them while providing exciting scenarios for our viewers. Remember: you don't race just for your own satisfaction, but for the millions of people who will be cheering you on over the other racers."

Everyone other than the Essex team and Roger were now watching Melody with worried glances.

"I believe that's all I have. Good luck, stay safe, and remember to save your interesting bits of conversation for the cameras! Are there any questions?"

Melody swayed again, staggered forward a couple of feet, and vomited all over Roger's shoes.

He looked up while she was still retching, doubled over with her hands on her knees. He pinned Tessa back with a look that should, by rights, have stripped the hair from her head. "You told her to do that, didn't you? You told her how you spewed all over my shoes the first day we met, and she decided to duplicate that event, didn't she?"

"Of course not. Don't be stupid," Tessa snapped, and rushed forward with Max. "She's sick! She has food poisoning!"

Melody wretched several times more, then collapsed, her face drained of all color and her flesh moist and clammy.

Paulie offered her services as someone who'd had numerous first aid courses, but there wasn't much she could do other than suggest that Melody see a doctor. After an urgent discussion with the translator and the hotel people, Max finally arranged for medical aid to check Melody out. They took her away to the hospital a short while later.

Max and Tessa followed the ambulance in Roger's car, while one of the production assistants drove the Ducal car after them.

"You come with us," Roger yelled from the passenger seat of the car, gesturing at the second film team. "Tabby and Sam can go with the other two. I just hope to hell that they don't get too far ahead, or Max and Tessa will never catch up . . ."

Ah. Paulie is done with her bath. I'll finish up another time.

Paulina Rostakova's Adventures

JULY 31
5:51 a.m.
*Astana, Kazakhstan, motel room with my new hunky
teammate and make-believe husband*

Man alive, what a start to my first experience abroad
yesterday was! As if the horror of finding Dixon's car
missing wasn't enough, Melody ending up at the hospital
was just icing on an abysmal day. Luckily, once Melody
was taken care of, things started improving, although I
didn't have confirmation of that until a few minutes ago
when I got Tessa's texts.

> July 31
> From: Tessa
> *Melody recovering at last. Stomach pumped last night
> when she went into shock. Doctors say it wasn't food
> poisoning. Something eels. Could be real poison.*

> July 31
> To: Tessa
> *Holy crapballs! Poison eels? I didn't see them at the
> lunch, but wasn't seeing much but my pretend
> husband.*

July 31
From: Tessa
Eels are electric, not poison. At least I think they are.
Let me ask Max.

July 31
From: Tessa
Yes, eels are electric.

July 31
To: Tessa
Then why did Melody eat one? I didn't see anyone else
have them.

July 31
From: Tessa
She didn't. Oh, I see. Typo in earlier message. No
eels. Poison, though, of some sort. Roger on his way
to you.

July 31
To: Tessa
I hope to arrest the Esses, because clearly they are
the ones behind all of this!

July 31
From: Tessa
Don't think so. Doctors tested food we ate, and noth-
ing in there, but couldn't find bottle of water she was
thinking.

July 31
From: Tessa
DRINKING.

July 31
From: Tessa
Max and I are staying here. Good luck with race. We're hoping you win. Don't eat or drink around anyone but Dixon!

I texted back a long message full of thanks, regrets that they were leaving the race, and hopes that Melody would recover quickly now that her stomach was empty. Then, after a moment's thought, I sent another message.

July 31
To: Roger
If you still deny the Esses are trying to wipe out the competition after they quite clearly poisoned Melody, you're delusional.

He didn't reply. Telling, that. I think . . . oh hell. Dixon's awake. More later.

AUGUST 1
11:53 p.m.
Petropavlovsk

I had to stop writing yesterday morning because Dixon woke up with me texting Tessa and Roger, and then . . . Well, let me tell it properly.

"What are you doing?" Dixon said when I'd just completed my text to Roger. He rolled over with a yawn and delightfully tousled hair.

"I just told Roger he was delusional. Oooh, sexy stubble is sexy." I gave a little wiggle and stroked a finger down his bristly cheek.

"Is there a reason you said that, or was it just a morning impulse?" he asked, looking sleepy and handsome and so sexy I wanted to bite him.

So I did.

"And now you're eating my arm?" he commented when I started nibbling on his shoulder and moved over to his neck. "Either you're starving or you woke up in an extremely good mood."

I slid my hand down his belly to where his penis was standing at attention, waiting patiently for me to turn my attention to it. "I think we both did."

"Any morning where I wake up with your delicious legs twined about mine is going to be a good one," he murmured, his voice still rough with sleep.

It was a roughness that made me shiver with anticipation, and as I pushed him onto his back I remembered something we'd said when we'd tumbled into bed the night before. "We didn't have a wedding night, Dixon. Do you think a wedding morning will suffice?"

His hands slid around my hips to my butt, his mouth doing amazing things to a breast. "I think that would work quite nicely."

"I swear," I said, swinging my leg over his body to straddle him and arching my back so he could have full access to everything he wanted to touch. "I swear you make little fires start up in my girl parts. Tiny little fires. Itsy-bitsy ones that combine to make everything down there burn."

He paused in the act of tormenting a breast, looking up at me with a cocked eyebrow. "That sounds . . . uncomfortable."

"What does?" I asked, busy with a mental image of me riding Dixon like a bucking bronco.

"Burning genitals. You don't think . . . This is awkward,

and I hope you forgive me for asking, but you don't think you have . . . you know . . . something down there to cause the burning?"

I stopped imagining me riding him while slapping a cowboy hat on his flanks and whooping with joy, and looked down at him. He looked concerned. "Did you just ask me if I have an STD?"

"Well . . ." Embarrassment crawled over his face. "You said you were burning in your female bits, and—"

"I said you make me feel like I have little fires in there, not that I have a burning crotch!" I said, pinching his nipples. "Sheesh, Dixon!"

"I apologize," he said quickly. "I just wanted to make sure that if you were having a burning sensation in those spots, you received medical treatment—"

"I do not," I said loudly, breathing heavily through my nose, "have anything in my crotch but a desire for your crotch to come visiting, although I have to admit that at this moment my crotch is having second thoughts."

He pulled me up so that his penis slid along my sensitive, STD-free parts. "What can I do to make your crotch forgive me?"

"Well . . ." I said slowly, considering my options. I leaned down to nip his lower lip. "Perhaps some gentle words of apology, along with well-placed touches and one or two twirls with your tongue would ease things along—oh, bloody hell."

We both looked at Dixon's phone, which had gone off with an alarm we'd set the night before. It buzzed along with blasting "The Imperial March" from *Star Wars*.

Dixon reached for the phone and turned off the alarm. He gave me a long look. "We should get up. It's six."

I nodded.

"We said we'd get up faithfully every morning at six,

no matter what we were in the middle of." He looked at my breasts, his eyes hungrily considering them. "No matter what."

"We should get up," I said, wiggling in such a way that he moaned and dug his fingers into my hips. "We can't let the Esses get ahead of us. God knows what sort of traps they'll set for us if they get the jump, and I know they couldn't have been very far behind us last night."

"That is sound thinking," he said, nodding, but his fingers moved around my front and dived downward, touching me in all those aching parts of me that so desperately wanted us to ignore the alarm and get down to business.

I leaned forward again to kiss him. "How fast can you be?"

"You mean at sex?" His brow wrinkled. He glanced at the phone, then obviously did some mental calculations. "Ten minutes. We can have ten minutes if we don't eat or take showers."

"Deal," I said, kissing him, and instantly slid downward to take his penis in my hands.

He looked startled. "Do we have time—"

"You get two minutes. Then I get two minutes. That leaves six for general shenanigans with my burning crotch. Sound good?"

"Sounds . . . glarm!" He grabbed the sheets with both hands when I put both hands on him and swirled my tongue around what I knew was sensitive flesh. He started to babble in another tongue while I allowed hands and mouth and even my breasts to go to town on him, all of which made me feel wonderfully powerful and filled with the feminine knowledge that men were putty in our hands (and mouth and breasts).

Then Dixon called time, and I was suddenly on my back with my legs over his shoulders and his whiskery cheeks rubbing on the inside of my thighs. His fingers did a delightful dance of their own, and by the time he bent to kiss intimate parts, I was doing my own babbling. "I'm putty, too! I'm putty, too!"

He looked up and cocked an eyebrow. "You're what?"

"Ignore me—my brain is talking straight through my mouth without checking with me first," I said, feeling as if I was a top that had been wound to the breaking point. "Hurry! There are only six minutes left. You used extra time on me."

"It was worth it," he said with a knowing grin, and crawled over me, his mouth kissing and nibbling a path upward.

I wrapped my legs around him and tried to pull him exactly where I wanted, but he resisted—damn him.

"Condom?" he asked, ignoring the demands of my legs. "Do we have time for me to find one?"

"Screw the condom!" I almost shouted, desperate now to have all my tingling bits sated as only he could sate them.

"I'd make a rude joke about that comment, but there's simply no time for it." And with that, he slid into me, and all my intimate muscles threw up their hands in joy and shimmied around him in a time-honored dance of utter happiness.

His hips seemed to have their own dance going on, and we moved together in an intense, if not technically perfect, unison. Fortunately for us both, it didn't take but a few minutes before Dixon's movements lost all grace and I began to thrash my limbs around in a desperate attempt to urge him on faster.

"Well," I said a few minutes later, exhausted, sweaty, and pleasured to the tips of my toenails, "that was a hell of a thing, wasn't it?"

"It was." Dixon panted, rolling off me. He looked like he'd just run a marathon. "I can't wait to do it again. That is, I can wait, because I think it would kill me to do it again without proper rest, a couple of solid meals, and a truck full of vitamins, but my anticipation of our next quickie is sky-high right now."

"Kind of makes you a fan of doing it fast, huh?" I got out of bed and hurried to the bathroom, where I had a superfast wash at the basin before pulling on my undergarments. "Can you do up my corset, please?"

Dixon was brushing his teeth. "I can, but it will mean I don't have time to shave."

"I like your stubble. I'd rather have it than no corset, because I don't think I can fit into my dress without it."

And so it was that seven minutes later we arrived at our car (which we'd placed in a secure parking lot with an overnight attendant), I in a dashing blue-and-white-striped skirt, red vest, and lacy white shirt with navy bolero jacket, and Dixon in a gray suit and a pair of red goggles. "I was saving these for photographic situations," he said, donning them and striking a pose so I could take a picture with my phone. "They're quite dashing, aren't they?"

"They're something—that's for darned sure," I agreed, and turned to face the car. That's when I saw it.

"Hey. Where are all our tires?" I pointed to the rear of the car. We'd already gone through about half of our spare tire stock, and Roger, having seen the writing on the wall while we were midway across the U.S., had ordered new ones to be waiting for us in Astana when we arrived. I did a count. "There are only seven here, and there should be eleven—five on the side and six on the back."

"They didn't fall off, did they?" Dixon asked, and we spent a few minutes searching the garage, but didn't find anything.

The attendant had no idea what had happened to the missing tires, saying he had just come on duty. He made a call, however, and managed to find the man who had been on duty overnight, and eventually wormed out a story that there had indeed been someone seen around the car during the night, but as the garage man had scared him off, and there was no visible sign of damage, he hadn't bothered to report it.

"It's the Esses," I told Dixon as we returned to the car and gave it a quick once-over to make sure that there was no sabotage. A half hour later than we had planned, we prepared to depart. "I just know it was them. They probably tried to take all our tires knowing full well that the Flyer goes through them like candy but got scared off before they could take more than four."

"I'll text Roger," Dixon offered. "I doubt if it will do any good, but perhaps he can order more tires to meet us somewhere in Russia. You can take the first stint of driving, and then we will alternate, all right?"

I gathered my own goggles (I only had white ones, since they matched my veiling), my hat, and my veil, and got into the Thomas Flyer. "Suits me."

He consulted his watch and made a note on the official logbook. Technically, we didn't need to record our arrival and departure times now that we were in the free-for-all section of the race, but Dixon thought it would be a nice inclusion in our journals.

We left Astana and headed northwest to Petropavlovsk, a town almost four hundred miles away. We passed a lot of land that reminded me of the Midwest—vast steppes of wheat and other grains, grand stretches of farmland, and even grander forests of what looked to be white birch trees. The road was pretty good, although we had hit a couple of patches where repairs were being made. During one of those patches, the stoppage was long enough that Tabby and Sam caught up to us.

"You were behind us?" Dixon asked when Tabby came forward from their car. We were all stopped, watching some big dump trucks maneuver loads of gravel and road-surfacing materials. "Dare I hope that means the Essex car is back there?"

"Lord, those goggles! You look like a cross between a comic book character and a steampunk adventurer. You may, in fact, dare hope. We all decided that since there are just two of you now, we'd each take a car and follow you. The Essex car should be rolling up soon with Roger and camera crew in tow. In fact, I believe that's them." Tabby pointed to the rear of the line of about sixty cars. I stood up on the seat and shaded my hand to see. Sure enough, the Essex car was in view at the end.

"Crapballs," I said, sitting down behind the wheel again. "But at least we know they aren't ahead of us."

"True," Dixon said, and proceeded to chat with Tabby about what the roads ahead in Siberia would be like. We'd had a warning that some of the roads were in a less-than-admirable state, but didn't know if that was just gossip by the Kazaks or a true indicator of potential trouble.

The road delay ended up costing us almost an hour, but with the Essex car so far back in the queue, we figured we had at least a ten-minute jump on them.

"Get ready for some fast driving," I called back to Tabby when the cars ahead of us started coming to life, indicating the holdup was about ended. "Because I'm going to floor it!"

"Will do," she shouted, and gave us a thumbs-up.

I adjusted my goggles, tied my hat on with a jaunty bow made up of the veil, and grinned at Dixon. "Ready for some high adventure?"

"So long as it doesn't involve car crashes, food poisoning, drunk drivers, or any of the other events that have befallen the race, yes." Dixon settled back in the seat. "Drive on, Macduff."

It was a long day, but we eventually made it to Petropavlovsk. Tabby and Sam were with us the whole way and filmed during a breakdown that we didn't diagnose. We ended up sitting on the edge of a vast wheat field, eating the sandwiches that Tabby had fetched and enjoying a little time sitting in the sun and chatting.

Until the end of the picnic, when the Essex team drove past with their camera car following. Roger pulled over to see what was the matter with the Thomas Flyer.

"She conked out and wouldn't start," Dixon told Graham, who rode with Roger. Dixon gestured at the car's engine, which we'd exposed by folding back the hood. "We thought it might be the radiator, so we've let it cool for about twenty minutes."

"That was damned nice of the Esses to stop and see how we were doing," I said loudly, stomping over to the car. "We could have been in serious trouble for all they knew, but nooo, off they go without so much as a glance back at us."

"I was right behind them," Roger told me calmly. "They must have known that Graham and I would see to any trouble you've had."

I sniffed with righteous indignation. "They could have at least stopped. Maybe had a sandwich."

"You wouldn't, by any chance, have wished for their company just so they wouldn't get ahead of you?" Roger asked with a blithe awareness that irritated me like a nettle on my flesh.

"Look, we all know they're cheating like mad by getting rid of everyone else, so I don't see anything wrong with wanting to keep them near us. Keep your friends close and enemies closer, and all that business."

Roger sighed. "I have no proof that the Essex team has done anything untoward except for the unfortunate accident involving Rupert and Samuel, and that was most definitely an accident. However!" He held up a hand to forestall my objection. "In the interests of safety and general concern for the well-being of everyone in the race, and since we haven't ascertained how Melody's water—assuming it was her water—was tainted, I have decided to pay closer attention to the Essex team, and will be spending the bulk of my time with them, rather than cycling between you and them."

"Thank god for that. It's like we're in an Agatha Christie movie," I said, waving an arm in a dramatic arc. A passing car honked, and several people stuck themselves out the windows to wave at us. I waved back. "One by one we're picked off, until the only one to remain is the murderer."

With a little roll of his eyes, Roger said, "No one has been killed, Paulie."

"Not yet! Who knows what would have happened to poor Melody if her folks hadn't gotten her to the doctor when they did? Just you wait. I bet the Evil Esses will try their respective hands at a little lethal elimination next."

"Bah," Roger said, and for good measure added, "Humbug."

"Is the car low on water?" Dixon asked Graham, who had been poking around in the Flyer's innards.

"No. Try starting her now."

Dixon did so, and the car roared to life.

"Just a bit temperamental," Graham said, giving the hood a pat once he'd closed it up. "She was feeling a bit needy, is all, and now she's calmed down."

"*He* doesn't get to be temperamental," I said, putting a definite emphasis on the pronoun. "*He* is a car, and he can bloody well keep his emo moods to himself, because we have murderers to catch up to. Thanks for the lunch, Tabby. Can I pay you for our sandwiches—that's very sweet of you, thank you." I climbed in beside Dixon and pointed in the direction the Essex team had taken. "Home, Jeeves, and don't spare the horses."

We are exhausted. I'm waiting for my turn at a communal bath. Paulie is asleep. She snores. Just a little, and it's kind of cute, but I can't help but think I shouldn't point that out to her.

It's been a hellishly long day, and we have the Essex team to thank for much, if not all, of that.

It began at the border crossing from Kazakhstan into Russia.

"It should be fairly quick," Roger told us before dashing off with Sam and Tabby to check on the other camera team, who evidently had been in a minor accident. "There's an official agreement with Kazakhstan to pass people through quickly. Just show them your visas and passports and this note from the government tourist agency, and you should be fine."

"So long as they don't go all Soviet on us," Paulie said darkly, but tucked the government document away in the logbook.

We were at the crossing a short time later and lined up behind a car filled with ducks going to market.

"How do you feel about blood sports?" Paulie asked out of nowhere.

I gave her a curious look. "I don't care for them. How do you feel about them?"

"I'm with you."

"What brought that up?"

She pointed to the ducks. "I feel bad for them. I mean, I know people eat them, and they were raised to be eaten, but still, they're cute little duckies."

"You ate chicken last night," I pointed out.

"Chickens are not quite as high on the cute meter as ducks, although I will admit that they have their points."

"Lamb, I suppose, is right off your diet?" I inquired.

"Oh, absolutely. No way I'd ever eat one. Or a deer. Or any of those cute things that are trendy to eat now, like emu and buffalo."

"Alligator?" I asked.

She made a face. "Not cute, but still wouldn't eat. I used to be a vegetarian, but kind of slacked off into eating chicken and fish."

"That seems fairly healthy. Ah. We're moving at last."

We jerked forward when an official lowered a barricade and gestured for us to stop on a black-striped line on the ground.

"Don't look now," Paulie said out of the side of her mouth, staring straight ahead in a manner that could be viewed only as uncomfortable and highly suspicious. "But there is a man with an Uzi standing on the other side of you."

I looked.

She smacked me on the arm. "I said, don't look!"

"Why shouldn't I?"

"Because they'll see you looking, and that's suspicious. You don't want to be suspicious at these border places. They pull you aside and do full-body cavity searches on you, and, thank you very much, I don't need anyone rifling around my girlie bits or butt."

"You let me rifle around," I said, smiling when an official marched over to me and spoke in Russian. I handed him our passports, visas, and Kazakhstan documents.

"That was not a full-body search, and besides, you didn't stray into no-man's-land. No one goes there but my doctor, and then she'd better have a pretty good reason before I allow that!" Paulie declared.

Another official approached, this one with a dog on a leash. Two more men came up to the rear of the car, one with a long device that I realized was a mirror to see under the car.

The first official said something and opened my door, gesturing for me to get out.

"You see!" Paulie hissed. "You looked at the Uzi dude, and now you're going to have your butt searched for contraband."

"You come," the man with the dog told Paulie, and opened her door.

"What? I didn't look at him, honest. Why do I have to go be searched? Dixon!"

"It's all right," I said calmly. None of the guards showed signs of suspicion, so I gathered we were being pulled aside as a mere formality. "No one is going to probe your depths but me, and only then wherever you allow it."

"I was going to say!" She marched along with me, twitching her long skirt in an irritated manner. We entered a low-ceilinged room filled with cubicles and were ushered into an office. Behind the desk sat a woman in uniform. She received the documents from the first border inspector, consulted them, then finally looked up at us. "American and British UK, yes?"

"Yes," I answered, relieved that someone spoke English. "We are part of a transcontinental race, as you can see by our documents."

"Race, yes. We have heard of you."

"Really?" Paulie was all smiles now that she knew her ass was safe. "I didn't think the local press had heard of us, because we hadn't so much as a reporter stopping by to see what we were doing. Roger—he's our producer—said that he tried to interest the press, but he didn't think they understood him because no one responded. Would you like a picture with us? We'd be happy to pose with you if you'd like."

The woman pursed her lips. "We have heard that you are carrying concealed weapons. How do you answer this charge?"

"Concealed weapons?" I was both outraged and startled. "What the hell gave you that idea— Oh. Don't tell me—it was the Essex team, wasn't it?"

Paulie had frozen at the woman's words, no doubt envisioning the body cavity searches, but she twitched at the word "Essex" and clutched my arm.

"The nerve of them, trying to sabotage us this way. You can take it from me, madam, that whatever they told you about us carrying anything contraband is utterly ridiculous. They are simply attempting to hold us back so as to increase their lead."

"Your car is being searched even now." She lifted a hand, and a man rose from his cubicle and darted over to us. "Now you will be searched. If we find weapons, it will be very bad."

Paulie's fingers tightened on my arm.

"You won't find weapons. We are part of a reality television show, not arms smugglers," I said, patting Paulie's hand to let her know she was hurting me.

"Um," she said, and gave my arm a tug. "Can I speak to you a minute, Dixon?"

I turned to reassure her that her body cavities were safe when I caught sight of the fear in her eyes. "What's wrong?"

"Um," she said, glancing at the woman.

"You aren't going to tell me . . ." I closed my eyes for a moment. "Where is it?"

"In one of the spare tires," she said softly, her eyes pleading with me for something. Comfort? Reassurance? I was damned if I knew, and I couldn't spend the time figuring it out. Not when I had a border guard to mislead. Or bribe. Whichever was effective.

"Just out of curiosity," I asked the woman, "what is the penalty for bringing a firearm into Russia?"

She just looked at me and snapped out an order to her minion. "You will go for search now. Man to the left, woman to the right."

"Oh god," Paulie said, looking as miserable as she could get.

"Stiff upper lip, sweetheart," I told her, following the man to a side room. A woman with a severe black suit had appeared to escort Paulie. "We'll get through this. Just stay calm, and don't borrow trouble."

"I didn't borrow it—it was forced on me by my father. Oh, I'm going to have a few things to say to him when I'm out of the gulag . . ."

To my surprise (and profound relief) the search of my person consisted only of a request to remove my clothing behind a screen, at which point they were examined thoroughly, then returned.

I was told to sit at a row of chairs against the wall opposite the offices and waited impatiently for Paulie to reappear. She did so about twenty minutes later, bustling out of the room breathless and with a sense of excitement, and followed by three female officers.

"Thanks for all the info, Katya. And, Anna, be sure to e-mail me the pictures you took trying to get me back into the corset. Tatiana, I hope your mom feels better. If you e-mail me her mailing address, I'll send her a postcard from California, OK?"

The ladies giggled and waved as they left her.

Paulie bustled up to me. "There you are! Did your

guys go where no man has gone before?" She took my hands in hers when I rose to greet her.

"No. You?"

"Unplumbed, thank god." She squeezed my hands and leaned in to give me a quick kiss. "They told me to strip, which didn't work very well because, as you know, I can't reach most of the hooks in the back, and of course there's the corset. Katya had to call in reinforcements, and Tatiana took the corset away to X-ray it for signs of bombs or something—I don't know—and when she came back, Katya told me all about the fact that the Englishmen who came through here a little before us told them that they'd heard we had guns. Anyway, I see now why Dad left Russia. It took Katya, Anna, and Tatiana together to figure out how to lace the corset properly. And then, of course, we had to take some pictures of them with the corset, and me with the corset, and them putting me in the corset, and lots of selfies, which I wanted because I'll need them to remember the last friendly people I see before I'm taken away to some distant camp."

"You will not be taken anywhere," I told her, allowing my lips to linger on hers. "If they find the object you mentioned—why on earth do you have it in the first place?—then I'll simply say it's mine."

"That just means you'll get sent away to break rocks in a chain gang," she protested. "I don't want that any more than I want to do it."

"You're mixing up your imprisonment scenarios." I was about to continue, but the two men who'd gone over the car with a dog and undercarriage mirror entered the room.

Paulie stiffened. I put my arm around her, swinging her around to face them, my expression calm even if my heart was racing with fight-or-flight adrenaline.

Perhaps the gulag wouldn't be so awful. Perhaps Paulie would visit me.

"Would you marry me for real if I was sent away to a Siberian camp?" I asked her quietly when the men consulted with the woman.

She unfroze long enough to blink at me. "I beg your pardon? Did you just propose?"

"Conditionally. I am conditionally proposing. Would you?"

"Why conditionally?"

I sighed. "If I am sent to a Siberian prison camp for the gun that you stashed in the tires, the only way we could have connubial visits is if we were married. So, will you?"

She thought for a minute. "If I was the type of person to allow another person to go to prison for something I did, then yes, I would marry you so we could get it on while you were serving out a sentence that should have been mine."

"That sounds like a conditional acceptance," I said suspiciously. "One that has far too many ifs connected with it."

"And that would be because your conditional proposal is entirely ridiculous. Dixon, I'm not going to let you take the fall for—"

She stopped when we were summoned outside by the two officers. Paulie took my hand in a firm grip, and when I held the door open for her, she murmured, "I'm sorry, Dixon. I really am sorry about this . . ."

The man with the dog strolled off while the other one handed us our visas, passports, and other papers, including a pass bearing the stamp of Siberia.

"What?" I asked, feeling stupid. "Are we supposed to take this with us? To the camp? Both of us?"

"Yes, yes, you go. You take papers," the man said,

and, turning his back on us, gestured at the car behind us to pull forward into the next bay over.

I stared at Paulie. She stared back at me.

"They didn't find it," she said.

"It must have been in one of the tires that the Essex team stole."

A beatific smile blossomed on her face, filling me with joy. "Serves the bastards right!"

"I will admit I was thinking something of the sort. Shall I drive?"

"Go ahead. At least get us a few miles across the border; then I'll take over. Holy bovines, Dixon! They didn't find it! We don't have to go to the gulags! We don't have to get conditionally married just to have wild, sweaty, naked-bunny sex!"

"A fact I'm profoundly grateful for, because at this point the naked bunny sex is uppermost in my mind."

"Really?" She shot me a coy look. "Because you can't stand to be parted from me for more than a few minutes?"

"Yes," I said, waiting for the count of four before adding, "And the fact that they didn't get you tucked into your corset properly."

She looked down and gave a little shriek when she realized her breast had breached the confines of the corset. She stuffed it back down inside with a little giggle.

As we drove deeper into Russia, I was possessed with a sense of well-being, of the fates, for once, casting a benign look my way and turning the wheels that allowed me to face the future with a song on my lips and a throb in my loins that was wholly due to Paulie.

"But not in an STD manner," I said, and then laughed.

"Huh?"

"I was laughing at myself because you aren't the only

one who is having symptoms in your genitals that could be grossly misinterpreted."

"Are you burning, too?" she asked with raised eyebrows.

"No, but I am throbbing."

"That sounds bad. Then again, so does burning. Is it a good throb?"

"Very good."

"Excellent." She patted me on the knee and then turned her attention to the scenery we were passing, no doubt making mental notes to add to her journal.

I smiled at nothing, feeling that, at last, life was good.

Paulina Rostakova's Adventures

AUGUST 2
9:34 p.m.
Small town in middle of Russia, hotel room,
lying exhaustedly on bed, waiting for Dixon
to return with food

We had a lovely night in Yekaterinburg, even though Dixon didn't want to do anything but stay in the hotel room and do naked-bunny-sex things to each other.

"This is a very historic city," I pointed out to him from the comfort of a small bed-and-breakfast on the fringe of the city. The place came with a small barn in the back, which we used to lock away the Thomas Flyer, allowing us to spend the night with each other rather than watching the car, figuring the likelihood of the Essex team finding us at a B&B would be much smaller than had we stayed at one of the mainstream hotels. "Czar Nicholas and his family were killed here. You can go look at the spot where their bodies were found. That sounds like . . . well, not fun, exactly. But interesting."

"Interesting to someone fascinated with government assassinations, perhaps," Dixon said, frowning at his phone. "Roger says they should be in Yekaterina shortly.

They were delayed because the Essex car had a break-down. A radiator hose, evidently."

"Rats. I would have liked for them to be held up as long as they held us up."

"I suppose we shouldn't be grateful that they had any sort of a breakdown, but I admit I'm petty enough to consider it an act of karma." He looked up. "You weren't serious about seeing the place the czar was killed, were you?"

"Actually, I was, kind of. Remember, I'm half Russian, and Dad always said we have Romanov blood."

He glanced at his watch. "It's rather late."

"Not even nine. Come on. We've gone halfway around the world and we haven't even had any time for touristy things. Let's stretch our legs and look at the site."

"I hate to take the Flyer out in case the Essex team are around and see it—"

"We'll take a taxi. Come on!" I danced out of the room, dragging a somewhat reluctant Dixon with me. I would let him rest, but he'd had a nap in the car while I drove, so I took no pity on his plaintive remarks about being no good to anyone in his current state.

"According to the notes I took before we left," I said, consulting my phone once we were in the taxi and on our way, "we are on the route that the original race took in 1908. Just think of it—more than a hundred years ago, another Thomas Flyer drove down these streets. Kind of gives you shivers, huh?"

"I'd be able to enjoy those shivers if I knew exactly where the Essex car was." Dixon brooded. "Perhaps we should have a quick nap and then drive through the rest of the night. We lost so much time at the border . . ."

"We promised Roger we wouldn't drive stupid like that. And besides, what would Tabby and Sam say? Tabby's

text said they are down for the night because both of
them are exhausted and they just want to sleep."

Dixon frowned. "Don't you care that the Essex team
is ahead of us by hours?"

"Not really, no. You know why? Because we still have
several days left in this race, and I know for a fact that
shit happens. They'll blow a tire or crack another radiator
hose, and we'll catch up, and then we'll be ahead for a
while. That's the way it's been the whole race."

"Yes, but that was before they so obviously cheated
by having us detained."

"What did Roger say when you told him about that?"
I asked, not having been privy to that conversation.

Dixon looked disgusted. "He told me it must have
been a mistake or a joke or something. The man is delusional if he thinks that team isn't behind all of the problems of the show."

"You've done a one-eighty about that," I commented.

"Being detained and searched will do that to you," he
said grimly, and I let the subject drop, feeling it was better to keep Dixon in a happy mood.

A half hour later, we arrived at the site where the
Russian Orthodox Church ran a memorial to Czar Nicholas and his family. There were rows of tour buses, and
although it was late in the day, streams of tourists poured
through the wooden gates that were bordered on either
side by kiosks loaded with souvenirs.

"OK, this is kind of . . ."

"Tacky?" Dixon suggested.

"I was going to say materialistic, considering the
church treats the Romanovs as saints, but decided I
wouldn't dis a religion as a whole. Although I have to
say, I wouldn't mind a couple of postcards. Oooh. Is that
a Czar Nicholas book bag?"

Dixon took my arm and steered me away from the

kiosk. "We only have half an hour before they close, so if you want to see the sight, we'd better get moving."

"All right, but if you don't get an authentic Czar Nicholas icon for your birthday, don't blame me." We passed a large bust of the czar and headed out into the birch and pine forest on a dirt path, swatting away moths and mosquitoes and stumbling over bits of roots. Once we'd seen the mine where the Bolsheviks had dumped the bodies, we had time to move on to view a simple cross embedded into the ground.

"Well?" Dixon asked a short while later, when we were headed back to our B&B. "Was that worth the time we could have been having a bath together?"

"I think so," I said, my mood somber after the experience. "For one, the tub isn't big enough for both of us. I know, because I checked. And for another, these were my people, or at least my father's people. My mom is Irish. And the whole revolution thing had an impact on my dad's family. One side left Russia right after the uprising and came to America. The other side—the one my dad belongs to—stayed put, until there was no one but my dad left alive. He emigrated as soon as he could leave the country and came to America so he could stay with his cousins. Wow, I really got into a lot more family history than you wanted to know, huh?"

"On the contrary," he said with a smile. "I like to know things about you."

I looked at him, aware of an emotion that seemed to run high between us, but just then I caught a flash of white in the darkness. Along the side of the road, a man in a Stormtrooper costume pushed a big baby carriage, from which a dog's head poked out.

"You don't see that every day," I commented.

"See what?"

"A Stormtrooper pushing a dog in a stroller."

He blinked. "Where was that?"

"It doesn't matter." I trailed my fingers across his thigh. "So, about this bath that we won't both fit into. Perhaps there's a way it can work. Say, if I sit on you . . ."

August 2
From: Julia
You haven't texted me in forever. How's lover boy? How's the race? Where are you? What time is it? I hope I'm not waking you.

August 2
To: Julia
He's in the bathtub with the B&B owner. Race is hairy. Yekaterinburg, Russia. It's almost midnight, but am awake.

August 2
From: Julia
He's what? Oh no, did he turn out to be a rat bastard? Don't worry. I'll find you another man, and we can leave nasty online comments for this guy. What's it called? Trolling? Yeah, we'll troll him. Will find out how to troll in the morning.

August 2
From: Julia
Also . . . with the B&B owner? Really? Dude!

August 2
To: Julia
Owner is man. They aren't bathing together. Tub isn't big enough. Dixon has toe caught in faucet and can't get it out. Owner is trying to pull it out. I was banished from room for laughing so hard I had an asthma attack.

August 2
From: Julia
You're kidding.

August 2
From: Julia
Isn't that an I Love Lucy episode?

August 2
To: Julia
Don't know. Laughing so hard I'm crying and can't see straight to Google it.

August 2
From: Julia
Do I want to know how he got his toe in there?

August 2
To: Julia
We were having bath together and I was on Dixon and he was adding water with his toes. Got cold water instead of hot. Made me shriek. Dix tried to stuff toe up faucet to stop cold water. I tried to turn it off. Foot twisted. Toe got stuck. All sorts of swearing.

August 2
From: Julia
Man. That sounds funny and horrible at the same time. Is toe OK or broken or something?

August 2
To: Julia
Not hurt. Just bruised. Oh, there is owner with faucet in hand, minus toe. Must go see how Dixon is. Smoochies.

August 2
From: Julia
And to you. Best regards to toe-boy.

August 2
To: Julia
Stop it! Trying to not laugh anymore! The look of outrage on his face . . .

Writing this in the car. Not the best of writing situations, not just because the Thomas Flyer's shocks are almost nonexistent, but because the blasted pram keeps hitting me on the back of my head.

What pram? The pram that accompanied our passenger, one Monsieur Vitale Barionette, Frenchman, Stormtrooper, and world wanderer. We saw him on the side of the road early this morning as soon as we left Yekaterinburg.

"Look," Paulie said, pointing at the figure ahead of us. She was driving, since I was recovering from the trauma of the night before concerning my toe and an extremely poorly made faucet. I will say no more about the subject other than the fact that Russian faucet manufacturers have a good way to go before they reach the standard of faucets in other countries.

"It's the Stormtrooper guy we saw last night. I wonder if he needs a ride?"

I looked up from the guidebook I was perusing. "Why do you wonder that?"

"Well, if you were pushing a dog in a baby carriage, wouldn't you appreciate a lift?"

"Perhaps. Perhaps it's his method of getting exercise."

She shot me a chastising look. "I'm going to ask."

"Paulie," I said in a warning tone of voice when she pulled to a stop on the shoulder in front of the man. "You don't speak the language, and besides, you know the rules as well as I do—we're not supposed to have unauthorized individuals in the cars unless it's a life-or-death situation."

"This could be life or death. He's got a dog with him, Dixon," she said, getting out of the car. "The dog may be sick or something."

"In which case, he would have seen a vet back in Yekaterinburg," I pointed out.

"Meh. I'm going to find out who he is and if he needs help. Or if his dog is OK. It's hot out today, and he may not have any water."

She gathered up her long skirts and marched back toward the man. I sighed and made a gesture, then said, "I have no idea why we are stopped other than Paulie is off on one of her Nellie Bly things," when Sam and Tabby's car pulled alongside and Tabby stuck an inquiring face out the window at me.

"Something wrong?" Tabby asked.

I stood up in the car and looked back. Paulie was talking to the man in the Stormtrooper outfit, absently petting the dog in the pram with one hand while gesturing with the other. "I don't know. I had better go see."

Sam said something, and they pulled ahead off the road. By the time I got back to Paulie, they were loading their equipment up and coming after us to film.

"—you can put the baby machine in the seat with you and Chou-Chou. It's very big," Paulie said in French. "The seat, not Chou-Chou."

"What's going on?" I asked in English.

Paulie turned to me with eyes bright with tears. "Oh, Dixon, it's just like I thought! Vitale here is desperate to get home to Paris."

"No," I said, shaking my head.

She blinked at me in surprise. "No what?"

"No, we are not giving him a ride to Paris."

"I wasn't going to suggest that, silly." She smiled at Vitale reassuringly and said in French, "Dixon is English."

"Yes, so I see," Vitale said, giving me the eye. The dog, a mix of something very hairy and something pie-bald, gave me a similar once-over before emitting an obnoxious odor. "The English, they are very proper."

"Very, but in this case Dixon will totally agree with me that you should let us drive you to Izhevsk, since we're headed that way anyway." She switched back to English and appealed to me. "Dixon, Vitale is a world traveler. He's walking around the globe, kind of how we're driving part of the way. Isn't that cool? The things he must have seen! I can't wait to interview him. But in the meantime, Chou-Chou, his dog, isn't doing too hot, and Vitale has a contact in Moscow who said he'd help him. I thought if we drove him to Izhevsk, he could rest up and his friend could take the train out to see him."

"That would defeat the goal of walking around the world, wouldn't it?" I asked.

The tears dried in Paulie's eyes and the look she gave me was anything but affectionate. "That is beside the point. His dog is sick, and Vitale is having an attack of the sciatica, and we're going to drive him to Izhevsk. You can help him get the baby carriage into the backseat." She switched to French. "Here, let me take Chou-Chou while you and Dixon get the baby machine into the car."

"Erm . . ." Tabby cleared her throat and lowered the microphone boom. "I should mention that taking on passengers is against the rules."

"Unless it's an emergency, and this is one," Paulie said, lifting the dog out of the pram and marching to the car with it.

I looked directly at the camera, sighed, and proceeded to help stuff the blasted pram into the backseat of the Thomas Flyer.

"Why are you in Stormtrooper clothes?" Paulie asked in French.

"It is because I stand out this way, yes?" Vitale answered. His dog was snuggled up against him on the red leather seat, the incongruity of the pair doing much to make my mind boggle. "People give me money for my journey and give Chou food. It works well, except in Russia people do not much like the Stormtrooper."

"Well, we'll get you to town and then you can get Chou to the vet." She said in a lower tone than the yell she'd used to converse with Vitale, "He's out of money. That's why he didn't get to a vet in Yekaterinburg. I've got some dollars I'm going to give him."

"You are aware that this could be a scam of some sort?" I asked, casting a look at the backseat. Vitale was leaning back, eyes closed, a blissful look on his face that was exactly matched by the dog. "He may prey on people's sense of guilt over the dog."

"Bah. Even if he is lying about Chou-Chou, it'll be worth a few bucks to get the story of his life for my journal. It's exciting, don't you think?"

"It's something," I muttered, and pulled out my journal to make some notes. "I just hope you won't be sorry you gave in to your generous impulse."

"You're cynical because your toe is purple," she said, and blew me a kiss. "Just you wait and see—we'll help Vitale, get a good story for our journals, and rack up some good karma all in one fell swoop. It's a win-win situation all around."

I had a feeling she was being naive, but forwent saying anything more.

Paulina Rostakova's Adventures

AUGUST 5
1:02 a.m.
Kazan, Russia

Vitale stole our car. And my passport, and my clothes, and Dixon's clothes, and . . . well, pretty much everything.
    Am exhausted. More later.

AUGUST 5
8:16 a.m.
Kazan, Russia

Dixon and I just had our first official argument. It started off when, while we were checking in to a motel on the outskirts of Kazan (keeping a low profile in case the Essex team was around—Tabby and Sam have been sworn to silence on their location, but from the looks Tabby keeps giving me, I think they're just barely ahead of us), Vitale drove off in the Thomas Flyer.
    "Hey," I said, spinning around when I heard a familiar roaring sound go past the tiny lobby of the motel. "Holy shit! Dixon, that's our car heading out—"
    "What?" Dixon spun around, then bolted. He was

through the door and running down the street after the
car before I could even finish my sentence.

"Sorry," I told the registration clerk, and, gathering up
my skirts (sky blue with cream lace edging that was gorgeous but a horrible dust collector), ran after them. Out
on the street there was traffic, but no sign of the Flyer or
Dixon. I ran a couple of blocks in the direction the car
had gone, but didn't see any sign of them and eventually
slowed down. It was late evening—about nine p.m.—and
the people on the streets were giving me odd looks.

"Does anyone speak English?" I asked loudly. "Or
French? Or a little very bad German?"

No one answered me. I spun around at the intersection, hoping to see Dixon or the Flyer, but the street was
full of modern cars only, and not one single Englishman
in Edwardian clothes. Tabby and Sam pulled up. They
had stopped to fill their car with gas and passed me on
the way to the motel at which we'd agreed to meet.

"Problem?" Tabby asked. A car behind them honked.

"Our car was stolen!" I wailed.

"Get in," Tabby said, and gestured toward the backseat.

I climbed in, beating back the fuzzy boom microphone, and shoving the camera over, just barely getting
my skirt tucked inside before Sam hit the gas. I explained
briefly what had happened with Vitale.

"We'll find them," Sam said grimly, gripping the steering wheel with white fingers.

"Should we call Roger?" I asked, peering out into the
lit streets, trying to see in shadows.

"Are you kidding? He'll have kittens," Tabby said,
snorting a little at the idea. "If we can't find the car, then
we'll have to, but it's going to stand out like a sore thumb,
so someone will see it. Left, Sam."

"Why?" he asked.

Tabby pointed. "Sign for Kazan, Novgorod, and Moscow."

"Done." Sam turned left and wove in and out of traffic, ignoring the honking of irate drivers. It was about two miles out of town that we finally saw the Flyer ahead on the road.

"Got you," Tabby said, and hooted.

"You bastard!" I yelled out the window when Sam, with a burst of speed, raced up and cut off the Flyer, forcing it to the shoulder.

"Where the hell did you learn to do that?" I asked Sam, momentarily flabbergasted.

He smirked as he pulled off his seat belt. "I used to drive cameramen in the Tour de France. After him!"

There was nothing to be after, thankfully, since Vitale didn't run. He did argue quite loudly and profanely when I wrenched the long flat key from him, and then ended in tears when Tabby demanded he gather up his dog and pram and leave the car, begging us to help him get to Moscow.

"Stealing our car isn't the way to go about getting help from people— Dixon!"

A car squealed to a stop behind us, a blue flashing light wavering drunkenly on the roof of the car. Out of it burst Dixon, followed by two men.

"You caught him! How did you— Oh, Tabby. Thank god. I saw a policeman and flagged him down. Luckily, he speaks enough English that he understood me."

"I watch American television," the man said with a huge smile. "I like *CSI Law and Order*. Is very informative. Book 'em, Danno!"

"Yeah, I think that's another . . . Never mind," I said, so relieved to see Dixon that I wanted to cry. Which was disconcerting as hell, because I'm not the crying-at-the-sight-of-a-person sort of woman. I was mulling over this strange situation when I realized what was going down in front of me.

"Hey, what are you doing?" I said, moving quickly to the Flyer when the cop brought out a zip tie and spun Vitale around to face the car. "No, no, no, don't arrest him!"

"No?" The cop hesitated when Dixon asked, "For god's sake, why not?"

"He hasn't done anything wrong other than take the Flyer."

Dixon breathed a bit heavily through his nose. "Repeat that last bit: he stole the Thomas Flyer. Our car. The one we need for the race."

"Yes, but he just took it because he's trying to get to Moscow. He's not a bad person, not really. He's just super focused on a goal." I pointed at Chou-Chou, sitting regally in the backseat. "And he has an old dog that he takes care of. Not many people would go to the trouble of wheeling their old dog around the world."

"He stole our car!" Dixon said, running a hand through his hair.

"Because he wants to go to Moscow and we were leaving him here in Izhevsk." I looked meaningfully at Dixon.

"No," he said firmly, and crossed his arms over his chest.

"Oh, come on. It's just a few hundred miles."

"It's over seven hundred miles, and I refuse to chauffeur a man who stole my car."

"It's partly my car, and I say he can ride in my half," I snapped, getting annoyed. Why couldn't Dixon see that this was the right thing to do?

His jaw worked for a second, but he said nothing.

The cop waved the zip tie around. "I arrest or not?"

"Not," I said, my eyes still on Dixon. He looked quietly furious. "We're taking him to Moscow."

Dixon turned around and got into the car behind the steering wheel. I told Vitale, who was looking miserable, that we were going to drive him to Moscow, but that he needed to behave himself and stop stealing cars. After thanking the policeman, he hurried around to the passenger seat.

To my surprise, rather than pull out and turn around, Dixon headed in the direction the car was pointed—away from Izhevsk. "What are you doing?" I asked him.

"You wanted to drive to Moscow—that's what we're doing," he answered grimly. "We'll try to make Kazan by midmorning, then go on to Novgorod."

"But we've been driving all day." I looked at my watch. "It's almost ten. I thought you were tired?"

"I *am* tired, but I'm not going to give our friend back there another chance to steal the car. Since you insist on bringing him along, we'll drive all night, taking turns sleeping. You go first."

"What about Tabby and Sam? You can't just drive off without telling them we're not going to the hotel."

"At this point, I don't particularly care about being filmed."

"Roger will have a fit if he hears about that," I murmured.

"I don't care." He relented after a moment, adding, "Sam and Tabby can catch up to us in Moscow. We'll be too exhausted to go on without proper rest."

I hurriedly texted Tabby.

August 5
To: Tabby
We're going to Moscow.

August 5
From: Tabby
The fuck you are! That's at least two days' driving!

August 5
To: Tabby
Dixon doesn't want to give Vitale another chance at taking the car. I think I may have broken him.

August 5
From: Tabby
Vitale?

August 5
To: Tabby
Dixon. He's making odd little snorting noises and talking to himself under his breath. And there's a muscle in his jaw that keeps twitching.

August 5
From: Tabby
Sam says we'll drive for another hour or two. Then we'll have to sleep. I'll text Roger your plans. He was going to come back to watch over filming with you for a day.

August 5
To: Tabby
Come back? Dammit, if he's with the Essex team, that means they are ahead of us!

August 5
From: Tabby
Hell. Pretend you didn't see that.

I eyed Dixon and considered whether or not I wanted to tell him that the Essex team was definitely ahead of us. As I watched, he growled something and flexed his fingers on the steering wheel. I was grateful I couldn't see his eyes through the lenses of his red goggles, because I had a feeling they would be shooting laser beams in my general direction.

We rolled into Kazan at about six in the morning. Neither one of us had slept much in the car, although Vitale appeared to snooze the entire trip. We stopped at a skanky-looking hotel, the kind where you don't want to touch anything inside, and took turns taking a shower and changing our clothing.

"Do you want to sleep?" Dixon asked, his face haggard and his eyes red-rimmed with exhaustion.

I looked at the bed and shuddered. "In the car, yes. Not here."

"Fine. Our guest can sleep here, and we'll take the car."

And that's how it worked out. Vitale was a bit confused, but grateful to have a room to himself, while Dixon and I curled up in the car for two hours. We had more than five hundred miles to go to Moscow, and I feared we wouldn't get there safely with only two hours' rest, but I couldn't complain since Dixon was doing as I'd asked.

I just hoped it wouldn't kill us.

JOURNAL OF DIXON AINSLEY
6 August
11:47 p.m.
Suburb of Moscow, Russia

We made it.

Barely.

Going to sleep for a week. Paid garage attendant to watch car.

Bonus: Roger caught up with us five hours out of Moscow, along with the second camera crew. Roger said we'd passed the Essex team while they slept in Novgorod. Ha. Take that, you bastards.

Paulie fell asleep on bed without even taking off her clothes. Managed to get her shirt and corset off. She didn't wake. Left the rest of her clothing. Too tired to take off so much as my tie. Screw the costume department. Sleeping in my clothes as well.

JOURNAL OF DIXON AINSLEY
7 August
6:33 p.m.
Moscow, Russia—still

We realized something was wrong when, while we were both asleep on the bed, a crash sounded from the attached bathroom.

Paulie sat bolt upright. "What was that?"

"Hrn?" It took me a moment to surface from the deep

sleep I'd been in. I tugged at my tie, which was partially strangling me. "What?"

"That's what I asked. I heard a noise."

"Dreaming," I said, and groggily sat up to remove my jacket, waistcoat, and blasted strangling tie.

That's when I saw the movement from the corner of my eye.

Two men emerged from the bathroom, both dressed head to toe in black, with black balaclavas over their faces obscuring their features.

One man held a gun, which was pointed directly at Paulie.

"Holy hellballs!" she said, staring with openmouthed amazement at the men. "Dad was right!"

"About?"

She pointed at the men. "He said I'd be kidnapped if I came to Russia, and I'll be damned if those aren't kidnappers. Hello. Are you kidnappers?"

"Yes," one of the men said in heavily accented English. He gestured toward me with the gun. "You. Get on your knees."

I thought about my options, and decided I didn't like any of them. "No," I said, getting to my feet and moving over to stand in front of Paulie. "I don't think I will."

"I shoot you," the man warned.

"I'd prefer you not," I said politely, trying to gauge how fast Paulie could make it to the door if I distracted the two men. "I have a race to complete, and for the first time in days, we're ahead. I'd like to build on that lead, not lie dying on a Moscow hotel floor."

"Yeah," she said, getting to her feet, hastily snatching up the discarded blouse and slipping it on. "What he said."

The man with the gun hesitated, then took three steps forward. I shoved Paulie toward the door, yelling, "Run!"

when a reddish black pain burst across my head, sending me tumbling down into a black pit of agony.

"—xon? If you've permanently damaged his brain, I'm going to come down like a can of whoop ass on you!" was the first thing I heard when I managed to claw myself out of the pit. I blinked at the lights and realized that my head was cradled in Paulie's lap. I turned my face into her belly and enjoyed, for a moment, the lightly floral scent of her, wondering how a woman who'd driven for more than twelve hours could still smell so good.

"I say we take a finger from each," came the low, almost guttural rumble of a man. "That way we have extra."

"What are they talking about?" I asked Paulie's delightful belly.

"You're awake! Oh, thank god." Her belly moved and soft lips commenced kissing my face. I turned my head to kiss her properly, but what felt like a massive lump on the back of my head brushed her thigh, causing red spiderwebs of pain to crisscross in front of my eyes. When my vision cleared, I found myself sitting upright, leaning against the edge of the bed. To my surprise, we were still in the hotel room.

"What happened?"

"Gun boy hit you on the head when you tried to get me to leave you. As if I'd ever do that." She brushed a bit of hair carefully from my forehead. The touch of her fingers did a lot to ease the massive headache centered on the back of my head. "I appreciate the attempt to save me, but we're in this together, Dixon."

I took her hand in mine. "In what? The race? Our faux marriage? Life?"

"All of them," she said, her eyes soft with an emotion I didn't want to examine too much at that moment. I simply relished for a few seconds the corresponding warm glow of happiness that seemed to start in my belly and radiate outward, and instead turned painfully to look at the two men, now seated at a minuscule table next to the window.

"Are they really kidnappers?"

"Yes, unfortunately." Paulie made a face. "If I understand their references to a friend who is in Dad's employ, I gather whoever this dude is ratted me out to his buddies here in the motherland. The buddies work for one of Dad's old rivals, and thus Rosencrantz and Guildenstern have popped up to hold us for ransom. Or so I assume all that finger talk is leading to."

"One finger," the man with the gun said, gesturing with it toward us. "Two is wasteful."

"How is it wasteful?" the second man asked, shaking his head. "One we send to Rostakova, and the other we send to the Englisher's family."

"Who is he? Does his family have any money? Do you know the answer to these questions? I do not, and I do not think it is smart to take a second finger without knowing the answers. Where will we keep the extra finger? I don't want it. You know how I am about blood."

"I like my fingers," I said, wiggling all ten of them and feeling a bit woozy in the head region. I leaned back against Paulie and allowed her to stroke my forehead, wondering idly what she'd think of living in England. "I like Paulie's fingers more."

"You're a bit wonky, aren't you, love?" She pressed a gentle kiss to my cheek.

I turned my head carefully to look at her. "You missed my mouth."

She smiled. "I'll kiss it later, OK? Once you're back to normal."

"With or without all my fingers?"

"I'll tell you a secret," she said, and then whispered into my ear, "These men are speaking in English."

"I know," I whispered back. "I speak English, too."

"Doesn't that strike you as odd? For Russian mobsters, that is, in the middle of Russia?"

I turned to consider the two men, who were now arguing over the proper method of storing severed fingers so as to ensure freshness. "That is odd."

"Quiet, you," the man with the gruff voice said, and pulled out a large hunting knife, which he waved at us. "We discuss how to send the ransom note."

"In English," I said, my eyes narrowing on them. "Rather convenient that, don't you think?"

The man looked confused.

I glanced at Paulie. She was watching me with concern. "Help me up," I told her, and got awkwardly (and painfully) to my feet.

The two men watched us in apparent amazement.

"Right," I said, tugging down the waistcoat that rode up on my chest and making an effort to not wince at the waves of pain that rippled across my brain. "I think we'd better get a few things straight. One, there will be no cutting off of fingers, either from Paulie or from me. Two, you may tell Mr. Rostakova that we are not intimidated, nor will we allow him to jeopardize our position in the race. And three, you both need to go to acting school if you wish to present yourselves as actual thugs capable of cutting off ransomable fingers."

"Um." Paulie tugged at my sleeve, and said quietly, "I think they really *are* thugs, Dixon, but you are dead right with the other assessments."

"And with that, we will ask you to leave," I said, striding to the door and opening it. "Now that you've woken us up, we have things to do and miles to race. Good day."

"What's this?" the gun toter asked, jumping up and shoving me away from the door.

"Uh . . . Dixon . . ."

"On your knees!" the other man said, his lip curling a little as he leaped to his feet.

"Give it up," I said, bored with their playacting. I made a mental note to have a word with Paulie about her father's actions and a discussion about what was, and what wasn't, appropriate in parental behavior. I attempted to retake the door, but the gunman suddenly lunged at me. Something in my head snapped, and I was back fifteen years to a martial arts class I'd taken my youngest brothers to and which I'd halfheartedly participated in. I kicked the gun from the man's hand, whirling around to slam him in the back of the head, which sent him staggering forward into his knife-bearing friend. The gunman screamed and threw himself to the side in order to avoid being gutted.

Paulie, with more gumption than I would have thought possible, snatched up a chair and brought it down over his head. He collapsed to the floor with a grunt of pain.

The knife-wielding thug snarled something that I was fairly certain was obscene, and hesitated for a second between Paulie and me. When he turned fractionally toward her, I leaped forward, slamming my fist into his nose, while punching out blindly with the other hand. Luckily, it missed the knife and landed on his collarbone, a nasty cracking noise resulting. The man screamed and dropped to his knees, making a halfhearted slash toward me with the knife before dropping it to clutch his shoulder.

"Let's get out of here!" Paulie shouted, snatching up our phones from the nightstand and leaping over the downed man. She grabbed my arm and spun me around, half dragging me to the door.

"We can't leave. Not until we call the police and a medic unit," I said, stopping her.

The look she turned on me told me she thought I was nigh on mad. "Are you freaking insane?" she asked, confirming my suspicion. "We have to get out of here right now. Thank god we were too tired after dropping off Vitale to bring in our luggage."

I'll give her this: she had more strength than it appeared. She had me out the door and midway down the hall before I managed to stop her a second time. "Paulie, we can't leave your father's men lying on the floor. We must call the police to report the attack—even if it was a sham—and get them some medical aid."

"Gah!" she said, slapping her thighs in annoyance. "They aren't my father's men, don't you see? Yeah, he must be behind this attempt to try to scare me so I'll sit at home and do nothing with the rest of my life, but I can assure you they are just hired goons and have no further allegiance to him, and therefore to me. And now you've hurt them."

"That's why I insist we get them medical aid. Honestly, Paulie, for a woman who made such a big fuss about helping a man who robbed us, you are being particularly unfeeling toward actually wounded men."

The sound of crashing furniture and breaking ceramics emerged from the room, followed by the knife man, bleeding from his nose and holding one shoulder higher than the other. He also held the knife, and snarled viciously when he saw us.

"You're adorable when you're noble, but I'd really rather not be kidnapped for real. Come on!" She dashed off toward the exterior staircase.

"Hell!" I swore, and ran after her.

"It's like we're in a James Bond movie!" Paulie cried when I jammed a trash can under the door to the exterior stairs, hoping to slow down the knife thug. Paulie streaked down the stairs, her skirts held high in her hands and the back of her blouse flapping open.

"I am not even close to being James Bond," I replied, leaping down the stairs two and three at a time. Above us, an ugly grating noise, followed by the sound of some-thing large and metal being thrown down the stairs, gave our feet wings.

"Do you have the key?" I asked when Paulie reached the bottom of the stairs and dashed outside, skidding when she made a sharp ninety-degree turn to head for the entrance to the parking area.

"Yes. Thank god we don't have to crank these cars to get them started."

"Meet me here," I said, taking up a stand at the entrance of the underground car park.

She glanced over her back, pausing to shout back at me, "What are you doing?"

"Making sure we aren't followed."

"How are you going to do that?"

"I have no bloody idea," I said softly, and shouted for her to go on and fetch the car.

She disappeared into the darkness, and I looked around for something to use as a weapon. There was nothing other than a kiosk where a bored-looking teen-ager sat with a cigarette clinging to his lower lip, the yellow-and-black-striped barrier that rose when cars were allowed to leave, another trash barrel, and a couple of orange traffic cones.

"Why didn't I watch that *MacGyver* show that Elliott loved?" I growled to myself as I picked up the cones and wondered if they could be considered lethal weapons. "I bet he'd have no trouble making nuclear warheads out of these."

The teen, a boy of probably seventeen or eighteen, watched me with an unmoving expression, his cigarette never wavering from where it hung off his lip.

"I don't suppose you have a gun?" I asked him.

He didn't even blink, just watched me with a look that said he was utterly bored by me, the parking lot, and probably everything in the world. A tiny bit of ash fell off the end of his cigarette.

Footsteps sounded loudly right ahead of the thug, who skidded to a halt at the sight of me. He was breathing heavily, his mouth, chin, and shirt bloody, and he still held that damned knife. I waved my cones at him. "Now, see here. We are not your enemies. Yes, I disabled you, but that is because you and your friend tried to kidnap us. Or pretended to. So really, you have no one but yourself to bla—"

He lunged before I finished speaking, and I swung first one cone, then the other, and finished up with a kick to his left knee.

"Well, what do you know?" I asked, eyeing him when he rolled around on the pavement, alternately clutching his knee and his shoulder. "They *are* weapons."

A roar sounded from within the garage. The Thomas Flyer raced up the incline to the exit, like some great white beast surging forward to consume its prey. Paulie was at the wheel, her hat jammed on her head crookedly, her goggles glinting in the dull yellow sodium lights, and her white veil streaming backward a good fifteen feet.

"Get in!" she yelled, waving one arm frantically.

"You'd better open it up," I said loudly to the parking lot attendant, but he stared dully first at me, then at the man on the ground, then finally to the Thomas Flyer as she roared up to me.

"Jump!" Paulie shouted, clearly not intending on waiting for the barrier to be raised. I thought of pointing that out to her, realized there was no time, and swung myself up onto the sideboard when she passed me, throwing myself into the backseat just as she hit the barrier and drove off into the night.

The last sight I had of the parking lot attendant was him leaning out of his window, watching us, the cigarette still dangling from his lip.

Paulina Rostakova's Adventures

AUGUST 9
5:55 a.m.
Warsaw, Poland

There are times when I'm surprised we're still alive. Then there are times when I'm convinced we're immortal. Fortunately, the latter isn't my normal state of mind. Although I did have to admit that I was filled with nothing but admiration for Dixon after he'd disabled the men Dad had engaged to put the fear of god in me.

"That man was on the ground again!" I yelled when we bounced over the edge of the curb and onto the street outside the Moscow hotel. "You beat the crap out of him, didn't you?"

"I wouldn't say that," Dixon answered, popping up from the floor of the backseat, where he'd been thrown when I gunned the car and crashed through the parking lot barrier. He looked back, his hair ruffled in the breeze. "We're going to have to pay for that, you know?"

"For the guys who attacked us? I don't see why. They must have some sort of insurance."

"No, for the barrier." He climbed over into the front seat, sliding down into it, swearing, rising up, and pulling his goggles out from where he'd sat on them. He donned them, then turned to look at me.

I giggled.

"What?" he asked.

"It's the goggles. They're bad enough with your driving hat on, but by themselves they're kind of . . ."

"Roguishly handsome?" he asked, lifting his chin.

"Steampunky."

"Yes, well, I can't help that. My cap is back in the hotel room."

"I told you to leave it in the car like I did with my hat. Would you gather up some of my veil, please? It's choking me."

He obliged, pulling it from where it was streaming the length of the car and wadding it up onto the seat, sitting on it to keep it from billowing out again. "I suppose we're going to drive all night."

"We shouldn't. We only had a few hours' sleep, and we were sorely in sleep deficit before that, but I have to admit, this escape was super exciting! I kind of got my adrenaline going, and now I'm all *Rawr!* Let's take on the world!"

He flexed his fingers and examined his knuckles. A couple of them were scraped. "I'd rather not, if you don't mind, although I admit the scene did wake me up fully. Roger won't be pleased with our change of plans, though."

"Probably not, especially since I saw Tabby and Sam's car in the garage, which means they made it to Moscow and were probably sleeping."

"I'll text him and update him as to recent events," Dixon said, and pulled his phone out of his pocket. A half hour later, he showed me the response.

WTH? the text read. *Why are you trying to sauber the program?*

"Sauber?" I asked, glancing quickly at the phone.

"Sabotage, I expect, is what he meant. Ah. Another one. *Will you stop trying to drive me insane and wait for the film crew?* Hmm. He seems to have disregarded the part of the explanation where I pointed out we were in danger of our lives."

"Did you tell him you went James Bond all over those goons' asses?" I asked, flashing him an admiring glance.

"Of course not. I'm British. We don't talk about our James Bond episodes," he said in a very correct voice, his expression prim.

I laughed, aware of a sensation deep in my stomach that was warm and squidgy and wonderfully exciting. "Dixon," I said, not realizing I was speaking until I heard the words, "I think I'm falling in love with you."

He said nothing for a minute. A very uncomfortable minute.

I slid him a glance out of the corners of my eyes.

"Well?" I asked at the end of the minute. "You've got to have some sort of a reaction to that statement. You can't just brush off an 'I might be falling in love with you' comment. It's a law that you have to reply. Please do so now."

"Ah," he said, and didn't look at me.

I glanced in the rearview mirror and managed to get us to the side of the road without accident.

"Why are we stopping?" he asked.

"Because an 'ah' is not a proper response to what I just said. Dammit, Dixon! I said I was falling in love with you!"

"You said you *thought* you were falling in love with me. That's not the same as actually doing the act," he pointed out.

"Stop being pedantic," I said, frowning a little.

"I'm sorry if you feel that pointing out the obvious is pedantic, but there is a difference between thinking you're falling in love and actually doing so."

"And this is what I get for trying to have an adult relationship where I speak my mind and am honest and aboveboard with my thoughts and feelings and yearnings for your naked flesh on my naked flesh. Particularly my female bits. They miss your male bits. A lot."

"Are your female bits perhaps confusing a perfectly normal and healthy lust for the more substantial and long-term love?" he asked.

"No!" I punched him lightly on the arm. "Dammit, Dixon. Is it your fiancée? Is it too soon? Not that I think nine years can in any way be considered soon, but still, people grieve at different rates. Is it because of her?"

He sighed, about to deny it, but stopped and finally said, "Yes. But not in the way you think."

"Oh? In what way, then?"

He toyed with the material covering his knees for a few seconds. "I told you about this, but you were asleep. I didn't love Rose. I'm not sure I ever truly did, even at the beginning when we first met and were together. She always seemed to take charge of the relationship, leaving me feeling as if my thoughts and preferences didn't matter. I was more or less without a say in the way our future was planned."

"That doesn't sound like you," I said with a little frown, and pulled out into traffic again.

"It isn't. Or rather, it wasn't then, but I lacked the confidence in myself to recognize what was wrong with our interactions. It's easy to see now that I allowed myself to be swept along with her visions, but that was not the case at the time. There was also a little oppositional defiance issue in that my parents disliked Rose intensely, and I was going through a rebellious stage."

"I tried to have one of those," I said with a little sigh at the memory of the time I tried to live on my own with only the money I made waitressing. I was a horrible waitress. "Not only was I a failure at it—my father made himself so sick with worry that I decided it wasn't worth it. It's hard to be defiant when the people who love you are so unhappy."

"You're luckier than me, then, because I clung to my defiance until I realized the situation was too complicated to bow out of with any sort of dignity. And then Rose became ill, and I couldn't leave then because . . . well, I just couldn't."

"You're a really nice guy—do you know that?" I kept my eyes on the road, but was very aware of Dixon's small movements next to me. He was making little "I'm embarrassed by your praise" twitches of his fingers. "I think it's admirable that you were there for your fiancée when she needed you most."

"She didn't need me. She hated me by the end, and I didn't blame her one bit. I wasn't any too fond of myself."

"Don't beat yourself up because you made mistakes," I told him from the wisdom of many years of therapy. "You can't control what other people think or do, and you certainly aren't responsible for either."

"No, but if I had backed out earlier . . . if she had met someone she really should have been with . . ."

"Bah. The world is full of ifs, and none of them are worth a damned thing. So how does the fact that you're not grieving for your lost love mean that you can't tell me that you've fallen for me just like I've fallen for you? And keep in mind if you tell me you haven't fallen for me, I am in control of this vehicle and I can easily see to it that you tumble out of it. While I'm driving. *Fast*."

He laughed, relieving the sense of worry that had filled me ever since I had made my declaration. "And I know you would never accept a profession of love made under the threat of death or dismemberment."

I cocked an eyebrow at him. "And . . . ?"

"And?" He looked somewhat surprised. "And I believe that you know what my feelings are."

I wanted to stop the car again just so I could look at him, but I'd be damned if I'd appear desperate after just telling him I loved him. I pondered what he'd said, gnawing my lower lip as I tried to determine if I was missing something. Should I know what he felt for me? Oh, I knew he was fond of me and enjoyed our sexual escapades, and he liked talking to me, but did he feel the same sense of burgeoning love that gripped me with painful fingers every time I clapped eyes on him? Did he think of me at all hours of the day, like I did of him? Did he mentally store up things to discuss with me, just as I did?

Dammit, why couldn't he answer my question the way I wanted him to?

"So . . ." I hesitated, fighting my pride with the need to get some clarity. "So you're not closed to the idea of a romantic relationship beyond that of a purely physical nature?"

"No. When the time is right."

"Huh?" Now I really was confused.

"I won't make the mistakes I did in the past. I will do things properly. I will declare myself and my affections. I will propose on one knee. I will be married in a ceremony where both families are in attendance, and it will be a celebration of our commitment to each other, and not a showcase bereft of good taste and emotions beyond greed and one-upmanship."

A sick feeling gripped my stomach. Was he saying I wasn't the woman of his choice? In my tired state, I didn't have enough brainpower to figure out just what it was he was trying to say. Was he gently letting me down? Or was he indicating that, at some point, he would follow his strategy and we'd live happily ever after?

I glanced at him, unsure how to respond.

He sat back easily, his fingers relaxed on his knees, his hair blown back from his brow by the wind.

Dear god, he was handsome. That straight nose, the bluish gray eyes that could go from pretty to steamy with just a bat of his lashes. And his jaw—oh, that jaw. I loved his jaw, almost as much as his chest. And his legs. And butt. And pretty much every other part of him.

Dammit, I loved him. There was no denying the fact—I wanted to wake up next to him every morning. I wanted to argue with him, and make up, and laugh and sing and dance with him. I wanted to hold him in the night and see his eyes light up with laughter when I teased him.

I just wanted him.

We drove on in silence. Dixon didn't seem to be bothered at all by our conversation, but I was badly confused and worried. And since I'm not a person who does either in silence for long, I finally blurted out, "Do you want to see me after the race? Or is this just a fling?"

The face he turned to me expressed utmost surprise. "What?"

"You heard me." I gritted my teeth and glared out the windscreen. The weather was starting to turn chilly for August, with cloud cover over the moon, leaving the night dark and uninspiring.

Pretty much like my life at that moment.

"Yes, I did, but my question was aimed more for why you would ask that than what your question meant."

"Man, you're going to make me ask it right out, aren't you?" I sighed, figuring my dignity didn't stand a chance against my raging curiosity. "The person you're talking about, the one you want to propose to—are you saying that's someone you've yet to meet, or someone you know now?"

The look he gave me was chiding. "Do you really have to ask?"

"Yes. Yes, I do. That's why I'm asking it," I said through clenched teeth.

His lips twitched. "Do I strike you as a Lothario?"

"Dammit, Dixon, answer the question!"

"Which one?"

"Gah! So help me, I will pull this car over and . . . and . . ."

"And what?" he asked, tipping his head to the side.

"Something you'll be very sorry about!" I finished, almost sputtering, so annoyed was I.

"Pull over," he said.

"Huh?"

"Pull over."

I glared at him for a second, then did as he asked and pulled onto the shoulder. "Look," I started to say, but got no further. Dixon was out of the car and coming around to my side, holding open the door for me.

"Are you kicking me out of my own car?" I asked, slowly climbing out.

"You have a very odd picture of me if you can declare your love and admiration for me in one breath and then suspect me of trying to get rid of you in the next." He pulled me forward into an embrace, his arms solid around me and the feel of his body so perfectly right for mine.

He squeezed my butt and gave me a quick peck before pushing me into the passenger seat. "You're tired and overwrought. Why don't you rest, and I will drive for a few hours?"

"I'm not overwrought! I'm a bit murderous, but not overwrought, and you only have yourself to thank for that state of mind," I growled.

"I'm sorry if you're so unhappy right now." He reached into the back for the lap blanket we kept there, mostly to take naps on. "Here, you cover up and rest, and I'll drive for a few hours."

I gave up at that point. I don't like to think of myself as a quitter, but I'd asked him point-blank several times, and if he didn't want to answer the question, then so be it.

The big idiot. "Roger will be pissed if we don't go find a hotel and park ourselves so they can find us."

"To hell with Roger," he said with blithe abandon.

I bit back some rather scathing comments and settled back, confused, emotionally vulnerable, and fearing a future of unrequited love, but realized that now was clearly not the time to discuss the future, so I tried to put the matter from my mind.

In the end, we did find a hotel, but only after we had crossed the border into Latvia.

I had hoped for some rompy time once we were snuggled into bed, even if the man refused to talk relationship. Dixon, however, had other ideas. When I emerged from a soak in the tub to warm up all my extremities (the misty rain had turned into a heavy drizzle that seemed to seep through my clothes to my skin), he was sound asleep, snoring up a storm. I stood looking down at him, wondering how I had started this adventure determined to find my wings at last and go my own way without ties to any family, and now here was a man who was so much a part of me, I couldn't even imagine life without him. And I had no idea if he reciprocated those feelings.

"You are just going to have to see reason," I said, snuggling into Dixon. He mumbled in his sleep and rolled on his side, his leg and arm over me protectively. I scooted in even closer to his chest, enjoying the scent and feel of him. "That's all there is to it."

We slept for almost twelve hours. Not intentionally, as I explained to Sam and Tabby, who had caught up to us by the following morning.

"Roger is about an hour ahead of us," Tabby said when we got dressed, and stopped at the hotel breakfast area for a little food. "The Essex team had an issue this morning when two of their tires blew at the same time and they only had one spare left. Roger had ordered the remaining tires stockpiled in Germany to be driven to Daugavpils."

"That's close to us, isn't it?" I asked.

"About forty miles," Dixon answered, looking at the map pasted into our logbook. "Damn. I was hoping we were ahead of them after all that driving."

"You were for a while. Then Roger mentioned how you'd driven to Moscow a day sooner than planned, and they drove all night to catch up." Tabby shrugged. "I guess Dermott and Clarissa were really annoyed by that. Roger, of course, gets by without any sleep."

Dixon and I exchanged guilty looks at the mention of the second camera team having to play catch-up. "We should apologize again for racing off without you," I started to say, but Tabby waved it off.

"It's all right. We kind of enjoy hunting you down. It's just good you can't go over fifty."

I made a face.

Dixon asked, "How did the Essex team pass us if they were missing a tire?"

"They got a temporary one from a local car dealership. I guess it makes the car shimmy something horrible because it doesn't fit right, and they can't drive over thirty miles per hour, but Sanders refused to wait for the actual replacements to arrive, so they're determined to be in Daugavpils when the spares arrive."

"That sounds highly dangerous," I said, glancing at the clock. "It shouldn't take us long to get past them if they can only do thirty. Let's see how much ground we can put between us and them."

"You haven't looked outside, have you?" Sam, a bagel in his hands, stopped by to comment. "It's pouring buckets out there."

"Ugh. We'll have to put the top up on the Flyer," I told Dixon.

"Worse, we'll be sopping wet by the time we stop." He rose and stretched. I was momentarily distracted by the sight of that movement on his chest, even though it was covered by an undershirt, shirt, vest, and coat. Really, the man was entirely too sexy for his own good. I narrowed my eyes on him, wondering if I was going to have trouble with women coveting him.

Tabby was chatting and joking about us needing to wear rubber suits in order to drive the Flyer when I turned my gaze on her. I knew from past conversations that she'd had both male and female partners, and now here she was with her hand on Dixon's arm while she joked.

I stood up, not wanting to draw attention to the fact that she was handling my man—because I liked Tabby; I truly did—but I wasn't about to put up with other women fondling him right there in front of me.

"What's wrong?" Dixon asked me when Tabby turned to gather up some food to go.

"What makes you think anything is wrong?"

He cocked an eyebrow at me. It was my favorite eyebrow, too. "You're glaring at Tabby as if she just took your favorite toy."

"Good call, Mr. Sexy," I said with much meaning, and went off to rearrange the storage boxes on the car so that we could put the convertible top up.

We'd had to use the top once in the U.S., but not since crossing the ocean. Putting it up required a complicated dance of turning cranks, hurriedly checking prop arms, and then cranking a bit more. One person had to guide the front part along its path until it was finally settled over the front seats.

"Do I want to know—" Dixon asked, following me out to the car.

"No. And I'm not jealous, just in case you were wondering, although you could keep your forearms to yourself, you know. You don't have to go flaunting them everywhere, so women are forced to touch them because they can't resist temptation."

"Sweetheart," he said in a drawling voice when I started to unsnap the cover that tucked the hood away. "I'm going to say this just once, but I hope you heed me: you have to stop smoking crack first thing in the morning."

"Oh, ha ha, very funny." I glared at him over the width of the car as we rolled down the cover. "I bet you're eating it up, you man, you."

"Eating what up? Hang on—this arm is stuck. There it is. Go ahead, both verbally and physically."

"I bet you love Tabby throwing herself all over your person."

He paused in the act of snapping one of the roof arms into place and had the nerve to look at me like I was the one encouraging strange women to feel me up. "Are you serious?"

"Yes. No. Oh hell, I don't know anymore. I just don't like the fact that you're so handsome women are going to be flocking to you. It's going to be hell living with a man who could beat women off him with a stick."

He stared at me for the count of five, then burst into loud, lengthy laughter.

I waited it out with a jaded look plastered all over my face.

"Oh, Paulie," he said finally, mopping at his eyes. "Only you could imagine that anyone, anyone else in the world would think I'm handsome."

"You are," I said, annoyed that he didn't understand what a burden I had to bear with his manly beauty. "You have a nice nose, and that jaw that makes my knees feel like they are made of pudding, and your eyes are so pretty, I just want to scream. And your chest! Holy hellballs, Dixon, your chest could make a sinner of a saint. I won't even *mention* what your ass could do to people!"

Still chuckling, he came around the car and took me in his arms, then kissed me on my nose. "You are the sweetest woman I know, and I have a very nice mother, sisters, and sisters-in-law. Thank you for thinking I have such a devastating effect on the female population of the world, but I can reassure you in all honesty that the only woman who ever hit on me was drunk and thought I was someone else."

"Don't try to sweet-talk your way out of this," I said, allowing myself to be mollified nonetheless. I'd have to be made of concrete not to be swayed by the lure of his voice and body and hands while he gave me another kiss, this one steamy enough to make me moan into his mouth. My tongue danced around his, and I was thinking seriously of us going back to the room and giving in to our base desires when he finally dragged his mouth away from mine.

"Now that is a kiss that will keep me going through the day," he said, squeezing my butt before returning to his side of the car.

"Just so long as you don't allow other women to put their hands all over you," I said grumpily, smiling to myself because it was clear that he was on his way to being in love with me. No one could put up with the things he put up with unless he was smitten.

Ugh. I hate it when I try to be cheery with myself.

Driving the Flyer in a heavy rain was a serious pain in the ass. It was hard at the best of times, but trying to see through the driving rain with no wipers on the windscreen made for tense driving. And then there was the fact that we had no side windows, so the wind and water blew in, soaking us and making our driving goggles fog up. By the time we reached Daugavpils, we were soaked and uncomfortable.

"Worse," I told Dixon when we stopped at one of the authorized gas stops to refuel, "there's no sign of the blasted cheating Esses."

Dixon glanced toward the car. "I'm glad you said that out of range of the dash cam. We should be careful to keep our opinions to ourselves, at least until Roger proves that they are the ones causing the issues."

"Hrmph." I snorted and made use of the station bathroom before we got back in the wetmobile and headed into Lithuania.

The weather got worse and worse the longer we drove, thunder greeting us when we crossed the border, along with rain that rode the wind until it was almost horizontal hitting the windscreen.

"This is miserable," I said after I finished an hour's stint driving. My arms ached, my hands were cold even in the leather driving gloves, my veil was sodden and dripped water all over me, and my face hurt from squinting to see through the rain.

Dixon and I swapped seats without getting out into the monsoon. He'd been doing the bulk of the driving duties simply because it was hell to steer the Flyer in the onslaught, but I was beginning to think we had better find a spot to pull over and see if we could wait out the storm when Tabby texted me.

August 8
From: Tabby
FYI our car just started making horrible grinding noises and the temp is rising. We're turning around and going to the last petrol station we saw.

August 8
To: Tabby
Oh no! Are you guys OK? Should we turn around?

August 8
From: Tabby
Lord no. We'll catch up once we have a mechanic look at it. Texting Roger to warn him.

I told Dixon what was happening.

"Ask her," he said, peering through the rain, his jaw tight, his fingers white on the steering wheel as he fought to keep the car from veering off the road in the face of the blinding wind and rain. "Ask her if the Essex team got their spare tires."

"Maybe we should stop for a bit," I said, eyeing him with concern. "We can't keep going on like this. We're both wiped out, and we've only been driving for five hours."

"I'll be damned if I get any farther behind them. We're so close, I can almost feel them."

August 8
To: Tabby
Dixon wants to know where the Esses are. I know you're not supposed to tell us, but I assume they are in front of us.

August 8
From: Tabby
Yes. Not far, though, according to Roger.

I contemplated keeping that fact from Dixon, since I knew it would keep him behind the wheel longer than was wise, but he was a grown man and he knew his limits. "They're not far ahead of us."

"Good." A grim smile played with his lips. "This storm is going to be just the break we need. The Zust will have an even harder time than the Flyer in it."

"Why?" I asked, reviewing the mental image of the Essex car.

"It's smaller and lighter. I bet this wind is all but tossing them around the road." He shifted the car into the highest gear, which let us zoom along at a dazzling fifty miles an hour. He brushed at the moisture on his goggles. "Cover yourself up with the blanket, love. No sense in you getting pneumonia."

A warm, fuzzy feeling swept over me at his words. My father had always been overprotective, but I'd never until that moment appreciated how nice it was to have someone concerned for my well-being. I pulled the lap blanket over so it covered his legs as well as mine, and snuggled into his side. "Let me know when you need a break."

Two miles later, we hit the detour. Evidently the storm had been raging in this area for a day and the bridge over a river had been damaged by some flooding upstream. We were rerouted off the highway to a single-lane road that wound through farmland, heading first one direction, then another, but slowly meandering toward a return to the highway.

Or at least that's where I assumed the road led. The sky was so dark, we'd had to turn on our headlights in order to help see, even though it was only four in the afternoon. We bounced along behind a small car that eventually turned off at the entrance to a farm. I felt oddly alone as the Flyer struggled down the pothole-riddled road.

"This is—*ow!*—horrible," I said, wincing when I bit my tongue at a particularly bad rut. "This road is more hole than paved surface."

"If it wasn't for the Essex team—" Dixon started to say, then suddenly swore and wrenched the steering wheel to the side. Looming up out of the near dark was the black shape of a person who was waving his arms. Beyond him was the familiar bulk of an antique car.

"Speak of the devil," I said under my breath when Dixon pulled up and Anton leaned his head in, water streaming off his hat onto Dixon's lap.

"Road's flooded ahead," he said, his breath coming in short gasps. "We only just got the Zust winched back out of it. Thought we might see you."

"Hullo," Sanders said, shoving his head in as well. "We thought we'd see you sooner rather than later. Road's impassible ahead. Stephen is talking to the local farmer to see if we can stay the night with him. Shall we declare a temporary truce?"

"Temporary?" I said, my ire rising.

Dixon patted my hand and said, "That sounds like the sensible thing to do. Is there somewhere we can park the cars out of the rain?"

"That's what Stephen's asking," Sanders replied, and withdrew his head when another figure stumbled around their car toward us.

"You haven't seen Dermott and Clarissa, have you?" Anton asked.

"No. Why?" I felt my nostrils flare, even though I knew it was a far-from-attractive look. "Did the Esses do them in, too?"

Anton didn't even look at me when he answered. "We lost sight of them about an hour back. They were ahead scouting out the road, but then the bridge closed and I think they were on the other side. What?" This last was said in response to a call from Sanders. "Ah. Good." He leaned back in to say, "Looks like the farmer said we can park the cars in his barn."

"What do you think?" I asked Dixon when he carefully backed up the Flyer, turning the great white car to follow the small black Zust down the driveway. "Can we trust this truce that Sanders mentioned?"

"Not for a red-hot minute," Dixon said immediately. "I'll sleep in the car tonight."

"We'll both sleep here," I said, knowing full well I wouldn't be able to sleep while he was guarding the car.

"No need for you to get a crick in your neck, too."

"There's every need. For one, I want to be with you. For another, we're partners in this race and we'll take turns staying awake and guarding the Flyer."

He flashed me a look that made me go all warm and fuzzy again inside. "Have I told you today how wonderful you are?"

"No, but we've had a hell of a drive, so I forgive you."

A very nice couple was on hand to greet us and show Dixon where to put the car (the Zust got the parking spot inside the barn, so Dixon had to make do with a freestanding carport arrangement where the couple's tractor normally sat), then hustled us all inside, where we were given vast quantities of soup and very strong tea.

We changed out of our wet clothing and, since no cameras were around, put on jeans and sweaters. The storm continued to rage, and we spent a few comfortable hours tucked away in the farmhouse, listening to the wind and rain try to beat its way in to us.

"You can sleep with me in my room," the daughter of the house, a pretty girl of about fourteen named Mirea, said in English when night finally claimed the already dark sky. Fortunately, with the darkness came an abatement of the storm. "Mama said the men can sleep downstairs."

I looked at Dixon. He nodded. "That would be lovely. Thank you."

As I followed her upstairs, I heard Dixon say to Sanders, "This truce of yours means we'll all be sleeping in the house, I assume."

"Of course," Sanders answered. "Where else would we sleep?"

I didn't trust him any farther than I could spit, and hoped Dixon didn't, either.

Mirea chatted away for a good half hour before finally getting into bed. "I'll just sit here in the chair for a bit," I told her. "Then I'll check on the car. You don't mind if I come and go, do you?"

"No," she said rather doubtfully. "But I have a nice bed. Mama and Papa just bought it for me."

"I'm sure it's wonderful, but our old car is very delicate, and it has to be checked a lot to make sure it's OK," I fibbed. "And Dixon is tired from doing most of the driving. Whew. Thank god the rain is letting up. I hope it means this storm is finally passing."

A half hour later I slipped down the back stairs and out through the kitchen, then scurried around to where the Flyer was parked. It was covered up to the windscreen in mud and dead bugs, and the interior was almost as wet as the exterior, but it was home, and I crawled over the front seat to claim the back when I landed on something soft that moved. "What the hell? Dixon?" I asked, freezing, half in horror and half in surprise.

"Paulie?"

The blanket beneath me shifted, and the vague image of Dixon's face came into view in the dim light from the house. "What are you doing here?" I asked.

"Protecting the car. I assume you had the same thought as me."

"That the Esses are bastards and not to be trusted any

farther than a snail can spit? Yeah, I had that thought."
He shifted so I could sit on the seat. "But you are pooped.
You shouldn't be out here."

"Neither should you. You'll be much more comfortable in a real bed."

"You're the one who fought the Flyer all day in the
rain. You deserve some serious rest." I made shooing
motions at him. "Go back to the house and get some
sleep. I'll guard the car."

Even through the muted darkness, I could see the
jaded look on his face when he said, "I prefer that you
sleep in comfort, which means you need to return to the
house and get a good night's sleep."

I sighed and slapped my hand on the seat. "We aren't
really going to have an argument about who goes back
to the house, are we?"

"No, but that's because I'm too tired. Would you mind
moving to the front seat? My leg is cramping with you
sitting there."

"Oh, I like that, Mr. I Want You to Be Comfortable.
The front seat isn't anywhere near as comfy as this one."

He nudged me with his toes until I gave in and clam-
bered over to the front seat. "I know it's not, but you're
smaller than me, and you'll fit there better."

I peered over the seat back at him. "We could lie there
on the comfy seat together, you know."

"Are you, by chance, propositioning me, madam?" I
couldn't see his eyebrow rise, but I felt it had done so.

"Depends. Have you ever made out in the backseat of
a car?"

"I can't say that I have."

"Well, I have. When I was sixteen, and Dad had a
newly emigrated friend of a friend whose name was
Misha. He was blond and gorgeous and smelled like rum,
and man alive, did he teach me things about kissing."

"Ah, it's Misha I have to thank for the way your tongue sets fire to my blood?"

"It's only fair since your tongue makes my knees turn to marshmallow. To hell with it. You can just be uncomfortable."

I climbed over the seat again, but this time I first removed the heavy blanket from Dixon, then draped it like a blanket fort over the seats so we were hidden from view. I proceeded to do an intricate and cramped shimmy that rid me of my T-shirt, jeans, and assorted undergarments. "No, don't get up. You can sleep on the seat—after I'm done having my wicked and wholly wanton way with you—and I'll sleep on you. Damn, man, you got out of your pants fast!"

I wasn't even through speaking before Dixon, evidently realizing what was on my mind, had shucked his shoes, socks, pants, and underwear. I helped him pull his shirt over his head before sitting on his thighs, feeling the lovely smooth, warm flesh of his belly and ribs. "I approve of your plan," he told me, taking my breasts in both his hands, which simultaneously pleased my boobs to no end and made me put an immediate halt to my idea of tormenting him with an endless array of touches, licks, and kisses so steamy he'd be putty in my capable hands.

"Putty!" I said mindlessly, writhing around when he sat up enough to take one breast in his mouth.

"Putty is good," he said around a mouthful of nipple. "I like putty. I like both your putties."

"I like a man who likes my putties. Breasts. Nipples. Whatever you want to call it, I like you liking it, but you're not letting me like you."

He stopped molesting one very needy breast, and I felt, rather than saw, the question in his eyes.

I slid my hands up to gently pinch his nipples. He froze beneath me. "You make me so mindless with pleasure

that I can't do the same to you. Lie back. No, my boobs
are fine now. Wet, but fine. They're happy and want me
to return the favor."

"I don't have the same sort of nerves in my nipples
that I understand women have in theirs—" he started to
protest, but the second I bit down ever so gently on one,
he almost came off the seat.

"Putty!" he shouted, and dug his fingers into my hips
when I attended to the second nipple.

I giggled. "I was trying to say that I was putty in your
hands, but that's all that came out. Dixon?"

"Dear god, woman, you're stopping?" He lifted his
head, presumably to glare at me. "Now? Right this
minute?"

"Yes, but only because I'm going to make your eyes
bug right out of your head in the very best cartoon
manner."

"You are? How are you— Lord, yes!"

I had slid down his legs while he was speaking and
taken his penis in both hands. "Now, let me see if I can
do this in the dark."

"Sweetheart, you can do anything to me you want in
the dark," he said with a profound note of gratitude in
his voice.

"Really? I'm going to remember that when the race
is over and I want to tie you down so I can use any number of sexual devices on you."

"What sort of sexual devices?" he asked, sounding very
interested. That made me pause for a moment. We hadn't
ever talked about adult devices, and although I had a single woman's usual collection of items that kept me from
jumping every man I saw, it hadn't occurred to me that he
might have a male-oriented version of my box of toys.

"Do you like toys, too?" I asked, inadvertently wag-
gling his penis as I spoke.

"Depends on the toy, and why are you using my dick to gesture with?"

"Oh." I looked down to where I could barely see the dark blob of his body. "I talk with my hands. Sorry. I expect you'd rather have action now than chitchat anyway, right?"

"Are you, by any chance, nervous about something?"

I sighed and gave his penis a friendly "so glad you understand me" squeeze. "It's the fact that someone could lift the blanket and see us. I've never been an exhibitionist."

"Would you rather we tried to get sleep instead?"

Absently, I tickled his balls. "No. I don't think anyone is going to peek in. And I really am desperate for you. The way your wet shirt stuck to your chest all day—I know it must have been horribly uncomfortable, but holy hellballs, Dixon, it just made me want to lick your entire chest."

He squirmed beneath me, his hips moving with little jerks. "Paulie," he said after a moment where I was remembering his wet-shirt-covered chest. He sounded breathless, as if he had been out jogging.

"Hmm?"

"If you don't stop in the next five seconds, you're bound to be disappointed with my performance."

I stared at the blob that I knew was his head and wondered what the hell he was talking about, until it struck me that his hips were moving faster and faster. "Wow, you really are anticipatory. And so hot. And dammit, are you bigger?"

He laughed, a rough laugh to be true, but still a laugh. And with some maneuvering, he managed to let his fingers go wandering in happy territory, where he was greeted by my intimate parts with much cheering and celebration. "I assure you I'm the same as I've always been."

"Tingle-making," I said, wiggling delightedly when

he hit an exquisite spot in my intimate parts. "Oh dear god, man, what you can do with just two fingers and a thumb!"

"I'd be happy to show you what my mouth can do in addition to my fingers."

"Another time," I said, biting back a groan of purest pleasure. "Would you mind if we did foreplay later? Right now I just want to do an internal measurement of how much bigger you've gotten."

"No, but I warn you that I won't be good for long," he said, his body moving beneath my thighs, his hands moving around to my back, positioning me where he wanted me.

"Good, because that little twirl with your thumb just about pushed me over the edge. Dear god, you are bigger!"

"It's just the angle," he said, panting, his hips moving jerkily while I tried to find a rhythm that worked for both of us. "And if you continue to squeeze me when you sink down, you're going to be very sorry!"

I laughed. "You're the only man I know who can threaten to make me sorry while thrilling me to the tips of my toes." I swiveled while I moved, enjoying the sensation of him so deep inside me, all my little muscles clinging to him, unwilling to let him go, and yet rejoicing with the movements. I leaned down to kiss him, feeling an overwhelming sense of lightness and happiness that I'd found this man. He was everything I wanted, funny and caring and smart. He wasn't the least bit needy, but his comfort with himself didn't lead to arrogance or narcissism. If anything, he was too modest, not realizing just what a wonderful, warmhearted, sexy-as-sin man he was.

"I love you more than anything," I murmured into his mouth just at the moment when his fingers gripped my hips, his body arching underneath me. The short, bucking movements sent me flying into my own orgasm, and it was only when I managed to kick-start my mind a long, long time later that I realized that he hadn't responded.

Dammit, what was wrong with the man? Why couldn't he admit his feelings.

Unless I was totally wrong about what he felt for me.

Oy.

There was a flood in Latvia, one that made it impossible to drive over what was evidently the only bridge in existence, or at least so you would have assumed, judging by the reaction of the local population.

"I'm not saying that I would have wished to drive through flooded areas," I told Paulie that night when we were lying together in the car. "But it is irksome to be here wasting time."

Paulie made a noise of agreement. She was warm and soft and lay draped over me like a delicious woman-scented blanket, the car blanket over top of us. I had a horrible feeling that my left buttock was glued by body moisture to the leather bench of the backseat, but other than making a little wiggle to see how hard it would be to shift the cheek, I decided not to worry about it.

Outside the tractor enclosure in which the Thomas Flyer was parked, the wind periodically gusted, making the thin material of the enclosure's sides flutter in the night. The lights of the house began to extinguish as we snuggled, and despite the fact that I was sleeping in the backseat of a 1908 car, with one butt cheek glued to the seat and Paulie's right elbow digging into my pancreas, I was happier than I ever remembered being.

"I guess I'd feel more like that if the Esses and Anton

weren't trapped here with us. At least we're all on the same footing," she murmured sleepily into my collarbone.

I wrapped my arms around her, feeling like the luckiest man alive. Just being with Paulie made me happy, and knowing she reciprocated all those feelings I'd been hesitant to express filled me with a sense of peace that I hadn't realized had been lacking from my life.

"Now I know what I've been missing," I mused into the top of her head, and gave it a kiss.

"Hmm?" she asked, scooting over until she was half on me and half in the space between me and the seat back.

"Nothing, love. Go to sleep."

"I like it when you call me 'love,'" she said, yawning hugely, and then snuggled into my side and promptly fell asleep.

I had vague notions of staying awake during the night just to make sure no one would try anything with the Thomas Flyer, but lack of sleep, long driving hours in horrible weather, and incredible lovemaking took their toll, and I drifted off without realizing it.

"Hrn?" Something clanged nearby.

"Mrrf?" came the answer from behind me.

I opened my eyes to find that at some point I'd rolled onto the floor and was lying stark naked on top of an oilcloth sheet that we'd used when changing tires. I sat up and met Paulie's blinking eyes. Her hair was standing up on end, sleep creases on one cheek. She squinted at me, and asked, "What are you doing down there?"

"Sleeping. Something woke me up." I grabbed my trousers, which were underneath me, and hurriedly got into them and my shoes before emerging from the car. The flaps of the enclosure moved gently, and I parted them to reveal daylight and a pale blue sky. From the barn emerged the form of a man, who waved and shouted something I didn't understand.

"Good morning," I called back, and waited until Paulie crawled out of the car in her jeans and shirt. "I intended on staying awake, but I guess you having your wanton way with me did me in."

"Can't talk—gotta pee like a racehorse," she said, trotting to the farmhouse.

I went to the side of the barn, remembering the farmer pointing with pride to the toilet and ramshackle sink that had been included in a lean-to that looked like it had been tacked to a wall, and with a cheery nod and wave at the two sons, I used the facilities. I was just heading to the farmhouse with thoughts of country ham and eggs, and perhaps some homemade marmalade, when Paulie burst out of the house, shouting and waving her hands in the air.

"They're gone! Those bastards, I knew it! I knew they would cheat! Hurry up—they have an hour on us!"

"What? How?" I dashed to the main entrance of the barn, swearing profanely at the empty space where the Zust had sat the night before.

"They left us here, those rotters." Paulie was panting when she got to me, her phone in her hand. Behind her, Anton emerged from the house, hopping on one leg while he tied the shoelaces of another shoe.

I paused. "Why is Anton here?"

"They left him behind, too. Oh, I am so going to rat them out to Roger." She started typing frantically on her phone.

Anton got his shoe on properly and met us halfway to the Thomas Flyer. "I just woke up. Is it true? Is the car gone?" he asked.

I waved at the barn. "So it seems. Why did they leave you?"

He made a face. "They wanted to do something to your car, and I said I wasn't having any of it. I'm not saying I wouldn't do many things to make sure my team was ahead of yours, but nothing underhanded. Nothing . . . devious."

"Devious and underhanded like telling the border guards that we were smuggling a weapon into Russia?" I asked.

Anton had the grace to look abashed. "I . . . that . . . I'm profoundly sorry about that. When they explained the plan to me, I thought it would simply mean a little delay for you. I had no idea they would strip-search you and retain you for hours. I'm just glad there was nothing for the guards to find."

Paulie started to say something about the gun, but at a quelling look from me, she changed it to, "Yeah, well, I notice you didn't bother telling Roger what you did."

He spread his hands in a placatory gesture. "I apologized for my part once Roger told me what happened."

"Was it you who took our spare tires?" I asked, one thought leading to another.

"No." He looked profoundly uncomfortable. "I told Sanders that was too underhanded and that, while I wanted to win the race, I didn't think we needed to be dishonest to do it. The Zust is a fast car, and we can easily outrun the Thomas Flyer."

Paulie snorted indignantly and glanced at her phone when it burbled at her.

"I don't understand why they would leave you behind," I said, mulling over what he'd said. I wasn't certain he was telling the truth, but if he wasn't, it meant he had been left behind as a plant. But for what purpose? To slow us up? Or to take us out of the race entirely?

"Got a response from Roger. He says it's not against the rules to leave before us. The idiot." Paulie looked disgusted. "I told him the Esses left Anton behind, and he said that also is not against the rules, although frowned upon, and asked us if we'd give you a lift to Warsaw."

"I'd appreciate that," Anton said, his expression worried.

"I just bet you would." Paulie narrowed her eyes on Anton. "And I'm going to ask you a question, and I expect a straight answer to it."

He stiffened. "I do not make a habit of lying."

"Uh-huh. Are you working for my father?"

He blinked twice. "Who is your father?"

"That's avoiding answering the question. Yes or no — are you working for him?"

"Unless your father is a member of parliament from a small constituency in the north of Scotland, then no, I do not work for him."

Paulie looked startled. "You work in Scotland? But you're Russian."

"I was born in Ukraine, but my parents emigrated shortly thereafter." He frowned at Paulie. "Who is your father?"

"The carpet king of Northern California." She chewed her lower lip. "Damn. That means I was all wrong about you."

I caught her eye and tried to mentally warn her about throwing all her trust in him when I wasn't convinced he wasn't working against us, but she was busy reading another text. "Roger says they're all stuck about ten miles back and are going to ditch the cars because of flooding between us and them. Wait — there's more . . . *taking a train to Warsaw*. They'll meet us there. Oh, good — we don't have to dress up until we get there. Come on. If the roads are as bad as Roger says, maybe the Esses are not zooming ahead of us."

She texted wildly while moving toward the car. I ran

inside the farmhouse, gathered up my suitcase as well as Paulie's, thanked the farmer's wife, and offered a handful of euros, which she refused. Anton was ahead of me with his own bag, which he tossed into the back of the car. I emerged from the house with a paper bag with warm muffins.

"Tabby and Sam are with Roger and the other film crew, and they said they heard on the news that all sorts of roads are washed out," Paulie said, turning to glare at Anton.

He shrugged and held up his hands. "I have nothing to do with their decision, I assure you."

"Hrmph."

"Lovely news," I said grimly, and tossed our luggage into the car. "At least it's not raining anymore."

"I'll take the first shift." Paulie took the key from me and slid over behind the steering wheel. "You eat and get some rest. You can't have slept well on the floor."

I climbed in next to her and was prepared to dispute the fact that I was sore and stiff, but was distracted when she started the car.

Immediately, the engine started knocking loudly.

"What the hell?" Paulie asked.

I sighed and got out, taking off my goggles and hat, both of which I'd automatically put on. "Keep it running. I'll take a look," I said, unstrapping the bonnet and pushing it back to stare down at the engine with incomprehension. Anton was at my elbow when I tried to find something that looked wrong. The knocking was even louder, and I could see an oily yellow puddle under the car.

"The hell?" I asked, prodding at a piece that did nothing.

The farmer came out at the noise and was soon joined by his sons.

"What's going on?" Paulie called.

"I don't know what the problem is. Everyone is looking and talking, but I don't speak the language."

"They say it's a crank bearing," Anton translated, asking
a question of the men. "We can't drive the car with it this
way. It would be very bad. The oil has been drained as well."

By this time, Paulie had joined us and swore under her
breath. Her fingers found mine and tightened in a show
of support and comfort. I squeezed them in return, grateful for the fact that she was there, shouldering the burden
of the car alongside me. It boded well for our future.

"Ah. Yes?" Anton held up a hand when Paulie asked
him what was going on. The oldest son ran for the house,
calling loudly to his mother as he did so. "Yes, yes, that
is good. It seems that our host knows of another farmer
who used to be a mechanic. They are calling him to come
and look at the engine."

"The engine that your team sabotaged," Paulie said,
and suddenly opened her eyes wide and sucked in approx-
imately half the air in the yard. She turned to look at me,
horrified.

"What?" I asked her.

She glanced at Anton and leaned into me. "They did
something to the car. While we were in it."

"Ah." I thought about that for a moment before
answering softly, "We had the blanket over us, if that is
what you are worried about."

"Still." She shivered and released my hand to rub her
arms. "It gives me the creeps to know they were poking
around the engine while we—"

I whispered in her ear, "While I was poking around
you?"

She made a delightful little half snort, half laugh, and
pinched my side.

"What do you know about this?" I asked Anton a few

minutes later, when he was done conversing with the farmer.

"I'm no expert on engines," he said, shaking his head.

"I meant about the sabotage. It's clear that your team is taking whatever steps are necessary to leave us in the dust."

"And I told you both that I refused to have anything to do with that sort of thing," Anton said firmly.

I looked closely at his face, but saw no signs of deception. I didn't put much stock in that, however. Despite his having been briefly a member of my team, I hardly knew him.

Half an hour or so later the mechanic arrived, along with three other men, and in no time there was a party around the engine. Tool chests were brought out, cloths were spread on the still-damp ground, and men donned filthy overalls in order to get underneath the big car.

Paulie watched and fretted, worrying aloud about how far the Essex team could get. I kept an eye on Anton, and a closer one on the men who started taking apart the engine. As each piece came off, the men would gather around it, examining it and holding a comprehensive discussion before moving on to the next piece.

Irritation and impatience rode high on me, but I repeatedly bit back the demands that they put the engine back together and just let us go on our way, knowing the engine would not stand up to travel in its damaged state.

Almost five hours later, we waved our good-byes again, my wallet quite a bit lighter after the repairs had been made.

"I'll reimburse you for my half of the cost," Paulie told me when I got behind the wheel. "Or better yet, we'll make Roger pay for it, since it was caused by the team he insists isn't behind all the trouble we've had."

"I'm not concerned about the money," I said, peering through the grubby windscreen. "It's the head start the Essex car has that worries me."

Anton sighed. "I wish I had some reassurance to offer, but alas, there is nothing I can say other than I regret my teammates have chosen this path."

"Oh, come on," Paulie said, shooting a glare over her shoulder to him. "You can't honestly expect us to believe you had no idea the Esses were responsible for damning the entire race from start to finish?"

"No, I assure you I did not. Yes, I knew they told the customs officials about you having a gun, but you didn't have one, so you were only slightly delayed. And I did know they intended to take all your tires, but Stephen was only able to get a few before someone came by the car. I felt you had enough left to see you through until Roger could replace what you were missing. As I said, those are regrettable instances, but I hardly see how that's damned the entire race."

"Don't belabor the point," I told her softly. "He will only deny it and you will simply seethe. I'd much rather you had a look at the GPS unit and see if there are alternative routes indicated."

We drove with few breaks for the rest of the day, sometimes able to follow the main route mapped out by the race officials, other times being led on lengthy detours. Mindful that the Essex team had at least a five-hour head start, we took turns driving with only necessary stops for petrol and to relieve ourselves. Anton had offered to take his turn driving, but it wasn't until we'd been in the car for eight hours that we finally took him up on his offer and allowed him to take the wheel, although I made sure I was next to him, awake and aware.

Just in case he had any ideas.

It was after midnight by the time we reached Warsaw.

We stopped at the first available hotel on the outskirts of the city and took two rooms.

"Get some sleep," I told Paulie when we straggled into our room. "I'm going to take a shower."

She collapsed on the bed, lifting a wan hand. "I'd join you, but I think I'd fall asleep even assuming your fabulous body all wet and soapy and naked was pressed against me. Damn."

"Damn?"

She yawned hugely. "I like you wet and soapy and naked, but I just don't have the energy to do anything about it."

I smiled. "Another time you may work your wiles, all right?"

"Deal," she said, and moaned when she snuggled herself into the mattress.

I had a shower, scraped away the worst of my beard, and donned fresh clothing. When I emerged from the steamy bathroom, Paulie was sound asleep. I pulled off her shoes and tucked her beneath the sheets, stroking back a strand of black hair that fell over her face, looking down at the woman who had so completely barged into my life and turned everything upside down.

I thought about my life back at Ainslie Castle, where I was a glorified clerk stuck in a job that anyone could do. Elliott's wife, Alice, was more than capable of doing the work, and it had crossed my mind more than once to simply turn it over to her. But what would I do then? I wasn't trained to do anything but estate management, and how could I ask Paulie to live with me, to love me, when I had nothing to offer her?

I sighed. I'd have to stay a steward. At least then I had the gamekeeper's cottage to offer Paulie as a home, and enough of a salary to feed and clothe her.

The night air was soft and warm when I left the hotel

room, making sure it was locked before I retraced my steps to the parking lot. We'd pulled the Thomas Flyer into a spot that couldn't be seen from the street, but there was no parking lot attendant we could pay to watch the car. "Well," I told it, shaking out the blanket, "at least this time I shouldn't end up on the floor."

I slept fitfully for three hours; then Paulie came down to find me. "What are you doing here?" she asked, waking me up. It was light out.

"Sleeping," I said, rubbing my face. "And guarding the car."

"Dammit, you should have woken me, and I'd have slept out here with you. Come on." She tugged me until I was in a sitting position. "I slept like the dead, so I can drive first thing. Let's get some breakfast in you, and then we'll go dump Anton on Roger, wherever he is, and get back to catching up to those stinking cheaters."

I allowed her to pull me from the car and give me a push toward the hotel rooms. "We shouldn't leave the car alone—"

"It's not going to be alone," she said, settling in the backseat and pulling out a small notebook. "Go eat. Take another shower if you want—I've had mine. And when you're ready to leave, get Anton out here."

I left her to her writing, making a mental note to jot down my thoughts just as soon as we were on the road again. "At least this time I have something interesting to write about," I said aloud while I made my way to our room. "It'll need a lot of editing, but there's a good deal of meat to it. Maybe too much. Hmm. Will have to consult another travel journal to see how they balance real life with interesting facts . . ."

Paulina Rostakova's Adventures

AUGUST 10
6:22 p.m.
Backseat of car, en route from Prague to Munich
Note to self: Copy this over to journal as soon
as I can find it

Writing a quickie update while Dixon is driving. He had a long sleep earlier this morning when we left Prague—poor guy hasn't had a lot of rest lately, what with the damned Essex team cheating all over the place.

Where did I leave off? There's been so much going on that I can't remember, and my journal is in my bag, strapped to the back of the car. Let's see . . . We got into Warsaw in the middle of the night and crawled into the nearest hotel. I crashed as soon as we got there, but Dixon, bless his heart, slept in the car to guard it against Anton (or the other members of his team).

"I have to admit," I told Dixon about six hours later, when we left a brief meeting with Roger, the two film crews, and Anton, "that Anton seems innocent of wrongdoing. I mean, he didn't do anything to the car when he drove."

"I was watching him pretty closely to make sure he didn't," Dixon answered, and yawned.

"You climb into the back and sleep," I told him. "I'll drive for a few hours. No, don't object—I can see how tired you are. Your normally devastatingly handsome face has lines of strain all over it."

He gave me a look of mock horror. "All over it?"

"Yes. Like plaid, crisscrossing hither and yon. Get some sleep before I change my mind about being in love with a man with a plaid stress face."

He bit my ear, but climbed into the back and dropped off almost immediately.

Two hours later, while I was fueling the car, Tabby and Sam stopped behind me. Roger had opted to take a train to Berlin, where he and the other film crew would rent a car and drive back toward Warsaw until they found the Essex car.

I glanced into the backseat, but Dixon was still asleep. Gesturing at Tabby, I pulled her away a few yards and said, "I know you're not supposed to tell me, but this is important. Those bastards cheated by sabotaging our engine and made us at least five hours late. Do you know where they are?"

"Yes," she said without a second's hesitation. "They're en route to Berlin. They should be there in the next couple of hours."

"Sons of seagulls," I swore, doing a mental calculation. It would take us more than six hours to get there. "Thanks for telling me, and not being all 'It's against the rules' and so on."

She gave me a little smile. "I might be more strict about it except Sam overheard Dermott telling the Esses you were just arriving in Warsaw. If their camera crew can help them, then I figure it's fair for us to do the same."

"Bless you," I said, giving her a quick hug. "I really appreciate it. We need all the help we can get."

"Then you'll love this tidbit—" She glanced around

and leaned in close to say, "You have a chance to catch up. Not just catch up, but pass them, if you can drive all night. I know Roger doesn't want you doing that, but if you and Dixon take turns sleeping, you might just pull it off."

"But they're still so far ahead of us—"

"They are, and they know it. And they've had a long, hard day after several long, hard days, and they have to be just as tired as you are. So with their lead time well in the bag, I don't doubt they'll spend the night in Berlin before setting off early in the morning."

"Yeah, but they wouldn't want to risk losing their lead."

She gave a half shrug. "Dermott told them you and Dixon looked like hell. No doubt the Essex team will assume that, even if you make it to Berlin tonight—and you know it won't be until at least midnight before you do so—you'll be too tired to do more than limp into town and collapse."

I gave her a keen eyeing. "How are you feeling, Tabby?"

"Me?" She looked startled.

"Slept well the last few nights, have you? Up to some hard-core driving?"

She grinned and punched me lightly on the arm. "I am. We both are. If you can do it, we can do it. Just don't leave us behind like in that rainstorm."

"Deal," I said, and shook her hand.

An hour later Dixon woke up feeling much better.

"I am pleased to inform you," I said, climbing into the backseat so I could get some rest, "that you no longer have a plaid face. I will continue to love you."

"You could do better, you know," he said in a light tone, and once again I was possessed with a doubt about his true feelings. Damn the man—why couldn't he just

come right out and tell me what he felt? Why did he have
to dance around the subject?

He had to love me. At least a little. He couldn't sleep
with me and want to marry someone else. Could he?

Damn him!

August 10
From: Tabby
You're swerving a lot. You guys OK?

August 10
To: Tabby
Yeah.

August 10
From: Tabby
*You know, there are no more autobahns here, right?
You can't just drive crazy like that.*

August 10
To: Tabby
*We know. I was trying to . . . uh . . . Dixon was being
all . . . um . . . never mind.*

August 10
From: Tabby
You didn't try to give him a BJ while driving, did you?

August 10
To: Tabby
Of course not!

August 10
To: Tabby
As if I would!

August 10
To: Tabby
*We are not the blow-jobs-in-a-car sort of people,
thank you very much!*

August 10
From: Tabby
Oh?

August 10
To: Tabby
*If you must know, I was trying to seduce him into tell-
ing me he loves me. By nibbling on his jaw. Nothing
more. OK, my hand was on his thing. But that's it.*

August 10
From: Tabby
You what?

August 10
To: Tabby
*Thigh! Leg thigh! Not thing. Stupid, stupid
autocorrect.*

August 10
To: Tabby
*You think he loves me, don't you? You and Sam see
everything.*

August 10
To: Tabby
*Tabby? You there? You were supposed to reassure me
that Dixon loves me and wants me and will marry me
because my dad won't let me live in sin. Although I think
that sounds like a lot more fun than living in non-sin.*

August 10
To: Tabby
TABBY???

August 10
From: Tabby
Sorry. Was reading something to Sam.

August 10
To: Tabby
You didn't answer my text. Don't think I didn't notice that.

August 10
To: Tabby
I knew it. He hates me. Sigh.

Paulina Rostakova's Adventures

AUGUST 14
9:14 a.m.
Paris, France. At. Effing. Last.

I'm going to do this properly and not foreshadow one damned thing. No, sir. It's all proper reporting, all the way. I am Nellie Bly personified! Except there's no way I'd have myself committed to an insane asylum, because I just know they'd do electroshock therapy on me, and just the thought of that weirds me out.

Where was I? Oh yeah, doing this properly.

We got into Berlin in the middle of the night. I don't know what time it was, because we only stopped long enough to get food and gas in the car, and have a potty break. We alternated driving and napping in the backseat. I won't say I slept every time I was back there, but I did my best to rest so that I was wide-awake and properly safe when it was my turn to drive. We crawled into Prague just as the sun was coming up.

August 11
To: Tabby
You guys OK? I don't see you.

August 11
From: Tabby
Tabby is sleeping. We're getting petrol. Probably about ten minutes behind you. Sam.

August 11
To: Tabby
We're all out, and going to find an out-of-the-way hotel. Will send you address.

August 11
From: Tabby
Thank god. I wasn't sure how much longer I could drive. My eyes are crossing. Sam.

"I think we're close to breaking Sam," I told Dixon from where I was bundled up in the backseat. "He says his eyes are crossing."

"I'm long past that state. I think mine have turned into glass," Dixon said in a voice that was rough with exhaustion. "What about this place?"

I peered out at the nondescript hotel. "Works for me. What street are we on? I'll send it to Sam."

"I'm going to have to sleep in the car again," Dixon said tiredly when we got a room and unloaded just what we needed to get through the next handful of hours.

"You don't really think the Esses are going to find us?" I asked, rubbing my face. My eyes burned, my ears were buzzing slightly from the constant noise of driving in a convertible, and my body felt like it was bound to lead weights. "Even if they leave Berlin now, and if we sleep four hours, would they be looking for us here?"

"It's not just them." He stretched, grimaced, did a couple of stretches to loosen up his back muscles, and waved when

Sam pulled in beside us. "Anyone could poke around the car if we leave it unguarded, and we're too close to the end to risk losing out because we both want to sleep in a bed."

I eyed him. Behind me, Sam woke up Tabby and helped her from the car. She murmured something at us and stumbled off to get a room. "It's your turn to sleep in the bed. I'll stay in the car."

"Don't do this, Paulie," Dixon said wearily, and, taking my hand, escorted me to our room. He dropped his bag of essentials and made a circle gesture. I spun around and waited while he unhooked the white pearl buttons on the back of my champagne-colored blouse and unlaced the corset.

I scratched my belly and back with sighs of happiness and unhooked my pale pink skirt with darker pink pin-stripes. "I'm not trying to be obnoxious," I told him.

He headed for the bathroom, peeling off bits of his suit as he went. "I'm too tired to point out that a woman sleeping alone in a car is more vulnerable than a man, not to mention I wouldn't allow you to put yourself in danger like that while I lolled about in comfort."

"But it's OK for me to be lolling?" I called after him, shucking the last of my clothes and slipping into a pair of sleeping shorts and T-shirt. "We can both sleep in the car."

He poked his head out and gave me a stern look that, for some reason, made me want to giggle. I blamed lack of sleep. That and the fact that he was so endearingly adorable. "Stop being noble. You'll get better sleep in the bed, and that will allow you to drive more. I'll be fine on the backseat."

"I have fond memories of that backseat," I said loudly over the sound of the water he'd turned on. I thought about arguing the fact with him but decided in the end that he was right—I would be more vulnerable alone in the car, and if I got a better quality of sleep, I could take on the bulk of the driving. And we were close, so very close to reaching Paris . . .

I didn't realize I'd fallen asleep until a buzzing noise sounded next to my head. I rolled over and saw that Dixon had set the alarm on my phone. It was almost ten in the morning.

"Holy shitsnacks!" I leaped up, made speedy ablutions, and tried to stuff myself back into my skirt and shirt but couldn't get the corset closed properly. Hurriedly, I texted Dixon to come back to the room to tighten me, then sent a wake-up text to Tabby.

Less than half an hour later we were on the road.

"We're going to push for Paris," I told Tabby when she loaded her luggage into their little blue car. Sam was busy stowing the video equipment he'd charged up during our brief break. "It should be about ten hours, plus time for stops. We figure twelve hours ought to do it. Will you guys be OK with that?"

"We'll be dead tired at the end, but yes, that's all right," Tabby said, then gave me one of her arm punches. "I think you have a good shot at winning."

I flashed her a grin and, with my eyes on Sam, asked quietly, "Does that mean you know something about the location of the Essex boys?"

"Only that Anton is with them again, and Roger knows where we are," she said cryptically, but her eyes were smiling.

I fought back the urge to do a little song and dance right there, instead taking my place behind the wheel while Dixon went around the car, doing his usual pre-setoff check. Sam filmed us waving as we headed out of the parking lot, but he didn't see me throw up my arms and let out a big "Woo-hoo!"

"What's that for?" Dixon asked, looking mildly startled. "Was the bed really that good?"

"It felt like baby bottoms and fluffy clouds, but that's not why I was celebrating. Tabby didn't say so much, but the Esses are behind us. It's sunny, we have good roads between here and Paris, and I feel like I could drive for hours and hours!"

"I'm glad to hear all of that." He gave me a warm smile that I wanted to investigate further, but I was driving, so instead I asked him how he slept.

"Moderately well. I think my body is getting used to the backseat." He rubbed the back of his neck. "I'm a little stiff but, like you, feel like I can drive without killing us."

"That's good, because—"

I never finished that sentence. At the moment I was speaking, we'd left Prague proper and were on the road that would take us near Pilsen, when a sleek black Mercedes passed us. As there were two lanes, I didn't think anything about it, but the minivan in front of us evidently didn't see them and made a left turn directly ahead of the Mercedes. The van and Mercedes, locked together, veered off into the barrier with a horrible scream of brakes and tearing metal. They slammed into a sign, sending it first careening into the van, then rebounding back toward us. I had hit the brakes as soon as I'd seen the Mercedes hit the van, but wasn't able to avoid the sign crashing onto the Flyer's hood and bouncing up to smash into the windscreen, which shattered into a billion pieces. The Flyer spun out to the side as I wrenched the wheel, while ahead of us the van finally came to a halt on the shoulder. Brakes behind us squealed as traffic came to a stop.

"Holy— Are you all right?" I asked Dixon at the same time he unsnapped his seat belt and asked me, "Are you hurt?"

"No," I said, looking down at my lap. My lovely skirt was covered with little squares of glass. "Although I'm thankful they used safety glass in the windscreen, because we could have been shish-kebabed by glass otherwise."

Dixon was out of the car before I finished speaking, running toward the van. A few people behind us pulled over onto the shoulder to see if they could help, but there was a lane left open and many drivers simply crept by and proceeded on their way.

It took me a minute to get my shaking hands under control, but I could see Dixon up at the crumpled wreck of a van, pulling people out. A couple of other people ran to the Mercedes, but from the looks on their faces, I feared the worst. I got out of the car, shook off all the little squares of glass, and hurried over to where two children were sitting on the side of the road, their heads bloody, but apparently all right otherwise. The driver looked like she was in worse shape.

"Is there anything I can do?" I asked Dixon when he helped a third child out. "Should I get a blanket? Water?"

"Blankets would probably be good. These kids are pretty shaken up."

I ran back to the car and fetched our backseat blanket, then wrapped it around two of the children who were sitting together, clutching each other and sobbing. In the distance, sirens began to grow louder. Coming from the other direction, a police car suddenly pulled onto the shoulder and the cop darted across traffic to climb the barrier.

"Can we help?" Tabby asked breathlessly when she and Sam made it through the crawl of traffic. I could see that she'd pulled over behind the Flyer.

"I don't think so. There's a cop here now, and it sounds like the EMTs are on their way." I turned to speak and felt my jaw drop at the sight of the car that slowly made its way past us.

Sanders was at the wheel of the Zust, shaking his head and tsk-ing. He didn't say anything, just drove on. In the backseat, Anton gave us an apologetic smile.

"What's—" Tabby turned and saw the back of the Zust. "What the hell? How did they get here? Roger said they were spending the night in Berlin!"

"They left early," I said. "Probably at the crack of dawn. No doubt they wanted to put more distance between us. Dammit all to hell and back again. Dixon!"

I ran back to Dixon, who was standing with the policeman, speaking in flawless German, telling him what we saw and who we were.

"I hate to interrupt, but our competition just drove past," I said in his ear. "If you think we need to stay and help out, I won't complain, but if we aren't needed, we really should get a move on."

"We aren't needed, but we can't drive without a windscreen," he said, glancing back at the Flyer. "It's dangerous."

"Life is dangerous," I told him, grabbing him by the wrist and pulling him with me toward the Flyer. Sam, who was filming us, followed. "But a life lived in fear is a life half lived. Come on. We have cheaters to catch up to!"

Unfortunately, it wasn't quite as easy as jumping in the car and zooming off. First we had to clean out all the glass from the windscreen. Then Dixon used a wrench to knock out the remaining snaggly shards that clung to the frame. He insisted I text Roger about the accident.

August 12
From: Roger
You can't drive without a windscreen! It's illegal!!!
You'll have to get it replaced.

August 12
To: Roger
Come on! The Esses just passed us! We have to
go now.

August 12
From: Roger
You cannot proceed without a windscreen. Rules say so.

August 12
From: Roger
Go to nearest repair shop. Then you can continue.

"Goddammit!" I snarled, then pulled up a list of windscreen replacement businesses around us. "OK, there's one half a mile from here, just off the highway."

"One what?" Dixon asked, brushing out the last of the glass. Tabby and Sam exchanged glances.

"Car repair. I don't know that they have windscreens for 1908 cars in stock, but they will have to give us something."

"Oh dear," Tabby said softly.

I pointed a finger at her and got behind the wheel. "None of that, missy. That's disparaging talk, and I won't have any of it."

She saluted and ran for their car when I started up the Flyer.

"You are aware that it will take hours for them to replace the windscreen," Dixon said quietly when I waved at someone who'd let us into the stream of traffic.

"Normally, yes, but we're going to put the full pressure of a reality TV show on this place and hope for the best." I took a quick glance at him. His face was grim. "It's not over until it's over, Dixon. Anything can happen in the next twelve hours."

"That is most certainly true," he agreed, but I had a feeling it wasn't in a good way.

The windscreen business we found was run by young, enthusiastic car aficionados who greeted the arrival of the Flyer with cries of delight. When Dixon requested a new windscreen, they pointed out they would have to custom shape the glass to fit the frame.

"Can you replace the existing frame with a new one?" Dixon asked the most excited of the men.

"No," one of the other men said, but was quickly drowned out by the other two.

I asked Dixon what the men said, my German being scant enough that I didn't catch much of the conversation.

"The first one said they can do a new windscreen, but it won't look right, and the second man said that it won't match."

"Tell them we care about function, not appearance."

"I have done so."

The second man whipped out a tape measure to measure the existing frame and gestured to his buddies. It didn't take them long to unbolt the existing frame, but they had to weld parts of the new one onto the car.

"I'm telling Roger that we're getting the windscreen replaced," I told Dixon a while later, when he asked me who I was texting. "But I am not telling him that we're welding it to the car. He might freak out about that."

"He's bound to notice," Dixon said when I sent the text. "We'll have to pay for putting the car back to its previous state."

I grinned at him and thought to myself what an astonishingly nice man he was. "Yeah, but he won't see until we're in Paris, and I'm fine with paying to have the original window put back on. We can toss the frame into the back, so they can reglass it. Oh, good. Roger says he's leaving the film crew with the Esses and taking a train to make sure he's in Paris before we get there."

Dixon took a long breath and gave me a curious look before pulling me up against his chest. He kissed my forehead. "You know we're going to end up well behind them. We will give it our best attempt, because to do anything else would be the sheerest folly, but I don't want you upset by the fact that we were held up by an accident and they weren't."

I bit his chin. "I'm not going to be upset if we do our best and lose. I will be upset if we give up, though. You don't want to stop, do you?"

"Hell, no!" The little laugh lines around his eyes crinkled delightfully, and he pinched my butt while adding, "We're going to give those blaggards a run for their money, as you Yanks say."

"I love it when you go all British on me."

"Then you're going to love tonight, my adorable one, because I plan on Britishing all over you."

"Oooh. Deal."

One of the men came up to report to Dixon at that point, so I had to stop flirting, but I sat in a warm glow of happiness until the car was ready to go.

Two hours later, we hit the road with a makeshift windscreen in place. It was big—poking out at awkward angles and reinforced by a couple of bars welded onto the side of the car in the role of support struts—but it was a windscreen, and we had Roger's blessing to resume the race.

"Floor it," I told Dixon when we left the parking lot.

"I will drive as fast as I safely can," he answered, giving the windscreen a dubious look. "I want to see how this holds up before I go our max speed."

"Caution is good, but catching up is also— What on earth is the matter with Sam and Tabby?" I looked behind us to where they were driving, Sam tapping on his horn to sound out a tattoo of warning.

"I don't know. Perhaps something is wrong with the car." Dixon pulled over into the parking lot of another shop and got out of the car, looking at the rear of it when Sam parked behind him. Tabby leaned out of the window, waving her phone at him. Dixon went over, spoke to her for a minute, then returned to the car.

"Can you pull up your GPS?" he asked, climbing in behind the wheel.

"Sure, but we stay on this road for a couple of hours."

He gave a look that a cat might have given after having eaten a small, particularly tasty bird. "It appears there's been an overturned lorry carrying toxic refuse just before the border, and the road is closed for a few hours while they clean up. Traffic is backed up for miles. We are to look for a detour."

"Oh. All right." I pulled up the GPS and told it to look for alternate routes, since it hadn't updated with the road closure. "How did Tabby hear about it?"

Dixon was silent. I glanced up at him, a bit startled by the warmth in his eyes. "Roger told her."

I narrowed my eyes on him. "OK, why are you looking at me like that?"

He started the car and tipped my phone so he could see the alternate route. "Perhaps it's because I like looking at you. Or that I like watching your face, which is charming on its own, but it also displays what you're thinking. Or it might be that Roger mentioned the holdup because he and the Essex team are stuck right in the middle of it."

Chills rippled down my spine as I yelled a hooray. "Holy guacamole! They're stuck? In a traffic jam?"

"One that is expected to take at least two hours, and

possibly three, before the traffic is routed off the con-
taminated area."

"Hoobah!" I shouted. "Karma's a bitch, eh, Essex
boys?"

Dixon laughed, and we headed out, taking it easy for
a few miles until his confidence in the replaced windscreen grew. We ended up taking a route that headed us
farther south than we needed, but when we crossed the
border back into Germany, Tabby reported that Roger
had only just made it to the train station.

"We've got them," I told Dixon when he read Tabby's
text to me. "This race is ours."

"Don't get cocky now," he warned, and nodded toward
the road. "Stay focused, and we'll see. It's going to be
close, since they are farther north than we are, but it's
entirely possible that, if nothing else hits us, we will make
Paris before them."

We had six hours of driving ahead of us at that point,
and I swear we felt every single second of it. We started
counting down the miles on the last one hundred, and
by the time we were seeing signs that gave the distance
to Paris, we were nervous wrecks. We knew from Tabby
that the Essex team was also in France but, because of
our detour, on a different route than ours.

"Ten kilometers," I said, reading the sign that flashed
by us. Dixon had the Flyer pushed to its limits now, the
engine and wind roaring away at us, bugs and dirt splat-
tering not only the car and window but our goggles, faces,
and clothing. Every now and again, when it was safe to
do so, Tabby drove alongside us and Sam hung out of
their car and filmed us.

"Five kilometers." I gripped the logbook with nervous
sweaty hands and checked the clock on my phone. It was
dark now, the night air cooling down with a hint of rain
and the lights of the suburbs and oncoming traffic started

blurring. Neither one of us had rested since we crossed into France, and I felt slightly nauseous. I realized with a start that we hadn't eaten since breakfast.

"You know where we're going?" Dixon asked for the third time.

I would have pointed out that fact, but knew he was just as nervous as me, so instead I pulled open the logbook to the printed map of Paris and instructions on the building where we were to meet. "The automobile museum on rue Béarnaise, yes. I have GPS ready once we hit our exit."

"Three kilometers now," he said, and flashed a grin at me. "We gave it a good shot even if we didn't do it."

"Do you think Roger would tell us if they got there before us?" I asked, breathing deeply to keep the nausea at bay.

"No. That's why Sam is sticking so close on our tail—they want to film us arriving, and our surprise at winning . . . or losing."

"Can I punch the Esses if we lose?"

"No, but you can write rude things in your journal about them," he said, laughter rich in his voice. "I certainly plan on doing so. One kilometer. Which exit?"

I reminded him for the fifth time of the exit, and then gave him the next couple of turns he needed to make after that as we came into Paris proper.

"I feel like there should be a brass band waiting for us, but here it is almost two in the morning and everyone is asleep. Golly, Dixon. We've driven around the world!"

"It certainly seems like it, doesn't it?"

"OK, we flew across the ocean, but still, we drove from New York City and here we are in Paris." Excited ripples of goose bumps prickled on my arms at the lights of Paris, shining brightly even at the ungodly hour. "Left at rue Béarnaise, then get in the right lane and make a right at the next intersection. It should be on the right side of the street. Oh man. I think I'm going to be sick."

He shot me a startled look. "Should I pull over?"

"You do and I'll strangle you where you sit," I said, gritting my teeth and ignoring the fact that Tabby had pulled alongside us again with Sam hanging precariously out of the window. I refused to turn to face him, instead nervously watching the road ahead as Dixon made each turn. "There it is!" I shouted, pointing.

Two blocks away a sign indicated the automobile museum. Dixon, with more presence of mind than I had, calmly pulled into the parking lot and proceeded around to the back of the building, where a couple of bright arc lights had been set up along with an awning and a cluster of people. There was a handful of cars there, but as I worriedly ran my eyes over them, wave after wave of goose bumps rippled down my back. "They aren't here! We did it! Holy hellballs, we did it! Dixon!"

"We did it—I know, I heard you!" he said, laughing as he came to a stop. Behind us, Sam burst from his car and circled around to catch our faces on camera. Roger, all smiles and with a big bouquet of flowers, broke free from the group of production assistants and network officials who had evidently stayed up all night to meet us.

"Congratulations, Sufferin' Suffragettes, our New York City to Paris race winners!" Roger said loudly, and paused while everyone applauded. Tabby did a little congratulatory dance behind Sam as I stood up in the car and whooped, then allowed Dixon to help me out of the car.

"We won, we won. We beat those"—I caught Dixon's eye and changed what I was going to say—"worthy opponent Esses. We won! I can't believe it! We won!"

And then I threw up all over the ground, only narrowly missing Dixon's feet.

Paulina Rostakova's Adventures

Had to stop writing in midexplanation of what happened when my father suddenly appeared in my hotel room. Which is also Dixon's hotel room, and since he was having a long shower to try to . . . Wait. Let me do this in the correct order. Man, that foreshadowing stuff is insidious.

"That's going to make the gag reel," I heard Tabby say when I clutched my pink skirt and tried to ralph up my guts.

"Literally," Sam agreed.

"Good god! Are you drunk or ill?" Roger said, doing a fast sidestep to get out of the way.

Dixon, a man of fast reflexes, not only moved out of the danger zone but also had the presence of mind to gather up my veil and hold it back so it didn't fall into the mess.

"Sorry," I said when my stomach stopped dry heaving. "I think it was nerves. It's been so stressful these last few hours, and we didn't have food or water, and I feel a bit woozy to be honest . . ."

Dixon flung my veil over his shoulder and caught me

when I weaved forward, pulling me well back from the puddle of bile and saliva. To my utter surprise, he slid an arm under my legs and lifted me up in the very best He-Man move. "Paulie is a bit overcome by all of this. Is there somewhere she can sit and have some water?"

Roger turned around in a full circle, but there weren't a lot of seating options in the parking lot behind a car museum. In the end, I sat on the running board of the Flyer and sipped a little champagne that Roger opened. I felt somewhat isolated, in a little cocoon of happiness, the bubbles from the champagne tickling my nose in a delightful way. In front of me, shielding me from the camera, Dixon stood chatting with Roger and the network people, telling them all about our adventures driving from Prague.

He was giving me time to recover, bless his heart. I suddenly had to know whether or not he loved me, and decided that there was no time like the present to figure out if I was going to spend the rest of my life with him. I tugged on the back of his suit coat. When he turned to look down at me, I repressed a hiccup and asked, "Who is the woman, Dixon?"

He looked confused. "Who is what woman?"

"The woman you intend on wooing properly, not sleeping with in a ramshackle mode as we are doing."

"Ramshackle . . . Paulie, what are you talking about?"

I stood up carefully, holding on to him for balance. "What I mean, sir, is whether or not you intend on honoring the marriage that we pretended to have? Because my dad is not going to let me just shack up with you, not that I even know if you want me to, because you haven't said so, you annoying man."

"Ow." He rubbed the spot on his chest that I'd punched when I spoke the last words. "I did tell you. I said that, this time, I wanted to do things properly. It's important."

I gawked at him for a minute, then said, "It's important to properly ask me to stay with you? That's what you're talking about, right? Me? Not someone else who you don't know, because you're not the kind of guy who'd sleep with one woman while planning on being proper with another woman?"

He took the glass of champagne from my hand. "I think you're a little tiddly."

"Probably. But I'm also madly in love with you, and tired of the mean part of my brain telling me that because you haven't said you love me, too, that means you are going to dump me, at which point I may well consider talking to my dad's bodyguards about ways to geld an Englishman."

He laughed and pulled me into an embrace, saying into my ear, "I would kiss you, but I suspect it wouldn't be the enjoyable experience either of us would hope for."

"Ew. No. No kissing until I sterilize my mouth." I pinched his side. "Say it, dammit!"

He sighed and backed up a few steps, pulling me with him, then got down on one knee, and, with a dramatic flourish at me, said, "Paulie Rostakova, light of my life, ache in my loins, and most incredibly wonderful woman in the whole wide world, would you make me a happy, happy man and marry me? Again. This time for real."

Roger started talking loudly, demanding that Sam be sure to film us, which of course he was doing, because Sam was not slow on the uptake.

I looked down at Dixon and blinked back a few tears of happiness.

"Please answer quickly," Dixon said, the arm held out toward me starting to waver. "There's a rock under my knee and my muscles are starting to spasm."

I grabbed his hand and pulled him to his feet, throwing myself in his arms and hugging him as tight as I could. "Yes, I will marry you. Yes, yes, yes. I hope to god there's a hotel around here, because I badly need to brush my mouth so I can kiss the living hell out of you."

Roger applauded and announced that, once again, his production had brought a real-life romance to fruition. More champagne was opened. I released Dixon, who looked absolutely exhausted, but extremely happy.

"He still hasn't said it," Tabby pointed out.

"Shut it," I said with a grin to take the sting out of it.

We spent another fifteen minutes being grilled in front of the camera about the last few days, and how we had fallen in love with each other, and anything and everything Roger could think of. And then the Zust arrived, speeding around the corner of the building and only just missing mowing us down. Stephen was driving and slammed on the brakes, then stood in the car to glare at us before turning to Sanders and starting to berate him with the most waspish, acid comments I'd heard in a long time.

"—had done what I told you to do, that would be us standing there guzzling the Bolly. But no, you knew best—you always know best. And just look what it's got us? Second! Second to *them*!"

There was more of that sort of tirade, all of which Sam got on film. (I found out later that the Esses had driven so hard they'd lost their film crew.) I stood next to Dixon, too tired to deal with their drama, and desperately wished I had a toothbrush.

It took another hour or so before we made it to a hotel and I could bathe and brush my teeth three times. After which I went out to molest Dixon in the manner he was due, but he was sound asleep on the bed, buck naked and holding a rose.

I smiled down at him, took the rose, and promptly fell asleep next to him. We slept for almost ten hours.

August 14
To: Angela
We won!

August 14
From: Angela
I know. The producer told us.

August 14
To: Angela
It made the news back home? Wow.

August 14
From: Angela
*No, dear. We're in Paris. Your father insisted. I'm
afraid he knows about your boyfriend. Rather, he
knows that he really is your boyfriend.*

August 14
To: Angela
Wait. What?

August 14
From: Angela
*He knows that you and Mr. Ainsley have been sharing
hotel rooms.*

August 14
To: Angela
Dammit! I knew Anton was spying on us!

August 14
From: Angela
Who is Anton?

August 14
To: Angela
The guy who tattled to Dad.

August 14
From: Angela
I don't think that was the name.

"I just got the weirdest text from Angela," I said to Dixon
when he entered our hotel room. He had an odd expression on his face, and his body language, when he closed
the door, standing with his back to it, screamed warnings
in my head. "Oh my god, what's wrong? Is it your brother?
I thought he was recovering nicely at your lord brother's
house."

"Rupert is just fine." He swallowed hard, his Adam's
apple bobbing with the motion. "Paulie, I . . . erm . . ."

"What?" I padded over to him, clad in a pair of jeans
and a tee. We didn't have to meet with Roger until din-
nertime, when we would have the official presentation
of the winners' purse. "You're scaring me! What is it?"

He closed his eyes for a second, and then said, all in
a rush, "I just ran into Roger. The Essex team has lodged
a protest, saying we broke the rules when we gave that
Frenchman a ride. Roger says they have a valid point,
and has stripped the win from us."

"What?" I shrieked the word, the echo of it harsh on
my ears. "Those . . . those . . . argh! I can't even think of
something obscene enough to call them! Goddammit,
Dixon! God*dam*mit!"

"I know, love, I know. But you have to admit, it was
against the rules, and we did know that when we invited
Vitale to go with us."

"But he needed us! His dog needed us! And what
about Anton? We gave Anton a ride, and no one said a

word about that. Or about the fact that they left him behind. What about that?"

Dixon kissed the tip of my nose. "It isn't against the rules to give a fellow racer a ride. It was only nonrace personnel that were forbidden."

"Well, then, what about all the shit they pulled the whole race? Poisoning Melody—"

"We don't know for certain they did that."

"And breaking Rupert's leg—"

"That very well might have been an accident."

"And all the other racers who were done in some way or another."

"Which also may have been accidents and cases of very bad luck."

I took a deep breath. "If they get to file a complaint about Vitale, then we are going to file a countercomplaint about the damage they did to our motor. We have Anton as proof that they hurt the Flyer's engine."

Dixon smiled. "I've already done so."

"We don't get the money? Any of it?" I asked, blinking back my tears.

"I'm afraid not."

"We don't get to lord it over the bastard cheaters that we beat them without once doing anything wrong?"

"No, but we will know that. As will others. The TV audience will see that."

A lone tear spilled out over my lashes. Dixon brushed it away. "It was all for nothing?"

"Hardly that." He pulled me against his body and I let myself relax against him, wonderfully filled with joy despite the devastation of this news. "I found you. I will have you to wake up to every morning, and every night you will have your wanton way with me. I can't think of anything in the world I want more than you."

"Oh, Dixon," I said, sniffling and laughing at the same

time. "That's the sweetest thing anyone has ever said to me. Where are we going to live? In England or California?"

His expression shifted. "I work for my brother. We can live in England if you want."

I watched him closely for a few seconds, discovering something that astounded me. "You really don't like your job, do you?"

He shrugged. "I used to. Lately, it's just . . . routine. All the machinery has been put in place. Alice—my brother Elliott's wife; you'll like her—she does a fine job running the tourist side of the estate, and I know she'd jump at the chance of managing the whole thing."

"Which means you can do anything you want, right?" I asked, not understanding why he looked so uncomfortable. Was there something he wasn't telling me? "What is your dream job?"

He was silent for a few minutes, then said slowly, "If you really want to know . . . what we just did."

"A round-the-world car race?"

"Not the race itself—the traveling from country to country. Only I'd like to be able to stop and see places, rather than racing through them. I'd like to go back to Russia. And Kazakhstan. And Poland, and Arizona, and all sorts of places. I liked writing about our trip, too. I thought . . . I wondered . . . I don't know if I can make a living at it, but there's a thing called travel journalism, and I thought it might be interesting."

I stared at him in openmouthed wonder for a moment. "Holy hellbells, Dixon! You want to be Nellie Bly, too!"

"Do I take it you approve of the plan?"

"Yes, yes, a hundred times yes." I let go of him to do a little jig. "We can get a blog! Travel blogs are huge. We can go to exotic places, and take pictures, and blog about it, and then write reviews of places. Oh my god, this is perfect! We can write a book about our trip and combine our journals into it! Oh! Oh! I can write stories about the people we see when we travel, and you can write about the places, and put those into books, too! This'll be so awesome! We'll travel around and have sex in all sorts of fabulous places, and there's nothing my dad can do to stop me, because I'll be with you, and you won't let me be kidnapped!"

He lifted me and spun me around, saying, "No one gets to kidnap you except me."

There was a tap at the door, and his face sobered. "Sam is waiting for us. He kindly gave me a few minutes to tell you what was happening, but they'll want our reactions."

"Pfft," I said, kissing him with all the love I had. I was breathless by the time I finished the sentence. "The race doesn't matter. You *do*."

We were out in the parking lot, standing next to the Thomas Flyer, while Roger prompted us to talk about the race, and losing it even though we technically won, when my father was suddenly in our midst, pulling me into a massive bear hug.

"You are safe! I knew you would be. You see, you listen to your papa. I know these things." He beamed at me and kissed me on either cheek. "You look tired. Angela, she looks tired. You are tired?"

"A little, but we're mostly recovered. I'm glad to see you both." I hugged him, then Angela. "And you in no way knew I would be safe. Because if you did, you wouldn't have stashed a gun in the car—which almost got us arrested in Russia—or sent your little spy on my tail. I have to admit, he had me fooled."

"He did?" Dad looked over to where Sam and Tabby were still filming us, although Tabby suddenly looked away. "You told her?"

I gawked at Sam when he lowered the camera. He gave me a sheepish smile. "Actually, no, we didn't tell her."

"You were the one spying on me? Sam!" I thought of throwing a hissy fit, but the other film crew had finally showed up, and they were filming the smug Essex rat finks standing next to their Zust. "I trusted you. We trusted you. How could you?"

"It was for the best—really it was," Tabby said, and I turned outraged eyes on her. "We just promised to keep an eye on you, and I thought it would be better to have us do that than someone you didn't like. And it's not like we were telling your parents what you were doing. Well . . .." She shot Sam a pointed look. "We weren't until the night in Kazakhstan when Sam got drunk and told your dad about Dixon being naked in your hotel room. But other than that, we just reported that you were fine and no one was trying to cut off your ears, or whatever kidnappers do these days."

"Fingers," Dixon said dryly, giving Dad a long look. "They go for fingers."

Dad pursed his lips and looked away for a moment.

"Forgive us?" Tabby said, giving us a winsome smile.

"I don't know," I said slowly, looking at Dixon. "What do you think?"

"I think they were good companions, stalwart cohorts, and good friends, and if they happened to keep a protective eye on you along the way, then so much the better."

"You!" Dad said dramatically, pretending he'd just noticed Dixon. "You are man who subtled my daughter!"

"Subtled?" Dixon asked.

"'Sullied,' dear, is the word," Angela said softly, smiling at me and Dixon.

"You sullied my girl. You will marry her. Today."

"I've already asked her and been accepted," Dixon said stiffly. "But we will be married on our own terms, in our own time. And it'll be held at Ainslie Castle, so my entire family can be there."

Dad's face grew red. "You do not tell me where my daughter will marry! I am father! I decide."

"No, sir. It's our wedding. We will decide," Dixon said calmly.

"You do not argue with me!" Dad roared. "Or it will be last thing you do!"

Dixon stepped forward until he was toe-to-toe with Dad. He said in a firm but polite voice, "No, sir. And you are not allowed to threaten me. I love Paulie. She loves me. We will be married in Ainslie Castle—" He broke off to turn to me. "Would you like to be married there?"

"Absolutely. It sounds fabulous."

"Good." He returned to my father and repeated, "We will be married in Ainslie Castle. You and your wife will be our honored guests. And after we are married, Paulie and I will leave for . . . for . . ."

"Zanzibar," I said, then added, when Dixon turned a questioning eye to me, "I like the name and have always wanted to go there. I bet Nellie Bly would have loved Zanzibar."

"I'm sure she would have. We will go to Zanzibar, and many other places. Paulie will keep in frequent touch with you so that you know she is safe, and you will trust both her and me to make sure that no trouble befalls her."

Dad stammered in Russian for a few seconds, then stopped and suddenly beamed. He clapped a hand on Dixon's shoulder and said loudly, "You ask her permission. This is good. You will make fine husband. You see, Paulina? I pick good man for you. He will take care of you."

I only just managed to keep from rolling my eyes, instead wrapping my arm around Dixon. "Yes, Daddy. He will take care of me and I will take care of him, and we'll all live happily ever after."

And so we did.

PRESS RELEASE
FOR IMMEDIATE RELEASE
VIEWERS TO DECIDE WINNER OF NEW YORK
CITY TO PARIS RACE!

Vision! Studios today announced that due to valid objections made by both the teams that finished the history-making race in Paris last August, members of the viewing public will be allowed to pick the official winner of the race by popular vote. The exciting journey, which took more than a month to complete, traveled across the breadth of the United States, Kazakhstan, Russia, Poland, Lithuania, Germany, the Czech Republic, and France, among other countries, and is expected to bring in a sizable viewing audience when it is aired on Go Britain! TV this December.

December 31
To: Angela
We won! Again! This time for real! Love to you both from us in beautiful Zanzibar.

Read on for a look at the first book
in Katie MacAlister's
Matchmaker in Wonderland series,

THE IMPORTANCE
OF BEING ALICE

Available now from Signet.

Expense Account
  Item one: ten pounds
  Remarks: Brothers are the bane of my existence.

"El-eeee-uuut."

"Oh lord, not that again."

"El-eeee-uuut. Phone home, El-eeee-uuut."

"There is nothing else on this earth that you can be doing at this exact moment but that?"

"El-eeee-uuut."

Elliott Edmond Richard Ainslie, eighth Baron Ainslie, and eldest brother to eleven mostly adopted siblings—mostly brothers, due to his mother's belief that boys were easier to raise than girls—donned a long-suffering expression and leaned back in his office chair. "Very funny, Bertie. Almost as funny as the first one thousand, two hundred and thirty-two times you blighted me with that movie quote, although I feel honor-bound to point out *yet again* that it was E.T. who wanted to phone home, and not the young lad who found him."

"Dude, you always say that, and I still don't see that it matters. I mean, Elliott would have wanted to phone home if he went up in the mother ship with E.T., wouldn't he?" Bertie, the youngest of his brothers, slumped into the armchair nearest Elliott's desk with the boneless grace of young men of seventeen.

"You're getting your alien movies mixed up again; the mother ship was in *Close Encounters*. What's set you off on this eighties movie binge anyway? I thought you were studying for your exams." Elliott eyed his laptop with longing. He really needed to get this book started if he was going to have it finished in time to join the family on their annual trek to visit the orphanage and school his mother endowed in Kenya.

"Whatev."

"Really, Bertie? *Whatev?* You can't even be bothered to add the last syllable?" Elliott shook his head. "If this is what time in America has done to you, I shall have to speak to Mum about letting you return there in the autumn."

Bertie clicked his tongue dismissively, swiveling in the chair until his legs hung over one arm. "Mum'll let me go no matter what you say. My family is there. It's my crib, you know?"

"Your family is from a small village two hundred miles outside of Nairobi," Elliott corrected him. "At least that's what the people at the orphanage told Mum when she adopted you, and I see no reason why they would confuse a small village in Africa with Brooklyn, New York. But never mind all that. Did you want something in particular, or have you just come to blight me on a whim?"

"Elliott!" a voice said sharply from the door.

Elliott sighed to himself. This was all he needed to utterly destroy the morning's chance at work.

"You will not be cruel to your brother! He is needful of our love and understanding in order to help him integrate into this family. If you abuse him like that, you will end up making him feel that he is a stranger in a strange land." Lady Ainslie bustled into the room, clutched Ber-

ie to her substantial bosom, and shot a potent glare over
his head at her eldest son.

"He's been a part of the family since he was two
months old, Mum. If he feels like a stranger, it's because
he's cultivating that emotion, and not due to any ill will
on my part," Elliott couldn't help but point out.

"You must love *all* your brothers and sisters," his
mother went on, smooshing poor Bertie's face into the
aforementioned bosom. Elliott winced in sympathy when
Bertie's arms flailed, indicating a lack of oxygen. "No
matter what their origins, color, or cultural roots."

"I do love all my siblings, although I will admit to
preferring those you and Papa adopted rather than the
two related by blood."

"Yes, well, that's because your dear papa and I were
first cousins," Lady Ainslie admitted, utterly ignoring
the fact that she was smothering one of her beloved sons.
"To be honest, we're lucky that your sister Jane's webbed
toes are the worst that came out of that. But I digress.
You must not pick on dear Bertie, or he will get a com-
plex."

Elliott gave consideration to the fact that Bertie's wild
gestures were now more feeble twitches than anything
else. "I don't think that will be a problem if you continue
to asphyxiate him like that."

"What? Oh." Lady Ainslie looked down, and with an
annoyed click of her tongue released Bertie. He collapsed to the floor, gasping for air, his face, already dark
due to his ancestry, now strangely mottled. "Silly boy
should have said something. Now, what did I come to see
you about?"

"I haven't the slightest idea. Is it something to do with
the builders? They haven't rescheduled again, have
they?"

"No, no, they're still coming on Monday as planned.

It will be terribly inconvenient having them underfoot for the monthly Mothers Without Borders meeting, but I suppose it is necessary to have the work done."

"If you wish for the walls to remain upright, then yes," Elliott said mildly.

He'd worked and saved and scrimped until he had, after seven years, managed to accrue enough money to start the restoration of the seventeenth-century house he had inherited. Along with a lot of debts, he thought sourly to himself, not the least of which was a nearly crippling inheritance tax.

If only his father hadn't been such a poor financial planner. If only his mother hadn't spent her own modest fortune on endowing any number of charities in her late husband's name. It wasn't that Elliott was against supporting such worthy causes—he was as charitable as the next man, doing his part to end child hunger and abuse to animals and to provide homes for needy hedgehogs—but he couldn't help but wish that supporting his large family and money-sucking estate hadn't fallen so squarely on his shoulders.

He had to get this book done. Hell, he had to get the damned thing started. Without the money the book contracts brought in, he'd be sunk. They all would be in desperate straits, everyone from his spendthrift mother right down to Levar, the second-youngest brother, who was recovering from a very expensive operation to straighten one of his legs. "Is there something in particular you wanted to discuss with me? Because if you've just come to chat, I will have to beg off. I really must get this book under way if I'm to meet the deadline. Bertie, for god's sake, stop with the dramatics. You aren't dying."

"I saw spots," Bertie said, ceasing the fish-out-of-water noises in order to haul himself up to the chair. "I saw a light. I wanted to go into the light."

Elliott bit back the urge to say it was a shame he hadn't, because he truly did love all his brothers and sisters. Even impressionable, heedless Bertie, who had recently returned from a two-month visit to see distant family members who had long ago emigrated from the small village in Kenya to the U.S. "Right. What have I told you both about my office door?"

"When the door is shut, Elliott is working," they parroted in unison.

"And if I don't work . . . ?"

"We don't eat," they answered in unison.

"So why is it you're both here when this is my working time?"

"I need a tenner," Bertie said with an endearing grin.

Their mother looked askance. "You just had your allowance. What did you spend that on?"

"Girls," he answered, his grin growing. "Three of them. Triplets with golden hair, and golden skin, and knockers that would make you drool."

"Bertie!" Elliott said with a meaningful nod toward their mother.

"Oh, well," Lady Ainslie said, dismissing this evidence of teenage libido. "Young men should be interested in girls. Unless, of course, they're interested in boys, which is perfectly all right no matter what the Reverend Charles says, and if he thinks he's going to make an example of dear Gabrielle simply because she ran off with his poor downtrodden wife, well then, he simply needs to think again. The Ainslies have been a part of Ainston village since the Conqueror came over, and I shan't have him blackening our name now. That brings to mind the letter I intended on sending Charles after that scathing sermon he read last week, which was quite obviously pointed at me. Elliott, dear, have your secretary send a letter expressing my discontent, and threatening to cease our donations to the church if he doesn't stop writing sermons about women who raise their daughters to become wife-stealing lesbians."

Elliott sighed and looked at his watch. "I don't have a secretary, Mum."

"No?" She looked vaguely surprised. "You ought to, dear. You are a famous writer, after all. No one can kill off people quite like you do. Now, much as I would like to stay and chat, I really must go write an article for *The M'kula Times & Agricultural Review* regarding the upcoming celebration at the Lord Ainslie Memorial School of Animal Husbandry. I've been invited to speak at the opening of the new manure house next month, and I want to alert all our friends in Kenya to that worthy event. Do give your brother ten pounds. Young men always need ten pounds."

"And, speaking of that, have you given any thought to my suggestion?"

"What suggestion?" Her face darkened. "You're not still intending on committing that atrocity?"

"If by 'atrocity' you mean requiring that the members of this family find gainful employment elsewhere, then yes." He held up a hand to forestall the objection that he was certain she would make. "Mum, I have explained it at least three times: I cannot continue to support every single member of this family anymore. All those brothers and sisters are a drain on the estate, one that cannot continue unchecked."

"You are exaggerating the situation," she said dismissively. "They are your family. You owe them support."

"Emotional support, yes. Help where I can give it, of course. But the financial situation has made it quite clear that only those members of the family who actually work for the estate will continue to be employed. Everyone else is going to have to find a job elsewhere. We can't afford to support them simply because they are family."

"You are heartless and cruel!" his mother declared, one hand to her substantial bosom. "Your father would turn over in his grave if he knew how you were willing to disown all your siblings without so much as a thought for their welfare."

"I have had many thoughts for their welfare, but I am also responsible for the estate, and everyone employed by it, as well as the many tenant farmers. Mum, I'm sorry, but there's no other way. If I don't cut out the dead-weight, we'll be foreclosed upon, and I don't think any-one wants to see that happen."

"But your brothers and sisters! What are they to do? How will they live?"

He smiled grimly. "Just like the rest of us. They'll have to get real jobs."

She gasped in horror. "You plan on throwing everyone to the wolves?"

"Hardly that. Dixon's job as the estate agent is quite secure—I couldn't do half the work he does. Gunner has employment elsewhere, so he doesn't come into the equa-tion. Gabrielle is excellent at managing the tour guides and gift shop, so her job is safe. Assuming she comes back from wherever she ran off to. But the others will simply have to find jobs outside of the castle."

"You are not the man I thought you were," his mother said, giving him a look filled with righteous indignation. "I would wash my hands of you except I believe that one day your sanity will return to you. I just hope you haven't destroyed the family before that time."

With a dramatic flourish, she exited the room.

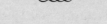